DEATH
IN THE
LIBERTIES

Published 2023 by Crimson
an imprint of Poolbeg Press Ltd.
123 Grange Hill, Baldoyle,
Dublin 13, Ireland
Email: poolbeg@poolbeg.com

© Poolbeg Press Ltd. 2023, copyright for editing, typesetting, layout, design, ebook

A catalogue record for this book is available from the British Library.

ISBN 978178199-691-1

www.poolbeg.com

DEATH
IN THE
LIBERTIES

TONY O'REILLY

POOLBEG
CRIMSN

ABOUT THE AUTHOR

Tony O'Reilly was born and raised in Dublin. He currently lives and works as a graphic designer in Dalkey, County Dublin. *Death in the Liberties* is his second novel and a follow-on from his debut novel *Murder in the Monto*. Tony based one of his main characters on his grandfather who joined the British army to escape extreme poverty.

ACKNOWLEDGEMENTS

I would like to thank Andy O'Donnell and Roger Cole who unlocked their libraries for my research. A special shout-out to Justin Nash, my agent, who, fortunately for me, is an expert on all things World War I, and who educated me about firearms used in that period. A big thank-you to Gaye Shortland, my editor, who, once again, cleaned up my musings and knocked them into shape.

DEDICATION

I would like to dedicate this book to my mother,
Josie O'Reilly (née Flinter)

CHAPTER 1

Levon Mordaunt – Dublin, 1st May 1916

Lower Talbot Street is coming to life again. One of the main thoroughfares that leads down to Amiens Street train station is almost as busy as it was before the Easter Rising. Shoppers and soldiers mix but ignore each other as the city tries to put on a brave face after the destruction of the preceding weeks. Housewives weighed down with heavy shopping-bags make their way home. A man sets up his fruit-and-vegetable stall in between chasing the young boys who dare each other to snatch an apple. A group of young women link arms and laugh at a shy soldier. Horses and carts make their way to the station, laden down with everything from canned goods to the latest copies of the daily newspapers. Carts coming in the opposite direction are full of vegetables, new potatoes, turnips, cabbages and clumps of carrots covered with fresh earth. The drivers shout at each other as they pass, cracking their whips over the plodding horses, happy to be working again. The metal wheels of the carts rumble over the cobblestones, the heavily laden loads swaying precariously, straining to break free from under their tarpaulins. The tramrails have been cleared of debris and one of the first trams trundles down Talbot

Street, slowing down to take the sharp turn onto Amiens Street. The sound of the brakes spreads outwards from the tram, a screeching metal-on-metal sound that permeates down through the very ground it travels over: on down past the cobbles, on through the foundations and down into the dark earth until it emerges in one of the tunnels underneath as a deep, rumbling vibration.

In the darkness of the tunnel, Levon Mordaunt's eyes flicker and open with the disturbance in the air around him. He knows he has been shot, but not where. The flash had blinded him and he'd felt a shock as if struck by lightning. Then he'd lost consciousness. How long he was unconscious he does not know, but he feels a terrible thirst. The tunnel is deserted so they must have presumed that he was dead. Maybe he is. Maybe he is in some kind of hell, the kind of hell his father had always preached about, with unrelenting darkness and pain. He reaches out with his right hand and it comes in contact with moist earth. He remembers that there were some areas of stagnant water that had filtered down through the roof of the tunnels between cracks in the brickwork. Gripping a handful of the damp soil, he lifts his hand over his face and squeezes. Before the precious drops trickle down, he opens his mouth. But that simple act of opening his mouth brings about a pain so excruciating that it feels as if he has been shot a second time. The phantom bullet is ricocheting around his skull in ever more concentric circles until it ends with an explosion of agony so intense that his mind cannot accept it and he relapses into unconsciousness again.

The second time – or maybe it is the third or fourth – he regains consciousness the tunnel is quieter. The rumblings from above have ceased. Now the only noise is the occasional screeching of the rats in the darkness and the wheezing noise he makes when he tries to breathe through his mouth. The pain he feels in his jaw convinces him that he has been shot in the face. Obviously, he's alive, but his attackers had thought him dead. So, the wound must be bad if they abandoned him here and hadn't bothered to send anybody down for him. But eventually someone will come to claim his body.

All of his plans and intrigues have come to nothing. But he has been in this desolate place before and he has survived; and he will survive this time. He lies quietly, breathing slowly through his nose, focusing. The English agent, Major Jonathan Byatt, played a large part in ending his grand plan. But he is dead and is of no use to him. On the other hand, the person responsible for bringing him down is very much alive. *Christopher Flinter*. He pictures him in his mind: young, able, pure, self-righteous, out to save the world, but not understanding that life is the survival of the fittest. What would happen if the meek inherited the earth? Chaos. And this narcissistic and self-aggrandising young fool who saw himself as superior to him, *to him*, would pay.

Mordaunt's whole being vibrates with the injustice of it all. But he will show them. In several, short movements he rolls onto his stomach and rests, as even those small movements have caused an explosion of pain in his jaw. Picturing Flinter again, he allows his body to build up such a fury that he's able to move his right hand and place it onto the side of his head. No sign of injury there except for a layer of filth from the floor of the tunnel. He moves his hand down in tiny increments: past his ear, onto his cheekbone, and down further. But after his cheekbone there is nothing except some grisly remnants of his jaw. Now it's the turn of his left hand. Again, he feels down the side of his face. His fingers reach a little further this time and he has a better idea of the extent of the wound. His lower right jaw is shot away and the rest of his lower face is hanging down one side.

Tears of frustration trickle from his eyes. Why should he go on? He's an animal dying in the back of his cave – why not just lie down here and let the rats have their day? But the idea that somebody as … what was the word he was looking for? Primitive … that's what Flinter was. A primitive man, hardly better than the native Indians his father used to trade with. He could not, *would not*, let him get away with it.

He rolls onto his back again and wrestles himself out of his jacket. The shirt underneath is clean and is made from a light cotton. Over the next several hours he works away with grim patience and extreme pain, making long strips from his shirt, some for bandages, some he would use for support. When he is finished most of the shirt is in tatters. He struggles back into his jacket as he can feel the cold beginning to seep into his body. Still on his back, he begins to apply the strips of shirt to his head, wrapping them carefully under what was left of his jaw, raising the mangled flesh and bone into position. He has to rest after each strip of bandage is applied and once or twice loses consciousness.

A wild, maniacal laughter brings him out of unconsciousness. Surrounded by pitch blackness, he thrashes out with his hands in every direction, mumbling through his broken jaw. He realises that he is becoming weaker and weaker as he flails his arms around. The silence is intense – there can't have been anyone down here with him. The laughter was coming from himself, whether in a dream or in some other part of his brain that he has no control over, he doesn't know. But the short burst of activity has taken away almost all of his energy reserves. Picturing Christopher Flinter in his mind again, he rolls onto his stomach. A bitter mixture erupts into his mouth, adding to his pain.

Now the only focus in his mind is Christopher Flinter's face, a face that he has to destroy as his own was destroyed. But not just the face. Anything to do with him: his brothers, sisters, parents, friends, children – he would kill anybody who had anything to do with him.

He begins to crawl back up the tunnel, using his arms and legs and sometimes even his stomach, like a snake.

After what he thinks is a long time, the blackness is replaced by a nebulous glow. He is coming home again, crawling over the rough terrain of his childhood towards the wooden cabin he had grown up in. His mother is at the door, waving, encouraging him towards her. Beside him, mocking him, telling him to crawl in order to survive, is not his father, as before, but a younger man, a man who has ruined his life. A man who would pay dearly.

CHAPTER 2

In the tiny bursar's office that looks out over Gloucester Street, Mother Mary Aloysius McCabe runs a pencil down a long line of figures that cascade down the length of the page in her leather-bound ledger. She flicks the page over: another full page of figures, and all in the credit column. Since the arrival of the giant brass double-cylinder washing machine all those years ago, in one fell swoop the laundry had more than doubled its output. This led to a new ironing hall, new hot-cylinder presses to take care of the bigger workload and more steam presses – in fact, more of everything. It seems that one purchase led to another and she is beginning to think she is now more of a businessperson than a Bride of Christ. Fortunately, or unfortunately depending on how you looked at it, there were plenty of girls and women to operate the now enormous laundry. Over a hundred, in fact. All fallen out of the grace of the Lord, but now, with her help and guidance, at least they had a chance to avoid the hot flames of Hell. Or even Purgatory.

The Magdalen Asylum for Fallen and Penitent Women, which backs onto that den of inequity, the Monto, is run by the Sisters of

Charity and is now a substantial business. The latest renovation is a whole new wing that includes a receiving room with wardrobes, a workroom with large presses, a sacristy stores, carpenters' workshops, can sheds, harness room, soap stores and a stoving room with a tall brick chimney that stands proudly above all the surrounding buildings in the area. Sometimes she feels overpowered by the sheer size of the laundry and she questions if this is what her vocation should be for. But Mother Aloysius is nothing if not pragmatic and believes in her heart of hearts that it is all for the greater glory of Our Lord.

The timid knock on the door is a welcome break from the boring ledgers. Closing over the thick leather cover she straightens her veil and calls 'Enter!'. It is not one of the other sisters to call her for lunch, as she had expected, but a seamstress, Margaret Yendell. The woman stands awkwardly in the doorway, in awe of the superior, and Mother Aloysius has to wave her in over the threshold. Margaret is about the same age as herself, fifty, and so one of the most experienced seamstresses in the asylum. She had arrived, heavy with child, from Tralee if her memory served her correctly, just before the census before last, which would make it early 1901. The poor child belonged to a local magistrate who had given the unfortunate woman a letter of introduction and a hundred pounds as a donation to the asylum. But for the life of her she cannot remember what happened to the child – there had been so many since then. She can't recall Margaret ever being in this part of the building before and her boredom is turning into curiosity.

'What can I do for you, Margaret?' she asks in her softest voice.

'Beggin' your pardon, Mother,' Margaret begins, her voice shaking with nervousness, 'but one of the girls from the lower kitchen found a man.'

Mother Aloysius straightens herself and points Margaret to the only other chair in the room.

'A man? Be specific, woman – what man?' she says as Margaret sits, perching on the very edge of the chair.

The lower kitchen, as everyone now calls it, is in the basement and was refurbished several years previously. But how did a man find his way down there? Had his lust got the better of him?

'He's a Catholic,' Margaret blurts out, 'and he's badly injured.'

'How do you know he's a Catholic? Did he tell you? Probably skulking down there looking for food. A scavenger most likely. I'll call the police.'

'No, Mother, he has rosary beads wrapped around his wrist. And he's horribly injured.'

'Go on.'

'Betty Cody was cleanin' out the main sinks when she heard a noise. It was comin' from behind that hatch that was left by those workmen.'

'The one that goes into the sub-cellar? I meant to get it blocked up – no doubt that is where the cockroaches are coming in.'

'Yes, Mother, that's the one. She had to force it open and, when she did, this man was reaching out for her as if out of the pit of Hell itself. But Betty is tough and slammed the hatch shut again. Then Kate Burke came down to see what the commotion was about. Kate has a big heart, as you know, Mother. She said that we should –'

'Yes, yes, get on with it. Where is he now and is he dangerous?'

'Well, we pulled him through the hatch and left him on the floor in the kitchen. We tried to find out who he was and how he got there, but it seems injury to his face won't allow him to speak – his face is all bandaged up – and he's so exhausted that he can't move. And we couldn't move him, we'd need more girls. So, I said to Betty and Kate, ye'd better not do anything else until I see the Superior.'

Mother Aloysius smiles. 'You made the right decision, Margaret. Could be one of those cowardly rebels who found a corner to skulk in. I had better go down and survey the situation.'

❋❋❋❋

The man could be a corpse except for the slight movement of the filthy bandages that cover most of his face. Mother Aloysius peers at the rosary around his wrist, admiring it. It is a simple wooden rosary with a crucifix carved from a single piece of wood. The beads themselves are dark-brown, almost black, and threaded through, holding them together, is a once-white cord discoloured from years of use.

A piece of paper and a pencil lie beside the man. Mother Aloysius picks up the paper. Scrawled across it is the word '*SANCTUARY*'.

'I gave him the pencil and paper, Mother,' said Kate. 'He asked for them – at least he made signs that he wanted to write.'

'You had no right to approach this person,' said Mother Aloysius. 'He could be dangerous.'

The man wears a well-cut but filthy suit. Mother Aloysius can make out a starched collar and all that remains of his shirt, the rest having been used for the bandages. The wound on his face is mostly hidden by the blood-caked wrappings and all she can see are his eyes, which are open and staring up at her. His skin is putty-coloured from the loss of blood and a terrible odour rises up from his body. She looks at the piece of paper with the word '*sanctuary*' scribbled across it and is virtually certain that the man has no hand, act or part in religion as pleas for sanctuary disappeared from most Christian faiths centuries ago. Only in gothic novels with stories of knights and maidens does it appear in modern times. But, still, there is something almost medieval about his desperate plea. It is from a different and possibly more simple age.

'Kate and Betty, you go back to your work – Margaret, bring me some boiling water and the medical kit from the recreation room.' She rolls up the sleeves of her habit and hitches her veil back behind her shoulders.

Kneeling down beside the man brings her closer to the stench rising from the bandages. But she is no stranger to the frailties of the human body. She spent part of her novitiate in the hospice for the dying run by her order in Harold's Cross on the far side of the city. That spell had banished all of the mysteries of the human form. She has seen it all: consumption, cholera, TB, diseases of the skin, women injured so badly in childbirth that they could not survive, and some unidentified sicknesses, usually brought about by people who had returned from their travels to foreign lands. These were the most mysterious, with some patients on the brink of death miraculously stepping back from that last glorious journey and walking out of the hospice cured, but not by the doctors or nurses. Every last one of them with promises of forever remembering the kindness and paying it back with all that they possessed – but, of course, they never did.

Margaret arrives back with the first-aid kit and leaves it on the floor beside the nun, then goes off to fetch the water. Mother Aloysius takes out a scissors and begins to cut through the many layers of dressing. The man must have suffered excruciating agony and her respect for the mysterious stranger grows. She snips away layer after layer of crude covering until the gory wound on his face is revealed. Margaret, who had arrived back with a basin of boiling water, gasps when she sees the full extent of the wound and Mother Aloysius waves her impatiently away. Whatever had caused the wound had taken away most of the lower jaw on one side, the other side held in position by strands of skin and tissue.

She looks into the man's eyes again and realises that he has been watching her reactions as if measuring the seriousness of his condition by her facial expressions. As she works on the wound, dabbing disinfectant around the skin and removing caked blood to get a better view, the man lies still with his eyes closed. She sets his jaw into a more comfortable position, puts some tincture of iodine onto cotton-wool swabs and places them gently over the worst areas of damage. She tears off a sheet of gauze and places it over his face, then uses an ointment to mark the position of his eyes, nose and mouth. Using a surgical scissors she fashions a rough mask with openings for his eyes, nose and mouth. After placing it onto his face, very gently, she wraps a bandage around it to hold it in position.

'I won't lie or belittle what has happened to you, is that understood?' she says and man blinks a few times. 'Most of your jaw is missing. The chances are that the doctors will excise even more of the remaining flesh to stop any further infection.'

The man blinks again.

'I have dressed the wound as best as I can and I'll send one of our girls over to the Mater Hospital, which is nearby, and organise an ambulance for you.'

The man's hand shoots out and grips her arm with surprisingly strong fingers. He pulls her towards him and shakes his head vigorously from side to side, the movement making the lower jaw flap to one side. She grabs one of his fingers and bends it back until he lets go of her arm.

'You need hospital treatment. What are you afraid of?' she says, rubbing her arm.

The man reaches down and locates the pencil and paper. He scribbles for several seconds and hands it to her.

'*MUST GO TO RICHMOND BARRACKS*'

She reads it, sighs and crumples it up.

'I'm sure you have your reasons and I don't want to know them, but are you certain you want to take your chances over there? It will be a longer and more uncomfortable journey. The best you can hope for there is a medical orderly.'

The man nods.

'Very well. If it is your wish, then who am I to get in your way? But you will have to stay here until I can organise some sort of transport for you. That may take time.'

The man reaches into the inside pocket of his jacket, takes out a large moleskin wallet and holds it out to her. She takes the wallet and opens it. On one side there is a substantial amount of cash and on the other some papers which she removes.

'So, our mysterious visitor has a name,' she says, glancing at his identity papers, 'and a place of birth. Welcome to Ireland, Mr Mordaunt.'

CHAPTER 3

Nell –
December 1916

Nell Flinter, on her hands and knees and breathing heavily with exertion, scrubs the bare wooden floorboards a third time in another vain attempt to remove the stains left by the old man who had lived in the flat before she and Christopher moved in as newlyweds. Her long curly auburn hair has come undone from her efforts and falls forward, almost touching the tainted suds before she whips it back in disgust. Devenish his name was, according to Christopher. She tries to push the source of the stains out of her mind as she forces the rebel strands of hair back into the hairband. She stands up to examine her work. To her eyes she has made little difference with the carbolic soap and the rough scrubbing brush. Small islands of stains are still spotted around the room. Maybe they'd have been better off staying in her little room in the Monto. Or, better still, Moussa's old converted stables in the yard – at least she knows its history. From Mary Sherry's flat directly overhead, she hears the footsteps of the poor woman's children as they run backwards and forwards across the floor. Tommy Sherry, Mary's husband, boasted about how he turned their shoes into hobnailed boots by hammering flat-head tacks into the heels and soles.

Another one of Mary's children join in. Two more hobnailed feet make their presence felt. Probably Tommy Junior as it is much louder and more incessant and no doubt driving Mary to distraction. Nell takes the broom from beside the bed and taps it on the ceiling until the noise abates and stops altogether. Minutes later she can hear Mary Sherry's footsteps coming down the stairs and then approaching her door – her first visitor in over a week.

Even though she had been expecting it, Mary Sherry's short sharp knock almost makes her jump. Nell goes over to the mirror and examines her reflection, turning to one side and then the other. Her brown eyes stare back at her from her sallow-skinned face with its high cheekbones – all inherited from her Moroccan father. Strange to think she spent most of her life unaware of his existence. She takes off the drab navy pinafore she wears when doing housework and smooths out the dress underneath before opening the door.

Standing in the doorway, her neighbour's face wears a tired smile and when Nell steps back to let her in she notices that she seems pale.

The Sherry's youngest child's head is resting on her mother's shoulder and she stares at Nell without any interest. Two streams of mucus flow unchecked onto her mother's dress. Her right hand is clasped around a sliver of moist bread coated in a thin layer of sugar. The sight of the tiny child brings out Nell's maternal feelings and she wonders, again, if she is going to make as good a mother as Mary when the day eventually comes.

'I see you're doing a bit of cleaning.' Mary nods towards the bucket of sudsy water.

'Old stains left by the previous tenant,' Nell closes over the door and stands with her back to it.

'Poor Mr Devenish. Couldn't help himself,' Mary says, glancing around the room to see if Nell has changed anything else since she was there the last time.

14

'Probably old porter stains.'

'Mr Devenish didn't drink, Nell.' Mary winks at her and bounces the child up and down in her arms to keep it amused.

'Jesus Christ, if not porter what are they?' Nell feels a shiver down her body.

'The poor man suffered terrible from the dropsy.' Mary bounces the child more energetically, only too ready to expand on the world of sickness she loves to talk about so much.

Nell can't stop herself. 'The dropsy?'

'Bad heart. Not strong enough to push the blood around the body. So, the legs get swollen with all kinds of poison. It all has to come out somewhere. Many a night I heard him scream out as the doctor relieved the pressure. Sometimes he cleaned up after the purge, but others …' Mary nods towards the stains.

Nell's hand goes up to her mouth – she's horrified.

'But maybe it's something else,' Mary adds quickly. 'Poor man, hadn't any luck since he moved into these rooms. Please God you'll change all that.'

Nell walks over to the only window in the flat and opens it wide, breathing in the air. Outside in the shared yard a dog is scratching himself vigorously and stops when he hears the sound of the window opening. From the outside privy she hears the sound of the toilet flush and Mr Cannon, whose door is across from hers, comes out, hitching up his braces. A newspaper is stuck down the back of his trousers – he takes it out, waving it at Nell. Behind her Mary Sherry is saying something.

'I'm sorry – I didn't hear you, Mary.' Nell turns.

'I said, do you need anything?' Mary says, a note of concern in her voice. 'When you knocked on the ceiling, I thought there might be a problem,'

'To be honest, I don't need anything, Mary, just someone to talk to. I'm going mad here. How about a cup of tea?'

Without waiting for an answer, she ducks behind the hanging blanket that they use to cut off their kitchenette. It's a tiny area with a square sink and a two-ring paraffin stove that Christopher set up. She pumps the paraffin stove and puts the lighted match to it. The tray is black but etched out in gold paint. Two Chinese lovers have reached the other side of a bridge spanning a stream and are making their way towards a tiny, perfect house. She hums one of the popular street ballads of the day, happy to have some company.

When she has finished her preparation, she pulls the blanket back, catching it up on the cord it is hanging from, then carries the tray into the living room, placing it onto the over-large dining-room table, a present from her mother. Nell and Christopher are among the luckier ones in the building. Although Mary and Tommy Sherry have two rooms also, they have to contend with seven children.

Mary Sherry looks down at the tray with the tea and biscuits.

'You shouldn't have, Nell,' she says, and almost throws the child under the table and takes one of the chairs, blocking the child's escape.

'It's no trouble.' Nell begins to pour out the tea.

'Tea strainer?' Mary interjects, smiling.

'I forgot. Here, I'll take that one, a few tea leaves don't bother me.' Nell goes into the kitchenette again to get the strainer.

When she returns the child has escaped from under the table and is crawling over to the bucket with the dirty water. She leans over and pours the tea through the strainer. Closer to Mary, she notices her neighbour's aging face: pale skin, sagging already, her eyes sunken back into her head. Christopher had told her Mary was only in her early thirties. She wonders if she will end up like that one day.

'That's enough, dear!'

Mary brings her out of her dream and she sees that the tea has overflowed the cup into the saucer.

'I'm sorry, Mary, I was daydreaming.' Nell takes a towel hanging on the back of the one of the chairs and mops up the tea from the saucer.

'*Jesus, Mary and the Blessed Saint Joseph!*' Mary shouts, pointing.

Nell turns. The baby is now over at the bucket and has somehow pulled herself up onto her two feet. She has plunged her face into the suds, probably thinking they were something she could eat. The shout from Mary frightens the child and she topples backwards, dragging the bucket over with her. The contents of the bucket pour over her and she begins to cry. Mary jumps up from the table and scurries over, snatching her child up from the floor. She turns her upside-down and begins to shake her vigorously. A small stream of water spouts from the child's mouth. The contents of the bucket are now spreading out in all directions over the floor. Mary is hugging the child close to her chest and moaning. Nell runs over and rights the bucket, then grabs the mop and tries to soak up as much water as she can before it trickles down through the floorboards. As she concentrates on getting as much of the dirty water as possible off the floor, Mary makes her way across the wet floor with the child and out through the door, leaving it ajar. Nell hears her heavy footsteps going back up the stairs and then her door slamming above.

Nell has just cleared the table of the cups and saucers when there is another knock on the door. The floor of the room is covered with loose newspaper pages to try and soak up the remaining wetness from the bucket. She doesn't even bother to check herself in the mirror, hoping that it's Mary Sherry come back to continue their chat. But when she opens the door, Phil Shanahan is standing there.

She nearly cries when she sees him. It has been months since she's been in his pub, just after the wedding in fact, when Phil had invited them all back to the Monto for a 'knees-up'. What a great night that was, though she didn't appreciate it back then. A lot of the girls from her mother's brothel had arrived to brighten the place up with gaudy streamers and decorations. Phil had found someone who could play all of the popular songs on his piano in the corner and he had even moved the tables around the bar so that people could dance if they wanted to. Thinking about that wonderful day, tears suddenly start flowing down her face and she throws herself at Phil, burying her head in his chest.

'There, there, Nell, what's the matter, love?' He pats her on the back and she can hear the embarrassment in his voice. 'Is it Christopher?'

Nell shakes her head and speaks into his chest. 'He's around in Donnelly's bacon factory. He got a part-time job there last week. He should be back soon.'

'It's something for the present, I suppose,' Phil says, lifting her head and looking into her eyes.

'That's the only job he could get. Not much use for an ex-British army soldier around here, Phil.' Nell smiles sadly. 'Come in, I don't want any of the neighbours to see me like this.'

'Most of my contacts are in Wales, under lock and key, since the Rising – so I can't help Christopher now, Nell, I'm afraid.' Phil steps into the flat, closing over the door behind him.

'You did your best.' Nell goes back into the kitchenette and puts the still-warm kettle back onto the stove.

When she comes back Phil is pacing around the room, looking idly at their few possessions and avoiding the newspaper pages scattered across the spillage. He picks up a photograph of her and Christopher on their wedding day. It was taken on the steps of the Pro Cathedral, just around the corner from the Monto, but a world away. On the steps behind the couple stands a motley bunch. One or two of Christopher's relatives from the country are standing to one side, most of the rest are friends of hers, including Phil Shanahan and some of the girls from her mother's brothel.

Upstairs Mary Sherry's children have started their playing again, their hobnailed boots clicking across the ceiling.

Phil holds the photograph up. 'That was a great day, Nell.'

And it was. The weather was kind, the cathedral magnificently stately and the main reception back in her mother's house – the house of ill-repute as one of Christopher's relatives whispered – was sumptuous. Then most of the guests finished off the day in Phil's pub. They even had a honeymoon, in the Esplanade Hotel in Bray, where they spent three days. Four days of intense happiness, then down to earth, arriving back in the Liberties to old man Devenish's flat.

A key rattles in the lock and Phil puts the photograph back onto the sideboard and straightens himself up. For a split second, as he walks through the door, Nell catches the despondency on her husband's face and it almost breaks her heart. But when Christopher sees that they have visitor and who it is, he perks up, or forces himself to perk up, Nell isn't sure which. Hand extended, he strides over to Phil, his face beaming. They shake hands for a long time then clap each other on the shoulders.

'You're looking good, Christopher,' Phil says, standing back and appraising him.

'And you too, Phil,' her husband replies, closing over his ill-fitting jacket to cover up his baggy trousers and frayed leather belt.

The two men stand looking at each other and it's up to Nell to cover up the silence. She brings in cups and saucers and chatters on about the fun they had at their wedding, the neighbours in the building, especially the Sherrys, about the repairs to the city after the Easter Rising and about the nervousness of the British troops, mostly young conscripts who had never faced a mostly hostile population before and, of course, about her mother's business which is picking up after several months of curfews and raids.

When they are all sitting around the table, sipping tea, Phil brushes his moustache with his fingers, a nervous habit she recognises. He turns to Christopher.

'I heard you have a job now?'

Christopher nods. 'Just something to keep us going until we get settled.'

'Donnelly's bacon factory?'

'The apple never falls too far from the tree, Phil,' Christopher says with a smile. 'Did I ever tell you that my father was a bacon curer, God rest him?'

'I suppose we all have to make do,' Phil says. 'If there's anything I can do?'

'No, no, you've done enough, Phil. Me and Nell are grateful for everything you've done. Especially helping me … you know …'

'Not at all. Sure, wasn't it Nell who fired the shot? Put paid to the most vile man I've ever come across. I've often wondered how someone like that was shaped. Was it something in his childhood? His upbringing, maybe. Imagine, taking pleasure in killing women, not to mention torturing your friend Major Byatt.' Phil grimaces with disgust.

After that horrific night in the tunnels under the Monto, it is something they rarely speak to each other about. In that dark cavern, Christopher had lain waiting for death at the hands of Janus, the mystery man. Under cover of the bedlam of the Monto, Europe's biggest red-light district, Janus had carried out his sick fantasies, killing, in the most horrific fashion, the very women who helped him carry them out. It was the sheer horror of what he had done that had kept that night almost unspoken between them and Nell is a little surprised that Phil has brought it up now.

Christopher nods in agreement with Phil.

'I suppose we'll never get to know the monster's name and maybe that's a good thing,' Nell says. 'If we knew his name that'd mean he was a real person and that's something I'm trying to forget.'

Phil wipes his moustache again and stares into the depths of his cup as if trying to read the tea leaves at the bottom. His voice lowers to barely a whisper: 'As a matter of fact, just in passing, we sent somebody down there, a few weeks after the British had carried out their man Byatt – and the unfortunate Moussa, of course. Just to see if we could find any identification.'

'I don't think I want to know about that.' Nell shivers. 'Let's not talk about him anymore.'

'Nothing to tell really – they didn't manage to locate the body,' Phil mumbles and sips his tea.

Christopher and Nell's hands creep across the table to each other.

'Are you sure they looked in the right place?' Nell asks.

'I'm sure – if I wasn't, I'd have gone down there myself. But, look, don't worry, Nell. I think it's safe to assume that your shot killed him.' Phil tries to make a joke of it, 'Sure, nobody could survive a wound like that. No, what probably happened was that he might have dragged himself away with the last breath in his body and died in one of the old cellars, like a cat does when it knows the end is near.'

'Jesus, Phil, now you're saying he dragged himself away, just after telling us he was dead. Which is it?' Nell says, squeezing Christopher's hand.

Phil looks uncomfortable and runs his finger around the inside of his collar: 'Maybe it was rats that got rid of him – they're as big as cats down there – I just didn't want to say that.'

'You should have gone back and finished him off, Phil.' Christopher shakes his head. 'A few rounds to the chest and one to the head to make sure.'

'Listen,' says Phil. 'What if he did survive? What sort of a monster would he be? Sure, he had no jaw left to speak of. If, in a thousand to one chance, he did manage to pull himself out of there with that horrific wound, we would have heard about it.'

'So, this is why you visited us today, Phil?' Nell stares him in the eye. 'To get that off your chest?'

'Of course not, Nell. I just wanted to see how you were doing. This other thing is something I didn't want to worry you about when you were … you know … newlyweds. In any case, haven't you got a fine ex-soldier here to defend you?'

Phil laughs, one of the phoney laughs that Nell has heard many times when he was behind the bar trying to ingratiate himself with a customer who was telling bad jokes.

'Nell,' Christopher says, 'Phil's probably right. Chances are he bled to death out of sight in some sewer, where he belonged. I've witnessed that in the war. Men just crawling aimlessly through no man's land searching for a place to rest.'

He squeezes Nell's hand tightly to give her reassurance and she squeezes back. In a way Christopher was the lucky one, she thinks, being semi-conscious through that ordeal in the tunnels and for several days afterwards. Those horrific few days in the Monto now come back to her in even more gruesome detail. The very chance of that monster's survival, no matter how slim, will stay with her forever. Sometimes, when she wakes up in the small hours, she relives that event again and again. She knows that whatever darkness lay in Janus's soul becomes darker the more she dwells on it, the evil in his heart even more evil, endowing him with superhuman powers he couldn't possibly have possessed. But what if his shadow grows and grows in the future, casting a blight across their lives forever?

Phil pushes himself away from the table, the noise of his chair scraping across the floorboards, bringing Nell out of her reverie.

'Anyway, it's good to see you pair again,' he says, playing with the brim of his hat.

Christopher rises. 'Thanks for coming by, Phil – let me walk you to the front door.'

The two men leave the flat and walk on through the shabby lobby to the entrance of the tenement. The smell of boiled cabbage, almost a permanent smell in the building, surrounds them until they step out into the raw, cold air of late morning. The bells of Saint Nicholas of Myrna church are beginning to ring out, the slow, steady peal signalling the end of somebody's funeral Mass. Passers-by bless themselves as they walk by.

Phil takes out a packet of cigarettes and offers one to Christopher. As they light their cigarettes from the match in Phil's cupped hands, an army tender goes past, the soldiers in the back at the ready, their eyes searching the surrounding streets.

'Here, you keep those.' Phil hands the box with the remaining cigarettes to Christopher.

'No, thanks, Phil, I've got some in the flat.'

But Phil is adamant and forces them into Christopher's jacket pocket. The two men stand outside the dingy building, each one caught up in his own thoughts, blowing smoke into the cool air.

'So you're working in Donnelly's,' Phil says eventually. 'Anna Macken said she offered you a job on the door in her place, is that right?'

'No interest, Phil. It was a good offer but I'm not going to spend my nights on the door of a brothel in the Monto, cleaning up her mess!'

Phil holds up his arms in mock surrender. 'That's your choice, Christopher. I've still got my ear to the ground, but things are tough. Most of my contacts are in prison in Wales at the moment, but there are rumours that they'll be released soon. There's a movement afoot.'

'And about time.'

'The revolution isn't over, Christopher. Take my word for it – when they get back to Ireland there'll be no stopping them.'

'I hope they won't make the same mistakes as they did at Easter,' Christopher says with sadness.

'No, not this time. They've a new man over there – Collins. They say he's a great organiser. From Cork, but worked in England for years. He knows the enemy inside out and he won't be afraid to recruit somebody who was in the British army after I put in a good word.'

'Really? Enough to pay the rent and get me out of that factory?'

'That's not the way it works, Christopher. But if he gets to know you and likes what he sees, he'll make sure you get a decent job. The wind's in our favour now so we'll need good men, soldiers and politicians.'

Christopher, hungry for any kind of good news, nods.

Phil puts a hand on his shoulder and squeezes it. 'You're a good lad, Christopher. Just concentrate on making Nell happy. I'll do what I can. And sorry about mentioning the other thing – it was just something I had to get off my chest.'

Christopher throws his cigarette butt onto the ground and stamps it into the pavement. 'Do you really think Janus might have managed to survive?'

'No. You saw the wound yourself. No human could have survived that.'

'Human isn't a word I'd use for him,' Christopher says.

'That's true enough. Anyway,' Phil puts his hand out, 'let's pray for better days.'

When Christopher returns to the flat, he can hear Nell stomping around in the bedroom and the slam of opening and closing drawers. Through the open door he sees her large suitcase, open on the bed. He stands in the doorway and watches as Nell, muttering to herself, grabs a handful of clothes from the chest of drawers and throws them into the suitcase, then goes over to the wardrobe and takes out one of the few dresses she possesses and folds it up.

'What're you doing?' Christopher asks, stepping into the bedroom.

Nell stops in mid-action and turns to face him. Her face is red and her lips are pursed, a sign that she has made up her mind about something and that she won't listen to reason. He is used to her by now and recognises the signs.

'You heard what Phil said, we should get to the Monto – that monster wouldn't dare to show his face there.'

'Phil should have kept his mouth shut,' Christopher says.

'But we have friends in the Monto. Wouldn't it be safer?'

'Aren't you forgetting – you have me?'

A flash of guilt passes over Nell's face and her breathing begins to slow down. 'I know I do, Christopher – that's not what I meant.'

Christopher walks over to her and reaches out. She comes into his arms and rests her face against his chest. He bends his head, taking in her familiar fragrance.

'Let's give it a bit more time, Nell. With a bit of luck, I'll get more permanent work and we can find another place, somewhere on the other side of the canal, away from here, and the Monto.'

Nell looks up into his face. 'Why do you hate it so much?'

'What would I do there, Nell? Work for your mother on the door? We'd be beholden to her even more then and we'd never escape. Anyway, you know as well as I do that the Monto's days are numbered.'

He feels the tenseness leaving her body and continues.

'We won't be here forever, Nell, I promise you that,' he whispers, trying to put as much conviction in his voice he can manage.

CHAPTER 4

Benjamin Stern 1917 – London

Captain Benjamin Stern stands just inside the door of the now-famous Room 40. A compact man in his late twenties, medium height and clean-shaven with thick, slicked-down auburn hair. His sallow skin still shows the residual scars of a mild form of smallpox he caught when he was a child. He holds his brown trilby in his hands, turning it constantly to mask his impatience. He regrets wearing his best suit (from Norton and Sons, Saville Row) as it comes with a waistcoat and the heat in the almost airless room is causing him to perspire. Already he can feel a build-up of moisture under his starched collar but he resists the urge to snap open the top button and grits his teeth. Why hadn't he just worn his uniform? All of this talk about him being sent over from Dublin Castle to assist the new Special Intelligence Service (SIS) had gone to his head and he had begun to dress as if he were already a spy. As things turned out, what a fool he had been! He was going nowhere. In Whitehall Court he was surrounded by typists, clerks and drivers. Most of the rest were wounded personnel too badly injured for active service, and well-connected men avoiding the front. Now he is desperate to be transferred to the Admiralty, where, he hopes, he has a better chance to rise through the ranks with the hope of a transfer to Palestine.

But located on the first floor, northern wing of the Admiralty's Ripley Building in Whitehall, his first impression of the office is a bitterly disappointing one. It was, when he had first heard it, an impressive address. But the reality of the tiny space is underwhelming. Two wooden desks that had seen better days sit, side by side, taking up most of the floor space. A lone fly throws itself against the only window again and again. A middle-aged woman is battering away on an old typewriter keyboard, head bent. Lying beside her, curled up in a wicker basket, is one of the largest cats he has ever seen. The obligatory battered filing cabinets run along one wall. He coughs politely again, hoping that she will interrupt her typing and at least have the courtesy to allow him to take a seat at the other desk. She looks up from the typewriter and frowns, her brow a sea of tiny furrows.

'I did say he would be only five minutes, didn't I?' she says apologetically.

'You did, ma'am,' Stern replies, gritting his teeth.

'Well, while Alfred may be one of the most intelligent men I know, I am afraid that he does not possess a pocket watch. Thinks they are, on the whole, a distraction and an abomination.'

'I would have thought that –' Stern is saying when the door to the inner office opens and there at last stands Alfred Ewing, Head of Room 40, the Admiralty's code-breaking department. More disappointment. He looks more like a schoolteacher than a spy, but then again what is a spy supposed to look like?

Ewing stands back from the door and ushers him into his inner sanctum.

Ewing's office proves not much dissimilar to the outer one, the overpowering smell of lavender now replaced with pipe tobacco. The only difference in layout seems to be that in here there is one desk rather than two. The rest of the floor space is taken up with several stacks of books that tilt precariously in different directions. Even the visitor's chair is laden with books and Ewing, lifting, bending and puffing, has to form yet another stack on the floor to give Stern somewhere to sit.

'Can I get you some tea?' he says, still out of breath after Stern has settled into an uncomfortably hard chair.

'No, thank you, won't hold you up,' Stern says. 'Just a quick visit to thank you for the heads-up on the arrival of the *Aud* and, of course, *U19* last year. All arms from the *Aud* secured, thanks to you.' He bows his head slightly in gratitude. 'The submarine got away, unfortunately, but we did manage to capture Casement.'

'You certainly did. Jolly Roger, we called him,' Ewing says with a smile.

'I heard about the Black Diaries. Bloody disgusting.' Stern grimaces.

'Ah, the Black Diaries. A detailed record of his ... what would you call it, his proclivities with young natives. But they were very effective. Support for him – powerful support – fell away when we circulated them. Without them Casement would only have received a jail sentence. You can thank your boss for them.' He winks.

Stern pretends to know what the old fool is talking about and smiles knowingly in return. Ewing edges himself back behind his desk and settles himself into his chair but not before Stern catches sight of a cushion. Through the window over his shoulder, he can see the other wings of Admiralty House. It is an impressive building with a long history, a building he would have preferred to serve in rather than the newer office building where he is located at the moment. It feels, at times, like an anthill, with all of the little people rushing around trying to outdo each other. But there is no sign of a promotion or even the opportunity of a promotion.

The new offices did have a lot more space than here, but they are drab and soulless, rows of box-like rooms, walls painted the same anaemic shade of blue. His superior, Captain Sir Mansfield George Smith-Cumming, the director of the Special Intelligence Service (SIS), is still getting over the death of his son. They had both been involved in the car crash. Sir Mansfield was injured quite badly and seemed to have lost his old resolve. A light had faded behind his eyes and the mandarins of Westminster passed his department from building to building without any objections from the once vibrant director. It did not take Stern long to realise that he had ended up in a cul-de-sac career-wise.

'And how is old C – is he any better?' Ewing asks, at the same time filling his pipe from a battered leather pouch. He tamps down the tobacco carefully, then rummages around his desk for some matches. 'C' was the way Sir Mansfield used to sign off on any letters or memos.

'He is still limping badly and has not been able to get rid of those damn headaches,' Stern answers, uncomfortable talking about his boss, 'but I can see an improvement.'

'Good. And you can tell him from us that he was very welcome to the information and I was only too glad to help with nipping that particular Irish problem in the bud.'

'I will,' Stern says. 'With those extra guns from the Germans, the Irish rebellion would have been a damn sight more complicated to put down and would have meant heavier losses on our side. And, of course, we can barely afford the men we have sent over there as it is.'

'Was it that serious?' Ewing asks. 'I remember reading in *The Times* that the Chief Secretary for Ireland was over in London, so I presumed that the so-called rebellion was just a couple of hotheads with no military training and not a great deal of arms letting off some steam. A distraction from the main event in Europe, if you see what I mean.'

'I don't think Augustine Birrell believed there would be a revolution after the boat was intercepted, so he decided to take his Easter break in London,' Stern says. 'An unfortunate decision. Mark my words, if that ship had been successful in landing the arms it would have opened up another front in the south of Ireland. God knows what would have happened. Luckily our chaps had it contained and are back in control, I assure you. Although the shooting of the leaders was a mistake, I believe. In any case, thank you for the offer of the tea and I hope that your intercepts continue to give us success. In fact, I think code-breaking is the future. That's why I was thinking of putting in for a permanent transfer over here.'

'Intercept? No, no, no, you can tell old C that the information we received was sent anonymously. Arrived some time last year, by courier.'

The colour drains from Stern's face. 'But I presumed that you received it through the usual channels,' he says.

'You mean the Berlin and New York cable? No, not this time.'

'Have you still got the message?'

'No, threw it away, I'm afraid,' says Ewing. 'Is there a problem?'

'I'll be honest, I'm not certain. I received a telegram recently, from my old unit in Dublin Castle. Apparently some unfortunate madman had turned up looking to communicate with someone in charge. Claimed he was responsible for information helping us overcome the rebellion. Also mentioned some hush-hush undertakings with the Germans and demanded to see someone higher up, if you wouldn't mind.'

'Really?' Ewing puffed on his pipe. 'Did he give any details?'

'Only that he knew Major Jonathan Byatt. But Byatt was killed in … unusual circumstances, so they couldn't corroborate his story and told him to be off in short order.' Stern waves his hand as if waving goodbye to an unwelcome guest.

Ewing begins to puff on his pipe with more energy, the tobacco in the bowl glowing with the effort.

'Byatt? Thought I recognised the name. He paid me a visit sometime at the beginning of last year. Got frightfully animated when I told him where our information was coming from. Or to be more precise, where it was not coming from. Took himself off to Ireland like a scalded cat. Can you tell me anything more about this mad chap?'

'Not really, but the telegram did mention that he was possibly unhinged from what they believed was a war wound. Apparently, he can only make rudimentary grunting noises. Most of his lower jaw is missing. But he writes very well and seems to be otherwise quite literate. In any case, they sent him packing – the Castle is overloaded with spies as it is.'

Ewing takes the pipe from his mouth and begins to tap it into an empty ashtray. A small mound of smoking ash ends up in the middle of it like a miniature smoldering volcano. He opens the drawer in his desk, takes out a small wooden box and opens it.

Stern watches as he takes out a small penknife and begins to clean out the bowl of the pipe. Was the meeting over? Should he go? He makes to stand up but Ewing holds his hand up, indicating that he should stay. He watches as the older man begins to disassemble the pipe and insert a pipe-cleaner into one end, pushing it in and out of the stem. When he has finished, he reassembles the pipe and places it into a pipe rack on the desk, straightens himself and looks into Stern's eyes.

'Would old C miss you if I were to suggest that you be transferred?' he says.

'Transferred? Here, sir? That would be splendid.' Stern, in his mind, is already celebrating the good news. If he is given a permanent position here, he will be a step closer to his real ambition: a posting to Palestine.

'No, not here, Captain Stern. Back to your old unit in Dublin

Castle. Would you be prepared to do that?' Ewing reaches out for the telephone on his desk and lifts the receiver, holding it in mid-air – making the point that it was not a request.

'I will go wherever I am sent,' Stern says and tries to hide the disappointment.

'Good fellow. Probably be a bit of a wild goose chase and, if it is, you can of course return to your post here in London and we can see about your ambition to be the next Lawrence of Arabia.'

Stern blushes and wonders how his ambition to go to Palestine had reached Ewing. He could have sworn that he hadn't mentioned it to anyone.

'I'll make all of the arrangements and explain the situation to old C,' Ewing says, 'but get yourself over there immediately if not sooner.' Then he turns his attention to the operator at the end of the line, dismissing Stern with a wave of his hand.

Stern marches past the startled middle-aged secretary and her cat, and on down the stairs. Outside he hails a taxi, trying to recall all of the conversation that he had with Ewing. In the back of the taxi, he takes out his notebook and begins to make a list of things to do before he leaves for Dublin. Then he jots down Byatt's name and puts a large question mark beside it. Byatt was not in his area in Dublin Castle, an enormous complex that stretched out from the gates in Dame Street, but he had come across his name several times since his death. What had been a feeble attempt at a transfer to the Admiralty Offices might turn out to be a promotion after all.

The driver, waiting for instructions, coughs politely. Stern looks up and gives him his home address.

'Take me directly there first. You'll have to wait for a while, I'm sorry, then I will need you to drive me to Euston.'

It's Friday afternoon and the traffic along the river is heavy. But the driver is an old hand and confident in his ability to weave his way through the clogged streets. In a few minutes he is turning up Oakley Street and into the warren that is Chelsea until he has reached the young gent's address. As he is applying the handbrake the passenger gets out and disappears inside. It's turning into a good day. The meter has been ticking away nicely since eleven o'clock that morning and it's still ticking away as he takes out his packet of cigarettes and puts one into his mouth. After this trip he will probably pick up a fare outside Euston in no time and then after that his day's work will be done. Billy Atkins would be playing the piano tonight in the Queen's Arms. Dotty likes him and they'll be serving their jellied eels too. Life was good.

CHAPTER 5

Nell –
September 1918

Nell sits at the kitchen table, rereading the Cumann na mBan Declaration that her friend, Sarah Murphy, had posted to her over a week earlier.

'*Because the enforcement of conscription on any people without their consent is tyranny, we are resolved to resist conscription of Irishmen.*'

Does that mean that Christopher could be conscripted? The thought of losing her husband to the British war machine brings a shiver of dread to her stomach. She reads on.

'*We will not fill the places of men deprived of their work through enforced military service. We will do all in our power to help the families of men who suffer through refusing enforced military service.*'

This was all very well but what could she do about it? It was all right for Sarah, a single woman, to join Cumann na mBan, the auxiliary women's organisation, headed by Constance Markiewicz. Sarah had worked in Anna Macken's brothel in the Monto as a maid and general skivvy. Sometimes Nell looks back on those days as the brighter, less responsible, ones in her life and, much to her shame late at night, she often dreams of going back there. Sarah had fallen in love with the doorman, Moussa, a giant of a man from Algeria who stood a good two feet taller than her. It seemed an idyllic match. They set up home in an unused stable behind the brothel on Montgomery Street and converted it into an exotic love-cave for themselves. But that was before Sarah and Nell had discovered that Moussa was not what he seemed, and, in fact, worked for the monster who had almost ruined all of their lives.

Before Nell found out that Anna Macken was, in fact, her birth mother.

Nell thought back to the last time she and Sarah had been at the brothel together. When they had discovered all of the money hidden at the bottom of Moussa's chest. It was the beginning of the end of a way of life for both of them. In her most frustrated moments Nell sometimes wished that they had never discovered that money. But then that would have meant not following Christopher down into the tunnels under the streets of the Monto. Not saving his life. Where would she be now? Probably still living with her mother in Montgomery Street and Sarah would have gone off to Algeria with Moussa and be living in the little white house on the beach he was always talking about. Or maybe not.

Nell folds the Declaration up and puts it with Sarah's letter into a drawer of the dresser. As well as the signing of the Declaration, Sarah also wants her to go with her to a protest in Foster's Place the following day. Something about the 'German plot' internees, locked up in prison on false charges for helping the Germans.

Early summer in the tenement has been stifling as the flat has only the one window which looks out onto the privy in the backyard that serves the whole building. On hot, airless days she cannot even open the window because of the smell. When she opens the hall door that leads into the lobby of the building, the smell of cabbage and bacon, one of the few dishes that Mary Sherry cooks, permeates the flat and seems to cling onto the walls and the furniture. She can even smell it off herself sometimes. Christopher says he doesn't notice it, but then he spends most of his days among the pig carcasses of the bacon factory.

She takes the letter out and reads through the contents again. Maybe she *would* go to the demonstration – why not? She can suggest to Sarah that they leave early and go up to Stephen's Green and make a day of it. It would be good to get out of the Liberties and into the city for a day. Although it is less than a mile to College Green it feels farther away in her mind. Perhaps it's the tall, narrow, dark-brick buildings that line the dreary streets and laneways of the Liberties that's at the heart of it. It's sometimes days before she can catch a glance at the open sky on her walks around St Patrick's Cathedral. Or maybe it's the gaunt-faced children of her neighbours, forced to spend most of their time on the pavements outside the over-crowded tenements. Or the constant smell of almost rotten food left outside the doors for the pigman to come and collect for the pigs in his nearby piggery. She knows that she shouldn't blame Christopher, he was doing his best, and she had walked into this life with her eyes open. But still, after the bawdy glitter of her mother's brothel and the excitement of daily life in the Monto, the Liberties feels as if it is closing in on her and squeezing out her very essence. That's it. She will meet up with Sarah, shout a few slogans and drag her up Grafton Street to look at the shops, before going up to St Stephen's Green.

As she leaves Thomas Street behind and passes Christ Church Cathedral the next day, the sky seems brighter, or maybe it's just because she is out of the Liberties. Dame Street, bustling with activity as usual along its full length, stretches down before her to the familiar grey façade of Trinity College. As she passes by Dublin Castle, the barbed-wired barricades and the nervous-faced young soldiers guarding the gates cast a slight cloud on the day. But it is only to be expected.

Phil Shanahan has become a more regular visitor to their flat and has kept her up to date about the attacks carried out on RIC barracks around Ireland. The elections are coming up soon and it is certain that Sinn Féin will be elected to parliament, he told her. Christopher, who had been sitting reading a newspaper, let out a skeptical laugh, but Phil had insisted and she had to step in to separate the two men. Also, he said, the Spanish Flu is depleting the British Army and the conscripts sent over to Ireland are young and innocent. She knew that this was a hint for her to come back and work for the movement at her old job: using her wiles to get her hands on soldiers' guns she could sell on to Phil. But she had shown no interest and Phil had steered away from any revolutionary talk after that.

As she crosses the busy road to Parliament Street, she thinks that she is witnessing an apparition. A disembodied head sticks up from the pavement opposite Dublin Castle and grins up at her, then a thin body rises from the pavement. It's a soldier, his face covered in mud. Out of curiosity she looks down into the manhole he has emerged from. Down in the darkness she sees another soldier feeding out barbed wire from a wooden spool to somebody underneath him. The sound of cascading water carries up from the darkness and she remembers that Christopher told her the River Poddle flows under the castle and empties into the Liffey. They must be really worried, she thinks, if they imagine that the Volunteers are going to attack from underground.

Passing the entrance of the Empire Palace Theatre, she tarries for a while in front of the colourful posters of past productions and wonders if she and Christopher will be able to afford the Christmas pantomime this year when the time comes. Drawing closer to Foster Place she's surprised at the numbers of Dublin Metropolitan policemen standing around chatting to each other beside the railings of the Bank of Ireland. She wonders if it is wise to join the protest as she can see from her location on the corner of Foster Place that the mass of women seem almost corralled into the short street. She feels an arm on her back and turns: it's Sarah, dressed in her ordinary clothes and not the Cumann na mBan uniform.

'I'm glad you made it, Nell, I was giving you up.' Sarah smiles and links her arm, walking her further into the crowd of mainly women.

'I just needed to get out of the house if truth be told,' Nell admits.

'Still, the more the merrier.'

They push through the packed bodies towards the front of the demonstration. A distinguished woman is making an impassioned speech from the granite steps of one of the old houses across from the bank. Nell looks at the faces around her. Mostly well-dressed women, some with placards, screaming their support for the speaker. It all seems so unreal, like walking into the middle of a play and not quite being able to join in on the drama. From somewhere behind her she hears a whistle. When she turns, she can make out the tall helmets of the Dublin Metropolitan policemen making their way through the mass. A scream goes up, then another. She becomes caught up in the surge of the crowd as it pushes back towards her. But it is a cul-de-sac and the women have nowhere to go. The police have drawn their batons and are swinging them in every direction. As the conflict draws nearer, she can hear the smack of wood on the bodies of the defenceless women at the back of the crowd, where she had been standing earlier. She becomes incensed at the sight of the belligerent, brutish policemen pummelling any women that are within reach. Instead of retreating from them, she finds herself pushing her way through the crowd towards them. *How dare they!* Sarah tries to pull her back towards the steps of a building on the side of the street.

'*Jesus, Nell, what're you up to?*' she shouts at her.

But Nell's sense of justice has taken over and she is determined to confront the police. As she pushes her way through the crowd, she finds herself at the heart of the pandemonium. The police, swinging and hitting everyone in their path are just feet away. One poor unfortunate woman has fallen under the batons, but the policemen, totally out of control, just keep up their flurry of blows onto her upheld arms and shoulders. When she can no longer stand the assault, she rolls herself up into a ball, but then they just concentrate on her exposed head. Nell throws herself at the policeman who seems to be doing the most damage, a tall, broad, red-faced man with a long moustache so covered with spittle that it drips down onto his chin. His face is full of rage and he has lost all sense of control. But, as Nell springs at him and claws at his face, he stops his assault momentarily and staggers backwards in shock. Recovering somewhat he draws back his baton to hit out at his attacker but Sarah springs from behind and hits him with one of the placards. It is a harmless blow but it distracts him for a few seconds. The rest of the police swirl around them, continuing their advance on the women. The shocked policeman stands, feeling his face. Two trails of blood run across his jaw and drip down onto the collar of his shirt. Incensed with his injury, he is just about to strike out at Nell when one of his superiors grabs his arm.

'*You've done enough, O'Brien – look at her, she's unconscious!*' he hisses into his ear.

The injured woman lies on the ground, eyes closed, her breathing coming in short, shallow breaths. The policeman's superior grabs him by the collar and shoves him after the line of police who are now running out of steam and just pushing the women out of their way. Nell bends down and gently rolls the woman onto her back, brushing her hair, which had come loose, from her face. Her skin has a grey pallor and when Nell puts her hand behind her head to put it in a more comfortable position, it comes away covered in bright, red blood.

'Do you know her?' Nell asks Sarah.

'I think her name is Josie,' Sarah answers.

'She didn't deserve that, nobody does,' Nell says. 'The bastards! Beating her when she was down and doing nobody harm.'

'They're all very brave when they come up against defenceless women,' Sarah says, turns and spits towards the backs of the policemen who have now completely surrounded the women and are taking down names and addresses. The crowd of bystanders who have gathered at the junction of Dame Street and Foster's Place are beginning to disperse. One by one, the protestors who have given their names and addresses and have been dismissed gather around the injured woman.

One of the women approaches and puts a hand on Nell's shoulder. Nell recognises her as the woman who had been addressing the protest.

'You've done enough, I've sent for a taxi. We can take over now.'

The woman is tall and striking and speaks with an upper-class accent – a toff, as Anna would have said. Her long, fair hair has escaped from under her hat in the tussle with the police and she is trying to tuck it back in. She looks to be in her late twenties, not much older than Nell, but she holds herself with such poise and confidence that she seems a world away from her. Nell stands up and brushes her dress down and she and Sarah are gently moved aside as a group of women take over from them. One of them has a shoulder bag and from its depths she takes out some cotton wool and a purple-tinted bottle. She empties some of the contents onto the cotton wool as one of her helpers rolls the fallen woman gently on her side. Now they can see the full extent of her wounds. A deep gash which runs across the

41

top of her scalp for several inches seems to be the most serious. The woman dabs at it with the cotton pad, clearing away some of the blood, and turns to the tall woman.

'She'll have to go to the aid station.'

'I've sent for a taxi,' the tall woman says and looks at Nell. 'It could have been worse if these young ladies had not been around.'

Nell's feels embarrassed as the circle of women turn to her.

'Anybody would have done the same,' she says.

'But they didn't,' the woman says and holds out her hand. 'My name is Cecile Saunderson.'

'Nell Flinter.'

Nell reaches out and shakes her hand but becomes flustered when she notices that her fingers are covered in blood. But Cecile doesn't seem to mind and draws her away to one side as the injured woman is tended to. Nell watches as a small bottle of smelling salts is held under the injured woman's nose. She revives somewhat but still seems groggy, her movements uncoordinated.

'I know Sarah from previous demonstrations, but I don't think I've met you before.' Cecile looks at her as if trying to place her face.

'It was my first time,' Nell admits and reaches into her pocket for a handkerchief to wipe the blood from her fingers.

'It looks as if you've made quite a sacrifice for our cause,' the woman says, reaching out to Nell's shoulder and pulling at a tear in her jacket.

Nell looks down at the damage and frowns. 'I can't believe it. I've only worn it twice.'

'Don't worry, Nell. I live nearby – I can have it repaired in a jiffy,' Cecile says.

'That's alright, I can patch it up,' Nell fingers the frayed ends of the tear, realising that her meagre seamstress skills will never repair it properly.

'I won't hear of it. Sarah will come with us, won't you, Sarah? We can have afternoon tea while the jacket is made new again.'

Sarah nods but says nothing. Nell has never seen her so stuck for words. She stands, not even up to the woman's shoulders and looks up into her face with a mixture of adoration and trepidation. A part of Nell wants to resist the woman's invitation. She had planned a day of window-shopping and a walk around Stephen's Green with Sarah. But, equally, she finds herself wanting to remain in the presence of this woman, who had stayed so calm and aloof even in such a threatening situation.

As they stand together, talking, a taxi draws up and the injured woman is helped into the back. Most of the women, who were huddled together in small groups, are beginning to drift away towards Dame Street and the policemen are left standing around, looking to their commander for their next orders.

Without waiting for a definite answer, Cecile links Nell and Sarah and walks, her held high, out of Foster's Place and away from the police lines.

She leads them across Dame Street, taking little heed of the traffic, then heads towards Grafton Street. As they stroll through the shoppers Cecile keeps up a patter of small talk but Nell notices that there are also some subtle questions being asked. Somehow, before they reach Stephen's Green, she has already found out that Nell is married and lives in the Liberties and that Sarah works somewhere over in the northside of the city, while the only thing that they definitely know about her is that she lives nearby. As they pass by the College of Surgeons, the bullet-pocked building that overlooks St Stephen's Green, she announces that they are almost there.

Her house, when they reach it, reminds Nell of some of the larger buildings in the Monto before the decline, but there the similarities end. Whereas the grander houses in the Monto are either brothels or tenements and mostly in various states of disrepair, all of the houses on Harcourt Street are in pristine condition. Four-storeyed and redbrick, they stand in long terraces on either side of the street which curves gently towards the far end. Cecile ascends the broad granite steps and opens the front door, standing back to let Nell and Sarah inside. Nell has no time to admire the grand lobby and staircase as Cecile walks ahead of them and into a room at the rear.

Half of the room is being used as some sort of office with two large desks facing each other and a row of filing cabinets behind them. The other side of the room looks like a normal sitting room with a coffee table surrounded by armchairs. A tall window with stained glass at the curved top looks out onto the rear garden which stretches away from the house. Cecile goes over to the window and pulls on a sash hanging to one side.

'We will have some tea while we get that jacket repaired,' she says and takes off her hat, throwing it onto one of the desks.

'There's no need, Mrs Saunderson, really,' Nell says.

'Call me Cecile, please.' She makes her way behind one of the desks and shuffles through some post left there. 'Please, Nell, take your jacket off and I will get Breeda to repair it for you. She's quite talented with a needle.'

'It's all right, really. A small price to pay compared to that poor woman who was attacked,' Nell says.

'I insist,' Cecile says and puts out her hand for the jacket.

Nell stands up and takes her jacket off, hoping that Cecile doesn't notice the small repairs on her blouse she has done herself over the years to save money. She'd been careful about darning the parts that were on view but had not bothered too much with the ones covered up by her jacket. She hands the damaged jacket to Cecile.

There's a knock on the door and a young maid enters.

'Gertie, can to give this to Breeda to repair immediately and then bring us some tea, please.' Cecile hands the jacket to the girl and then motions Nell and Sarah over to the armchairs.

As soon as the maid leaves, she takes one of the armchairs opposite, bending forward conspiratorially towards them.

'I don't like to speak in front of Gertie about my dubious activities,' she whispers with a smile.

Nell nods tentatively, feeling the remark is a little frivolous in the circumstances.

'This is a beautiful house.' Nell stares up at the intricate decorative plaster moulding that runs around the wall and the giant, circular rosette in the centre of the ceiling.

'Much too big for me,' Cecile says, 'but where else could I live?'

'Do you live here alone?' Nell asks.

'I do, most of the time, I'm afraid. My husband travels a lot. At the moment he is in the United States trying to buy something or other. I have Gertie and Breeda, of course, and Maura who does the cooking, but I'm afraid most of the house is unused – but not unloved.'

She reaches out to a silver cigarette case that stands in the middle of the coffee table. She opens the lid and offers the cigarettes to Nell and Sarah, who, after a glance at each other, accept.

'So, you see, I have a lot of time on my hands to fill,' she says, holding out a lit match to the two girls. Then she lights a cigarette herself and blows a cloud of blue smoke up towards the ceiling. 'Which brings us back to our protest today. What did you think of it, Nell?'

'To be honest, I don't know much about what the protest was about,' she answers. 'I was really just there to meet Sarah.'

Cecile laughs at her answer, tapping her cigarette into the ashtray. 'Good for you. I like an honest answer. It sets a good tone in any new relationships.'

There's a knock on the door and the maid enters with a tray which she puts on the coffee table. She unloads a teapot, milk, sugar and a plateful of tiny triangular sandwiches without their crusts. She places teacups, side plates, cutlery and napkins in front of the three women then pours the tea.

The women watch her silently. Nell feels rather awkward, wanting to say something to the girl.

'Thank you, Gertie,' says Cecile.

Gertie withdraws with a slight nod.

Seeing the freshly made sandwiches, Nell's first thought is how hungry she is, but then she feels a pang of guilt about being served by another person roughly the same age as herself, who probably goes back every night to a tiny tenement room somewhere in the city. Or maybe lives in the maid's quarters in the basement under where they are sitting now.

They stub out their cigarettes and begin to eat.

Cecile keeps the conversation light, and it is Nell who returns to the subject of the protest.

'Do *you* think the protest was a success?' she asks her hostess.

'Of course. What we did today will be picked up by the newspapers, national and international, and hopefully will embarrass the government enough to set the internees free. Remember the war is almost over now and the British may be victorious, but it was with the help of the Americans. And in America there are thousands of first- and second-generation Irish people who vote.'

'But do you think that those poor women being attacked by the police, maybe even seriously injured, was worth the price?'

'It's the price we have to pay, Nell. Tomorrow the papers will have headlines berating the police for attacking unarmed women.'

'I hope Josie is all right,' Sarah suddenly says.

'I'm sure she will be.' Cecile waves her hand as if she's tired of justifying the protest, then gets to her feet. 'Excuse me while I check on the progress of the work on your jacket.'

'What do you think?' Sarah nods towards the door after Cecile leaves.

'Well,' Nell says slowly, 'I suppose you have to give her credit … if you think about it, she doesn't have to take part in any of those protests. She's rich, has a fine house. And yet she puts herself in danger.' She knows she sounds grudging.

'*And* there are rumours that's not all she does,' Sarah says, keeping her voice low.

'What do you mean?'

'They say that this house is a safe house, used by the higher-ups in Sinn Féin. It's been raided a few times, but Sinn Féin are too clever for them.'

Nell is astonished. She really has underestimated Cecile.

'And she runs a secretarial training college, for girls who want office skills.'

Nell gets up from her seat and walks over to the window. The back garden at the rear of the house is long and narrow. Halfway up there is a gazebo surrounded by low bushes and behind that what looks like an orchard of trees laden down with apples. In the garden next door, she can see the neighbours' children playing a game with sticks and a ball. The sound of their laughter drifts up and she wonders about the different areas of this tight-knit city of Dublin she calls home. Not two miles away in the Monto, her mother, Anna, is probably getting the brothel ready for tonight's customers. While over in the Liberties Mary Sherry lives in two tiny rooms in a miserable tenement building with her seven children.

Cecile comes back into the room with the jacket, holding it up to the light.

'You'd never know it was torn!' she announces, handing it to Nell.

And she's right. Nell examines the jacket and the tear is hard to find. She puts it on and remains standing.

'Please thank Breeda for me,' she says. 'And thank you for the tea.'

'Do you have to leave so soon?' Cecile asks, a bit taken aback.

'I'm afraid my husband will be home soon and I need to get his dinner.'

'Of course, I understand,' Cecile says, but looks disappointed.

She leads them back into the imposing hallway and opens the front door for them.

Sarah says goodbye and walks out but, as Nell walks past, Cecile puts her hand on her arm.

'Can you hang on for a minute? I'm sure Sarah won't mind waiting,' she says.

She goes back to the office and comes back with a business card which she hands to Nell.

'I'm not completely useless, Nell. I run a secretarial college not far from here. I'd be delighted if you could attend. I think you have great potential.'

Nell is taken aback and more than a little embarrassed that Cecile has sensed some disapproval from her. She takes the business card. It looks expensive with Cecile's name in black heat-raised type and an address on Earlsfort Terrace printed in black on the front.

'I really couldn't afford it, I'm afraid,' she says.

'Don't worry about that. Nell – you were honest with me so I will be honest with you. You might think that I'm just filling in time while my husband is away. But that's not the case. We need women like you more than ever.'

'We?'

'Sinn Féin, Nell.'

'So, the rumours are true?'

'I can't comment on rumours, but what I've just said to you would land me in jail if you ever reported it. All I can be certain about is that our country needs to be free to decide its own destiny once and for all. I think you feel the same way. If I'm wrong about that, so be it.'

'But how could I help anyway?'

'You can begin by expanding your mind, and your skills. After that, we shall see.'

Nell looks at the card and considers it. In another few hours Christopher will be home from his dead-end job in the bacon factory. After his dinner he'll go out again, wandering around the Liberties, passing by the old cottage where he grew up, remembering better times before his parents' death.

'I'll think about it,' she says.

'Just come to this address, any time during weekdays and we can talk,' Cecile says, leading her out through the door and into the warm September sunshine.

As they walk back down Harcourt Street towards Stephen's Green, Nell turns to Sarah.

'You knew what was going to happen, didn't you?' she says accusingly.

'I had a good idea, Nell. But things are going on that you're not aware of, great things. And you could be part of them. I know you love Christopher, but I also know that you're not the person who used to be full of laughter and joy back in the Monto. Just go along with Cecile for a while and see if it will bring any of the old you back.'

Nell links her friend again and for the first time in over a year feels alive. They walk down Grafton Street, taking in the shop windows and admiring the well-dressed crowds that mill around them. She knows that she could have taken a shorter route, but she wants the unfamiliar feeling of lightness to last longer.

When she and Sarah finally part company outside Trinity College, she turns up Dame Street towards the Liberties. She looks over at Foster's Place, the scene of the protest earlier. Now it is virtually empty, no protestors and no police, just some well-dressed businessmen coming and going from the well-appointed doorways, unaware that somewhere on the cobbled roadway the blood of an innocent woman had been spilt. She reaches into her pocket and finds the business card that Cecile has given her, turning it over and over in her hand like a rosary.

CHAPTER 6

Skagway, Alaska
1897

Jefferson Randolf 'Soapy' Smith stares out through the grimy window of his bar – Jeff Smith's Parlour – onto the main street of Skagway. It is a long, appraising look as Jefferson is constantly on the lookout for any opportunity to come his way.

The frontier town is now a temporary home to about eight thousand people, most of them transient prospectors on their way to the Yukon. A heavy rain has just ended and is causing chaos on the dirt street outside the bar. Known to the more permanent citizens of the town as Main Street, it is now a churned-up mixture of brown mud and dirty water. Mules are being whipped unmercifully as the owners try to dislodge their wagons from the deep swampy mess. Men and women plot their way around the deeper ruts caused by the countless wagons on their way to or from one of the four docks that now supply the town.

But Jefferson is not paying attention to any of the tumult outside. His shifty, searching eyes have now settled on two figures on the opposite side of the street.

Outside Clancy's Saloon two poorly dressed figures are huddled together. The older of the two, a tall gaunt man – the father, he guesses – is handing a tightly wrapped package to his teenage son. He is bent down, speaking intently into the boy's ear and the son is nodding, his face pinched up in concentration. Jefferson spits on the glass window and rubs it around with his handkerchief to get a clearer view. At the same time, he clicks his fingers to catch the attention of his gang, most of whom are sitting at the bar arguing loudly among themselves on the merits of the new model 1894 Winchester rifle versus the older but more reliable earlier model.

Immediately two of the men, John L 'Reverend' Bowers and Slim-Jim Fraser, join him. Jefferson points over towards the man and the teenager who are still in deep discussion. The boy is busy shoving the package down the front of his trousers, which look like hand-me-downs from the father. They hang limply from his thin hips and are held up by a length of thick cord. When he is happy that the package is secure, he buttons over a sad-looking homemade overcoat.

The two gang members gaze across the street. Jefferson is wearing his usual dark, three-piece suit, a white shirt with a starched collar and a thin leather bootlace tie. Thick black hair sprouts from under his hat which he wears indoors and out. The bottom half of his face is covered by a luxurious beard. The jacket of his suit is pushed to one side to show the army Long Colt pistol that he always wears in the saloon. He uses the deadly-looking firearm as a warning to any of the suckers he has swindled since he arrived in the town over two years previously. Some have ideas of getting their money back, but always retreat when they look into the dark maw of his Long Colt.

'Where's Old Man Triplett?' he asks.

'Bog house,' Bowers answers, still gazing across at the man and boy. It is an unexceptional scene, but he respects the instinct of his boss.

The man and boy opposite who are now separating.

'Why don't you get Old Man Triplett to take hisself over to that boy and show him how to play three-card Monte,' Smith says, pointing his cheroot.

'What about the father?'

'That yonder man has a thirst on him and I reckon he's headin' to cure it.' Smith nods towards the man who is now disappearing through the door of Clancy's Saloon.

Bowers smiles at his boss and turns, shoving his way through the crowd towards the rear of the bar and then leaves through a side entrance. In the yard outside he notices cigarette smoke drifting up through the cracks in the rough-hewn timber of one of two wooden outhouses that serve the saloon. It is the cubicle marked 'WOMEN'. Even though few respectable women had ever squatted in there, his boss insisted it added sophistication to the bar. Most of the whores preferred to bring their customers to the upstairs rooms and it is an unwritten rule that members of Soapy Smith's gang have the use of the seldom-used female outhouse.

Bowers picks his way through the mud towards the outhouse, grumbling to himself about the wasted nickel he had just paid to the half-breed shoeshine. He hammers on the wooden door with his fist, inspecting his ruined boots.

'*You in there, Triplett?*' he shouts out.

'*Can't a man have a shit in peace anymore?*' Old Man Triplett shouts back.

'*The boss has a job. A young mark, standing outside a' Clancy's!*'

'Why do you need me, goddamn it?' the petulant Triplett says through the crack in the door.

'It's a three-man job. Now git your trousers up and outa that damn shitter – he's not goin' to be hangin' around while you take a dump!'

Bowers makes his way back into the bar.

✳✳✳✳

The awestruck boy stands outside Clancy's Bar, taking in his surroundings. Facing him across the street, a row of neat wooden buildings look out over the muddy thoroughfare. They are nothing like his own log cabin, a squat, no-nonsense building thrown up by his father, with a sod roof and a few mean openings covered with burlap. Unlike his own home, all of them have actual glass windows that reflect the sun that has just made an appearance. One of them is even two storeys high and he wonders why somebody had ruined a good, solid, wood cabin with an addition that looks just plain unnatural. On the street more people than he has ever seen in his life go about their daily business. A woman steers a carriage down the street, concentrating on avoiding the worst of the deep ruts now filled with water. Two angry prospectors try to move their pack mules who have decided not to go any further. A tiny man with a yellow face and pigtail runs across the street towards the boy, his baggy pants flapping in the breeze and he has to step aside to let him jump up onto the wooden walkway.

'First time in the big city, son?'

The boy turns. A tall man in a frock coat is leaning against a hitching post to his left and smiles over at him. The man goes back to filling his pipe, which, unlike his father's corn pipe, is a complicated affair. The stem protrudes from the man's heavy moustache and curves downwards, ending in a deep bowl of dark, shiny wood. The boy watches as the man holds a lit match over his makings and sucks vigorously until the clump of tobacco changes into an orange glow. A plume of blue smoke rises up and over his head and drifts away. The man removes his pipe and strolls over to him, holding out his hand.

'The Reverend John L. Bowers, at your service, son,' he says, bowing slightly.

The boy stares at the stranger's outstretched hand uncertainly.

'Have yeh never been told it's bad manners not to shake a hand that's being offered, son?'

'No, sir.'

'Well, I do declare standards seem to be slippin'!' The man laughs good-naturedly and shakes his head from side to side.

'I'm sorry, sir. My pa told me never to talk to no strangers.'

The man laughs again.

'But, son, I ain't no stranger. I am an ordained reverend in this here town and versed in the ways of the Lord. Have you ever heard of the Lord, boy?'

'Yessir. He's creator of everything under the sun,' the boy says proudly.

'Good. We're gettin' somewhere now. And, by the way, what name do you go by?' He draws nearer to the boy.

'My name is Levon, sir,' the boy says after a pause.

'Levon …' The man seems to consider the name and taps his brown teeth with the stem of his pipe. 'A good strong name, son, for a strapping young man like yerself.'

'Levon Mordaunt,' the boy adds, pleased.

'Glad to meet your acquaintance, Levon,' Bowers says, putting his arm around Levon's shoulders, 'and welcome to Skagway.'

'Thank you, sir.'

'You can call me Reverend, everybody here does. Tell me, have you ever been to Skagway before?'

'No … Reverend.'

'Well, it's a good thing we bumped into each other, Levon, because this here town is full of every type of bad people out to do a young man harm. Plain evil, in fact. Tell me, Levon, where do you hail from?'

The boy thinks about this for a while. 'It ain't got a name,' he answers, 'but you follow the big river for some days and then follow a smaller river into the hills and there you are, I guess.'

'You must be somewhere along White Pass,' Reverend Bowers says, almost to himself.

An elderly man with a sparse grey beard approaches and shouts out a greeting to the Reverend. He is carrying what looks like a small suitcase in his left hand.

'Well, hello, Mister Triplett, fancy meeting up with you!' The Reverend shakes the old man's hand vigorously. 'Let me introduce you to this fine young gentleman and a stranger to Skagway – Levon Mordaunt.'

'Hello, son,' Triplett says and doffs his hat towards the boy. 'Always a pleasure to meet an acquaintance of Reverend Bowers.'

The three of them are standing in the middle of the boardwalk outside Clancy's Bar. A constant stream of customers coming and going from the bar press around them, some elbowing their way past and muttering under their breath. Reverend Bowers shakes his head sadly and takes the old man and the boy by their arms, leading them to a narrow alley that runs down the side of the bar.

Triplett mops his brow with a huge, check handkerchief and puts the small suitcase onto the ground beside him as if he is going to sit on it.

'Now, isn't this more convivial?' Reverend Bowers says to the old man and the boy. 'If there's one thin' I hate it's being jostled, especially by men with one thin' on their minds. And we all here know what that is.'

'Well, good evening, gentlemen. Anyone for a game of Chase the Lady?'

A well-dressed man strolls down the alleyway towards them and lifts his hat to the two men.

'Well, if it isn't Jim Fraser, as I live and breathe!' the Reverend says good-naturedly. 'Are you not tired of losin' your savin's to this old man yet? What's yer good wife goin' to say?'

As the two men are shaking hands, the Old Man Triplett opens the suitcase. Levon has never seen anything like it. In a few seconds Triplett has turned the suitcase into a table and a deck of cards appears in his hands.

CHAPTER 7

Queen's Hospital, Sidcup

D
r Harold Gillies isn't a great admirer of the odd design of the pre-fabricated buildings that they had constructed for him on the grounds of the Queen's Hospital, but he had to admit that they were bright and functional. Their functionality came about by accident in that most of the patients had to be separated into various wards scattered among the wooden prefabs that radiated out from the main building, where most of the surgery and recovery took place. This forced separation of patients had helped him in grading the soldier's facial injuries from the moderate to the very severe.

Gillies, a New Zealander, is now performing miracles in facial reconstruction to the soldiers and sailors lucky enough – or unlucky enough? – to survive the horrendous wounds from bullet or bomb. As he began his work on the intricacies of rebuilding broken faces, he had learned one thing that surprised him. As he unwrapped the faces of the injured, he found that it wasn't the injuries that gave them nightmares, it was the after-effects of the war itself. In fact, most of the men accepted their damaged faces eventually and, before they had even left the hospital, some had begun to plan their lives into the future. He introduced photography into his path of healing. From the first admission to the final discharge, he used the camera as a witness to what turned out to be the miraculous transformation from a horribly damaged face to a face that was not entirely unlike the original. Not all, of course. To some it was all too much and no amount of healing could bring them back to their old lives as they were rejected by wives, or lovers or even their own children.

Sunday afternoons are his rest periods. An accomplished golfer and violinist, he spends his spare time either on the golf course or playing his violin, sometimes giving impromptu recitals in the local pub much to the amusement of the locals. On this particular Sunday it is the golf course. After a dreadful round of golf and then a long drinking session in the clubhouse, he decides not to go home, but to spend the remainder of the night in the hospital where he has a spare cot in his office. Tired after his two rounds of golf and the meal and wine afterwards, he is preparing his bed for the night but then decides to step outside the building for a last cigarette.

In the grounds to the rear and one side of the hospital, a copse of mature oak grow, probably as a windbreak, he thinks, as the rest of the area where the hospital is situated is quite flat and featureless. These appear as darker silhouettes against the pitch black of the surrounding countryside. As he pulls on his cigarette, he sees a pale shadow flitting between himself and the woods. Probably a doctor, or even a nurse, getting out of the wretched wards for some fresh air. A wind blows across the open side of the grounds and seems to make the pale shadow flicker. Then he realises that it must be one of the patients and the flickering is the wind disturbing the long, white, hospital gown issued to the men. How odd!

As the pale shadow approaches the hospital buildings and takes on a more solid outline, he steps back into the shadows. It is definitely a patient, with the tell-tale bandages around his head covering everything but the eyes. As he watches, the man stops and throws himself on the ground. Flat out and face down, he begins a series of push-ups. Dr Gillies watches in fascination but loses count. Every time the man pushes himself up he lets out a low grunt, like a wounded animal. When he has finally exhausted the strength in his arms, he pulls himself into a squatting position and begins to do thrust squats, forcing his hips backwards until they almost touched the ground, then pumps his legs until he is in an upright position.

Normally, if Dr Gillies had witnessed this kind of dedication to rehabilitation, he would have congratulated the mysterious patient heartily. But something about the animal-like noises and the total concentration of the patient, almost an obsessive concentration, keeps him from emerging from the shadows. Is it that he feels embarrassed by the sight of the man pushing himself to the limits in the darkness, he questions himself? No. He realises that at some subliminal level, he is actually afraid. Frightened of one of his own patients – absurd? But no, he feels as if he is in the presence of a wild animal, a powerful wild animal, one that would pounce on him if it had the chance.

As if he senses that he is being observed, the patient stops his exercises and stands, sniffing the air and looking around him.

Dr Gillies takes the opportunity and strides out of the shadows, making a lot of noise as if he has just emerged from the hospital. The man stiffens but, when he sees it's the doctor, relaxes and walks towards him.

'Good evening,' the doctor nods affably, 'and a fine evening it is.'

The patient nods back and passes him by, disappearing towards one of the free-standing units at the back of the complex. The doctor steps further out into the grounds but looks back, following the patient's progress. The man disappears into the George Ward and closes over the door silently behind him.

Dr Gillies rushes back into the main building and makes his way directly to the general office. Inside he opens the filing cabinet and shuffles through the various names of the patients in the ward. He is acquainted with most of the men, knows their names, and now he realises who the patient must be: Levon Mordaunt.

Dr Gillies might have known. Mordaunt is one of his more peculiar patients. He communicates by using the written word, which is normal, but what is contained within those messages is negligible. Before initial surgery on patients, Gillies always takes a photograph to show the progress after the wounds have healed somewhat. Then, after subsequent operations, he repeats that, believing that the progress shown would improve the men's state of mind and chances of recovery. But Levon Mordaunt had resisted all of his attempts to photograph his face. When he had questioned the decision with him, he had simply written: *NOT NECESSARY.*

After a year of constant painful surgery, during which Mordaunt has never complained, Gillies has finally given up on him. There is a little improvement, but not much. Most of the right side of his face is open and gaping, but had settled down, and the left side is improving. But the wound is still horrendous and would have made another man lose his will to live. But not Mordaunt. He had even ruled out the 'tube pedicle', the method that Gillies had perfected to reduce the risk of infection by using flaps of skin from undamaged areas from the face and neck. He made Gillies aware that it would be too complicated and take too long. It was as if, behind those bandages, Mordaunt was biding his time until his discharge from the hospital. What are your plans? Gilles had asked him once, but Mordaunt had ignored the question and written nothing down on the slate he kept beside the bed, just stared straight up at him with those lifeless eyes as if Gillies himself was the one with the problem.

Mordaunt has no visitors, no family, no friends – another anomaly – and Gillies wonders where he would go when he is discharged. He just lies in his bed – or so Gillies had thought before he'd witnessed his nocturnal exercises. He has no personal visitors, that is true, but there are visits. Every few weeks men, usually uniformed, ask to speak to him. The format is always the same: the men arrive, the screens requested are wheeled around the bed, and afterwards the men depart for another few weeks.

Gillies had heard rumours that his mystery patient could be heard mumbling. But he put that down to a mixture of the bad feelings of his fellow patients and idle gossip.

Even the men in the beds around him have given up trying to communicate with him. Now they just leave him be and the hospital bed and the patient lying on it seem to have just disappeared from the day-to-day life of the ward. And, if Gillies is to be frank, he suspects that Mordaunt has disappeared from his own mind as well. He is just a breathing body, waiting. For what? This he does not know and does not want to know.

Mordaunt had arrived in an ambulance, with few accompanying notes, just some scribbled messages from a nurse attached to a barracks in Ireland. So, presumably, that's where he would go back to. And, Gillies hates to admit it to himself: good riddance.

The only person who has got near to the strange patient is one of the most unlikely. The Reverend Stanley Tompkins, the new spiritual pastor to the hospital. He seems to pique Mordaunt's interest in that he at least reacts to his presence. The Reverend Tompkins, a Catholic priest from Birmingham, is the most irritating man Gillies has ever met, yet there he is, sometimes daily, sitting down beside Mordaunt's bed, reading out tracts from the Old Testament under the steady gaze of those dead eyes. Tompkins' official parish is in nearby Bromley.

What makes him leave the church of St Peter and St Paul, Gillies at first wondered, and brings him to the hospital?

After a few weeks of the priest's daily visits, Gillies began to realise there was a problem. On his daily rounds of the wards, he became aware of the priest's incessant nasal drone as he sat beside the beds of the other patients who sometimes pretended to be asleep. A discreet phone call to his parish priest gave him his answer. It was obvious, after a short conversation, that the parish priest of Bromley was reluctant to send another priest in his place as this would 'set a precedent'. The unspoken message was: he was glad to be rid of him.

In a strange way Dr Gillies is grateful to the Reverend Tompkins and his visits to Mordaunt's bedside as this means he can curtail his own visit to him without feeling guilty. Over the course of a few months, the priest has gravitated to the only bedside where he is welcome. On Gillies' daily rounds through the various wards, he has noticed that he has begun to change his order. Now he leaves the George Ward until the end of his rounds and finds himself hoping and praying that Reverend Tomkins will be in his usual spot beside the bed of the strangest patient he has ever had.

Several days after he witnessed the bizarre form of Mordaunt, alone, doing his exercises in the dark, comes another surprise. The body of Reverend Stanley Tompkins is found, naked and lifeless, in the grounds of the hospital. The last person he suspects is Mordaunt. He informs the police, when he is being interviewed, that he has no idea who has committed the dastardly crime, but he can make a good guess at the only person who is above reproach. On the day following the discovery of the body, while the police are still combing the grounds of the hospital looking for clues, the nurse in charge of Mordaunt's ward informs him that the patient, Mordaunt, has disappeared.

'Are you sure?' he asks the nurse, a middle-aged no-nonsense Irishwoman. 'Perhaps he's just upset that Reverend Tompkins has been murdered and he's wandering around the countryside.'

'Positive, doctor,' she states. 'We thought that he might be outside with the police, seeing that the good Reverend was the only poor cratur in the hospital who he listened to, but he missed his midday meal. Then he missed this afternoon tea and sandwiches. He's never missed a meal before.'

'Surely you're exaggerating?' Dr Gillies says, annoyed that he hadn't noticed that before.

'No. The poor man never missed a meal, even though every chew must have been torture.'

'Tell the police sergeant I want to speak to him,' he says wearily.

Gillies sits down on a nearby chair and rubs his temples. Mordaunt's disappearance is beginning to make sense. Only the previous week he had been fitted with his tin mask. Under precise instructions from Mordaunt, the most animated Gillies had ever seen him, the artist had spent hours adding accurate skin tones and even a narrow moustache to the mask. Why? He should have recognised that in a gruesome way, Mordaunt's face, with the addition of the mask, began to resemble the poor priest's. Why did he not pick up on it? Who knew the deeper depths of the minds of men and he includes himself in this.

After all of the horror and mystery, a germ of relief has risen within him. Why? He is almost ashamed to admit it, but over the course of a couple of days he is finally rid of two of the most annoying people he has ever come across.

CHAPTER 8

Christopher –
February 1919

In Browne's Public House nestled in the middle of Patrick Street, Christopher Flinter nurses the dregs of the porter at the bottom of his glass, swilling the remaining dark-brown mixture around and staring at the changing shapes made by the agitated froth. Out of choice he sits alone, down at the end of the bar and deeper into the interior of the pub, away from the window and the door. His father, when he was alive, used to drink here and, as a child, Christopher remembers being sent to fetch him home on Friday nights. It was the only night his father went out drinking and, even then, it was only for a couple of hours. On the way home they would drop into the local chipper, run by an Italian family. His father would order fish and chips for the dinner and after that feast Christopher and his younger brother, Ned, would have their weekly bath in the giant cast-iron tub his mother used for washing clothes. In the earlier years Ned and himself would fit into it together, flicking water at each other before their mother called a halt and took them out, wrapped towels around them and let them dry off in front of the open fire.

He finds this end of the bar matches his mood. Hunched over and away from the daylight seeping in through the windows, he tries to work out what he is doing here and, more importantly, how he can escape? If he had less pride he would ask Anna Macken, Nell's mother, for a loan so that he could buy a sailing ticket for America. He's heard that it is safe to cross the Atlantic now and that there are plenty of jobs over there. Once there he could work night and day to get Nell across to join him. But that would mean being beholden to Anna, who, no doubt, would string him along with empty promises.

Towards the front of the bar, three men are throwing rings at a worn-out board. One of them, Tommy Sherry, shouts down at him to see if he wants to join them.

Christopher shakes his head, drains the rest of his drink and calls for another pint of plain porter, the cheapest drink in the bar.

Tommy Sherry scuttles down to him.

'Havin' another one, Christopher?' he says.

'I've only enough for the one more pint, Tommy, sorry,' Christopher apologises.

'I don't want a drink,' Tommy says, a hurt look on his face. 'I'm just sayin', you've a beautiful young wife at home, so what are you doin' here by yourself?'

The irony is that Tommy is right. Christopher often asks himself that same question. What drives a man into a dreary bar to wallow in his own dark thoughts? After deserting the British army to exact revenge on the same Tommy Sherry for not looking after his young brother, Ned, then his capture by an army patrol, why hadn't his life ended then? What higher power saved him, and for what? And why doesn't he appreciate the luck that was bestowed on him after escaping from a firing squad and then meeting the love of his life?

That act of redemption, handed to him by Major Jonathan Byatt, was a double-edged sword. In the course of the following few days, he had met and fallen in love with Nell and had helped apprehend and bring down the monster they called Janus. When it was all over, Tommy Sherry had forgiven him and had even helped him to get old man Devenish's flat. Now they are friends, of a sort.

So, what has him lurking in the dark corners of a public house rather than being at home with Nell?

The truth, he realises, is deep anger brought on by frustration. The ending of the Great War last year had at first brought a temporary relief. But when all of the victory parades were over and the last of the soldiers had returned home, the day-to day struggle for survival continued unabated. Nothing had really changed. The poor were still poor and crowded into filthy tenements. The Irish were still subjugated by their masters, the British. Yes, there had been progress on the political front – after Sinn Féin's landslide victory in the general elections in December, on a manifesto promising an Irish Republic, the party had created an Irish parliament named Dáil Éireann. But would the British accept that? Many still believed independence could only be won by the sword. So now the war for independence was beginning, but he was not allowed to fully take part. He had presumed that he would be recruited by the Irish Volunteers, who were beginning to take up arms. But it looked like they still didn't trust him because of his time in the British army.

Phil Shanahan had promised him he would try and find him something better than standing at a butcher's block all day in a bacon factory. But the only 'mission' he had been given so far was the previous September when he had helped slaughter a herd of pigs that had been requisitioned for the poor people of Dublin by the Irish Republican Army. They were driven into a local council yard near Dorset Street and it was only then that the Volunteers who had carried out the rustling realised that they would have to kill the pigs properly first before they could begin to butcher them.

When he received the message from the commander of the unit, he thought at first that it was for a military operation and not for his skills at slaughtering pigs! And, to add insult to injury, when he had been dismissed he had been handed a brown-paper parcel with some of the meat. At first, he had been insulted, but then he realised that he *was* one of the poor of the city.

The barman puts his pint of porter in front of him and waits for payment. As Christopher searches through his pockets for the money, somebody behind him places a ten-shilling note onto the counter and pushes it towards the barman.

'The same for me,' a man's voice says, 'and take for the two out of that.'

Christopher turns. With the light shining from the window behind the newcomer, it's hard to make out his features. But, as soon as the barman leaves to get the drinks, the stranger takes the stool on the other side of him. Now he is sitting near one of the flickering gas globes that hangs from the ceiling behind the bar. The man paying for his drink is in his mid-twenties, about the same age as himself. Whereas Christopher is wearing his much-repaired work jacket and ill-matched trousers, the stranger is dressed in a dark suit with a matching waistcoat. As he sits down on his stool, he takes great care, pulling up the trouser leg of his suit so as to maintain the perfect crease. He's clean shaven with a slight razor-nick on one of his cheeks and Christopher recognises the smell of bay-rum aftershave lotion. The strength of the lotion and the shaving nick makes him suspect that the man has prepared himself carefully for his night out.

'Thank you,' Christopher acknowledges as the barman places another pint of porter in front of his benefactor.

'Not at all.' The man tips his hat, a trilby.

'Do we know each other?'

The man takes a tiny sip from his drink and makes a face, wiping the froth from under his nose with a handkerchief he has taken from his breast pocket. He folds the handkerchief back to its original shape and places it back into his pocket again.

'We have a friend in common,' the man says, pushing the porter away from him. 'Phil Shanahan.'

'Did he send you?' Christopher picks up his own drink up and takes a large gulp.

'How do you drink that stuff?' the man says, making a face, and he calls for a small whiskey and water.

'It's cheap,' Christopher says, 'and it's the working man's drink'.

The man shrugs apologetically. 'To each his own,' he says and smiles. 'Anthony Caprani, at your service.'

The barman brings back the whiskey and jug of water, then takes his time picking the price out of the change on the counter, but Christopher suspects he's trying to eavesdrop and remains silent until he leaves.

'Christopher Flinter,' he then says simply, and waits.

'I know all about you.' Anthony pours a tiny drop of water into his whiskey, picks up the glass and takes a sip.

'From Phil?'

'Phil ... and other people I can't name.' He shrugs.

Christopher looks closely at the young man's face. His pomaded hair, an unusual shade of auburn, is combed back and held in place by hair oil. Under a high forehead his eyes, dark-brown, are continuously glancing over Christopher's shoulder. His build is slight, and this, together with his pale hands give him the appearance of an office worker or a clerk of some kind.

'You're Italian,' Christopher states.

'They never told me you were a detective,' Anthony replies. 'With a name like mine, how did you ever guess?'

'I meant that you're probably first generation, that's all,' Christopher explains, 'I can hear your accent coming through, but only slightly.'

'First, second, third, who cares, we're all God's children – didn't your parents ever teach you that?' Anthony says in a slightly irritated tone.

'I meant no offence. I just want to know who I'm dealing with.'

'OK, you guessed right. My mother and father are from a little town outside Rome and I was born on the ship to Ireland from Naples. They still call me Antonio no matter how much I argue with them about it.'

'My surname is Flinter. Not exactly Irish either.'

The barman, out of boredom or curiosity, drifts down to where they're sitting and begins to polish some glasses, but they nurse their drinks in silence until he gives up and makes his way back up the bar again.

'I was told you are reliable and handled yourself well in Dorset Street,' Anthony says. 'People were impressed.'

'All I did was slaughter some pigs and helped with the butchering.'

'But you kept your nerve, did what was asked of you and never complained,' Anthony insists.

'You've heard I was in the British army?'

'Of course. Phil told me everything.' He leans in closer to Christopher. 'We're looking for volunteers who can handle themselves. There's no shortage of men coming forward, but most of them have never been in combat or even shot a gun. We need experienced soldiers to train them.'

'You mean marching them around Dublin with pikes over their shoulders?' Christopher says, and takes another gulp from his drink.

'No, we're reorganising – now there's a Dublin brigade,' Anthony says with more passion, moving his stool closer. 'We train in the mountains,'

'With real guns?'

'Yes, thanks to the Royal Irish Constabulary,' Anthony says with a laugh.

'I've heard about the barracks raids.'

'They're only a part of what's happening. We have a new commander and he has plans. And with our big win in the election last December, independence is on the way. Make no mistake, Christopher, the country is rising up and you can be a part of it.'

'For what it's worth, I think you made a mistake in Tipperary.'

'Those two unfortunate RIC men should have laid down their arms,' Anthony says, tapping out the words on the counter with his finger.

'That's not what the newspapers said.'

'The newspapers are liars and they'll be taken care of.'

Christopher attempts to hide it, but he can feel himself coming alive for the first time in months. Nell had other interests, why not him? Every weekday now she takes her hat and coat and her satchel and makes her way over to a secretarial college on Earlsfort Terrace. When he had asked her why she wasn't being charged, she just shrugged it off and said that she didn't know herself but suspected it had something to do with her mother.

'Either way,' Christopher continues, 'they've just declared war on a country with one of the largest standing armies in the world.'

'I know. That's Dan Breen for yeh! He pushed our hand. But now it's too late. Well, are you with us or not?'

'What's in it for me?' Christopher asks, trying to make it sound casual.

'How about a Luger Parabellum for a start?' Anthony whispers.

'I prefer a Mauser C96.' Christopher takes out his cigarettes.

'Phil said you'd say that!' Anthony laughs and takes a cigarette out of the offered packet. 'Unfortunately, they only go to the top men.'

'The Luger will do, I suppose – for now,' Christopher says, and strikes a match for their cigarettes.

As their faces draw together over the flame a weight seems to lift from his mind.

CHAPTER 9

Levon Mordaunt

The exterior of the house in Fitzwilliam Square is in better condition than he had thought it would be. The spare key, placed behind a loose brick at the bottom of the steps leading down to the basement entrance, is where he left it. After he lets himself in, he checks the gas geyser in the lower bathroom, but there is no gas supply. He makes his way upstairs to the ground floor of the house. A pale light shines through the stained-glass fanlight over the front door and picks out the surprisingly small clutter of old post that lies scattered around the floor under the letterbox. He gathers the post up and takes it with him to the main reception room to the front of the house. A light layer of dust lies over the furniture, but other than a stale smell that hangs in the air, the room looks exactly as he left it.

He puts his post on the walnut table in front of the tall window and looks out at the familiar scene. Fitzwilliam Square is an upmarket Georgian square on the south side of Dublin and he had paid handsomely for it. Surrounded on all sides by somber five-storeyed redbrick houses, it was the perfect location for his enterprise: not overly ostentatious to bring attention to him, yet almost in the heart of the city of Dublin. The houses around the square overlook a large private garden, really a small park. The park was established when the houses were originally built and was for the private use of the owners and, as an owner, he had used it often for contemplation and for dissecting and examining all of the intricate interlinking parts of his schemes.

A large bunch of keys lies in a cupboard in his office and he intends on crossing the street, entering the park and sitting on his favourite bench to reformulate his plans. The need for money is pressing and there is money to be made here. The Great War is over, the treaties signed, but the failed 1916 rebellion that he had played a small part in is beginning again. Now the election has lent a kind of legitimacy to a so-called Irish government and it is becoming more established.

He walks over to the huge ornamental mirror that hangs down over the marble fireplace and wipes a layer of dust off with his hand. The face that stares back at him is not his own, but it will suffice. Most people in London studiously ignored him, thinking him one of the brave soldiers who had been disfigured for the great cause. On the overfull train down to Liverpool he had been given a seat by, of all things, a priest. He was glad of it as he was beginning to get tired. The elimination of Reverend Stanley Tompkins had been more complicated than he had thought.

But it was all worth it. Turning to one side and reaching behind his neck, he unties the string that holds the mask in position and lets it slip down by degrees. The left side of his face comes into view. Very little damage except for the white pallor of the skin from wearing the mask. Then he turns around in tiny increments. As more of the right side of his face comes into view, the rage that he had been storing somewhere in the back of his consciousness begins to manifest itself. It comes from somewhere below his solar plexus and rises up to his misshapen mouth, erupting in animal-like grunts through the shattered side of his face. Gillies, for all of his faults, had done as good a job as he had allowed him to, but his mask was going to be a part of him for the rest of his life. The doctor had connected the loose skin from his upper face to what was left of the lower jaw. It was only a temporary solution to keep as much life as possible in as much skin as possible. As Doctor Gillies had explained to him, because he had not allowed his new treatment it would eventually have to be cut apart again and sutured as soon as the blood vessels had recovered from the shock of the initial injury. Now his mouth runs from the left side of his face and extends almost to his right ear. Some of his teeth and part of his jaw are missing so he is now left with a gap-toothed extended grin on one side. Speech is difficult and he sounds like a drunk, but after hours of practice he has mastered it as best he can.

Now he turns the disfigured side of his face in all of its gory detail to the full light of the room. From the side he can see his exposed tongue, which is really only a stump. Viewing his disfigurement like this adds impetus to his new mission: the complete destruction of Christopher Flinter. It would take time and patience, but he had those in abundance. He would sketch a concentric circle starting on the outside with his close friends, then relatives and, if they existed, lovers. He would plan and carry out their destruction in such a way that Flinter would eventually have no doubt who was coming for him. And when it was Flinter's turn, he would take his time with him, finding out the name of the person who pulled the trigger from the darkness inside that tunnel on that fateful night.

Tying the mask back into position over his lower face, he stares at his reflection again. The artist had done a good job. There is no way to disguise the fact that it is a mask, but the thin line between it and his skin is almost like a skin blemish. With the use of a scarf, it is non-existent.

He goes over to the bookcase by the window and opens the glass doors. The spines of the books that face out are perfectly matched except for one. When he puts pressure on the spine the secret door clicks and swings outwards and the contents behind it are revealed. Hanging from the wooden panel behind the books are his tools of the trade. He reaches out, ignoring the handguns and knives, and selects one of the many garottes that hang down from hooks. It is the first one he ever used, his prized possession. Using this thin length of piano wire with the simple wooden grips on either end, he had taken away the life of a useless whore and her gambler boyfriend on a paddle-steamer that plied its trade on the Mississippi river.

The gambler had sealed his own fate. Levon lost a middling amount of money to him playing five-card stud in the casino on board the boat. The whore, who had attached herself to Levon after he had entered the casino, was, he surmised later, working for the gambler, Jacques Dupont. Their mistake was that after they had cheated him, they flaunted that relationship in front of him. Jacques even tipped his hat, like a gentleman, and smiled at him the following morning. Levon had shrugged, as if to say, 'That's life'. But biding his time he had shadowed Jacques and his whore back to a rundown hotel off Jackson Square in New Orleans. His initial plan was to just shoot Jacques and get his money back. But somehow that didn't give him enough satisfaction as it seemed too fast and final and he wanted the gambler to know why it was happening to him. The whore had to die as well, of course. And that was why he used the garotte for the first time, a weapon he had found out about from an Italian he had met in Lafayette on his way back up from Mexico.

It was also the first time that he had used ether, although he probably didn't need it as the unlucky couple were drinking heavily after a night at the card table. After slipping into their hotel room, which was at the rear of the hotel, he had put the ether-soaked rag over the whore's mouth and nose. The only indication that it had worked was her breathing became deeper and louder. After looping the wire around the gambler's throat and dragging him from the bed, struggling, he brought him over to the mirror on the wall so that he could witness who his executioner was. As the gambler's eyes bulged and the wire bit deeper and his face turned red, Levon could feel the life leaving the man's body. It was an exhilarating feeling, over all too quickly.

Then it was the turn of the whore. By the time she came around he was becoming bored, but perked up again when he saw the horror on her face once she realised what was happening. What he did to her and the way he did it, opened up a Pandora's box in his psyche that needed to be satiated again and again through the following years. He had read somewhere that the Jesuits use to say 'Give me the boy and I will show you the man'. But he wasn't certain of that. Sometimes, when he was alone, he would look back over his life with complete detachment, from when he grew up to Skagway through all of the years learning his trade, selling controlled mayhem to the highest bidder. He worked for rich industrialists, governments, all kinds of despots, carrying out their wishes in what was becoming a very complicated world. The money was extraordinary and he could have retired back to America a wealthy man. But it was never about the money, really, he thinks, as he grips the familiar wooden handles of the garotte and stretches it out to its full extent. The piano wire looks old with rust running along most of its length. But only he can tell what those rust stains really are.

CHAPTER 10

Nell

The white porticos of the secretarial college are becoming a symbol of hope for Nell. Once she walks between them, she feels that her own identity is returned to her again. She is no longer Mrs Flinter, wife of Christopher Flinter. She is Nell Claffey, strong, independent, intelligent and, according to Cecile Saunderson, a beautiful young woman. Nell doesn't really care about that part, but the rest gives her a lift in her spirits that lasts until she arrives back at their flat in the Liberties and sometimes beyond.

The door to Cecile Saunderson's office is closed, which is unusual. She usually likes to stand in the open doorway in the morning as the trainees pass by on their way to their classrooms. Nell's first class is Pitman Shorthand, her favourite class. When she first saw the sample pages of dots and squiggles and angled lines, she thought that she would never learn such an alien representation of language. But she discovered that she had an aptitude for it and before long she had left the beginners' class and was now near the top of the intermediate class. Her typing, too, after a few weeks of frustration trying to find the right feel and rhythm for the keyboard, is now up to forty words per minute and she sometimes even has to rein in her enthusiasm so as not to overshadow the other, younger girls in the class.

Before she pushes open the door to the classroom, she hesitates for a second to compose her face. She has to remember to smile more as the other students in the class, all girls from good backgrounds and slightly younger than her, seem to be living in a different world to hers. Their world is a place where most of life's little details are looked after by their parents, which leaves a lot of time for talking about what she would consider frivolous activities. Activities such as their boyfriends, where they went the previous weekend, what the latest fashions are and on and on about subjects that she's not the least bit interested in. Cecile had warned her not to mention her husband and as little about her private life as possible and it was good advice. Now she is considered just one of the girls. Not that her fellow pupils pay any attention to the auburn-haired young lady who usually sits at the back of the classroom and keeps to herself. Nell is convinced that half of them are there to put in time before they 'catch' a suitable husband and move into a nice house in Rathgar or Kingstown to raise children and perform the day-to-day domestic tasks that their mothers had.

Today, instead of the usual chatter of young women's voices in the classroom there is silence. When Nell pushes the door open fully, she sees why. Cecile Saunderson is standing at the top of the classroom beside their usual teacher, Mrs Donohoe, and they are holding a discussion over various sheets of light-blue pages strewn across the mahogany desk – the previous weeks Pitman tests. Cecile, although on friendly terms with Nell, is regarded with awe by the other, less mature, pupils. She is considered strict but fair, and personally writes the monthly progress letters to the parents of the pupils. Sometimes these letters are positive, other times less so, and in some cases a student would abruptly disappear from the daily roll call never to be heard from again.

When Cecile looks up and sees Nell, she smiles, which is a relief. Excusing herself to Mrs Donohoe, she walks over to Nell, takes her by the elbow and escorts her outside, closing the classroom door behind them.

'I see you are doing extremely well with the Pitman script,' she says, guiding Nell towards her office, 'and Mrs Donohoe says you are working well within your capabilities.'

'She's very kind.'

'Nell, everybody knows that she's not particularly kind, but she is fair.' Cecile unlocks the door to her office with a key that she keeps around her neck.

Nell has never seen Cecile locking her door before and assumes that the office must contain exam papers for the following month. But, after Cecile ushers her inside, Nell is surprised to see that there is a man seated to the side of Cecile's desk, a cigarette in his mouth, bent over and wiping his shoes with a white handkerchief. When he hears the two women enter, he stands up, takes off his hat and stubs out his cigarette in the ashtray on Cecile's desk.

'Roads a bit of mess – the rain, you see,' he says, smiling and holding up a pair of bicycle clips.

'May I introduce Mr Billy Jones,' Cecile says with a deference that Nell has never heard from her before. Normally it's Cecile, owner of a successful business and living in one of the grandest houses on Harcourt Street, who dominates most situations. Not to mention her work within Cuman na mBan and the part she plays in other protest organisations. Now she seems to be almost tongue-tied, a faint blush on her otherwise composed face.

'Nell, take a seat.' Billy Jones nods to an empty chair and puts his cycle clips in one pocket and his dirty hanky into the other.

Nell feels slightly annoyed, both at his attitude and at the off-hand tone he uses in the presence of Cecile, who to Nell has become one of the only women she has ever looked up to. She sits in the chair and appraises this stranger as he takes his own seat again. Billy Jones is a tall, broad-shouldered man, not that much older than Cecile, possibly in his early thirties, with a shock of dark-brown hair swept to one side. He's wearing a navy woollen suit and a shirt and tie, but he seems uncomfortable in his clothes, fidgeting with the collar of his shirt or pulling his cuffs down. Not that he lacks confidence. In fact, she was surprised when it was Mr Jones, and not Cecile, who indicated that she should take a seat.

'I've told Mr Jones all about you, Nell,' Cecile says, and sits back in her chair as if withdrawing from the conversation altogether.

'All about me? Like what?' Nell says, slightly alarmed.

'Nell, you know what we've discussed about your past and your … procurement of weapons from the British soldiers,' Cecile says.

Nell flushes. 'But that was personal information! You had no right!'

Mr Jones puts up his hand. 'Nell, relax. The past is another country. It's the future I want to discuss with you.'

Nell is completely confused. Is this man a prospective employer? If so, why was he locked up in Cecile's office? Procurement of weapons? He must have some connection with undercover operations. As for the man himself, she is beginning to take even more of a dislike to him. Although his soft-featured face is handsome in its own way and he smiles easily, the smile doesn't seem to reach his eyes, which are deep-set and wide apart. His jovial face seems to Nell to belong to somebody from a farm, but the eyes staring at her, weighing her up, are a lot more dangerous.

He reaches into his jacket for a packet of cigarettes and offers one to Nell, who shakes her head. Then he takes his time lighting up his cigarette and seems to be gathering his thoughts.

Nell feels an urge to put an end to this situation.

'Cecile should have informed you that that part of my life is all in the past,' she says firmly. 'Now I'm married and I have responsibilities which I take very seriously.'

Billy Jones claps his hands together and laughs. 'Nell, I apologise for all of this,' he waves his hand around, 'secrecy!'

Nell, annoyed, wants to walk out. But if she leaves now and returns the following day, will Cecile even let her back inside the college? And where would she go then? Back to the Liberties and the daily drudgery of her life? Back to Mary Sherry who was beginning to take heart from her success here in the college? Little by little, her neighbour seemed to be taking more of an interest in the outside world. She would have to tell her that she gave up on the college and that would break Mary's heart.

'Nell,' Mr Jones leans towards her, 'what you did before 1916 is less of a concern to me than the courage you showed when you tried to protect that poor woman. Cecile told me everything.'

'I did what anybody would have done.'

'But you were the one who took it upon herself to take action. Unfortunately, that poor woman didn't survive … another martyr for Ireland.'

Nell looks over at Cecile who nods in confirmation.

'I didn't want to upset you, Nell, you had enough on your plate. She died the following week, I'm afraid.'

'I didn't know,' Nell says, and feels her voice catching as she remembers the battered face of the fallen woman and the animal-like howls of the police as they laid about them with their batons. She remembers the red-faced panting policeman who beat the poor woman with such savagery and can almost smell the odour of sweat coming from his body as he brought his baton down again and again and again. Her face burned with indignation and she felt a lump lodging somewhere in her chest and wondered was this how hatred began.

'It's only the beginning, Nell, believe me,' Mr Jones continues. 'As we speak the British are getting ready to sign the Treaty of Versailles. We have sent requests to Paris to be considered a sovereign, independent country, able to take its place among the other nations of the world, but the Allies, encouraged by the British, will have nothing to do with us.'

'We?'

'Dáil Éireann, Nell, the elected representatives of the people of Ireland.'

'Yes, I supported Countess Markievicz and she was elected of course.'

'The first woman ever elected to the United Kingdom House of Commons. She didn't take her seat, of course, in line with Sinn Féin policy, but instead is a member of the Dáil.' Mr Jones stands up and begins pacing around the room, waving the lighted cigarette around. 'We know that the British are more concerned now than at any time in the long, bloody history of their illegal occupation of this country. But we don't know what they're going to do about it. We desperately need information on what they're up to. Rumours are that they are going to flood Dublin with agents. We've failed before, we can't fail again.'

Nell prefers this side of Mr Jones, the look of fervour in his eyes, the seriousness of his demeanour. Gone is the laconic man she was introduced to – now, in his place, is a man with total commitment and intensity. She realises also that Mr Jones – probably not even his real name – isn't here to interview her for a job. He is here to enlist her. Cecile is in Cumann na mBan and was part of the anti-conscription campaign, but it now seems more likely that she is part of something more than a protest movement. The mystery of the waived fees is now beginning to make sense.

'But what can I do?' Nell asks. 'And did Cecile tell you that I'm married, so it's not just –'

'Ah, your husband.' Mr Jones stops walking and turns to her. 'Christopher Flinter.'

'How do you know about my Christopher?'

'I know that he was in the British army once, but now his heart lies elsewhere.'

'What has that Caprani peson told you?' Nell says. 'The pair of them take to the hills some weekends and play soldiers, but that doesn't mean he's willing to risk his life.'

'That's not important, Nell.' Mr Jones waves his hand. 'He's occasionally helped us with training young volunteers. Nothing more. What we're discussing here is far more vital for the cause, and more dangerous. If you decide to join us, you can't tell Christopher what you're involved in. And it will mean taking an oath.'

'You want me to say nothing. To my husband?'

'No, that would be the worst thing to do. Dublin is a small city and he'd find out sooner or later. Get him used to the idea. Tell him that you're thinking of applying for an office job in Dublin Castle, but nothing more.'

'I'm not sure he'll be pleased with that. He was a guest there three years ago and nearly ended up paying with his life.'

'How you get around him is up to you. I'm sure you'll think of a way. Are you with us, Nell?'

Christopher's humour *had* improved over for the last number of weeks and they were beginning to go back to the way things used to be in the early days. She had thought it was something to do with his job, but now she is beginning to understand why.

'I am, with one condition,' Nell turns to him.

'Which is?'

'I will do anything you ask of me, but I want you to promise me that you won't use Christopher for any dangerous missions.'

Mr Jones sits down again, takes a drag from the cigarette he had forgotten about, and blows smoke up at the ceiling. Nell can almost see his mind at work. Is she worth enlisting if they lose a young volunteer, a volunteer with experience on the battlefield?

'I'll have a word with the OC of the Dublin Brigade, Nell,' he says finally. 'That's about as much as I can do. I'll ask him to keep Christopher on a short leash.'

Nell considers the answer. 'But what do you want me to do?'

'Well, as you know, Cecile has many business and local government contacts in and around Dublin who recruit their secretaries through her, including Dublin Castle. At the moment they are looking to hire a typist who can use Pitman Shorthand. Thanks to Cecile, you'll be the only candidate. The position isn't very senior, but a lot of communication will come across your desk. All we need you to do is to keep your handler informed of anything notable happening.'

'My handler?'

'You'll get a handler to look after you. He's a young man, Mick Crotty – he'll be the one. You don't need to look for him, he'll find you, and you can work something out between yourselves on where and when to meet.'

Cecile leans across the desk then and takes Nell's hand.

'You can save lives, Nell … and the pay isn't bad,' she says and smiles.

'What happens if I'm caught?' Nell says, and shakes her hand free.

'Nell, I can guarantee that you won't get caught,' Mr Jones says, getting up from his chair again. He seems to be a man who can't stay easy very long and now he strides backwards and forwards across the room, gesticulating with his cigarette. 'You won't be stealing documents or anything, just memorising things seen and overheard. If anybody gets caught it'll be Crotty, but he's doing it with a willing heart because he knows it's the right thing to do. Every day the British are building up a network of spies in Dublin. We know some of them, but not all. With you on the inside it might help us catch the very spy who could bring everything down around our ears.' He turns, staring into her eyes. 'Is that something you can live with, Nell?'

Nell bows her head to escape the intensity of his eyes which seem to bore into her. But still she hesitates. As she considers her answer, the memories of that poor woman being beaten up flood back, and for what? For lending her voice to the innocent men locked up in a jail somewhere over in Britain. If she turns down this opportunity now, she knows that the image of that battered woman will haunt her forever.

'OK, I'll do it,' she says.

In an instant the mood in the room seems to change. Gone is the impassioned man whose very personality had convinced her to risk all. He claps his hands together and his smile widens.

'You won't regret this, Nell,' he says and, without waiting for a reply, he grabs his hat from Cecile's desk and, with a curt bow to the two women, rushes out of the room.

After he leaves it seems as if he has taken something with him from the room. Vibrant in the man's presence, it's now a drab office again. In the vacuum that he has left, the realisation of what she has volunteered to do dawns on her.

Cecile is standing at the window that overlooks Earlsfort Terrace, her attention fixed on something outside. When Nell joins her, she is staring out at Mr Jones, who is unlocking his bicycle from the railings outside. She can see that his mind is already on something, or someone, else as he checks his watch before mounting his bicycle and heading back down Earlsfort Terrace towards Stephen's Green. As he disappears from view, lost among the traffic, Cecile seems to revert to the woman Nell has come to know.

She turns to Nell. 'I will see to the application forms and go over what you might be asked at the interview,' she says, looking her up and down, 'but it's a formality and I can't see any hot-blooded man, especially a soldier, turning you down.'

Nell feels her face flush. 'Who was that man?' she asks.

'Mr Jones?' Cecile says, returning to her desk. 'I suppose you'll find out sooner or later. That was Michael Collins – and, mark my words, a future leader of Ireland if the British don't manage to get their hands on him first.'

Michael Collins. Nell has heard of him, but usually in hushed tones. He's the ghost that haunts Dublin in the daytime, avoiding capture by hiding in plain sight. Even Christopher reluctantly admires him.

But has she the same courage to do what was asked of her? As a teenager living in the Monto, she had felt no fear, but there was only herself to look after. It was exciting, getting the young soldiers drunk and using her wiles to get her hands on their weapons, then selling them on to Phil Shanahan. Days of innocence. But now she's a married woman and Christopher seems to be getting further away from her every day. But, in the end, it was her decision and her decision only.

'Are you really certain you want to do this?' Cecile looks into her eyes and seems to search them for any hint of uncertainty.

'I said I'll do it and I'll stand by that promise.'

'Very well, let's get started then,' Cecile says, all business again. 'Lesson one today, how to portray yourself to your interviewer. You might have to hold back some of that spirit of yours,' she smiles, 'and, lesson two, from now on, as far as Dublin Castle is concerned, your name is not Nell Flinter. It's Nell Claffey. Flinter is an unusual name, so it's best not to draw any attention to yourself.'

'I don't know,' Nell says, feeling a slight hesitation. 'It feels disloyal to Christopher.'

'I've never met him, but I'm sure he'd cope with it, if he ever found out. But as for your family and friends, they must never know.'

'I hope I can make them believe me.'

'It'll only be a small lie. You can say you've got a job in Healy's. It's in Dame Street, near the Castle. They'll never have to know – and remember it's for their own safety too.'

'Jesus! That's easier said than done,' Nell says.

'That's another thing, Nell. You'll have to watch the way you speak.'

'What do you mean?'

'Sometimes your turn of phrase can be … a bit too … colloquial. But we have a few weeks until the interview and we can work on that.'

CHAPTER 11

Robert Byatt

The well-maintained military cemetery ends abruptly with a painted wooden fence. Beyond the fence he is standing among a scattering of haphazard graves. He consults the diagram again, but he is not mistaken: his brother's final resting place is not as he had pictured it. Grass and weeds have taken over the sunken earth. There is no gravestone, just a simple wooden cross tilted to one side and almost rotted away. He can just about make out the name of the person – *MAJOR JONATHAN BYATT* – carved awkwardly across the arm of the cross. It tilts to one side, the nail that holds it rusted and exposed. He kneels down on the damp earth, takes out a small, leather-covered Bible and opens it at the Book of Psalms. He finds what he is looking for, Psalm 23, and whispers out the words: '*The Lord is my shepherd …*' continuing until he reaches the end. He snaps the Bible shut and puts it into his inside pocket, then changes his mind and takes it out again.

'You didn't deserve this, Jonathan, and I swear on this Bible that I will make amends. I know that it's nothing less than you would do for me, brother.'

Across the graveyard, in the tidy military section, he sees two men bent over, shovelling earth into an open grave. They struggle with the damp earth and stop now and again, holding their aching backs. He approaches them across the mucky soil and stands and stares as the clods of turf fall into the rectangular hole. One of them becomes aware of his presence and stops, leaning on his shovel. Realising that he is working alone, the other gravedigger also stops and looks up at the tall, distinguished-looking figure who stands, looking down at them.

'Can we help, sir?' one of them, the better dressed of the two, says, tipping his cap.

'Those graves over there – beyond the fence – why are they left so?'

The gravedigger, the one who seems to be the spokesman, stares over to where the man points and scratches his head.

'That there's the non-maintained plot,' he says, sensing a possible windfall, 'and we have no special instructions.'

'But they're a disgrace. My brother deserves better than that.'

'And who might your brother be?'

'Major Jonathan Byatt.'

'Ah. Poor Major Byatt, abandoned by king and country in his final hour. And no sign of a family to mark his burial. It's tragic!' The man says, takes off his cap and shakes his head sadly.

'I want to put it right. How do I go about it?'

'Well, you could go through the army records, find out his regiment and approach them for permission. But,' the gravedigger says, scratching his head, 'it's most unusual that a commissioned officer wasn't given a decent burial. It is as if the powers that be are almost ashamed of the gentleman.'

'My brother was one of the bravest men in the army.'

'That may be so, but somebody, somewhere higher up in the ranks, didn't agree, wouldn't you say? My advice is to skip past all that nonsense with the military. We'd be delighted to look after his last resting place – for a small commission.'

Byatt takes out a notebook and begins to write, squinting in the approaching dusk. He rips out the page and hands it to the gravedigger.

'I want a proper gravestone, something that befits a hero. And I want these words carved on it. I also want a surround and the grave needs topping up. How much?'

The gravedigger takes the note and counts up the words, then stares up at the sky and calculates the price, adding on extra for himself and a little for his colleague.

'Won't be much change out of fifty pounds, sir.'

'Very well. I want you to start immediately and I will return with your money. When I come back, tomorrow, I want to see the grave cleared up completely and covered in new earth.'

'Of course, sir. I will talk to the mason tomorrow, order the headstone and give him the wording. It will take a while and you'll need to approve the lettering.'

'I intend to remain in Dublin for as long as it takes,' Byatt says, almost to himself, turns, and walks back through the graves towards the entrance.

In mid-afternoon the Kildare Street Club for gentlemen is infused with an air of somnolence. Some of its members stand in the bay windows that overlook the grounds of Trinity College trying to catch a glimpse of the cricket match. Scattered around the members lounge, deep leather armchairs envelop the after-lunch brigade, mostly middle-aged and elderly men digesting their substantial meal and nodding off after their glasses of good port and cigars. Loud conversation is not tolerated and the only sound is the faraway click of billiard balls coming from the games room in the floor below. Two of the armchairs are pulled together for privacy and the men facing each other are almost touching knees.

'I didn't expect to see you in this neck of the woods, Robert.' Peter Cuffe raises his brandy glass and takes a sip.

'Neither did I,' Robert Byatt shrugs, 'but we never know what rocky shore fate will wash us up on.'

'I've done some preliminary enquiries, all very discreet. It seems your brother was killed in 1916, several days *after* the rising.'

'I was overseas and only found out last year. Of course I was upset, but we were both busy and hadn't really communicated with each other over the years. I've been to his grave, to pay my respects.'

'Good for you.'

'Not really. It's a disgrace. What's going on, Peter?'

Peter Cuffe's slim shape seems to press further into the armchair and he scratches his head, a trait Byatt remembers from their days together when they were based in Calcutta. It usually signified that he knew something but was unsure as to whether to share it or not. Now he takes the opportunity to wave to a fellow-member who has passed by their armchairs.

'Robert,' Cuffe finally admits, 'it's difficult. State secrets … and all that.'

'Jonathan was a soldier, dammit.'

'He was. But he did dabble in espionage as far as I can ascertain. And part of the reason he was in Dublin was in that capacity.'

Robert shook his head, refusing to be side-lined, even if it is by an old friend.

'I don't care what he was involved in, he was army through and through. Gave his life for it. Now all he's got to show for it is a miserable grave. The army hadn't even the decency to bury him at home.'

His voice has risen in volume and Peter is becoming aware of the disgruntled glances of some of his fellow members.

'Please, keep your voice down. I'll tell you everything I know but, I warn you, some of it isn't pretty.'

'Good, let's start with the state of his grave, shall we?'

'That's the easy part. The order came directly from London. No honours were to be bestowed, discretion was to be shown. And I think you know why.'

Robert sighs. 'So, Jonathan's crime was to be in love with another man. I should have known.'

'I am so sorry, Robert.'

'But the whole business still doesn't make sense. He took great pains to avoid any unpleasantness. He had an unblemished record and served gallantly until the injury to his leg.'

'Who knows how these things work? Maybe one of the higher-ups in Whitehall took offence.'

'I can tell you some tales about Whitehall.' Robert takes a sip of his brandy, then he stared at some spot over Peter Cuffe's head.

'I don't want to know any of that.'

Peter reaches into his inside pocket and takes out a slim, black leather notebook and hands it over to Robert.

'I managed to get my hands on this from his personal effects. It's his notebook. I didn't read it, of course.'

'Thank you.' Robert eagerly reaches out for it and slips it into the inside pocket of his jacket.

'It's as much as I can do, I'm afraid. I don't get into Dublin Castle as much as I used to.'

'Of course not – you're going up in the world.'

'I think these big companies like to see a name on their letter headings along with any old war decorations.'

'They were justly deserved, Peter.' Robert finishes off the rest of his brandy and gets to his feet.

'You know I'd trade the lot of them for your Victoria Cross,' Peter says.

Robert nods and makes his way towards the door.

Peter Cuffe watches his old comrade as he makes his way across the lounge, past the nodding members and the afternoon fire. He takes in his erect stature and the still purposeful stride that he remembers so well. The wine Peter had with his dinner and the brandy afterwards takes away some of the guilt. He had lied. Much to his shame he had been curious and had worked his way through the notebook, even swapped gossip with some of his old acquaintances in Dublin Castle, and for that he was sorry. But no man deserved the death that was inflicted on Jonathan Byatt and afterwards the disavowal of his superiors. And if anyone were to find out answers, he had no doubt that Robert Byatt would.

Byatt does what he usually does when he arrives in an unfamiliar city: he buys a detailed map. Opening it out on the hotel bed, he consults his brother's notebook and marks the areas that he thinks might be relevant. Sipping a cup of weak tea, he studies the Liffey's course through the centre of the city and decides to split the city into two. On the south side, the side where his hotel is located, there is Dublin Castle of course, and the location of the newspaper that Jonathan had mentioned he was going to visit. Also, among the writing, there is a list of items of clothing his brother had bought on George's Street, each one itemised in a way that makes him think that he was buying them for somebody other than himself. The address of the restaurant where his brother dined regularly is mentioned, but not the name, which he thinks is odd.

The notebook is in fairly good condition and he suspects that his brother started a new one at the beginning of each investigation. There are two names that stand out: *Janus* and *Christopher Flinter*. The first one, Janus, makes no sense. It's obviously a codename he had for some person or a project. That leaves Christopher Flinter. Was he an ally or an enemy? Frustratingly there are no details of either, just meetings, suppositions and lots of question marks. Whatever case Jonathan was investigating was obviously at the early stages.

The bells of a nearby church ring out the hour of seven o'clock and he realises that he hasn't eaten all day. He consults the map again and sees that the restaurant Jonathan frequented is a short walk from his hotel, The Royal Hibernian. Not knowing what type of restaurant it is, he puts on a formal dinner jacket and bow tie and decides to wear his top hat. As he passes through the hotel reception, he tells the concierge that he won't be dining in the hotel that evening.

'Are you dining in town?' the concierge enquires.

'Yes. Is that a problem?'

'No, no, not a problem. It's just that tensions are rising on the streets and we have to advise all of our guests to be careful.'

'Understood.' Robert raises his cane and leaves.

The streets outside the hotel are as busy as they were during the day and he feels more reassured. The dark shape of a tram trundles past, upsetting a cabman's horse. The cabman steps down from his carriage and comforts the animal until the tram has disappeared round the bend towards what he remembers from the map as St Stephen's

Green. On seeing a gentleman dressed in evening clothes standing outside the hotel, the cabman opens the door and stands to attention beside it.

'No, thank you. I'm going to walk,' he says, and strolls down Dawson Street towards Trinity College.

On the corner of Dawson Street and Nassau Street he consults the map. In his estimation the restaurant should be no more than a ten-minute walk. In his notebook Jonathan had mentioned a laneway located somewhere between Dame Street and Aungier Street. Memorising the approximate location, he makes his way along the walls of the college, enjoying the fresh air after spending the day in his overheated hotel bedroom. The only difference between Dublin and London, as far as he can see, is the presence of soldiers on patrol and every so often a military tender passing by. But the buildings in this part of the city all seem to be intact and people go about their business as usual.

When he reaches College Green, he takes his time to admire the surrounding buildings: the frontage of Trinity College which stares out at the busy traffic, and the magnificent sweeping Palladian style building that is now, he believes, a bank. He continues up Dame Street and turns. A short way up the street he reaches his destination, a laneway on the right. He consults his map again to make sure he is in the right place, and then proceeds up the lane. Most of the doorways are merely rear entrances to bigger buildings.

As he makes out what he thinks might be the entrance to the restaurant, he becomes aware of movement behind. Turning, he sees that two shabbily dressed men have followed him into the laneway.

'You seem like a proper dandy,' one of them, the taller of the two, says. 'Do you think you could spare a few coppers for a couple of poor old soldiers?'

Both men are wearing heavy overcoats and caps which they have pulled down low over their eyes. The smaller of the two begins to circle to one side of Robert, looking him up and down.

'Isn't he a pretty one?' he says. 'Off to see his boyfriends.'

Robert fishes around in his pocket and takes out some change, holding it out.

'Here, take this,' he says to the taller man who looks at the coins in his hand with disdain.

'Not enough for a decent meal – why don't you try your wallet,' he says, moving the opposite way to his friend.

Robert backs up against the wall and puts the coins back into his pocket.

'Well, in that case, you get nothing. Now, be good chaps, turn around, and crawl back to that hole you came from,' he says, a slight smile playing across his face.

The two men exchange glances, uncertain of his reaction. The smaller one reaches into his inside pocket and, with a glance back up the laneway towards the street, produces an open-edge razor, which he opens out and slices through in the air.

'You're very brave … for a nancy boy.'

Robert has had enough. In a fraction of a second, he pulls the blade from his cane and swishes it through the air several times in quick succession then holds the point of it to the taller man's chest, keeping up the pressure as the man backs away and eventually ends up with his back to the wall. He puts his hands up in surrender and turns to his companion with the razor.

'Put that away. Can't you see the gentleman has misunderstood our intentions,' he says.

'Very good,' Robert says, as the man puts the razor away. 'Now, take off your caps and give me a good look at you.'

Both of the men take off their caps as he withdraws the blade but keeps it at his side. The two men are younger than he had thought and both are unshaven and pale-faced. He has seen lots of men like this in London, back from the war and demobbed without any prospects for their future. But it was no excuse for what they had done and again he thinks of what his brother had to put up with in his daily life, meeting other men furtively in places like these and putting up with the abuse thrown at them. He stares at them for a few seconds as if committing their faces to memory, then points the blade towards the entrance of the laneway.

'Be off, and don't let me catch you do this again,' he says.

The two men turn and rush down the laneway, looking over their shoulders as they go. He inserts the blade back into his cane and waits until they have disappeared.

The door to the restaurant opens and a man comes out, tips his hat, and makes his way down the lane towards the street, leaving the door ajar. Robert goes through the door and into a long, dim hallway. The smell of spices fill the air and the crackling sound of music being played on a gramophone drifts up from further down the hallway. He makes his way towards its source, pushing aside a curtain of beads and entering into a small reception area. A waiter emerges from behind the desk, holding a menu.

'Table for one?'

Robert nods, taking off his hat and placing it onto the hat rack beside the desk, but he keeps his cane in his hand. The waiter walks ahead of him and he follows him into an intimate dining room. The space is illuminated with paper lanterns that cast an orange glow onto the walls. Several tables are occupied, all by men of various ages, who look up when he enters. He is led to a small table in the corner and the waiter goes through the dishes of the day, then asks if he wants something to drink with his meal. Robert looks at the short wine list and orders a half bottle of claret, then one of the dishes, all of which, much to his dismay, are Italian. The waiter, a tall slim youth who looks bored, writes down his order and prepares to leave.

'Excuse me. I wonder if you can help me? My brother used to eat here regularly. I wonder if you remember him – Jonathan Byatt?'

The waiter shrugs his thin shoulders. 'Perhaps – when was this?' he says in accented English.

'A few years ago,' Robert says.

'No, that is impossible. I am here only one year. But I can ask.'

'No, don't bother.' Robert waves him away. 'It was an off-chance.'

A man rises up from one of the tables and approaches Robert. He walks with the careful steps of one drunk. He looks to be in his twenties, but seems overdressed for his age, wearing a dark blazer and a cravat and sporting a monocle. His hair is overlong and flops in front of his face and in the dim light Robert can detect that the man is wearing some kind of dark make-up around his eyes. He waits for him to speak, but the man just stares at him, swaying slightly and brushing back his hair with his hands as if to get a better look at him. The seconds drag on and some of the nearby diners are now watching.

'May I help you?' Robert finally says.

The man pulls out a chair and flops down into it.

'You asked for Jonathan?' he mumbles. 'How do you know him?'

'Jonathan Byatt? He was my brother,' Robert says.

'You said "*was*".' The man leans forward and Robert gets the strong smell of aniseed from his breath.

'Jonathan died some time back. Were you … acquainted?'

The man slouches back in his chair and stares at the tablecloth. 'We all wondered what had happened to him,' he says, glancing back at the table he came from.

'Then you were … close friends?'

'We are all friends here – it's the only place where our kind of friendship is acceptable,' the man says with a look of disgust.

'Well, for what it's worth, Jonathan's friends were always my friends,' Robert says and holds out his hand. 'Robert Byatt, glad to meet you.'

'Harry Irvine. Likewise.' The man clasps his hand and shakes. For such an apparently effeminate man, the handshake is firm.

Harry fumbles with his jacket and reaches into the fob pocket of his waistcoat, taking out a pocket watch and dangling it from its chain in front of Robert. It is a distinctive watch and most of the gold layer is worn away with age and use. But, for all that, he remembers it immediately. The last time he had seen the watch it had been left beside a wash-hand basin by his brother, Jonathan. They had not seen each other for several years and, at Jonathan's insistence, they had spent a few days together in a hotel in Brighton. When he opened the watch, out of curiosity, he realised the real reason behind their short holiday. Seeing it now, under these circumstances, raises a lump in his throat.

'How did you come by that watch?' he asks sharply. 'He never would have parted with it.'

'A waiter appeared with it one day. A nasty piece of work – he said he bought it in a pawn shop. But I knew that watch better than I know my own,' Harry says, unclips it from his pocket and hands it across to Robert.

The watch is still warm to the touch and still keeping time. He turns it over and reads the inscription on the back: *I wish you God speed and a safe return, love – H.* The H, Jonathan had explained to him, was for Howard, his lover, who had been murdered in New York, how or why Jonathan had never explained. Before he opens the watch, he hesitates. Tears well up in his eyes and Harry reaches across and pats his hand. He opens it. Enclosed in the back there is a sepia photograph of his brother and Howard. Both men are smiling into the camera, unaware of the fate that was to befall both of them.

'May I purchase it from you?' Robert says, closing the back.

'It's not mine to sell, it belongs to you,' Harry says.

'But you must be out of pocket?'

'No. I threatened the waiter with the police and he handed it over. Disappeared soon after that.'

'I will treasure it always. Thank you,' Robert says and carefully puts it into his inside pocket.

'Be careful. Unfortunately, the restaurant also attracts the wrong sort of person to the neighbourhood, if you know what I mean. I'd hate to see you get robbed when you have just found it.'

'I've met some already.' Robert smiles and raises his cane.

'Just like your brother,' Harry says, tears forming in his eyes.

'Have you any idea what happened to Jonathan?'

'No. One day he was here, the next he was gone. The last time I saw him I made a fool of myself and regret it to this day,' Harry says and takes out a packet of cigarettes, offering it to Robert who accepts one, more to keep the conversation going.

'Jonathan had a thick skin,' Robert says. 'I shouldn't let that worry you unnecessarily.'

'You're too kind.' Harry lights up the cigarette and blows smoke up towards one of the orange lanterns, making it sway slightly.

'Can you remember anything unusual about that time?'

'Only that he was with a younger man ... not in that way, I can sense these things. But Jonathan gave me short shrift and I kept out of their conversation.'

'You are certain that this man wasn't a *special* friend, as you call it?'

'Certain. I remember they had an argument towards the end of their meal, which was very unusual for Jonathan. But it simmered down after and they left on good terms.'

'Had you ever seen the man before?'

'Never. He introduced him to me as some kind of assistant, but I didn't believe it. I thought it was one of his agents.'

'How did you know about Jonathan's background?'

'Dublin is a small city, Robert, everybody rubs shoulders. We all knew he was British, didn't wear a uniform and worked from Dublin Castle. It didn't take a genius to guess he was an agent.' Harry shrugged.

'That place is a bloody sieve.'

'They say there are more spies in the Castle than soldiers!' Harry laughs at his own joke and is then hit by a spasm of coughing.

'The man with my brother – I don't suppose you remember anything about him?'

'In fact, I do. I might have been in my cups but I remember he had a German-sounding name, which was ironic.'

Robert reaches into his pocket and takes out Jonathan's old notebook. He flicks through the pages towards the back.

'Would that name have been Flinter? Christopher Flinter?'

The look of surprise in Harry's eyes gives him his answer.

CHAPTER 12

Christopher

On Friday evening Christopher strides out through the gates of the bacon factory, looking forward to his weekly bath. The smell of pigs – their fat and blood and even their shit – clings to his clothes. Even after scrubbing himself with carbolic soap there will still be a lingering smell that slowly goes away over the weekend. But before it has entirely disappeared, he will be back on the line again, curing, chopping, segregating the offal and by Monday night he will smell as bad again. He stops on the corner of Francis Street and lights a cigarette, the first of the day, sucking the smoke into his lungs.

'Well, if it isn't Christopher Flinter!'

Anthony Caprani, dressed in a suit, even though it is a warm evening, is standing in front of him with his hand extended. Christopher shakes his hand, still unused to Anthony's habit of shaking hands. They had last met only the previous weekend. They had both been up in the Dublin mountains, playing soldiers again. Christopher is tired of the constant exercises with nothing to show for it. Even the commander of the brigade, a young solicitor called

O'Malley, is becoming impatient. When Christopher threatened to leave, telling him it was a waste of time, the young solicitor had given him an old Smith and Wesson .38, not his favourite revolver, and five rounds of ammunition, and told him to go into the trees with it and get some of the boredom out of his system. In the darkness of the woods, he had picked out a target, a boulder beside a stream which was the approximate size and shape of a head. After the first recoil of the gun and the familiar smell of the cordite, he was back in Flanders again, and that strange stillness had come over him as he aimed the revolver again and shot at the imaginary head, hitting it repeatedly.

'What brings you to the Liberties on a Friday evening?' Christopher asks Anthony. 'I thought it was your cards night?'

Anthony raises his shoulders upwards and stretches his arms out to either side, an old habit he has inherited from his Italian forebears.

'Can a man not drop over to see his friend?'

'You're not going to get me traipsing around the Dublin hills again? Nell's been called into the office for the weekend and she's left me with a list of jobs to do.'

'The road to success is filled with women pushing their husbands along,' Anthony jokes, taking hold of his arm and steering him out of the path of passersby and into a doorway. Standing almost as closely as lovers, he whispers: '*I think it's time.*'

'Time for what?' Christopher says, letting the comment about Nell go as he senses by his friend's expression that it's not about a training exercise.

'O'Donnell wants to see us.'

O'Donnell is the brigade quartermaster, a no-nonsense Dublin man. A summons from him means only one thing. They are to be given arms to carry out a job. Weapons, Christopher has learned since he began training young recruits in the Dublin hills, are in short supply still. Nobody, except the higher-ups, have their own. When a job is done the weapons, he has learned, are handed back to O'Donnell, who then sends them on somewhere else to be cleaned and prepared for the next job. It is a complicated but necessary system, and at any one time there are only a small amount of people who know where an arms cache is located.

'At last,' Christopher says, grabbing Anthony's arm and squeezing it. 'I thought it would never happen. I was beginning to wonder if I would ever be picked.'

'I don't understand that myself,' Anthony says, 'but now's our chance.'

'Who's the target?'

'I'm not sure, but the last one, I heard, was a detective, lives over on the northside. He's been giving some of our lads a lot of trouble. They sent a unit out, four men, to get him but they failed.'

'With the .38s no doubt. Bloody rabbit guns. You need a .45 at least.'

'They took five bullets out of him, but the bastard's still alive,' Anthony says, shaking his head. 'Should've gone back and finished him off with a few to the head.'

'And you think that's got to do with us meeting up with O'Donnell?'

'I think the higher-ups tore strips off him for sending out boys to do a man's job,' Anthony says, 'and now they need somebody with a bit of experience.'

'I've got plenty of that,' Christopher says, 'but what about you?'

Anthony stares down at his shoes for a while, then looks up at Christopher.

'I sort of told them that if I didn't go, you wouldn't either,' he says with a laugh.

'You're some chancer!' Christopher says, tossing his friend's well-groomed hair.

They stand in front of O'Donnell, who sits behind a battered wooden desk and looks like a schoolteacher, except that in front of him there are two .45 Webley revolvers. Lined up beside each one are six bullets and Christopher can see that they have been fixed with a tiny cross-notch carved onto the top of each one. He won't say anything to Anthony in case his already nervous friend becomes even more nervous. The bullets, when they enter the body, will splinter and cause massive damage. He doesn't like them, but can see the point of their use if you have a limited number of arms and a limited number of experienced Volunteers. Even the rawest recruit will cause the maximum amount of damage with little experience. His only concern, if everybody is using them, is to keep out of line of fire because if you're hit by friendly fire with one of those bullets, no matter where in the body, it will be a catastrophic injury. The guns themselves, heavy and cumbersome, are, Christopher knows, well able to do the job they were designed for and seldom jam.

The small room over the grocery shop in Middle Abbey Street has only one circular window that overlooks the offices of the *Irish Independent* newspaper. Only weeks before it had been raided by Volunteers and the presses and machinery destroyed because of the newspaper's coverage of an ambush by the IRA. Christopher was on that raid as a lookout but felt sorry for the various printers and compositors who stood around as their livelihood was being smashed out of existence with sledgehammers.

'Your target is this man.' O'Donnell shoves a faded photograph across the desk to Christopher.

Christopher picks it up and goes to the window to look at it under the light. The man looks to be in his forties with a heavy moustache. The suit he's dressed in and the hat he wears, a plain, dark-brown homburg, make him seem more like a businessman than a soldier. He studies the man's face, which is round and soft-featured and this lends it an air of innocence. Behind him in the photograph he can make out the gates of Dublin Castle with the barbed-wire in place, so it is a recent photograph.

'Shouldn't be too difficult, with the right plan.' Christopher puts the photograph back on the table.

'Keep it,' O'Donnell says.

'Who is he?' Anthony asks.

'That's Mr Nigel Reynolds. We've tried three times to get him, but through bad luck or bad planning he's avoided us. Like most good spies, he seems to have a sixth sense. And, more importantly for us, he's the man who runs a lot of the agents from Dublin Castle. What I'm telling you is, no matter how genteel he looks in that photograph, the man's nobody's fool. He got away from the Squad a couple of times and that's not something you can say any day of the week.'

'The Squad. I've heard about the Squad. If they didn't get him, what makes you think it will be any better for us?' Anthony says, taking the photograph from Christopher.

'Who are the Squad?' Christopher asks O'Donnell.

'I forgot, you're new. The Squad are a few handpicked men. They're used for special jobs. They've all proved they've the stomach for the close-up stuff. But Dublin is a small city, and we think that their identities might be known, or at least their faces.'

'Bigshots!' jeers Anthony. 'They spend most of their time in the Cairo café rubbing shoulders with the plainclothes G-Men from the Castle, trying to outwit them.'

'You've a bit of a lip on yeh – just sit down,' O'Donnell says to Anthony, who hands the photograph back to Christopher and sits down in a huff.

'If they're so good, why us?' Christopher says.

'Nobody knows you, for one. You can get nearer to him, get the job done, get away,' O'Donnell says, reaching into a drawer and taking out a folded sheet of paper which he opens out and lays across the top of his desk.

Christopher leans on the desk and looks down at the paper. It is a crude diagram, drawn in pencil and smudged with greasy marks. He can make out some of the roads, the main one being in Ballsbridge where a large X is marked. Parallel lines denote the tramline from Dalkey into Dublin city centre. He studies the diagram, taking note of the compass points marked on the map which are obviously not accurate. The words '*between nine and nine thirty*' are scribbled on one side of sheet beside an X. Four crosses are scattered around the X.

'What do you think?' O'Donnell asks.

'You're going to carry it out here, I suppose,' Christopher says, pointing at the X.

'Go on.'

'I presume that it's going to happen on one of the morning trams, so Mr Reynolds is coming from Kingstown.'

'Blackrock, to be precise. You've got a good brain, Christopher. I can see why Collins wanted to keep you for himself, but my motto is: a good manager always picks his best team.' O'Donnell lights up a cigarette without offering them around.

Christopher is puzzled, but doesn't want to show it. If O'Donnell is talking about *the* Michael Collins, the man, according to Anthony, who single-handedly runs the war of independence against the British, why has he not been used before this? Was he still not trusted because of his time in the British army or was it something to do with Nell's job? He was fed up reading accounts of botched assassination attempts in the newspapers. Most of these were a bad reflection on the calibre of people sent out. Young and enthusiastic, but nervous and amateurish. He read about two of the would-be assassins tracked down to a house in Drumcondra after an assassination attempt. The house was in a dead-end street and it was by the grace of God that one of them was shot but only wounded and was now in hospital. The other one drowned in the canal when he tried to swim away from his pursuers. Although he would lay a bet that the man was dragged down by the lead in his back. And worse again, both men were carrying their revolvers on them when they were captured. Another loss.

'Nobody's ever contacted me before now, except for the Dorset Street pig job and the newspaper thing,' Christopher says, nodding through the window towards the *Irish Independent* office across the street.

'That's stuff for kids and all in the past. If you make a go of this, I'll use you … no matter what anyone says. What else can you say about the plan?'

Christopher sits in the chair beside Anthony and taps a finger on the plan. 'You're going to use four men. Two waiting on his tram and two further up and down the road as lookouts and to dissuade anybody from interfering. You're not sure what which tram he'll be on, that's obvious, so that's your first problem.'

'What do you mean?' O'Donnell says, leaning over the plan and spilling the ash from his cigarette in the process. He brushes the ash impatiently away and examines the plan again. 'It's a simple plan, granted – there've been too many complicated plans that've failed and taken good men with them. So, you see, to my mind simple is best.'

'That may be so, Mr O'Donnell, but with all due respect even simple plans have to have a chance of working. See here? Between nine and half past nine is rush hour. The tram stops for only a few seconds – how are you going to be certain which one he's on? Mr Reynolds is a very ordinary-looking man. No distinguishing features. He's wearing a homburg hat in this photograph, so it's safe to say that he'll be wearing one on the tram. Along with every other businessman on it. If the men make a mistake and pick out the wrong man, it will be not just a failure – it will be a disaster. If speculation reveals that it was a mistake and an innocent man has died, we will lose support and credibility. It will appear in the newspapers. Plus, the next time you see Mr Reynolds on the way to work will be in a Crossley Tender surrounded by soldiers. All I'm saying is it's not a well thought-through plan.'

O'Donnell sits back in his chair, takes a puff from his cigarette and blows a cloud of smoke towards the ceiling. Christopher hears Anthony's intake of breath and can feel the tension in the room. But he has been asked and he has given an honest answer. O'Donnell stubs out his cigarette and throws a pencil across the desk.

'What would you do?'

'It's a six-man job, at the very least. One to signal which tram he's on …'

'How do you propose to do that?'

'Station a man near his house.'

'But his house is well guarded,' O'Donnell says with a look of triumph on his face.

'The man stationed outside the house will have a bicycle. He can pretend he's fixing a puncture, happens every day. Who would suspect that? When he sees the target leaving his house he follows him, confirms which tram it is and follows it. After the first stop he can overtake it and give a warning to the men at the tram stop.'

O'Donnell, who has been silently counting off the men asks, 'What's the sixth man for?'

'He takes up position at one of the stops and as soon as he sees the cyclist go past, he knows he has to get onto the next tram. He takes a seat downstairs at the front and waits.'

'Why the front?'

'He makes sure Reynolds can't get off that way.'

'If the men do their job properly and kill him, he won't be needed.'

'Did you ever shoot a man?'

O'Donnell looks uncomfortable. 'No,' he admits.

'Even if he's shot, he'll struggle and fight for his life – he's a soldier. Is that what you want the other passengers to see? A dying man being executed in front of their eyes?'

'Point taken. What would you propose?'

'We force him off at gunpoint and tell the driver to get on his way as fast as the tram can take him. Then, we put one of these,' Christopher points to one of the bullets, 'into his head, and another in his chest.'

'I'm glad you're on our side,' O'Donnell says and lets out a phlegmy laugh.

'I told you he was good,' Anthony pipes up.

'You did, Anthony. Now, would you mind leaving the adults alone for a few minutes?' O'Donnell says and points to one of the guns and the bullets. 'And you can take those with you.'

Anthony picks up the gun and bullets and leaves without saying anything, but Christopher can see from his face that he's annoyed.

'Anthony's a good man but he can be a bit excitable,' O'Donnell says. 'And he's very fond of the ladies, which I've no problem with, but not at times like these.'

'To be honest, when we first met, I was surprised that he was a volunteer in the IRA.'

'What do you think makes any young man risk his life, Christopher?'

O'Donnell sits back in his chair and stares at him through the smoke.

Christopher shrugs. 'Love of his country?'

O'Donnell's laugh comes out like a bark and he hits the table with the palm of his hand, making everything littered across the top bounce.

'That's one reason. But there's more, and I've seen them all. In Anthony's case it's for the excitement. I know his father, Benito, a dour aul shite. And, of course, Anthony loves to wear the uniform at weekends – for the ladies, do you see?' O'Donnell winks.

'I thought he'd earned the right to wear that uniform.'

'Don't believe everything he tells you. Don't you know he hasn't been tested yet? Anyway,' O'Donnell slaps a blank piece of paper onto the desk and hands the pencil to Christopher, 'let's see how good you are.'

From memory Christopher draws the main road again and puts the various men into their positions. He writes in the times again but puts '*to be confirmed*' beside them. He indicates the crossroads near where the attack is happening and puts in several arrows.

'Escape routes,' he explains to O'Donnell. 'We don't want a bunch of men going in the same direction.'

O'Donnell turns the plan around the studies it, nodding his head.

'I'll organise the two extra men,' he says.

'Good.'

'Just one other thing. I think we should keep this to yourselves. No need to pass it up the chain for now.'

'I've no problem with that, Mr O'Donnell. I just want to do my bit.'

'Very good, Christopher. And I believe you're married?'

'Yes. What's that got to do with it?'

'I don't need to tell you that you can't even hint to your wife what's going on.'

'Of course not, although she has done her bit in the past.'

'The past is the past, Christopher. 1916 was just boys playing with guns – they never had a chance. This time it's going to be different. It's going to get bloody.'

'I understand.' Christopher nods.

'One other thing before you go. I have certain funds at my discretion. It's not a massive amount, but I'm going to give you a weekly wage, same as you're earning in Donnelly's. You're now a paid member of Sinn Féin and my second-in-command, but that's between you and me and nobody else, not even your nearest and dearest.' O'Donnell holds out his hand.

Christopher shakes his hand, already working out ways to avoid telling Nell. He would have to pretend to go to work every morning, as usual. Even wear his bloodstained working clothes. But then Nell would guess when he returns with the same clothes day in and day out. So he will tell her he has been moved to a different section, a packing section.

As he leaves the office, he can feel a change coming over him. The old feelings of danger and excitement are returning and it is almost like an awakening. He can almost feel his stance straightening and his blood growing hotter. By the time he reaches the bottom of the stairs he is a new man.

Outside, amid the hustle and bustle of Middle Abbey Street, Anthony is waiting for him. Unobserved, Christopher studies his friend. He is smoking incessantly and spends most of his time looking at the girls who are leaving the offices for their lunch break, tipping his hat to them if they look his way. He's constantly touching his tie and pulling down the cuffs of his shirt, then examining himself in the window of Lawlor's, the printing and stationary shop. Can he be trusted in a dangerous situation? He had heard young men in the barracks boasting about their exploits with women, strutting around in front of the other soldiers like cockerels, passing photographs of their girlfriends around. But when the going got tough, especially in the hand-to-hand bloody struggles in the enemy's trenches, they were nowhere to be seen.

Anthony spots him and rushes over. 'What was that about?'

'What?'

'Asking me to leave, the arrogant bastard! I brought you to him and he asks *me* to leave? *Bastard!*' Anthony flicks his cigarette at a passing tram. It explodes against the side, sending out a shower of sparks.

'*That's* why!' Christopher points to a passenger on the tram who is turning to his friend, pointing out at Anthony, disapproval written on his face as the tram trundles past them.

'Who cares? The only reason he picked you was to get one over on Collins. He hates culchies like Collins, especially ones from Cork.'

'First thing to learn, don't draw attention to yourself. I've seen too many fellow soldiers getting their heads shot off when they stuck them up where they weren't wanted.'

Anthony shakes his head. 'Are we together in this or not?'

'We're together, but I give the orders,' Christopher says, tapping the pocket where his new plans sit.

Anthony's mood changes and now he is almost dancing around with delight. Another problem of his – he seems to be able to go from one mood to another in the blink of an eye. Christopher makes up his mind as to the task he is going to allocate to him – the man repairing the puncture outside Reynolds's house – that way he can do no damage and still maintain he was on 'a job' as he likes to call it.

'Another thing. I've told O'Donnell that I don't want to know the identities of any of the men who're on this. As far as I'm concerned, it'll be Mr North, Mr South, Mr East and Mr West. I want to see what they're made of before I work with them again – our lives might depend on it.'

'Mr West – is he the jeweller on Grafton Street? Am I to be called Mr North East?' Anthony jokes.

'Listen, Anthony. Now's not the time for joking. I have a wife. I need to be there for her and not put behind bars again by some slip-up or betrayed by somebody I don't know. And that's why I came up with a new plan.'

'What did O'Donnell think of that?' Anthony grabs his friend's arm in excitement.

'In fairness, the man knows when he's wrong and has agreed that it's now a six-man job. You have a good bicycle, haven't you?'

'*Hey, mama mia!* I'm *Italiano* – so of course.'

'Good. You've got the most important job. You have to figure out the right tram that Reynolds will be on and signal that to the next man. After that, you can make yourself scarce.'

Anthony draws himself up to his full height and puts his arms around Christopher, crushing him in a bear-hug.

'I knew you were the right man,' he says into Christopher's shoulder.

When he finally releases him, Christopher can see that there are tears of emotion in his eyes. He takes a hanky from his pocket and turns away, dabbing at them.

CHAPTER 13

Anthony

Anthony Caprani, or Mister C as he now calls himself, stands beside his upturned bicycle turning the back wheel for what feels like the hundredth time, searching for a puncture. It was easy for Christopher to give him what he thought was the safest task, but the two soldiers standing inside the gate of the large suburban house, Reynolds's residence, are glancing over at him more often. He has no choice but to lift the bike into its upright position then stare at the back wheel again, scratching his head for the soldier's benefit. He props the bike against the brick wall of the house across and up from Reynolds's house and begins to pump up the tyre he had let down earlier.

Christopher had been right, as usual. Wearing his suit had been a bad decision. His efforts are causing him to sweat profusely and he can feel the chill of the dampness under his arms. That and the glances from the two soldiers are making it worse. He was thinking about what to do after a sufficient amount of time had passed. Should he take a chance on which tram stop – there were two close by – cycle off and hide in some nearby garden to wait? No, he couldn't take that risk.

By the time he has pumped up the tyre and settled himself back in the saddle, there is movement across the road in front of Reynolds's house. The two soldiers have snapped to attention. A small, dapper man emerges from the driveway and says something to them and they both laugh. It's unsettling. This is the first time Anthony has seen Reynolds in the flesh and he's taken aback at how ordinary he looks. He could almost be his father. And now they are going to take his life away and probably leave a widow and children.

Reynolds, with a briefcase in his hands, claps one of the soldiers on the shoulder and leads them away from the house towards the tram stop.

It's not too late, Anthony thinks – he can back out and tell Christopher there was a mix-up. Christopher was right, he's not cut out for this. Not that his friend said it directly to him, but he knew by his attitude that he had doubts. But he would show him. Buoyed up by hurt pride more than anything else, he straddles his bicycle and waits until the three men have disappeared around the bend, taking the turn to Sydney Terrace, then follows them, pedalling slowly. He wonders why Reynolds doesn't let the soldiers accompany him on the tram and puts it down to British pig-headedness. Probably the same pig-headedness that refused to accept that the Easter Rising of 1916 was about to take place, even though the clues were all around them. Or maybe he just wants the soldiers to return and take up their position outside his house to protect his family?

Anthony had excused himself from attending most of Christopher's briefings after his part had been discussed. The meetings, usually held at lunchtime in St Patrick's Park, included all of the tiny details that were known of Reynold's personal life. This was one of his friend's natural aptitudes that he hadn't had opportunity to witness before. The way he could discuss so dryly the killing of another human being knowing that the man, Reynolds, had a wife and children – and all under the shade of a leafy tree and in the shadow of St. Patrick's Cathedral. What disturbed him most was the way he could plan a killing like a game of chess with the pieces on the board represented by the assassins, the victim and the bystanders. Each piece had a place to be on the board but, like any game of chess, things could go wrong. It was Christopher's first mission and he was endeavouring to make sure that it went well: including everybody's task afterwards and, in the case of an unforeseen event, where to go.

The other men had objected to Anthony's constant absences at first, but Christopher had explained this away by telling them his mission would end after he identified the tram. Now, still nervous about what is about to happen, he waits until the tram comes into view. When he sees Reynolds stepping on board the tram he pushes himself away from the kerb and cycles ahead of it as fast as he can, raising his hat when he cycles past the tram stop where Mr North is waiting. On down Merrion Road he cycles until he has left the seashore behind and is into the suburbs of Ballsbridge proper. He glances sideways as he passes the tram stop where it's all going to take place. At first, he can't identify Christopher in the queue, but then recognises his friend who is wearing an unfamiliar cap pulled down over his eyes and a long overcoat. He is reading a newspaper and standing beside him is Mr South, whose real name is Liam Twomey. He used to be an apprentice stonecutter to Anthony's own father when he worked on the altar of Saint Peter's Church in Phibsborough. He had pretended not to recognise Twomey at their first meeting in St Patrick's Park and Twomey had done the same.

Coming up to the junction at Ailesbury Road, he can see the other two men loitering on opposite sides of the road, covering the eventuality of any soldiers or police straying onto the scene from either direction. Instead of turning left and cycling back towards the city as ordered,

he stops his bicycle and locks it to a lamppost, then walks back towards
Merrion Road. When he reaches the corner, the tram is just about to
stop. He watches as people shuffle onboard. After a few seconds there
are shouts and he sees Reynolds emerge from the tram and after him
Christopher and Twomey, who shouts something back at the driver.
The tram moves away from the stop. Christopher is standing in front
of their target who has his hands up in the air. Anthony wants to close
his eyes but can't. Reynolds gets down on his knees, whether begging
or having been told, he doesn't know. Twomey's right hand extends,
the muzzle of the gun against Reynold's forehead and Christopher
turns his head away, whether to shield himself from the blast or
because he doesn't want to witness the cold-blooded killing, Anthony
doesn't know. A sound of a single shot rings out and he sees the back
of Reynolds' head erupting and then his body falling backwards with
the impact of the bullet. Twomey steps over Reynolds and fires two
rounds into his chest and it's all over. As Twomey walks quickly away,
Christopher stands alone over the dead man and blesses himself, then
he too walks away in a different direction.

All of the men are to meet up later in St. Patrick's Park in the shadow
of the cathedral. Christopher, now without his cap or overcoat, sits on
the bench, a rucksack at his side. Anthony watches from the shadows
of one of the side entrances to the cathedral. After a few minutes
Twomey comes up and sits beside Christopher, then leans over and
puts something into the rucksack – his gun. Over the course of the
next hour each of the men deposit their guns into the rucksack as
Christopher, seemingly oblivious, throws pieces of bread to a flock of
pigeons strutting around his feet. Now it is his turn.

As he takes his place beside him Christopher turns to him and says: 'Look at that big dark one, he's taking most of the bread. No matter what I do, he just jumps onto the piece, pushing all the other ones away.'

Anthony looks into his eyes to see if his friend is acting nonchalantly about what had occurred earlier, but Christopher's eyes are impossible to read. Anthony looks around him to see if there is anyone nearby and, when the time is right, he takes the revolver out of his pocket and slips it into the rucksack.

'That's everything,' Christopher says, closing up the rucksack and standing up, tossing the rest of the bread towards the pigeons. 'Let's go back to O'Donnell and then for a pint.'

'How can you even think of drinking after what Twomey did?' Anthony shakes his head in disgust. 'I saw it all. I'll never sleep properly again.'

Christopher sits back down on the bench beside him.

'Is that his name? He's a good man, held his nerve, as the rest did. I'll use them again now that I know I can trust them. But you weren't supposed to be there – that was the plan.'

'I couldn't help it,' Anthony admits. 'It was terrible.'

'You're right, Anthony, but we're at war.'

'Then why didn't you pull the trigger yourself?'

Christopher puts his arm on Anthony's shoulder: 'Everybody had their job to do and he volunteered for that one. I haven't got it in me, but I'm not ashamed. I can exchange fire with anybody who's armed, and probably will, but I'm no executioner. Men like Twomey lack something, and that makes them invaluable. Anyway, do you want me to tell O'Donnell that you're not up for it anymore?'

'He'll think I'm yella – he'll tell everyone.'

'No, he won't, I'll make sure of that. I'll say it's for religious reasons.'

'I don't know, Christopher. I think I'm done.'

'Did you know O'Donnell's never shot anyone himself?' Christopher punches him playfully on the shoulder and takes out a pack of cigarettes, offering him one.

'I didn't know that,' Anthony says, and takes one. 'I suppose it's not everyone who can do that.'

Christopher holds out a match. 'No. But you did your part, other than disobeying my orders!' He slaps him playfully on the back of his head.

'Yes, sir, won't happen again, sir.' Anthony, fingers trembling, pulls on his cigarette and inhales deeply.

'That man, by the way, was the one responsible for bringing in more agents. It'll send the British a message that we won't sit idly by.' Christopher pulls on his own cigarette and sits back. 'He knew the risks and died like a soldier. His last words were "Shoot straight".'

Anthony begins to cry then, letting out the pent-up tension that had been building up since he had begun to watch Reynolds's house. He stares down at the ground, imagining Reynolds' wife when she hears the news; and the children. What was once a game to him is now a reality. The British would now hit some of their men and they would hit them back and on and on it would go until some form of bitter agreement would come about. Would he even be alive to see it? He throws his cigarette onto the ground and stands up.

Turning to Christopher, he holds out his hand.

'That's me finished, Christopher. I can't do that anymore.'

Christopher ignores his hand. 'You don't have a choice, Anthony. It's a war and it's going to get worse. I'll take these guns back to O'Donnell. You go home and get some rest. Tomorrow we'll meet up again and talk about it.'

CHAPTER 14

Skagway, Alaska
1897

The old man Triplett shuffles the deck and puts three playing cards onto the table, face up. One of the them is the Queen of Hearts and Triplett turns the cards face down and begins to swap them around and around in slow, awkward movements, even letting one of them slide off the suitcase onto the ground. Levon stares, fascinated, and wondering what's going on. The new arrival, Fraser, laughs out loud and takes out a thick leather wallet from the inside pocket of his suit.

'Yeh have to give a man a chance to git his money back,' he says and waves a dollar bill in the air, 'but this time I want to see the Lady before yeh begin.'

'So be it,' the old man says, 'all yeh have to do is find the Lady.'

He lays out the three cards onto the top of the wooden crate, turns them over again, places the Queen of Hearts in the middle and a non-coloured card on each side. Flipping over the cards he begins to shuffle them around again in his slow clumsy way and then stands back from the table.

Jim Fraser holds his chin, shakes his head, then turns to Levon.

'I reckon the Lady has stayed put and is in the middle – what do you think, boy?'

'I would have to say it's the one on the right, sir,' Levon answers.

'Naw, I think you're wrong there, son,' Fraser says, leans over and flips the centre card.

A Five of Hearts stares back up at him and he lets out a loud groan. He hands over the dollar bill to the old man and shakes his head. The Reverend laughs good-naturedly at his misfortune, reaches over, picks up the card on the right, showing it to the other two men: the Queen of Hearts.

'That boy sure knows how to play! Have you ever played before?' Triplett says.

'No, sir.'

'I find that hard to believe, son. But let's do it again,' Fraser says, taking a five-dollar bill out of his wallet, 'but this time I listen to the boy.'

Triplett puts his fingers on the cards again and begins to shuffle them around each other. When he stops, he looks up at Fraser with a twinkle in his eye.

'I want to say the Lady is on the right, but I'm just not sure.' He turns to Levon. 'What do you say, son?'

'It's in the middle, sir,' Levon says eagerly, drawn into the game.

'Well … if you're sure,' he says and tips the card in the centre with his finger.

Triplett seems disgusted as he flips it over. The Queen of Hearts stares up at them and he puts five, clean one-dollar bills on top of the box. Fraser picks them up and looks at them.

'Easiest money I ever earned, Reverend,' he says, turning to Bowers.

'Yeh mean the easiest money the boy earned for yeh. Why don't you give him a reward?' Reverend Bowers says. 'Yeh would've been losing if'n it weren't for his young eyes.'

Fraser seems to consider this for a while, then hands Levon one of the brand-new dollar bills before he turns back to the table.

The boy's hand trembles as he holds the crisp note, the first time he had ever held his own money in his life.

Downcast, Triplett is shuffling the cards around again, slightly quicker this time, but still not too quick for the boy to see that he had left the Queen in the middle.

'Hey there, old man,' Fraser says, taking out his wallet again, 'I've got to be headin' off soon myself. Why don't you change the stakes? Let's have one last game.'

'If that's what you want, but you're goin' to bleed me dry,' Triplett says, shuffling the cards around. 'Twenty dollars to play, winner takes all.'

Levon watches intently as the old man, now looking tired and dispirited, begins to move the cards around with little enthusiasm, his old fingers fumbling awkwardly. If anything it is even more obvious which card the Queen is as he had noticed a slight crease in one of the corners. Fraser scratches his chin and puts two ten-dollar bills, the biggest denomination Levon has ever seen in his short life, onto the wrong card, the one on the left.

The old man looks up at Levon.

'Do you want to play, son?'

Levon looks at the dollar bill in his hand and is devastated. He's certain where the Queen is and can imagine what his father will say when he produces the twenty dollars he's just about to win. If he only had more money!

'A'course, it don't have to be legal tender,' Old Man Triplett says as if reading his mind. 'It can be something of equal or greater value. Say, gold dust for instance. It's used all the time in Skagway. Isn't that right, gentlemen?' He looks at the two men.

'Of course it is,' the Reverend says. 'Why, all the time it's put on our collection plates. Praise the Lord!'

'It's make-up your mind time, son,' Triplett says.

Levon turns away and puts his hand down the front of his pants. He takes out the packet his father had given him earlier and considers it.

'Let's make it the very last game, gentlemen. I got to get back to work,' Triplett says and looks at Levon. 'Are you in, or are you out?'

Triplett begins to fan a line of notes across the crate. Ones, tens and twenties sit side by side. More money than he has ever imagined in his life. Levon looks at the bag containing his father's gold. He isn't sure of its value and doubts if there is enough in it to go up against all of the money on the table.

'I don't know,' he says. 'I don't think I have enough to play.'

The two men look at each other.

'Well, I'm sure that Mr Triplett will make an exception this once. Isn't that right, Mr Triplett?' says the Reverend. 'What say you?'

Triplett seems to consider this and runs his fingers through his scraggly grey beard.

'Hell, OK, since you put it like that,' he says, and holds his hand out to Levon.

'Thank you, sir,' Levon says gratefully, and hands over the bag.

'OK, son – to show that there's no cheatin' going on here, you get first pick,' Triplett says, and stands back.

A feeling of guilt makes Levon hesitate. He doesn't really want to take the old man's money. Maybe he can give some of it back to him, he thinks, or the Reverend for his church. He reaches out and, as he turns the card over, he looks with sadness and shame at the old man, hating to have to do this to him.

'Well, bless my soul, the Lord works in mysterious ways!' says Triplett, smiling.

Levon can't understand why he is so happy at losing and looks at the upturned card. The Five of Hearts. It can't be. It's the same card with the crease, the same card he has seen the old man trying to hide. A shock of cold travels down his body and he stands rooted to the spot. The old man whips up the money and the gold and stashes them into an inside pocket of his jacket and takes the table apart, turning it into a suitcase again.

The Reverend shakes his head sadly and pats Levon on the shoulder, then follows old man Triplett and Fraser down the alleyway.

The reality of what has just happened sinks into Levon. His father will kill him. He feels a warm gush of urine as it trickles down the inside of his leg and he begins to tremble. He stumbles out of the passageway and into the main street and spots the three men. They're approaching a building across from where he stands, talking and laughing together. The sign over the door reads *Jeff Smith's Parlour* and, as the men push open the door, a cloud of smoke pours out from the interior and he can hear the clamour of voices and the sound of a piano. He sits down on the wooden walkway and stares at the entrance to Clancy's Bar until his father finally comes out.

Before his father can say anything, he jumps up and cries out, pointing over to the bar across the street: '*I was robbed, Pa! The men went over there! They took the gold!*'

His father staggers slightly and, judging by his slack face and unfocused eyes, Levon can tell that he's drunk.

'What do yeh mean, took the gold? How could they take the gold?' his father says, trying to understand what his son is trying to tell him.

'They swindled me, Pa, I swear it. They had playing cards and they cheated, then they went off laughin' together over to that bar!' Levon points again.

'*You were playin' cards with our gold?*' his father shouts at him.

Levon can smell the alcohol on his breath, and something more, the sweet scent of perfume.

'Maybe you shouldna' left me, Pa, on my own, while you were –'

Before he has finished the sentence his father's fist explodes into his face and he falls backwards into the mud. A small crowd gathers around the father and son but nobody intervenes. His father jumps down off the wooden sidewalk and grabs him by the hair, turns him around and kicks him in the behind towards the bar across the street.

'*Never you mind what I was doin'!*' his father shouts. '*Just point out those men!*'

Levon half walks half stumbles across the muddy street towards Jeff Smith's Parlour. The small crowd of onlookers had grown, sensing some entertainment. At the window he points out the three men, who are all drinking at the bar with several other men. He is shocked to see that Reverend Bowers has his arm around a woman dressed in a red, silky dress while Old Man Triplett is nodding to Fraser, who is counting out the money and putting it onto the counter along with the sack of gold dust.

'Wait here and don't let them out of your sight,' his father says, and heads off in the direction of the livery stable where they have left their horses.

When he returns, he has his rifle with him, an old one-shot ex-army rifle with a battered stock. When the crowd see the rifle, they clear off the wooden walkway back into the muddy street and stand, gaping. His father cocks his weapon and pushes open the door to the bar. Levon looks through the window and can see his father approaching the men and shouting something at them that he can't make out. Most of the drinkers around the bar scatter when they see the rifle and now his father is facing the three men. They have their backs to the bar but look unconcerned. A tall figure in a black suit detaches himself from the crowd of onlookers, says something to his father and pulls back his jacket. A silver star stands out from the dark waistcoat he is wearing. He begins talking to the three men at the bar and then to his father who gradually lowers the rifle in defeat, turns away and comes back out onto the street. The crowd, seeing that the entertainment is over, have drifted away. His father points down towards the livery stable.

CHAPTER 15

Levon

Sergeant Samuel McBride of the Dublin Metropolitan Police is coming up to retirement. The buttons on his police uniform look strained over his well-rounded stomach. That's just to cover up my muscles, he jokes good-naturedly to the younger policemen who taunt him over his weight. As his years of service stretch out behind him, so too does his distance from Dublin Castle. Once his beat would have taken in the tougher areas around Dublin – the Liberties, the Monto, the docklands – now he patrols the more sedate area around Fitzwilliam Square where the only criminals are the hawkers who sell their wares to the rich inhabitants of the square or the occasional pickpocket trying their luck on the well-heeled ladies out for a stroll around the park before lunch. But Sergeant McBride, after a lifetime's experience, can spot them a mile away and gives them a sharp rap over the knuckles or a Size 10 boot in the arse and tells them to be on their way.

The denizens of Fitzwilliam Square appreciate his experience and every Christmas he receives a lot of gifts from them for his vigilance. In return and as a mark of respect, he has memorised all of their names so that when they press that envelope on him, he can say 'Thank you very much, Miss Delaney' or 'How thoughtful of you to remember, Mr Fry'. This also encourages their perception of him, not alone as a good policeman, but also as a personal protector who looks after them and their property. From their day-to-day movements in and out of their homes, he can usually surmise their marital status, their type of employment, and even their wealth. The wealthiest of them have several servants, take delivery of their groceries from Findlater's, one of the more expensive grocery outlets in Dublin, and even employ a liveryman to take care of their horse and carriage.

But now Sergeant McBride has a mystery on his hands. One of the houses, which has been vacant for a number of years, is inhabited again. The lamps in the parlour are lit every evening and the windows in the front of the house have recently been cleaned. The post, which he had been in the habit of helping through the letterbox when a postman didn't bother to do his job, is now no more a problem. He has tried, several times, to meet the owner – one Mr Levon Mordaunt – if the name on the post is correct – but he is a difficult man to bump into. It's as if the man is peeking out the window and leaving the premises just as Sergeant McBride is on the opposite side of the square.

On a warm September evening, to test out his theory, he changes his routine and instead of patrolling the entire route around the square as usual, he cuts back through the park. As he emerges through the gate, his timing is perfect and he at last gets a look at the owner of the house for the first time. As he leaves through the door with the hall light behind him the man, tall and well built, has a quick look around, then bounds down the granite steps, two at a time, and makes his way towards the city before disappearing around the corner onto Baggot Street, leaving Sergeant McBride bemused. At first he thought he could make out a clerical collar but maybe he was mistaken. And in the hundred yards or so the man seems to have changed shape. Leaving the house, he was tall, broad and upright and his gait was almost animal-like in its movement. But by the time he approached the corner of Baggot Street, he seemed to have shrunk somehow, his shoulders folding in on themselves, his steps more hesitant. Before he continues his patrol of the square, Sergeant McBride decides to finally take his wife's advice, forget his pride, and begin wearing his spectacles to work.

Fonsey Whelan and his dog Butcher are in their usual doorway in Mabbot Street. It's a pawnbroker's, but it closes at six o'clock and he is the occupier of this small porch until the following morning. The swells and toffs, students and soldiers walking past on their way to Montgomery Street hardly ever register him, never mind throw him a few coppers. But every now and again, just like tonight, somebody good comes along. An angel who alights beside him and hands him down some loose change or even a hot crubeen, hardly touched, which he shares with Butcher. Tonight is one of those nights. The man sharing his doorway is well dressed but, in some ways, is more unfortunate than him.

The mask he wears is life-like but there is nothing life-like about his voice. Like a wounded cow it sounds, and it takes him some time to be able to understand its cadence, but it becomes easier the more he listens. But the poor creature has promised him a florin and Fonsey's patience can last the night. The man claims he is a soldier, an officer, who has spent many a night in the Monto in the past. But, as well as the wound in his face, there is also a wound in his mind. What he wants to do is to relive his past but he can't, for the life of him, remember quite where he had spent his nights when he was on leave.

'But why bother with that? Sure money is the same in one or the other,' Fonsey says, anxious to get hold of the florin.

'*Noooo*,' the man grunts. '*It must be the same.*'

Fonsey wonders if this person is one of those funny men with unusual appetites? But no, the man seems genuine, if not a little simple in the head. Keeps grunting about a mouse on the door. What would a mouse be doing on the door? Fonsey wonders. Then a light switches on in the back of his addled mind. Does he mean Moussa, the exotic giant of a man who used to work on Montgomery Street? That would have been a few years ago, before he adopted Butcher.

'Do you mean Moussa?'

The man's eyes, which up to then had been soft and beseeching, stare into his and widen. Fonsey thinks he has struck a gold mine. That look, so desperate, so excited, eyes bulging, head nodding so hard that his mask is in danger of falling off. Fonsey holds up his hand to quieten the poor creature, then takes Butcher, a mongrel Jack Russell, onto his lap. He rubs his head and plays with his ears.

'I know all about Moussa,' Fonsey says.

'*Tell me!*' The stranger lets out a strangled cry.

'Do you mean where?' Fonsey helps, and the stranger nods.

Fonsey is about to tell him when some part of him stops him from blurting out the answer. When he was younger and sober, Fonsey worked hard on the barges that made their way from the Guinness brewery on the upper quays, down to the ships that waited in the docks. Then he worked on the hack boat – the barge that used the Grand Canal dock and moved along the Grand Canal, that manmade waterway that sliced its way through Dublin city and on into the countryside, delivering kegs of stout and porter to all and sundry. In his thirties he had bought his own hack boat, with an engine, and took up with a woman from Carlow, who he eventually married. Life was good for a few years. The hack boat was their home and his workplace. But every time the barge stopped to make a delivery, Fonsey never refused a drink from the bar owner. He liked to think of himself as a clever man in those days. But looking back from his stinking doorway, he can trace the downward spiral of his life from a proud owner of a barge to a broken pauper. He used to spend his time telling the other street drunks what had happened and blaming his wife for abandoning him after he lost the boat, until they tired of his tales. Older and wiser now, he only has Butcher to confide in. But now some of his old acumen comes back.

'You said a florin,' Fonsey reminds the stranger.

'*esss*,' the stranger hisses and takes a shiny florin from his pocket.

'That's good. For a start.' Fonsey winks. 'How about another one and I'll bring ye there personally?'

In a movement that he can hardly follow the man drops the florin, grabs Butcher by the scruff of the neck with one hand and holds him up. An open razor appears in his other hand and he rests the blade across the exposed belly of the little dog. People pass by, oblivious to the drama taking place in the dark doorway. Tears flood down Fonsey's cheeks and he tells the stranger everything he knows and some things he thought he had forgotten. And then he is gone, just another passer-by in the long line of men on their way to a night's cavorting.

It's dusk as Levon Mordaunt makes his way down Talbot Street. Wearing his ecclesiastic clothes and making use of the Reverend Tompkins identity papers he walks past the young, nervous British soldiers with a benign salute. They carry rifles that look taller than themselves and their restless fingers hover over the triggers. Wouldn't it be a perfect irony if he was shot by mistake by a twitchy-fingered English boy? And there are unexpected advantages to his wound. If and when any get too close to him and can make out the strange appearance of his lower face, he is amused to find that it makes them even more reverential towards him, as facial disfigurement from the war is becoming a more familiar sight in Dublin.

It's his fourth foray into the Monto and he has learned to button up his overcoat once inside the famous red-light district, where he is relieved to see the curfew is being ignored. Here his collar is a bit more remarked upon and he has found it a magnet for some of the streetwalking women. Believing that he is a clergyman looking for some relief, they assume he will be a good payer, at least better than the soldiers who still drift around the streets looking for a bargain, haggling intensely.

He had first bumped into Moussa in a bar on Montgomery Street, one of the more popular bars which Levon sometimes frequented back in 1916. The amount of information picked up from the mouths of drunken soldiers – and officers – had always amazed him. Later in the evenings, as the drink flowed and the more presentable prostitutes were allowed to mingle with the customers, it became evident that the bar was a kind of no-man's land where hostilities between the occupiers, the British, and the occupied, the Irish, were put to one side as they rubbed shoulders in man's greatest pastime: the pursuit of lust.

But Moussa was an exception. He had observed him a few times in the evenings, as sober as himself, his eyes darting around the pub, his great height giving him an advantage. It amused him to see Moussa's eyes fixing on his prey, a drunken gentleman or an officer, and using large hands to split the crowded drinkers apart with a gentle smile on his face and, with the cunning of a prowling coyote, cut the man off from the herd. Moussa's bearded face would lower towards the unwitting victim and whisper … what? After witnessing the performance over several nights, it became evident that the well-dressed gentle giant was some kind of go-between who worked for one of the better brothels in the area and came to the pub presumably before he took up his night-long post as doorman.

Levon never found out which one, and it didn't, at the time, bother him. But, he realises now, it was a clever move of Moussa's to have withheld that information. In a way Moussa was a great survivor, like himself. Not on the same level, of course, but it was only a matter of scale. Like sharks they were both predators, gliding through the innocent shoals of tiny fish that swam about in the sea of existence. And all put on this earth for the amusement and gratification of people like themselves. Where Moussa was using his wiles to bring back customers to his employer and getting paid for it, Levon also, in a way, made his money by dangling tasty morsels in front of the hungry American industrialists, or the warmongering Germans or British, in fact anyone who would pay his substantial fee. But, in the end, it was never really about the money, although that helped. It was because it gave him control over – or dominance of – his power-hungry, money-grabbing clients. A subtle difference and he could never decide which. Maybe they were sides of the same coin?

But, unfortunately, all of his intricate plans had to be put to one side because of Christopher Flinter, the young, ignorant upstart who had no concept of the coming evolution of a new type of man. No more kings or prime ministers, presidents or czars, no more wasteful wars brought about by petty arguments. No. Future countries would be ruled by more pragmatic minds. Minds that would understand the needs of the masses, but minds chosen by a select few with fully evolved minds, like his own. A movement was starting, he could feel it, and he was a part of it.

Moussa had to be eliminated, and he was forced to do it sooner than he would have liked. In a way Levon thinks that Moussa had suspected this would eventually happen, so had never revealed much about his personal life, just the comings and goings of the flotsam and jetsam in the Monto. A pity, as he was one of Levon's best sources of information. Moussa also had that sixth sense of a true predator: he understood and recognised weaknesses in people. Levon's obvious one was his need not to be seen on the streets of the Monto creating suspicion in that tight-knit community – hence Moussa remained his well-paid eyes and ears. Pity ... he would have made a good partner.

Now, eating shellfish from a vendor outside the brothel owned by Anna Macken, he has a clearer picture of Moussa from the people he has talked to and who were only too glad to share the story of the giant, bearded foreigner. How he had appeared one night on the door of the brothel in a fancy suit that Anna made him wear. How everyone now missed his booming laughter and his very presence outside the door of that high-class brothel. About his relationship with the tiny girl-like servant girl who worked for Anna and, of course, his murder. The aforesaid diminutive woman, Sarah Murphy, might go to the top of his list. With her it will be the beginning of the end of Christopher Flinter and, when that task is done, he can at last move on with his own life. It will be a trickier task than any before because it will have to happen during daylight hours, as constant curfews by the British will hinder a nighttime abduction. But in daylight hours his disfigurement will be a disadvantage.

It will be a calculated risk but one he must take. He must find out who had fired that shot that had almost taken his life away and had left him for dead – but instead turning him into a monster who might be better off dead.

What if he was caught? No. Not Sarah Murphy. Too risky. Instead, the new doorman with the ridiculous cap at the top of the steps that led into the promised land of Anna Macken's brothel, might be a better choice.

Kevin Brennan lumbers down Talbot Street, an overladen shopping bag hanging out of each hand. It's Monday evening and the shopping list from Anna Macken is almost complete. His last stop is the fishmonger's where he has to pick up a sack of oysters which he can hang from his thick neck. She has promised him a lad to help him with the messages but keeps putting it off, telling him costs are going up due to ongoing tit-for-tat killings between the British and the Irish rebels which is getting worse every week. Kevin is a simple man and believes everything his boss, who he looks up to, tells him. She pays and feeds him for standing at the top of the steps seven nights a week, so why shouldn't he?

The momentary sharp pain on his buttock feels like the sting of a wasp or a bee. He drops one of the shopping bags and brushes the seat of his pants with his free hand to get rid of the insect, then lifts the bag again. For some reason his right leg seems to have seized up on him and he puts the bag down again just in time. His right leg is now numb and he topples to his side, letting the second bag drop onto the ground. The captain's cap he wears in the evenings falls off his head and into the gutter. It was given to him by Mrs Macken to wear on the door at night to make him look more distinguished, but he has taken to wearing it in the daytime too. Now it lies on its back, the dirty water soaking into it. He sits dazed as passersby stare and the little street gurriers begin to run off with the groceries that have spilled from the bags, ignoring his curses and his threats.

Luckily the day is saved by the one true gentleman who has come to his rescue. The man shakes his fist at the remaining urchins and helps him to stand on his one good leg. With the gentleman's help, he hops towards the waiting carriage that stands further down the street. When he has been helped inside, the gentleman leans in and covers his legs with a blanket, then goes back for the remaining groceries, which he gathers up, along with the cap, and places in the carriage beside him.

As he is thanking his benefactor profusely, the man leans in and puts a cloth over his nose and mouth. He struggles as best he can, but without the strength in his right leg he has no purchase in the confines of the cramped carriage. The struggle lasts barely ten seconds.

CHAPTER 16

Nell

Nell skips across Dame Street onto Parliament Street and begins her circuitous route towards home. Crossing Capel Street bridge, she stares down into the River Liffey below. It's a tidal river and the tide is in, making the water almost clear. Large shadows clumped together swim upstream. She used to think they were salmon or trout, until Christopher had put her right. He told her they were mullet, scavengers of the sea. They were almost impossible to catch and even if caught they tasted foul because their diet consisted of all the filth and pollution that found its way into the Liffey from the various streams and sewage outlets that fed into it. The worst polluter, the one that gave the Liffey its greyish colour, was the Camac River, he told her.

When Christopher talked about his younger brother, Ned, he would reminisce about their walks deeper and deeper into the countryside as they got older. It was on one of these walks that they discovered the reason for the grey colour: Clondalkin paper mills. As young teenagers they had explored the Clondalkin area with its round tower and old woods, stopping in the village to buy sweets before their long journey home. On one of these walks, they had come across the paper mills. Fascinated, they looked through the fence into the giant factory, the biggest they had ever seen, listening to the sound that the giant paper-making cylinders made, like a giant, mechanical heartbeat that made the air around them throb.

Nell loved when he told her these things. In those rare moments she caught glimpses of his true self, the person he was before he joined the British army. Added to that, of course, there was the loss of his younger brother, Ned, to the so-called Great War. She never understood why it was called 'great', maybe it made the generals feel more important, as if previous wars were not quite up to this one. All of those hundreds of thousands of young men from both sides, for the most part buried under foreign soil in unmarked graves, and for what? And the survivors had their wounds as well, visible and invisible.

Memories, she thinks, are a funny thing. Now, the river reminds her of those earlier, happier days of their marriage which, in turn, makes her sad at the secret she has to keep from Christopher. Thankfully she doesn't have to witness low tide too often and, if she had her choice, she would have picked a different way to get home. But this is the route she has been instructed to take every day. From the bridge she can glance to her right back up towards Dublin Castle, the place where she now works, or up and down the quays on either side of the Liffey and see if she can identify any suspicious person. But she never can tell if she is being followed or not, that was up to somebody else.

No matter how hard she tries she can never spot her handler, Mick Crotty. She knows that he is shadowing her and that once or twice, in the early days, he had informed her he had spotted a likely candidate checking up on her movements. Although nothing had happened for several weeks now, he insisted she follow the same route. After her five-minute stop on Capel Street bridge, she continues onto Capel

Street until she comes to Lafferty's chemist shop. Lafferty's has a curved window and is ideal for checking anybody suspicious behind her without them knowing, but everybody seems to be rushing past, anxious to get home after a day's work. Her next move brings her down one side of Capel Street until she reaches the end, over to the other side and back down again. It's only then that she catches her first sight of Crotty. He's standing outside Gogarty's tearooms reading a newspaper, the sign that it's all clear to meet up.

Nell enters the tearooms and goes to the rear where she orders a cup of tea and a scone. After ten minutes Crotty enters, sees her and waves, then greets her as a friend who had just happened to be in the same place at the same time.

Crotty is a good choice as a handler. Quite tall, he walks with a stoop which makes him look unassuming. He is dressed in a shabby gabardine coat and a check peaked cap and has that same pinched, pale face that is common among young Dublin men. He always sits in the chair that faces the entrance and always has a rolled-up newspaper sticking out of his pocket. Their conversations are random: the weather, people they have in common, general gossip. In a few sentences Nell can tell him that it was a warm day in the office, meaning that she has something for him, or that her boss had nearly caught her taking a break, meaning there were too many people around for her to examine any communications that were lying around. Today, even though it's late in the year, she tells him that it was very warm in the office and slips a folded-up piece of paper under his newspaper which he has left on the table, saying: *My husband's name has been mentioned in a telegram.*

Crotty's hand slips under the newspaper and takes the note. Holding it below the table he scans it then tears it up and puts the pieces into his pocket.

DEATH IN THE LIBERTIES

Nell likes to think that the results of her work in Dublin Castle are going directly to Michael Collins, but it is probably being delivered to some other member of the backroom boys. The names she passes over to Crotty sometimes appear in the headlines over the following days. Usually, the victim of a shooting or a bombing. Some died, some were horribly injured. The first one was the worst as she had been introduced to the man who was quite likable. He was from Northern England, but both of his parents were Irish. His cover was as a salesman and he lived in a hotel in Sackville Street. His one task was to try and get a meeting with Michael Collins on the pretext of offering himself as a double agent. But Nell's information had meant a death sentence instead. The shock of the man's execution had almost made her give up, but she had justified it to herself by believing that she had probably saved Michael Collins' life. After that assassination she purposefully skimmed past the headlines that mentioned any names she had handed over.

Usually, after a short meeting, Crotty would leave, hot-footing it to whoever his masters were with the information. This time he stays, his long fingers beating out a nervous tattoo on the table. Eventually he says, 'Let's go for a walk.'

They make their way in the general direction of Smithfield Market, using the warren of busy laneways and byways behind Capel Street. Crotty takes a zigzag route, cutting backwards and forwards in such a way that Nell is disoriented. British soldiers stroll through the area, their rifles shouldered, smoking and chatting to each other but Crotty seems more interested in the unseen enemy. They finally emerge onto the cobbles of Smithfield Market, quiet now after the morning's cattle market.

Nell picks her way through the cowpats that splatter the cobblestones, lifting her dress off the ground so it doesn't become soiled. Crotty ignores her discomfort and leads the way over to a horse trough. He picks up a handful of straw from the ground and, putting his foot on the side of the trough, wets the straw and uses it to brush the cow dung from his shoe.

'What did it say about Christopher?' he asks.

'I couldn't make it out, it was just in a column of names being forwarded to London.'

'Who was it addressed to?'

'Sir Mansfield something or other. I remember the Mansfield, I knew a doctor Mansfield once but –'

'Could it have been Sir Mansfield George Smith-Cumming by any chance?' Crotty cuts her off, now dealing with his other shoe.

'It could've been. I told you I didn't get a chance to read it properly. I only got a quick glance and it was upside down.'

'Alright. I'm sorry I snapped.'

'I'm sure that it's nothing big. Probably just a list of ex-soldiers or something. Christopher has nothing to do with any of this, thank God. He's working away in Donnelly's and keeping his head down.'

Crotty straightens up, rinses his hands in the water and, pulling out his handkerchief, uses it to dry his hands.

'What should I do?' Nell asks.

'Stay calm, it could be nothing. But maybe you could find out a bit more?' Crotty is looking everywhere except into her eyes.

'How can I do that? The information has been filed away. The British file everything away and keep it under lock and key.'

Crotty turns and looks at her. 'Listen, Nell. You were picked for many reasons: bravery, intelligence, loyalty. But, also, you are an attractive young woman. Perhaps you can flirt with one of the officers, work your way around him?'

'I'm a married woman! Do you want me to debase myself?'

'Steady on. I didn't mean debase yourself. Just a bit of innocent flirtation. You've done it before, Nell.'

'That was different. I wasn't married then.'

'As far as the British are concerned, you're a young, attractive and *single* young woman. Why not take advantage of it? Play the role, like an actress, that's all I'm sayin'.'

'Is this something Mr Collins would ask me to do?'

'Michael Collins has asked a lot more from other women volunteers, Nell. Some of them have gone to jail for it. Do I tell him you said no?'

Nell plays for time and looks around her as Crotty waits for her answer. A stray dog runs past with a dried-up cowpat in its mouth. Dogs will eat anything to survive – they're not much different to people, she thinks. How far would she go? If she did toy with some of the officers, she could be helping Christopher as well and it wouldn't be the first time she has used her looks for the good for the cause. But the young officers that surround her during the day are not the innocent soldiers she had cajoled arms from in the past. In a way, this is the first time she has been asked to do anything distasteful – up until now she has enjoyed her days in Dublin Castle. She feels as if she has been living a protected life, but now she must make a decision: leave the IRA or do as they ask. The smell from the nearby Jameson whisky distillery taints the air around her and she feels like getting sick.

'Very well. I'll do my best, but I'm not promising anything,' she says, and walks away from Crotty.

She makes her way towards the Liffey, crossing the market square and negotiating her way through the empty metal animal stalls. When she reaches the corner of Smithfield Market, she looks back. Crotty is still standing beside the horse trough, trying to dry his hanky by waving it in the air. It looks to her as if he is waving a flag of surrender and she smiles at the awkward young man and almost feels sorry for him. Like her, he is only a small cog in Michael Collins' large machine.

As she makes her way up the hill on Winetavern Street and towards the Liberties, a niggling thought comes into her mind. The more she goes over her conversation with Crotty, the more concerned she becomes. Why, for the first time since she has been handing over information, had he reacted that way? Was it because Christopher is her husband and is ex-British army? But what if they believe that he is some sort of spy?

At the busy junction with High Street an elderly Franciscan monk in a dark-brown habit stands on the edge of the pavement, looking around him in a confused manner. She goes over to him and asks if he wants to cross the road, but he looks at her and takes a step backwards, crossing himself. Nell apologises and leaves him be. When she looks back a younger monk is now linking the elderly monk back down Winetavern Street towards the Franciscan priory.

She cuts across High Street towards the Liberties. Is Cecile right about a new day dawning for independent-minded women in Ireland? Will they not always be cast as second-hand citizens and looked upon as such? Will things be any different if Ireland does achieve independence?

Turning up the familiar laneway towards her home, she ignores the local children who are standing around a car that looks out of place outside her tenement building. It is a Hupmobile, dark-green in colour and she knows it well: her mother is paying her a visit. She curses inwardly. All she wants to do is cook the evening meal for herself and Christopher and have a pleasant evening listening to the phonograph. She tries shooing the children away from the car but she knows they'll be back, like flies, as soon as she goes into the house.

Anna Macken is walking up and down in the hallway outside her door, smoking. Around her feet there are already several stubbed-out cigarettes so she must have been waiting for a while. When she sees her daughter, Anna gets rid of her cigarette and crosses her arms. Nell has seen that look on her face before, and it was usually when she had been caught out for something.

'Hello, Nell. I need to talk to you.'

'Mam, what a surprise, is something wrong?' Nell fishes in her handbag for her keys.

'It can wait until we get inside,' Anna says.

Nell finds her key and lets herself into the flat, hoping that Mary Sherry won't make an appearance. Anna has taken a dislike to her neighbour and is not afraid to show it. As Nell puts her handbag down onto the dining table and takes off her hat, Anna lights another cigarette and is pacing the room, mumbling to herself.

'Would you like a cup of tea?' Nell asks her mother.

'No. Something stronger, if you have it.'

Nell goes behind the curtain into the kitchen and takes out the bottle of whiskey they keep for special occasions. She puts a small measure into a glass and goes back into the sitting room where Anna is now sitting at the table. Anna takes the glass and throws it back in one go, handing the glass back to her.

'Do you want another one? But it's only six o'clock,' Nell says.

'So keep your precious whiskey, Nell!' Anna snaps.

Nell goes back behind the curtain and pours her mother a stiffer drink. She hands her the glass and this time, thankfully, Anna takes a sip out of it and puts it down.

'What's got into you?' Nell asks, joining her mother at the table.

'It's Kevin, the doorman. He's been kidnapped from the street, in broad daylight.' Anna lifts the glass again.

'Kidnapped? By who?'

'If I knew that I wouldn't be here, would I? I'd be up in the bloody police station,' Anna says, taking out the hatpins that hold her hat in place. She places the hat on her lap, throwing the hatpins inside. 'I've been wanting to do that for the past hour. Where were you anyway?'

'I had to work a bit late. I'd some typing to do.'

'You should ask for a rise – they're taking advantage of you, Nell, mark my words.'

'Tell me about Kevin.'

'So yesterday I send him out to do a bit of shopping for last night. I wait and wait and wait. No sign of Kevin. I think, that bastard is after running away with my tenner. So, I go out myself to Talbot Street to see if there's any sign of him.'

'But how do you know he was kidnapped?'

'Will you wait until I tell the whole story! So I go into Wright's, the fishmonger's, because that would be his last stop. Oul' Stephen Wright starts to give me lip about an unpaid bill. I don't even argue with him, just give him what he asks. Then I say, "Did you see our Kevin?" He says "Why don't you ask dem louts?", and he points out the window at the gang of young fellas playing marbles outside.'

'That was good advice. They know everything.'

'Talking about young fellas, will my car be alright outside?' Anna says, getting to her feet.

'Don't worry. All the kids are afraid of Christopher – they won't go near it.'

'Where is your nearest and dearest, by the way?' Anna asks, looking around as if he is hidden somewhere.

'Might've dropped in for a pint on his way home.'

'Isn't it great for the men? Anyway, I went outside to the young fellas, took out a thrupenny bit, and said that it was for anyone who could tell me anything about my Kevin. Big man, wears a fancy suit and that stupid captain's hat I gave him for the door but that he wears all the time. Thinking to myself I'm wasting my time. Then they run up to me straight away and try and grab the thrupenny bit, shouting "I seen him, missus, I seen him, missus!" So I pick out one of them and take him to one side. I look into his eyes and say: "Would you swear on the Bible?" But he nods straight away and I know he'll tell the truth.' Anna takes another sip of her whiskey.

'So, what happened? Was it the British?' Nell says impatiently.

'Not a bit of it. They saw him take a fall on the street. Then a gentleman came to help him up, but he was limping badly. He helped him into a carriage and then took off towards Amiens Street like a bat out of hell.'

'Maybe he was taking him to a hospital,' Nell says.

'Hospital, my arse! The boys saw Kevin put up a struggle, then he just flopped onto the seat. Kevin might be a bit slow, but he's a fighter. No, I think something bad happened, I can feel it.'

The door to the flat opens and Christopher comes in, whistling to himself.

'Hello, Christopher, you're looking well,' Anna says.

'Can't complain,' Christopher says, coming in and taking off his cap.

'Christopher has a new job in Donnelly's. No more bloodstained clothes, thank God!' Nell says and goes into the kitchenette to heat the remaining coddle that she had put aside for their evening meal. She calls out: 'Would you like something to eat, Mam?'

'No, too early in the day!' Anna begins to place her hat back on her head again, pinning it into place. 'I've got to go back to the Monto. I've a new man starting tonight and I suppose Sarah will have to babysit him in case he assaults somebody, so I'll be short a pair of hands inside.'

'What are you going to do about Kevin?' Nell comes back into the room, a metal ladle in her hand.

'God only knows,' Anna says, rising from the chair. 'Maybe I'll try the police. Superintendent Clancy is due in tonight – I'll ask him. He owes me a few favours.'

'What's happened to Kevin?' Christopher asks.

'My mother thinks he was kidnapped.' Nell laughs. 'Mam, I think those kids were pulling your leg.'

'You're probably right, Nell. Anyway, I'd better be off. Good to see you, Christopher.'

Christopher is already at the door, opening it for her. Nell will have to have a word with him – it looks as though he's trying to be rid of Anna. But Anna doesn't seem to notice and leaves their flat, her hand in the air, waving goodbye to them.

'Go after her, Christopher,' Nell says. 'She'll break her arm trying to start that ridiculous car of hers.'

Christopher throws his eyes to heaven and goes out after Anna, slamming the door behind him.

CHAPTER 17

Captain Stern

Captain Benjamin Stern peruses the printed menu which has been placed on the table earlier by the stiff-backed waiter. The same waiter drifts past again and stares at the unoccupied chair opposite him, then gives him an accusing look, and walks on. If, by chance, the invitation was a hoax and his host doesn't make an appearance, he is attempting, in vain, to pick a dish that he can afford. He supposes that just a pot of coffee would be frowned on but is just about to ask when his host finally arrives, handing him a written note, and taking the chair opposite.

'*SORRY TO KEEP YOU WAITING,*' it says, no other explanation.

The man's appearance is not as disconcerting as he had feared. From the description of the soldiers who had been on duty at the gates of Dublin Castle the night the man had turned up, he was expecting much worse. Stern was glad that 1917 had been a fairly quiet year, otherwise it would have been a hell of a job sifting through the files for it. According to that report, filed away in 1917, the man was described as being deranged (or 'a lunatic' as it was written) and his lower face seemed to be all but missing. But the man across from him, was, to all appearances fairly normal, helped, he supposed, by the dimmed gas lights that lined the walls of the restaurant. The mask on his lower face was barely noticeable, disguised in part by the sideburns and moustache. His upper face was almost as still as his lower face but the eyes, light-brown with a greenish tinge, look like the eyes of another man, or even the eyes of a wild animal trapped inside the body of a civilised man.

The waiter returns to the table and hands his host a menu. There is a moment of embarrassment as the waiter tries to leave their table to let them decide, but the man grabs the waiter's arm, forcing him to stay. With a quick look down the menu he points an item out and hands the menu back. Caught unawares, Stern points to the most expensive dish he can see, *caviar frais* at fifteen shillings. If this is a wild goose chase, he is going to make it worth his while. Before the waiter leaves to get their order, the man takes off his hat, a bowler, and, without looking up, thrusts it at him. Stern would have felt sorry for the waiter if he hadn't been so rude earlier.

'So', Stern begins, 'you knew Byatt, Mr eh ...'

The man replies, ''esss', which he presumes is yes, ignoring his invitation to identify himself.

'A tragic death. Under any other circumstances he would have been given a hero's burial. But as the facts emerged about his ... weakness, it was thought better to have a more modest affair.' Stern takes note now of the man's impressive physique, which wasn't mentioned in the report. Over six foot tall and with wide shoulders, the chair he is seating in just about contains his bulk and creaks every time he moves. The fact that they are sitting at one of the smaller tables at the back of the restaurant, which is long and narrow, makes Stern a bit nervous. The man's bulk seems to lean in towards him, enveloping him as he listens to his every word.

'Not to seem too rude, but what exactly am I doing here?' Stern asks.

The man takes out a paper pad and turns it towards him. Written in large capital letters is: '*MY NAME IS LEVON MORDAUNT, I WORKED WITH MAJOR BYATT.*'

'I see, Mr Mordaunt,' says Stern. 'I wasn't aware of that. Byatt played his cards very close to his chest. Like all good agents.'

Mordaunt throws up his arms as if in despair and shakes his head. Stern leans in closer to the man.

'Were you responsible for the tip-off about the *Aud* ... and Roger Casement?'

''ess.'

'That was very useful information,' Stern says, then adds, 'at that time. But the world is now a different place. The war in Europe is over and I think the Irish are coming to their senses and will accept Home Rule.'

Stern at first found it hard to believe that this man is the reason he has been condemned to languishing away in Dublin. But, reading between the lines in Byatt's files, it appears that Mordaunt was thought of as some kind of super-human entity with contacts spread across both sides of the Atlantic. A dangerous man who could possibly be working for all sides. Byatt's last notes had also intimated that there was a suspicion that Mordaunt had a much darker side, but that was never fully proven. Byatt, ever the secretive agent, kept few notes and, after his death when his files were examined, they contained lots of rambling suppositions, gossip and hearsay. The rumours in the officers' mess was that Byatt was deranged, possibly because of the death of a man-friend.

Mordaunt is writing something in his pad. He holds it up and Stern wonders is he a mind-reader as well as everything else.

'*MAJOR BYATT WAS BLINDED BY THE DEATH OF HIS LOVER – ANOTHER MAN.*'

151

'Sadly, it appears so,' Stern agrees and raises his hands in surrender.

Two waiters wheel in a small cart with their food. Under a large cloche, Stern's caviar is served in a small, silver bowl placed in the middle of a large bowl of ice. On the metal tray around it there are several, smaller side dishes in miniature bowls. The only one that Stern can identify are tiny pieces of onion. On a side plate there are what look like miniature round pancakes. Stern glances over at Mordaunt's choice of food and is dismayed to see that it is a large dish of raw oysters served with wedges of lemon. As soon the waiters leave, Stern watches in fascination as Mordaunt grabs up an oyster, shucks it and squeezes some lemon on top of it. Should he look away? But Mordaunt solves his dilemma by bowing his head and lifting his mask away from his mouth so that Stern doesn't have to witness his wound. The oyster disappears from sight and there is a sickening, slurping noise. The empty shell is put to one side and he begins again but, before he does, he waves his hand at Stern, indicating that he should start his meal.

Stern takes up the tiny silver spoon and scoops some caviar onto a slice of pancake. He takes a little out of every side-dish and puts them on top of the caviar then puts the lot into his mouth. The combined flavours are disgusting, and he regrets not going for one of the more familiar dishes, even if they are less expensive. When he looks up, he sees that Mordaunt is studying him closely. He feels as if the man has read his mind even though he'd thought that he had disguised his disgust at the food, and has put him down as somebody from the lower classes desperate to join the more privileged.

''eave it,' Mordaunt grunts, pointing to the caviar, and Stern pushes the dish to one side.

'I thought it was Russian,' Stern says. 'Obviously from an inferior country.'

Mordaunt stands up and waves his hand at the waiter who pretends to ignore him but his dining companion simply pushes his chair backwards and it crashes onto the wooden floorboards. When the waiter arrives, apologising to some nearby diners for the disturbance, Mordaunt reaches over and takes hold of Stern's tray, shoving it at the waiter and waving him away. Mordaunt sits and the restaurant settles back down again. He makes his way through the oysters until he has slurped the flesh from the last one. When he is finished, he belches loudly and Stern catches a whiff of shellfish from his breath.

'What can I do for you, Mr Mordaunt?'

Mordaunt turns a page of his pad and shoves the pad across the table at him. He taps the open page with his finger. Stern takes up the pad and reads the list of names written down. Most of them he recognises as small players in the IRA, couriers, lookouts, owners of safe-houses, but the name Dan Breen stands out. Mr Breen was the latest *bete noire* of Dublin Castle and it would do his chances of returning to London no harm if he were to catch him. He hides his excitement and pushes the pad back.

'I don't see Michael Collins' name there,' he says, taking out a cigarette and lighting it.

Mordaunt becomes agitated and writes something down, pushing the pad back across the table to him.

'*QUID PRO QUO*,' is written under the names and underlined several times.

'And what do you want from me?' Stern asks.

Mordaunt takes the pad again and writes one name, the lead of the pencil digging into the paper: *CHRISTOPHER FLINTER*

Stern is surprised. Christopher Flinter, he knows, used to live within a stone's throw of Dublin Castle, in a tenement area known as the Liberties. According to Byatt's files, he had been arrested in 1916 for desertion from the British army but offered a reprieve from the firing squad for reasons that were classified. Whatever those reasons were, Flinter must have honoured them, thus regaining his liberty. Last place of residence unknown, but presumably somewhere in the Liberties, probably keeping his head low and staying out of trouble. But the opportunity presenting itself had to be handled with care. The thought of sending a telegram to Sir Mansfield George Smith-Cumming or, better still, Ewing, informing him that he had the location of the elusive Michael Collins would earn him a recall to London for his services and escape from this dismal city. He looks at the name again and hands the pad back.

'I believe I have information that might be useful in finding this man. But in return I need Collins' location. The rest of the names I'm not too concerned about. They'll eventually be found and dealt with. You do realise that there are a lot more of our agents in Dublin now?'

Mordaunt begins writing rapidly again and seems to be becoming more impatient.

'*AMATEURS – THEY MEET REGULARLY IN THE CAIRO CAFÉ UNDER THE NOSES OF COLLINS' MEN*'

'I wasn't aware of that,' Stern lies and makes a note to have a word with some of the newcomers drafted into his department.

In fact, it had been his suggestion that some of the agents, ex-army mostly, should go there and improve their bastard Irish accents if possible. One or two of them had been brought up in England but had Irish parents. But he'd put a stop to that now. And how did this man know that they had been under surveillance by Collins' men? Maybe he was a double agent.

'Very well. Quid Pro Quo. I will find out Flinter's address and you give me Collins,' he says, not believing it could be as simple as that: the elusive Collins in return for the location of some injured ex-serviceman.

Mordaunt nods quickly, calls for the bill and takes the pad back, seeming to accept his offer.

As his host pays the bill, Stern would like to question him more closely as he suspects that his speech is not as bad as he makes out and used, no doubt, as an excuse to avoid close questioning. Maybe another day. He tries to conceal his excitement and holds his hand out to seal the agreement. The hand that reaches out to his is large and surprisingly rough for a man who dresses like a gentleman. Mordaunt stares into his eyes, shaking and squeezing his hand tightly, and then ever more tightly until Stern can feel the bones in his hand being crushed together. He is just about to cry out when Mordaunt lets his hand drop. Before he can take him to task, Mordaunt is already making his way through the crowded restaurant and disappearing through the door. People's heads rise at his passing, some sixth sense telling them that a dangerous presence has just touched their lives.

CHAPTER 18

Benjamin and Nell

The following week Stern, dressed native in a long gabardine and a flat cap, is confused. Trekking through the laneways and alleyways of the Liberties he has ended up again outside the church of St. Nicholas of Myrna. The Doric columns of the church are familiar to him now that he has seen them so many times. An old man goes by pushing a cart full of bric-a-brac, women wrapped up in dark shawls shuffle past, some holding onto grimy children, others with shopping bags that look half-empty. Most of the shop windows on Francis Street are dirty and the pubs look decrepit. From one of the doorways he can smell boiling cabbage.

He makes his way up to Thomas Street again, turns left and wanders past the stallholders who try to interest him in their wares, but he ignores them. What he must do is to roughly map in his mind the extent of the Liberties. He plods on for another twenty minutes and turns left down another street that is even more rundown than Francis Street. He follows the cobbled road that leads downwards, past the dark entrances of more tenement buildings that reach upwards almost blocking out the sky. The smell is suffocating. From over a redbrick wall, he hears the squeal of pigs. Onwards he walks, becoming more dispirited.

Eventually he comes to an area called the Coombe and turns left again which should, if he is correct, lead him back down to St Patrick's Street. Once he can see the cathedral he can continue on to Christ's Church, keep that on his left and on to Dame Street, back to Dublin Castle and civilisation again. Then he gets an idea and kicks himself for having dragged his body around this damned Dickensian landscape – surely one of the workers in the Castle is familiar with the area. But how would he approach it without raising suspicion? No, it should not be too difficult – a bland memo with a list of names, including Flinter's. Something to do with the War Office's attempts to update their records. Now why hadn't he thought of that before? Better still, he could just go through the employment records of the staff working within the Castle's walls and see if any of them come from the area.

The task proves longer than expected. He hadn't realised that so many of the local population were working in the Castle: cooks, waiters and waitresses for the canteen, tradesmen of every description, groomsmen for the horses, women in the kitchens, women employed undertaking clerical duties. Though he shouldn't be so shocked as he hasn't visited every building in the sprawling complex. And there were constant changes to some of the political appointees, including different regiments who were assigned there. In view of the hundreds of names he decides to focus on the women, as he believes the women would be more naïve than the men. He finally locates three possible contenders and is surprised that one of them, a Miss Nell Claffey, age 23, works in his department as a clerical typist. Marital status: single. Resident in the Liberties.

He finds her hidden away on the second floor of the building and is surprised at her appearance. How does someone so pretty and well-dressed emerge from the Liberties every day and, more puzzling, how do they face going back? Fortunately, the office is home to an enormous amount of filing cabinets so he can loiter around these and observe. The amount of filing undertaken by the army never ceases to amaze him. When he was starting off his military service, his first posting was to Gobindgarh Fort in Amritsar. There he had his first experience of the British army filing system and had been taught to file everything away. The system had worked while he was there and a file of everyone of note and the various internecine rural movements existed so that the army could play one side off the other. Although it didn't always work or prevent the massacre the previous year. He takes a random file and makes his way down to her desk.

A shadow falls across Nell's desk and she knows immediately who it is. The young officer has been observing her for several minutes and making a bad job of disguising it. Her years of working for her mother has made her an expert on men. But Captain Stern is different. She had seen him from a distance and he seems to spend a lot of time wandering around the grounds of the castle, smoking a pipe. She had made discreet enquiries. The rumours were that he had been promoted and had returned to London several years ago, a young intelligence officer on his way up in the service. But he had then come back to Dublin for some reason and now seems adrift. Maybe he is trying to mend a broken heart?

'Miss Claffey?'

For a moment Nell forgets the name she is using and continues typing. Stern coughs and taps on the desk with his fingers and she realises her mistake.

'I'm terribly sorry, I was caught up in my work,' she says and looks up, smiling apologetically.

Closer up, Stern looks like a more contained version of her Christopher. His eyes are a dark-brown colour and his skin is sallow with small, pale blemishes scattered unevenly across his face. Nell has seen something similar in the past, usually on sailors who visited her mother's brothel: smallpox. Whereas their scars were more numerous and larger and stood out starkly on dark, sunburnt faces, his are barely noticeable and look more like freckles in reverse. His uniform is immaculate which makes the worn holster he wears at his side out of place. She can't imagine him in a war, wallowing around in the mud and confusion of no-man's land. Christopher doesn't talk often about Flanders, but sometimes in his cups he talks for hours, staring straight ahead. It feels as if she is there, with him, so vivid are his descriptions.

'I wonder if you could help me, please? I believe that you live locally,' Stern says.

'Yes, I do,' Nell replies.

'Oh good. I'm following up on a report my predecessor left. It was to do with a local man. Injured in the war actually, but never followed up on his disability pension.'

'Oh.'

'Yes. A Major Byatt made some use of this man. Byatt was here before your time.'

'I've never heard of him,' Nell replies, hoping that the hot flush she feels rising in her face is not obvious.

'The man's name is Flinter. Christopher Flinter. Believed to have come from this area.'

Nell struggles to conceal her shock. 'Can't say that I've ever heard of the name,' she says.

'I'm sure you'd remember it,' Stern says, a disappointed look in his eyes, 'Oh well, never mind.'

He turns to move away from her desk.

'Perhaps I could ask around?' Nell blurts out.

Stern turns back and smiles at her, a wide smile showing his even, slightly tobacco-stained teeth. Nell doesn't know why she has said that. Is she feeling sorry for him? Now she is beginning to feel relieved. At least that explains Christopher's name appearing on the list. She'll tell Mick Crotty the next time they meet. How did they ever believe that the British were after Christopher? An honest, hard-working man. Or is she being naïve?

'That would be very kind of you, Miss Claffey,' Stern says and looks at his watch.

Nell feels another blush rising to her face and wonders why.

'What do you normally do for lunch?' he asks suddenly.

The unexpected question takes Nell by surprise and she says the first thing that comes into her mind. 'I have a sandwich. In the gardens.' She takes out the small brown-paper bag from her drawer to show him. She looks at the bag and realises how grubby it is, covered with so many grease stains that you can see the sandwich through it. Embarrassed, she puts it back into the drawer and closes it over.

'Well, one good deed deserves another. May I take you for something to eat?'

'Well ...'

'Please. I don't get a chance to go out much. Most of my men work outside the castle and it's been a long time since I had the company of a young lady.'

Nell remembers Crotty encouraging her to make use of her good looks – and this is the perfect opportunity. Why shouldn't she? It isn't as if she is going to have an affair, even if he does consider her to be attractive. Outside the window a light rain has started and she realises that she will be having her sandwich in the office, alone.

'I would like that, Captain Stern.'

'Please, Nell, call me Benjamin. Thank you ever so much.' Stern's face radiates such gratitude that he looks like a little boy who has just been given a prize. 'I just need to change. Back in a mo.'

Before she has time to reply he has turned and left the office. What is she doing? Benjamin Stern looks like a nice young man. Could she really use him as Crotty would probably suggest? Then Nell has a thought that repulses her. What if she's ordered to take him to some place where there are men waiting? She is aware of the Squad, the handpicked group of men who have no qualms about killing in broad daylight. No, she would never do that.

Benjamin comes back into the office, wearing civilian clothes. He stands in front of her and holds his arms out, turning around.

'No uniform and unarmed. I am completely at your mercy,' he jokes.

Nell forces a smile and rises to get her coat. Together they walk outside and Benjamin steers her by the elbow past the Chapel Royale and towards the main entrance on Dame Street. Outside the gates he holds his arm out to her. She feels herself blushing again. She glances around her in case there's anybody who might recognise her, but the passing people are mainly bowler-hatted businessmen making their way out of the surrounding offices. She tucks a hand inside his arm and he turns down Dame Street towards the city centre.

'Were you expecting to see someone you know?'

'No,' Nell says, realising how observant the captain is. 'I'm just a bit nervous. There's been so much violence lately.'

'Of course. Violence from both sides,' Benjamin says. 'Unfortunately, that's the way these things work. First one side, then the other. And it goes on and on. I've buried a colleague recently, I'm sure you've heard.'

'Yes.' Nell lowers her head.

'Wife and children. But he knew the risks he was taking.' Benjamin takes quick glances around as they walk, but glances that take everything in, like Crotty's when he sits across from her drinking his tea.

The rain has stopped and the clouds part as they near Trinity College. Shards of light reflected back from its window lift the building's appearance from the dull grey of the brickwork into something that looks magical. Benjamin turns up Grafton Street and for a moment Nell is concerned that he will take her up towards Harcourt Street and Cecile's house, afraid that one of the maids might recognise her. But he turns down Nassau Street and they walk along the walls of the college. Halfway down Nassau Street, Benjamin stops and looks over the wall. Several students dressed in white are playing cricket. The smack of ball against bat reaches them and she looks up at Benjamin. His face is sad, his eyes drinking in the sight of the students playing a game that Nell has never understood and has never really wanted to.

'Do you miss England?' she asks.

Benjamin looks down at her. His eyes are almost tearful and he nods.

'Can you not go back?'

Benjamin seems to straighten himself. 'A soldier's life is complicated, Nell. We have to do things we don't want to and, sometimes, are even ashamed of.'

'I've never looked at it like that before.'

'We're not all monsters,' he says with a smile.

'I know. I've met some nice people since working in the Castle.'

'Good for you,' Benjamin says and looks up and down Nassau Street, waiting for a gap in the traffic.

They cross the road. He leads her up Kildare Street and then around onto Stephen's Green, ending up in front of the Shelbourne Hotel. On the road outside the entrance there are two carriages. One is a hansom cab but the other is a beautiful, ornate coach drawn by four horses. A driver sits in the front seat, erect, staring ahead. The door of the carriage has a large crest. She takes a peek through the windows to try and see who's inside but the blinds are drawn down. At the top of the steps, a doorman stands in full uniform.

Nell thinks they have stopped to admire the building but Benjamin starts up the steps. Nell holds back, unsure of herself. She has never been in such a place and worries in case she does something stupid in front of Benjamin, showing up her ignorance.

'What's the matter?' Benjamin stops, looking down at her.

'It's very grand, Benjamin. I'm not used to this,' she says.

'Neither am I,' he says with a laugh, 'but let's be reckless, just for today. Tomorrow will be here soon enough.'

They make their way up the steps and the doorman touches his cap and opens the door for them. Nell walks through the doors on Benjamin's arm, noticing that the doorman is wearing white gloves. They continue on into the carpeted lobby and she can feel her shoes sinking into its deep pile. Inside, the air is warm and scented with perfume and the people who pass through the high-ceilinged lobby look as if they're from another world. Hanging from the ceiling is an enormous chandelier.

He leads her down a long, wood-panelled corridor and on into the dining room.

They wait just inside the door until a waiter comes and leads them to a small table tucked away near the back of the busy restaurant. He stands beside the table and takes their coats before disappearing again.

Nell is about to sit down when Benjamin comes around the table, pulls out the chair for her and waits until she is comfortably seated, her handbag placed at her feet, before taking the chair opposite.

The drone of conversation and clatter of cutlery around them seems to draw them closer together.

'Now that I'm here, I realise how famished I am,' he says.

Another waiter appears and hands Nell a menu. The menu is bound in leather with the hotel's name printed in gold on the cover. When she opens it and turns the heavy, parchment-like pages, all of the choices are set out in such a delicate script that she finds it difficult to take in. Benjamin, who had been studying his menu looks over and sees her confusion.

'Allow me to order,' he says. 'They make such a fuss over something so simple but I believe the beef is very good here. Would you like that?'

Nell nods and when the waiter returns, he orders soup to start followed by roast beef and vegetables for them both, then adds a bottle of wine, almost as an afterthought.

The volume of conversation has risen further and Benjamin has to lean over the table closer to her to be heard. 'Sorry for the racket.' He smiles and shrugs. 'I'm from a loud family so I'm used to noise. What about you?'

Nell gets flustered and doesn't know what to say. She decides to appeal to his gentlemanly nature and hopefully end the small talk about family which she is not prepared for. She must bring up the question of her history, a good back story, with Crotty the next time they meet.

'Unfortunately, both my parents are dead and I live with an aunt, a widow,' she says, lowering her eyes as she answers, 'and meal times are very quiet'.

When she looks up again, she sees by Benjamin's expression that it has worked.

'I'm terribly sorry, how stupid of me,' he says, fidgeting with the pieces of cutlery on the table in front of him.

'How could you have known?' Nell replies.

'That's no excuse,' Benjamin says and looks relieved as the waiter approaches with the wine, shows him the label and pours a little for him to taste.

At Benjamin's nod, the waiter pours them both a glass and departs.

Nell takes a sip of her wine and recognises from her time working in her mother's brothel that it's expensive.

'Tell me about your family,' she says, breaking the uncomfortable silence that has descended on the table.

Benjamin looks relieved. 'Well, I grew up in London, in a place called Highgate. It's a large family, four brothers and two sisters.'

'That must've been fun.'

'I didn't realise it then, of course, but it was. Especially on Friday nights when my mother insisted we all sat down at the table together.'

'Why Friday?'

'My background is Jewish,' Benjamin says, waits for her reaction, then adds, 'but I don't really practise anymore.'

'That must've been interesting. There's an area in Dublin called Little Jerusalem.'

Benjamin becomes more animated. 'Our day of rest begins at sunset on Friday and extends to sunset on Saturday – we call it the Shabbat. So on Friday evening we have a festive meal. I remember the table was covered with food: poached fish dumplings, matzo ball soup, brisket or roast chicken, potato kugel, and tzimmes, all traditional dishes.'

'You must be bored with the local food,' Nell says, looking down at the bowl of soup that the waiter is placing in front of her.

Benjamin asks the waiter for extra bread.

'For the ducks in the park,' he confides. 'We can feed them later.'

Nell smiles, though she's wondering if there will be time – she'll have to get back to work.

'As for being bored with the local food,' Benjamin says, 'you forget I'm in the army. Have been for over ten years. The officers' mess soon puts a stop to all that nonsense.'

'I can imagine.'

Nell takes a spoonful of her soup. It tastes watery and she thinks that it's probably some sort of consommé.

She takes a sip of her wine and looks over at Benjamin. His glass is almost empty and he now seems to be in a mellow humour.

'Benjamin – that man you asked me about earlier – was he called Flynn or something like that?'

'No. Flinter, Christopher Flinter.'

'As I said, if it's important to you, I can ask around.'

Benjamin waves his arm. 'No, it's not important. In fact, I was asking about him for an ex-colleague and, to be perfectly honest, I don't think I'll be having any more dealings with him. The poor fellow has lost his relevance and is finding it hard to come to terms with that.'

He changes the subject, asking her if she enjoys her work at the Castle.

The waiter comes back to remove their soup dishes. Almost immediately another waiter appears wheeling a trolley with their two plates covered with stainless-steel cloches. He places them on the table and lifts the cloches, making such a performance of it that Nell and Benjamin smile.

'This looks delicious.' Benjamin says as the waiter departs. He pours them both another glass of wine.

Nell has begun to notice two well-dressed businessmen at the only table nearest to the entrance. One of them, a portly man with a florid face and a drooping moustache keeps glancing over at their table. He looks vaguely familiar. Every so often he plays with his moustache and seems distracted as if he is trying to remember something. Eventually he rises and makes his way towards their table.

Benjamin is side-on to the man and doesn't notice his approach until he is standing, slightly unsteadily, looking down at them. The man puts one hand on the table for support and points the other at Nell, smiling.

'I know you,' he says with a wink, ignoring Benjamin, who has turned towards him.

Nell, who had presumed that the man had come over to talk to Benjamin, momentarily loses her composure. She takes up her napkin to dab at her mouth. The man continues to stare at her and she has a vague recollection of seeing those pale-blue eyes before. His nose is a blueish colour and his lower eye-lids droop down exposing two pink half-moons of flesh.

'I'm afraid you're mistaken, sir,' she says with what she hopes is an apologetic smile.

'Oh, don't be so coy, young woman. Never forget a face. Anna Macken's, the Monto. Good to see you doing so well.'

'I'm really sorry. You must be mistaking me for someone else,' she says, but the man persists and his smile becomes even wider. He is now resting his hand on Benjamin's shoulder and squeezing it gently.

Benjamin shoves the man's hand off his shoulder and stands up, pushing back his chair. He throws his napkin onto the table and faces the intruder, standing erect, his eyes locked into the other man's, a barely suppressed look of contempt on his face.

'I believe the lady has given you an answer. If you want to continue this conversation, I suggest we go outside,' he says.

Benjamin's face has transformed. All of the boyishness has disappeared and in its place there's the rigid face of a soldier ready to fight. The man's demeanour changes and his body looks as if it has shrunk inside of his clothes. His mouth opens and closes like a fish in distress.

His dining companion, who has heard what has transpired, rushes over to their table and takes him gently by the arm.

'Come now, Daniel, don't be interrupting this young couple's lunch,' he says, and gently guides the man away from their table and straight out through the restaurant's doors.

Benjamin remains standing, looking after them until they have disappeared. He sits down again, reaches across the table to Nell and puts his hand over hers.

'I apologise – that man is a cad,' he says. 'If you only knew what he was insinuating.'

He removes his hand quickly and looks embarrassed, taking up his napkin again.

Nell feels a moment of regret – she misses the fleeting warm touch of his hand and the look of concern on his face.

'I've met drunks before,' she says, in what she hopes is an off-hand tone.

'Of course you have.' Benjamin smiles back. 'You are a very pretty girl, so you must be used to unwelcome intrusions.'

'I'm hardly a girl, Benjamin. And what do you think the man was insinuating? I've heard of the Monto – who in Dublin hasn't? Do you think he mistook me for one of those women?'

'He was obviously under the influence. I don't think we should discuss it further. Our food is going cold – let's not allow that man ruin a good lunch.'

He begins to talk about his time in the army, first in India and later to Ireland, and soon the mood at the table has lifted. Most of his stories are about India: the people, the animals, the exotic buildings.

He brushes over his time in Ireland, especially in 1916.

After they finish eating, Benjamin suggests dessert but Nell declines, saying she really needs to get back to work.

'Oh, of course,' he says, looking embarrassed. 'I must apologise. I was enjoying our conversation so much I forgot you are under time constraints.'

'That's alright,' she says with a smile.

Benjamin drinks the last of his wine, then puts his glass down and gazes at Nell.

'Would you like to do this again sometime, Nell?'

Nell is caught off-guard. She is feeling slightly light-headed from the wine and from the attentions of a man, something she has not experienced for several years. For a moment she almost agrees, but then the reality of her situation sinks in: she is a married woman.

'Perhaps it's not such a good idea,' she says. 'After all, you are my superior.'

'Of course. I'm being impractical. Forgive me.' He raises a hand to summon the waiter. 'Let me pay the bill.'

Nell realises he is a little hurt and is confused by the fact that this upsets her. She hopes it's the wine but, as she watches him paying the bill, she recognises that it's something more.

They walk to the door where he stands, holding her coat. She slips her arms into it, trying to ignore his closeness.

After he has put his own coat on, he stands back to let her precede him. She remembers the almost-full bread basket and is almost going to remind him about the ducks they were going to feed, but says nothing. There would have been no time to do it anyway.

CHAPTER 19

Robert and Harry

Robert Byatt sits in the corner of the hotel lounge, rereading his dead brother's notebook. Jonathan always had an unusual mind and his notebook reflects this. Random words and names cram the pages of the notebook, some encircled and leading to other words, also encircled. Some of these circles are allotted numbers which coincide with almost illegible notes in the back of the notebook. To make matters worse, it is all written in pencil and over the years a lot of the writing was smudged from the many hands that perused it.

'Thought I'd catch you here, lurking in the corner,' a voice says.

When Robert looks up, he is relieved to see that Harry Irvine is dressed in a normal dark navy suit, his untidy hair slicked back from his face. The difference between the man that stands in front of him now and the man he had met in the restaurant is remarkable. He stands almost to attention, hands behind his back, as if addressing his classroom. Irvine, he was surprised to find out on the night they had met, is a lecturer in English and history in the university. But that said more about Byatt's preconceptions than about the actuality of living a hidden life in plain view. And there was a steeliness about Irvine that had surprised him, a determination to find out what had happened to Jonathan.

He stands and shakes hands with him.

'Sit, please,' Robert says, gesturing to an armchair.

Harry settles himself into the chair. When he sees the notebook opened out on the table, a sadness descends on his face.

'I see you're not giving up on that artifact,' he says, pointing to the notebook. 'We used to jeer at Jonathan about it. In the middle of a conversation, he would take it out and jot something down that had suddenly occurred to him, then put it back into his pocket without losing the thread of a conversation.'

'That was Jonathan all over,' Robert says and raises a hand for a waiter. 'What'll you have?'

'Ginger ale.'

They wait until the waiter has left to get Harry's drink and then Robert points out the last page in the notebook which has the names *Maybury* and *Irish Gazette* with a time beside them.

'George Maybury is the owner,' Harry says. 'It's a publication for emigrants mostly. Bit of a rag, wouldn't read it myself.'

'It was the last meeting, official meeting, that Jonathan had.'

'We must question him, so.'

'We? Are you sure? You've no obligation to help me.'

'I know that, but I want to. Anything else in there?'

'The name *Monto* appears a few times along with *Janus*. And, of course, Christopher Flinter's name.'

'Janus, the Roman god of beginnings, gates, transitions, time, duality – take your pick. The Monto is more straightforward. It's Dublin's infamous red-light district. Full of soldiers, sailors and ne'er-do-wells, and … students.'

Robert raises his eyebrows. 'You've been there?'

'As a student, of course. Like all rebellious students, I followed my peers. But I was always the one too drunk to go upstairs. But, for what it's worth, I don't think Jonathan would have been a customer.'

The waiter returns and puts Harry's ginger ale on the table and Robert gives him his room number.

'Jonathan must have been in the middle of some investigation,' Robert says then, 'but none of it make sense.'

'Why don't we start at the end and work back?' Irvine says.

'George Maybury?'

'The very man.'

They stroll up Merchant's Quay together, Harry with a handkerchief held up to his nose. The Liffey, a tidal river, is at low tide and smells of sulphur. The bed of the river is laid bare, city refuse exposed for all to see. Below the quay wall, urchins pick among the muddy stones, shouting and arguing together. A few British soldiers lean over the wall, smoking and jeering, occasionally tossing farthing coins towards the boys who scramble around in the mud. Overhead noisy seagulls dip and dive towards the river. One of them grabs some unidentified morsel and climbs up into the sky, pursued relentlessly by his fellow gulls.

Harry stops suddenly and points across the road: 'That's the *Gazette*.'

It is an unimpressive redbrick building of three storeys. Most of the windows have their shades pulled down against the afternoon sunshine. Robert notices that the comings and goings through the front door are sparse, nothing like an average newspaper office on Fleet Street.

They dodge through the traffic towards the entrance, Harry in the lead. The arrangement they have is simple: Harry will do most of the talking. At the top of the steps, they come to a wooden panelled door with a brass knocker. The name *Irish Gazette* is etched onto a brass plate on the wall and seems to be the only thing that shines, throwing back their reflections.

Harry pushes open the door, a beaming smile on his face.

'Good afternoon,' he says to the receptionist who sits alone behind a tall, wooden counter.

She is a middle-aged woman and beyond her smile Robert can sense a harder core as she eyes them up and down, trying to categorise them. Prospects or time-wasters?

'Good afternoon, gentlemen, what can I do for you?' She gets up from her chair and leans against the counter.

'We would like to meet Mr Maybury,' Harry says.

'Do you have you an appointment?' she replies, still smiling.

'No, but my friend here,' Harry points to Robert, 'is only in Dublin for a couple of days. He is interested in taking out some advertising in the *Gazette* and was assured down in the Kildare Street Club that Mr Maybury would be the very person to see.'

'I'll see what I can do – he's just putting the latest edition to bed,' the receptionist's smile has grown broader and she turns to leave.

As soon as she opens the door to the factory, the thundering sounds of the printing presses and the shouts of workers pour into the tiny reception area, enveloping it with noise and confusion.

They wait until the door closes again, dampening the sounds within, then Harry turns to Robert.

'Did you see that? Things aren't going well for the owner of a newspaper if he can meet somebody at such short notice.'

'I hope you know what you're doing,' Robert says, but Harry's answer is swallowed up in noise as the receptionist opens the door again and beckons to them to come through.

A young apprentice leads them across the factory floor, between the beating printing presses, towards a raised office which overlooks the whole enterprise. Through its glass surround they can see a middle-aged man with silver-grey hair putting on a jacket and fixing his tie.

Harry strides confidently behind the boy as he leads them up the steps to the office, knocks on the door, and then withdraws back to the factory floor.

The door opens and Mr Maybury stands there, hand extended.

Harry marches up the steps and grabs his hand, pumping it and even clapping him on the shoulder. 'Mr Maybury, I presume,' he says in a loud, confident voice. 'May I introduce you to my colleague, Mr Byatt.'

At the mention of his name a look of uncertainty descends on Maybury's face. He takes a pair of spectacles from his pocket and looks Robert up and down, settling his gaze on his face as if trying to place it. They can almost see the mind behind the eyes diving backwards in time, then reaching some point back in the past he does not wish to visit again. His face hardens and he ushers them into the office, closing the door behind them. Without offering them a chair he goes back behind his desk and takes a seat.

'I presume you're not here to buy advertising,' he says brusquely, and reaches for a bottle of whiskey on the bureau behind him. He sits, pours himself a glass and takes a sip, contemplating the two men in front of him.

'Would you have seen us otherwise?' Harry asks.

'And you,' Maybury says, looking up at Robert, 'must be a brother?'

'Yes,' Robert acknowledges.

'Very well. I'll tell you what I told the detectives who came to question me. I have no idea what happened to your brother. He came into the factory investigating the death of one of my apprentices, Daniel Joyce. I gave him all the help I could on the matter. And that was the last I saw of him.'

'But why was he investigating the death of a boy?' Robert says.

'I don't know. It was after the rebellion in the city. Everything was in confusion. Later, two detectives investigating your brother's disappearance came here, just like you, to ask questions.'

'And?'

'And I told them I was sorry to hear that your brother had disappeared, but that I couldn't help them,' Maybury said and took a long drink from his glass.

'My brother is dead,' Robert announces, taking out Jonathan's notebook and shaking it in the air. 'Dead and buried in a pauper's grave in your godforsaken city. Forgotten by all. But not by me. I am going to find out what happened to him and, according to his notes, you know more than you are letting on, sir.'

Maybury's face turns red. 'How dare you, sir! Coming in here and making accusations! It's been several years since that day and now you have finally decided to take an interest in your poor brother's affairs?'

Robert closes the notebook and puts it back into his pocket. He slides the blade from his cane, slams it onto the desk and stares into Maybury's eyes.

'I've been on the far side of the world, Mr Maybury, but I am back here now. And I swear to you, on the Bible, if necessary, that I will not leave this city until I find out what happened to my brother. You have two choices. You can tell us everything you know, and we will leave you in peace, that I promise. Or you can sit there and lie, in which case I will return, and return, and return!' Robert slams the wooden desk with the narrow flat of the blade, over and over.

Maybury's eyes take on the glazed look of a person thinking and calculating his best interests. A man dressed in a dark-blue apron puts his head around the door and asks if everything is all right. Maybury dismisses him with a wave and, when he closes the door, points at the two chairs in front of his desk.

'Please sit. I will tell you everything I know. But after that you must leave me alone. I have had enough of this nightmare.'

The two men take their seats and Robert slips the blade back into the cane. They wait while Maybury fills up his glass and sits back in his chair. He looks up at the ceiling.

'Your brother came to me, as I've said, enquiring about Daniel Joyce, a young apprentice compositor who disappeared one evening and was found, dead, in the Liffey. I only found out later that he was murdered, his throat almost severed through. The suspect in the death of poor Daniel was a Reverend Mordaunt, although I doubt if he was a real minister of the Church. Mordaunt was mixed up in some skullduggery and involved my newspaper in it. Unbeknownst to me, of course.'

'Mordaunt. I didn't see his name mentioned in my brother's notes.'

'Believe me, it should have been,' Maybury says. 'He was the devil himself.'

'And where is this Mordaunt now?' Robert asks.

Maybury shrugs. 'I honestly don't know. He left and I never heard from him again, thank God.'

'Does the name Janus mean anything to you?'

'Isn't it one of the Roman gods?'

'Yes. And the Monto?'

'Everybody knows the Monto.' Maybury gives a knowing look.

'Think, were there any links between the Reverend Mordaunt and the Monto?'

Maybury looks up at the ceiling, reminiscing. 'One of the detectives who visited later did advise me that Daniel had been mutilated and that the type of mutilation was similar to that of some prostitutes who were murdered in the Monto.'

'Then would it not seem logical to you, Mr Maybury, that this Mordaunt person had, in fact, killed your apprentice and could have been responsible for the killing of some whores?'

'To tell you the truth, I banished the whole sordid event from my mind. Not because of the death of some whores – that happens all the time in the Monto, I believe. But I mean … poor Daniel, a lad in the prime of his life. Are we finished now? I've got a paper to put to bed.' Maybury stands up.

'Two more questions,' Harry says, holding up a hand. 'Have you ever heard of Christopher Flinter?'

'Never.'

'What about Shanahan's pub?'

Maybury hesitates for a split second. 'Doesn't sound familiar. Now, please, gentlemen, I have told you all I know.' He walks towards the door and opens it.

Reluctantly Robert rises and bids Maybury goodbye. Harry follows him out of the office. They make their way through the printing hall again and on through the reception office.

On the street outside a patrol of British soldiers are checking the papers of passing pedestrians. It is almost six o'clock and cars, trams and horses reluctantly share the narrow quays. The sound of the bells of Christ Church Cathedral competes with the noise of the traffic and the shouts of newspaper boys who flit in and around the crowds making their way home.

Robert turns to Harry.

'What do you think?'

'Seems to be a man who wants shut of that period of his life, I would say.'

'But did you believe him?'

'Most of it. But everyone knows of Shanahan's pub in the Monto, even a businessman like Mr Maybury. Perhaps he just didn't want to link himself to that place.'

'Well,' Robert says, pulling up his collar against the wind coming down the quays, 'at least we probably know who Janus is.'

'Who?'

'The Reverend Mordaunt, the man of many faces, not just two.'

'What do we do now?' Harry asks.

'We?'

'Yes, we. I said I was in this to the end and I meant it.'

'There's really no need, Harry.'

'You do realise where this is leading us, don't you?'

'The Monto?'

'Exactly. And you wouldn't last ten minutes there without me.'

'So be it,' Robert says, and they turn and make their way through the oncoming tide of people.

CHAPTER 20

Christopher

The note, which he had to destroy after reading, had instructed Christopher to go to Phibsborough, an area he is unfamiliar with, and from there he would be taken, blindfolded, to meet one of the leaders of the IRA. When he read the note, he was immediately on guard.

Tit-for-tat killings between the IRA and the British in Dublin are becoming more frequent. The picture in Dublin is confusing and there is talk of more British agents operating out of Dublin Castle – good ones. Everything was on a need-to-know basis and he had to take the word of O'Donnell that the missions were sanctioned by HQ, whoever they were. O'Donnell keeps everything close to his chest, but Christopher gets the impression that as Anthony's star is declining, his star is rising. In a way he is glad that Anthony is not included in direct action now, but is only used as a lookout or a glorified delivery boy dropping arms and ammunition to safe houses. But Anthony is a proud man and they are slowly losing contact with each other.

Walking along the banks of the Royal Canal towards Cross Guns Bridge, Christopher goes back through the last operation he has been on. Has something gone wrong? As well as British targets being hit, there are rumours of double agents being routed out of the IRA. These are usually English-born but with Irish backgrounds. The last one was an ex-British soldier shot dead in his room in the Gresham Hotel on Sackville Street by several masked men with Irish accents, according to the newspaper reports. It didn't take a genius to know what had happened there. Maybe, in all of the claims and counterclaims, his name had come up as being an ex-British army soldier. But he had done all that was asked of him, and more, cleaning up the messes of some of the younger recruits who, in their excitement, more often than not botched up a killing. Could it have been one of those, he wonders, who had brought up his past again out of jealousy?

A family of swans drift by, hardly disturbing the water in their passing, an adult and several downy cygnets. On the far side of the canal an excited dog runs up and down, barking at them. According to his watch, he has another fifteen minutes or so to make up his mind. It wouldn't take him long to retrace his steps down the canal and make his way into Amiens Street train station. He could make his way up to Belfast, send for Nell, maybe head over to Scotland. She would complain, he knew, about leaving her job, but he would explain to her that Dublin was now more dangerous than Flanders in 1916. At least in Flanders the enemy were coming at you from the front and not behind you as was happening more often now in Dublin.

But he suspects he is making things out to be worse than they are. If there is a problem, he can talk his way out of it as he has nothing to hide. He reaches Cross Guns Bridge just before three o'clock and lights a cigarette. In the canal down below a long, dark barge is puffing its way into Dublin, throwing up clouds of smoke and soot. As he backs away from the parapet a hand is placed on his shoulder. He turns quickly, ready to take out the Webley concealed in the deep pocket of his coat.

'Easy, Christopher.'

A man, younger than himself, stands facing him, his coat open to show that he is unarmed. Behind him a car is parked, ticking over, the driver leaning back in the front seat, his hat tipped over his eyes. They certainly don't seem like assassins – in fact, the man who spoke to him seems more nervous than him.

'Where to?' he says as he accompanies the man over to the car.

'You'll have to wait and see,' he replies and directs him into the back seat.

'I have to be home before six – my wife will be back around then and she'll be expecting me.'

'Nell won't mind,' the young man says and taps the driver on the shoulder.

'How do you know my wife's name?'

There is no response.

The car pulls away from the curb and takes a right turn immediately back towards Dublin. The young man makes Christopher sit on the floor, takes out a blindfold and, apologising, ties it around his head.

Christopher accepts the cigarette pushed into his mouth.

'Have a smoke and relax. By the way I'm Mick Crotty and that old man up front is Eddie Ryan.'

The fact that they have revealed their identities is a relief to Christopher and the atmosphere in the car seems relaxed. Occasionally he hears the driver commenting on a pedestrian, usually a woman, and Crotty telling him to concentrate on his driving as it wouldn't do to be pulled over by an army patrol. At the end of the road the car takes a right and he is now certain that they are going back into Dublin city, but after several turns he loses track of their location. After about fifteen minutes, the sound of traffic increases. He hears the bells of several trams and feels the jolts as the car makes its way across tram tracks. The car is now stopping and starting in the traffic so they must be in the city centre. He can sense the young man beside him growing more tense and he knows that they are about to arrive at their destination soon.

'Who am I going to meet?' he asks.

'You know better than to ask that, Christopher.'

'I had to try.'

The car pulls up and the driver puts his handbrake on, leaving the engine ticking over. Crotty removes the blindfold and the sudden light blinds Christopher for a moment. When his sight returns to normal, he gets back up on the seat and sees that they are parked in a laneway. He glances back through the window and can see a busy thoroughfare behind them and thinks he recognises Harcourt Street. Crotty taps him on the shoulder and holds out his hand. Christopher takes out his Webley and hands it to him and Crotty gets out of the car. He stands on the pavement and looks around, then indicates that Christopher should get out. Together they walk towards Harcourt Street, Crotty behind him with his gun, no doubt, at the ready.

'You do know I was born in the Liberties not far from here?' Christopher says over his shoulder.

'We know. But if we hadn't used the blindfold you might have thought it was a one-way trip,' Crotty says, chuckling.

When they emerge onto Harcourt Street Crotty guides him across the road then walks beside him until they come to a hotel, the Standard Hotel. They walk into the hotel together and past the reception desk where the man behind the counter nods to Crotty. On down a long corridor they go and out into a small yard at the rear of the hotel. Crotty points to a metal fire-escape ladder.

'All the way up,' he says.

Christopher starts to climb, staring straight ahead as they get higher and higher until they reach the roof. Crotty joins him and leads the way across the roof to the next building. Thankfully the access to this one is through a doorway and, once through, they descend a wooden staircase that opens out onto the top floor of the building, which is a short corridor with two doors leading off it.

Crotty knocks on the door farthest away.

Christopher automatically takes off his cap and smooths down his clothes.

'Don't worry about that,' Crotty says.

A voice calls out 'Come in!' and Crotty pushes the door open, standing back for Christopher, but doesn't follow him into the room, closing the door behind him.

The room is tiny with one square fanlight and a lone bulb hanging from the ceiling which is almost at his eye-level. Because it is the topmost room in the house, the air is still, the smell a mixture of cigarette smoke and body odour. Most of the floor space is taken up by an enormous wooden desk which is covered with neatly stacked piles of paper. In front of the desk there is a small, wooden stool. Behind the desk, writing away on a sheet of paper, is a man not much older than himself. He is working away with his shirtsleeves rolled up, his jacket draped over his chair.

The man takes a typed sheet from a pile on his left and examines it closely, crossing out passages with his pencil then flipping it over and making notes on the back. Then he puts it onto the pile on his right.

'*Done!*' he says with relief and stands up, extending his hand to Christopher. 'Sorry about the wait, Christopher, and the rotten air in here. I've told Crotty he should give up the fags. I'm Michael Collins, by the way.'

Seated behind the desk, Collins didn't look like much of a specimen, but standing up he almost has to crouch because of the low ceiling. He is above average height but seems taller as he is powerfully built. He has a broad face and deep-set grey eyes spaced wide apart. His hair, thick and dark-brown, is parted on one side. His chin juts out, giving him a slightly aggressive look. Although he is smiling pleasantly, Christopher can feel those eyes drilling his, taking his measure.

Christopher reaches out and takes his hand which grips his tightly and pumps it with vigour.

'I didn't mind waiting,' Christopher says.

'Please, take the load off your feet.' Collins points at the stool and sits back down again. 'You're probably wondering what you're doing here,' he says, leaning back into his chair.

Christopher sits. 'I admit I was a bit worried.'

'No need to be, Christopher. You've made quite an impression on O'Donnell. He's certainly taken advantage of your … skills.'

'It's all for the cause,' Christopher answers.

'Ah yes, very good, the cause. Let me ask you about that. What do you think it means?'

Christopher hesitates. 'I think it means getting the British out of Ireland and winning independence so that we can rule ourselves.'

'How do we get the British out?'

'We fight them the best way we can with whatever we have. Show no mercy. Force the politicians to believe it's more trouble than it's worth to stay here.'

'Very good. Yes, we do fight them, but there's many ways to skin a cat. Take you, for example. It's obvious that you've a calm head on your shoulders, you follow orders and you don't mind getting your hands dirty. In other words, you're a damn good soldier.'

'Thank you, I try my best.'

'Some people don't have your qualities, Christopher, but can be equally valuable in the fight. Your friend Anthony Caprani, for instance. Not very good in a tight situation but, then again, he brought you into the fold, which was a good day for us.'

Christopher is trying to work out where their conversation is going but is at a loss. Is he going to be asked about Anthony's behaviour? If that is the case, he will politely refuse to answer any questions about him.

'Is this about Anthony?'

'No, it's not about Anthony, not directly anyways. It's about the many ways people can help the cause. Take Nell, for instance.'

Collins is watching his face closely, presumably for a reaction, but Christopher is confused. Is he saying that Nell is a brave woman for letting her husband volunteer? But he hasn't even told Nell of his escapades and has been very careful to keep it that way.

Almost as if reading his mind, Collins says, 'Don't worry, Christopher. Nell doesn't know a thing about your activities lately. As far as she's concerned, you're still working away in the factory packing meat and occasionally give us a hand, like in the Dorset Street raid for example. In fact, I made a promise to her that you wouldn't be allowed to get involved in any dangerous situations. Other than a bit of training up in Ticknock.'

Christopher thinks he has misheard Collins. 'You've met my Nell?'

'I have. Several months ago. She works for us in Dublin Castle. In fact, she's a very valuable asset to us.'

Christopher jumps off the stool and lunges across the desk. But Collins is quicker and a gun materialises from somewhere and is pointing at his face, stopping him in his tracks.

'Wars are fuckin' messy and confusing, Christopher, I shouldn't have to tell *you* that.'

'*Nell is an innocent woman! What do you think you're doing putting her in danger?*' Christopher shouts.

Behind him the door opens and Crotty sticks his head in but Collins waves him out.

'Sit down and I'll explain. If you're not happy you can go on your way,' Collins says. 'Nell is in no danger. As far as the British are concerned, she's a secretary working away in the background, taking notes and typing up reports. The person she gives the information to is very well trained and makes sure that she is never followed from the Castle when they meet and he even shadows her home.'

'I can't believe it,' Christopher says, shaking his head and sitting down.

'At this moment, Christopher, Nell is the most valuable agent we have. More important than you or any of us, and we're grateful.'

'Let me ask you this, is there nobody sacred to you?'

Collins immediately shakes his head. 'No. When it comes to the greater cause I'd use anyone and everyone, including kith and kin. But I always calculate the risks. In Nell's case, part of the reason she joined up was to protect you.'

'Me? I don't need protecting.'

'She thought you did. She knew about your little trip to Dorset Street to help us out. She also knew that you wanted to get back into the action. So, I made a promise to her that you wouldn't be involved in the more dangerous end of things.'

'Is that why it took so long for me to be trusted? I thought it was because I'm ex-British army!'

'As I said, war can be confusing. You were never supposed to be as involved as you have been. I was out of Dublin for a while. O'Donnell must have got fed up, I suppose, and decided it was a good chance to use you, and here we are.' Collins shrugs and lowers his gun. 'Can I put this away now?'

Christopher nods.

'And in a roundabout way it has all worked for the best,' says

Collins. 'The British, I'm afraid, are on to you. Nell saw your name mentioned on a telegram and told Crotty. She doesn't know exactly what it's about and thinks it might have to do with your army days, some nonsense about a pension. And she might be right, but we can't take the risk. The British are pouring agents into Dublin because of all of our attacks. We are presuming one of them got lucky with an informer and you were singled out.'

'Does that mean I'm finished?'

'I'm afraid you are, in Dublin anyway,' Collins says.

He slides a map over the desk towards Christopher.

It's a map of Europe.

Collins points to somewhere near the top of Italy.

'What's this?' Christopher asks.

'Your next mission, if you're willing to go. Mr Gabriele D'Annunzio has just declared the Republic of Fiume or something like that. Seems he's a supporter of the downtrodden and a hater of the bourgeoisie. Rebels are flocking to his cause.'

'You want me to go down there?'

'As a representative of the new Republic of Ireland and representing the Dáil. We'll write a letter of introduction, stamped with an official Dáil stamp. The place is full of Russian arms and he's willing to put some our way. So, you see, Anthony Caprani will come in useful after all. He has fluent Italian and he's pretty harmless.'

Christopher looks at him to see if this is some kind of joke, but Collins' face is serious and he's waiting for an answer.

'Does Nell know about this?'

'Not yet. That's up to you. If you decide to go, you'll have to tell her. If not, I'm afraid there's nothing for you here. If you want to risk staying in Dublin, we can organise that you get your old job back in Donnelly's, as you won't be on our payroll anymore. Or if you want to go on the run, we can probably find you a safe house down the country somewhere.'

'What would I have to do if I agree?'

'That's the easy part. We'll organise a berth for you and Caprani down to Fiume. We'll give you the letter of introduction to our friend D'Annunzio and you take it from there. If there are guns down there, well and good. I'll give you the authority to buy them and ship them back to Ireland. If not, look on it as a holiday.' Collins laughs. 'I've heard stories about what's going on down there. It would frighten a bishop!'

Christopher imagines what it would be like going back to work in Donnelly's meat factory in the winter. Getting up in the dark, going home in the dark, the stink of blood and flesh coming off his clothes. The crude jokes of the men on the packing line, then back to the pub to drown his sorrows. All that and at the same time knowing that Nell is in Dublin Castle carrying out her work for Collins. Jealousy of his wife might be a factor, but he doesn't dwell on that. On the other hand, if he did agree to go, he could be away from Nell for weeks or possibly months. But it was still a small price to pay to hold on to the dignity and meaning he has felt in his life since joining the struggle. If he was to lose that and go back to the factory, he feels certain that he would be swamped with depression and his marriage would probably be over.

'When does the ship sail?'

'Day after tomorrow. Well, are you in?'

Christopher nods.

'Good man,' Collins says.

Then the interview, or whatever it was supposed to be, is over.

Collins is already starting on a new stack of paper and shouting out for Crotty who sticks his head through the door. Crotty nods for Christopher to follow him and they go back along the roof and down again into the hotel where Crotty gives him back his gun. Once outside the hotel, Crotty shakes his hand and starts up Harcourt Street to carry out his next mission. Christopher looks at his watch. It has been less than half an hour in all, and in that time his whole life has been changed. He's not looking forward to making his way home and waiting for Nell, but it has to be done.

A tram trundles past, electric sparks coming out of the overhead lines. The passengers inside, mainly men, are reading their newspapers, oblivious of the fact that a few yards away Michael Collins is plotting to bring about a change in their lives such as they've never seen before.

CHAPTER 21

Partings

Nell waits in the café for Crotty to show up but, as it's past six o'clock now, she knows that he won't be here. Sometimes it happens like that. She has learnt that spying isn't an exact science. Sometimes she thinks the information she provides is valuable, but is then informed that they have already received it from another source within Dublin Castle. She doesn't know if that's just to keep her on her toes or if one of the other secretaries or even the cleaning lady in her office is also passing on the information. However, it's Friday night and all she can think of now is getting home and waiting for Christopher to come home with fish and chips from Leo Burdock's in Werburgh Street, just around the corner. Then they can sit around the phonograph and enjoy some music.

As she turns down Engine Alley, she is half expecting to see her mother's car parked outside the building, but the street is clear. Inside the house the sound of voices arguing comes down the stairs from Mary Sherry's flat. Mary seems to be arguing with Tommy about money, or the lack of it. She makes a mental note to ask Crotty the next time they meet about what happens after the revolution? Is Sinn

Féin going to help people like Mary and Tommy out of the poverty trap that they find themselves in? It's alright for Collins and his men to go galivanting around the countryside to rid Ireland of the British. But what happens when they win? Nell closes over the door to her flat and looks around. Christopher is sitting at the table, smoking and nursing a mug of tea, reading a newspaper without a care in the world. The room looks a lot more habitable than it did when they had first moved in. A large rug now covers most of the old floorboards and she has placed some framed pictures around the room. The new lampshades she bought add some muted colour to the painted walls, and the second-hand furniture from the Iveagh market is waxed and shining. The only regret she has is that Mary Sherry has curtailed her visits and she suspects it's to do with the growing difference in their fortunes.

'You'd better sit down, Nell,' Christopher says, and folds up his newspaper.

She sits down at the table and Christopher pours out a mug of tea so dark that she can taste the tannin. The last time her husband had made her tea was the time he had told her about getting the job in Donnelly's and she wonders what the matter is now. Has he now lost his job? Or worse, has he finally found out about hers? Dublin is a small city and Christopher is training more people for the IRA, so somebody might have let it slip. She has planned for this day to come and regrets that it has happened so soon. She takes a sip of the strong tea and places the mug back on the table.

'What's the matter?' she asks.

'I met Mick Collins today. We had a long chat.'

Nell was expecting anything, but not this.

'What about?'

'About you, mainly, and your real job in Dublin Castle.'

'I can explain everything ...' Nell tries to interrupt but Christopher holds up his hand.

'There's no need to, Nell. I've some explaining to do myself.'

'What do you mean?'

'Collins told me about the promise he made to you, about my part in all of this. You tried to protect me, isn't that true?'

'It is. I was thinking the worst ...'

'You might've talked it over first.' Christopher takes hold of her hand, squeezing it.

'I know, I just thought at the time –'

'It doesn't matter now because, you see, Collins' orders were ignored. I've been an active member of the 3rd battalion Dublin Brigade for several months now.'

'*But he made a promise!*' Nell says loudly, pulling her hand away from Christopher.

'Settle down, Nell. He kept his promise. I *was* a glorified messenger boy for a while. Even when Anthony Caprani –'

'I knew it had to be him. I never trusted him, with his suits and the way he flicks his hat back when he's passing women, thinks he's some kind of film star!'

'That's not fair, Nell – he's a good man. It was through Anthony that I became more involved in the movement but, even then, I did nothing more than take part on some training in the Dublin mountains. Then the quartermaster came under pressure from his superiors because he was losing some of his men due to their stupidity. So that led him to use me, aware of my army experience, despite Collins' orders to the contrary. That's the way it works in war, Nell – people just do what they have to do to survive.'

'I suppose you're right.'

'And then there was that telegram you caught a glimpse of.'

'But they agreed that it was probably nothing, just something to do with you being an ex-British army. You have all your paperwork.'

'They agreed with you because they didn't want to worry you, Nell. Collins has just found out that I was more deeply involved in several missions than I should've been. So, you see, that telegram took on more of a meaning.'

Nell needs to think. She tastes her tea again which is even more bitter and now getting cold.

'So, what does all this mean?' she says.

'I have to get out of Dublin, for a while at least. Until this dies down. I know you work in Dublin Castle as Nell Claffey. But if they find out that we're married, both of us could be in danger.'

'I knew I shouldn't have become involved, it was stupid,' Nell says.

'What's done is done. Collins has asked me to go to Italy for him. I'll be out of danger down there.'

Nell stands up from the table. 'Italy! What in the name of God are you going to do in Italy?'

'It's not Italy exactly. It's a place called Fiume. The people down there are only too happy to help a small country get rid of an oppressor.'

'You can't even speak the language, Christopher! How're you going to manage?'

'Anthony Caprani is coming along. He speaks Italian.'

'I don't like the sound of this, Christopher. How will you get there? Most of Europe is a mess and the British army will surely pick you up.'

'We're not going by land. We're taking a ship from Dublin. It's all been arranged.'

'You've decided this without telling me?'

'It was either that or go on the run. Either way I won't be able to see you for a while. By the time I return I'll probably be forgotten about.'

Nell rises from the table and begins to pace the room. She can see now how people's lives can be shaped and changed by forces outside of their control. She feels like a leaf being carried down a river, caught up in the currents in this brutal war of independence, a war with no end in sight. And Christopher too. What choice did anybody really have? She turns and looks at his profile. His face has filled out more since they married and even before his thirtieth birthday there are tiny flecks of grey in his hair. But they hadn't been caused by his latest exploits – no, they were caused in Donnelly's factory, doing a job that he hates but had accepted because of her.

'Well?' he said. 'What do you think?'

Nell looks around their flat, taking in the new paintings she and Christopher had picked out so carefully, the comfortable furniture and the new rug on the floor. It was all she had ever dreamed of having, a cosy home, a loving husband and, hopefully, someday a family. But how could she really take pleasure in any of it if everyone else living around her is destitute and oppressed?

'I think you should go, Christopher, and do whatever you can to get the British out of our country – and I'll do the same,' she says, putting as much conviction in her voice as she can,

CHAPTER 22

Sarah Murphy

Levon Mordaunt prepares himself for another foray into the Monto. Down in the basement the body of Kevin Brennan, late of Anna Macken's brothel, lies festering under a layer of quicklime and loose earth. After several days of questioning, the doorman to Anna Macken's brothel had proved to have little knowledge of the inner workings of Macken's empire or her circle. In between screams of pain and pleadings to stop, the only information he gained was a vague reference to Christopher Flinter possibly living somewhere in the Liberties, a tenement area near St Patrick's Cathedral which was several times larger than the Monto. Almost useless information.

In a way he wasn't overly surprised at Mr Brennan's lack of knowledge. After all, it was Moussa's betrayal which no doubt made Anna Macken more cautious about the people she employed. Which was not alone unfortunate for him, but also for Kevin Brennan, the now ex-doorman to the brothel. But he's not too despondent. In his questioning about the people who worked for Anna, it was confirmed that the miniature woman, Sarah Murphy, was his only option after all. It would raise the possibility of alerting Flinter if he ever found out, but that was a chance he was prepared to take.

In the sitting room of his house, he peruses the various tools of his trade. Due to her small stature, a child's really, he can't use the small phial of heroin he had used on Brennan. It had to be chloroform. It would be messier, but at least it wouldn't kill her. As in the case of kidnapping Brennan, his unusual appearance will be heightened during daylight hours but the weather is becoming colder and a large scarf won't look out of place. The Monto, as well, will play its part. Who will pay any heed to a gentleman and a worker from a brothel tussling on the street?

Later that afternoon he strolls past the brothel, crossing the road further up Montgomery Street, stopping to look into the window of a bakery to allow the natural flow of people on the street to change before returning again. The woman, Sarah Murphy, is not a prostitute. She normally leaves the brothel before midnight and arrives the following afternoon, probably to oversee the cleaning-up from the night before and then the restocking of the kitchen. Not ideal. Sometimes she appears to carry out her errands in the many shops of Talbot Street, but sometimes she sends one of the other maids out. He has parked his carriage several times on Mabbot Street, the entrance to the Monto district, but twice she has already taken different routes on the days she does emerge.

But today he is in luck. Her slight frame looks even slighter against the tall entrance to the brothel's doorway and, after making her way down the steps, she turns right. The weather, too, is in his favour. It is a still day with heavy clouds that hang so low they seem to touch the roofs of the taller buildings. But there is also a chill in the air so many fires have been lit. Nobody casts a look in his direction as the few gentlemen strolling in the area have also covered their mouths and noses with their scarves. She walks along Mabbot Street ahead of him, an empty canvas shopping bag hanging from her hand. As she passes by his carriage though there are too many people about. He crosses the street and takes up a position near a grocery shop and waits.

His patience is rewarded. Barely thirty minutes later she reappears and approaches his carriage, laden down with her shopping bag. She is bent to one side with the weight of whatever is inside and is stopping and starting, changing the grip to ease her burden. A slight rain shower has begun and people are walking faster with their heads down. Crossing the street, he stands beside the door to his carriage and fiddles with the handle. As she is passing by, he opens the door suddenly, blocking her path. She is startled and drops the overladen bag of groceries. Of course, he is the perfect gentleman and offers to help her to pick up the spilt groceries. By providence, a large tin of pineapples in syrup has rolled under his carriage. She bends to reach it and, in an instant, he has taken out the small bottle of chloroform from his pocket, holds his breath and pours some onto his handkerchief then applies the handkerchief to her face, covering her mouth and nose.

Barely the weight of a child, she faints into his arms and he wonders if he has overdone the chloroform. But he bundles her into the carriage, slams the door and climbs up into the seat, grabbing the reins. As he pulls away from the footpath the groceries, strewn about the pavement, are being fought over by the local street rats, the true survivors in this city. As they continue fighting with each other among the parcels and bags, he is already at the end of Mabbot Street and turning onto Talbot Street. A quick turn at the bottom and he will be heading back to his house and that much closer to finding out if the woman is still breathing or if he will have to dig another grave in his basement. A bit of company for Mr Brennan, he supposes.

❋❋❋❋

Sarah Murphy wakes up in darkness, her head pounding. There is something obstructing her mouth. She realises she is gagged. She tries to move her hand to her mouth but her hands are tied tightly behind her back.

She is lying stretched out on a rough floor which feels cold and damp. Overhead she can hear footsteps pacing backwards and forwards. Beyond the footsteps she can make out the familiar background hum of horses clip-clopping over cobblestones and the voice of a young newspaper seller shouting out headlines. The air around her is damp with an underlying sweet smell that makes the hackles at the back of her neck tingle.

Upstairs the footsteps slow and stop. She holds her breath, waiting. The person begins to walk again, heavy footsteps. A door opens and closes with a sharp rap and she can hear the footsteps coming downstairs becoming louder and louder. She hears a key being inserted into a lock, the sound of chains and then a horizonal bar of light falls across her face, blinding her. A man steps into the doorway and she opens her eyes. All she can see is a tall shadow but she has no doubt it is the man who had pretended to come to her rescue on Mabbot Street. He walks across the room and bends down, grabs her by the scruff of her neck, pulling her face closer to his. He looks into her eyes, sniffs at her like a dog then lets her head fall back onto the ground.

Those eyes, that face. She has seen it before, but can't remember where. The bottom half of the face is motionless, the mouth a thin line painted in the shape of a mouth. A mask. He makes a grunting noise and leaves again, slamming the door behind him and putting the chain back on. From the brief look she had when the door was open, she knows that she is in a large cellar. She saw that one side of the cellar is full of old furniture and household rubbish and the other is empty with a metal table against the wall. When the light from the doorway had fallen across it, she could make out leather straps and bloodstains running down the sides. The sight of the blood makes her panic. She begins to choke on the gag. She tries to wriggle her wrists together but they feel sore so she gives up trying, to save her strength in case she gets an opportunity to fight back.

Somewhere in the back of her mind she feels that this man is somehow associated with her dead lover, Moussa. But how? Was he one of the sailors that Moussa had introduced her to? Then she remembered the monster who had killed her lover. But discounted him as he was dead, shot by Nell. In the face. Her mind leaps back to that nightmare in the tunnel. Nell had grabbed the gun from Phil Shanahan and fired at the figure. She could still picture the explosion of blood and bone. Surely he must be dead? But what if he had survived? She begins to shiver, remembering all of the horrible crimes that he was responsible for. All of those poor women. She pulls at her bindings again and feels a slight give. Her childlike wrists, slippery with sweat, have a certain amount of movement.

She tries to roll on her side but with her hands tied up it is almost impossible. Then she starts to rock from side to side and finds that the momentum carries her onto her stomach. She rests for a moment, gathering her strength, then repeats the same movement and turns on her back again. It is tiring but the thought of the man coming back into the dark cellar spurs her on. She rolls onto her stomach again and her face is pressed into loose earth. The smell emanating from it nearly makes her sick and she rolls onto her back again, escaping the putrid stench. With her strength leaving her she makes one final push, choking on the gag with the effort. This time she comes up against a solid object. She pushes her back against it and tries to feel it with her fingers. It feels like an old metal frame, possibly for a bed. One of the edges seems quite sharp and she gets her wrists into position and begins a sawing motion. Every time she slows down or loses heart, she just pictures the dead body of her lover, Moussa, and continues. She loses any sense of time, guessing that it must be between midnight and early morning as the sounds from the streets outside have ceased altogether. She begins to nod off, promising herself that it would only be for a few minutes, but then she hears the sound of footsteps upstairs and continues even faster.

It takes her a while to realise that she has worn through her bonds. Her two hands just fall away from each other and she lies back. But then an intense pain develops in her fingers as the blood begins to circulate again. When the pain begins to subside, she pulls the gag off and lies there for a few moments, breathing deeply. Then she gets carefully to her feet with her arms extended out in front of her. She finds the wall, inches her way around the room and reaches the door. She tries it, to no avail. Then she continues her slow journey, past the metal table she had seen earlier and onwards until she comes back to the corner of the cellar. One wall left to explore. She begins to trace her fingers along the rough brickwork of that end of the cellar with little hope but then she feels a slight draught of air on her face.

Moving as fast as she dares, her hands come in contact with some kind of a metal hatch set into the wall. It is about three foot wide and the air is coming in from the outside around its edges. There is a metal handle in the middle of it which is at her eye level. She pulls it towards her but, although the hatch begins to swing down with a screeching sound, it sticks and she hasn't enough strength to get it all the way down. Would it be worth the effort anyway, she wonders, as if she makes any more noise it might attract her kidnapper back to the cellar. She remembers the table she has seen against the wall and makes her way around to it. Pulling it back towards the hatch is slow progress as the metallic feet drag through the earth of the cellar, digging in.

After what seems like hours of pushing and pulling, she finally gets the table up to the hatch. Now she can get onto the table and use all of her strength to push down the hatch. The door finally screeches opens to its full extent and stops. She puts her hand inside to investigate and her fingers come in contact with what seems like sand and pebbles. Then she realises what the hatch is: it's the opening for a coal chute. Coal is delivered into the cellar by the sack-load by way of the small, circular opening on the pavement outside. It then lands in the chamber behind the hatch and spills out onto the floor of the cellar when the hatch door is opened. There is no coal in the chamber at the moment. But her way is blocked as the hatch when it's open on the inside shuts off access to the outside. Despondent, she begins to close it again but then she has an idea. She clambers through the hatch and into the circular metal drum-like container. If she's right, when she pulls the hatch door behind her the whole container should swivel, giving her access to the chute.

Pulling the door up behind her is easier than she thought it would be. Suddenly the draught of air coming down the chute is more pronounced. She looks up through the dimness of the chute and can make out a faint halo of light. She thinks it must be light seeping in from around the metal coalhole cover. Judging by the occasional noises coming from the outside world, it's early morning. The chute slopes up and away from her at a steep angle and she begins to climb. Using her hands and legs as anchors against the walls, she moves upwards towards the coalhole cover. When she reaches it, she pushes upwards with one of her hands until the metallic cover opens and falls back onto the pavement with a loud noise. But the opening she had hoped to escape through is too narrow. With the last of her strength, she reaches up one of her hands up through the opening as far as it will go and waves it about, at the same time screaming for help.

✳✳✳✳

Sergeant Samuel McBride is standing on the corner of Fitzwilliam Square, contemplating what he will have for breakfast after his shift finishes. He hears a shrill noise from somewhere across the street and turns in its direction. Damned seagulls, he thinks, worse than the pigeons. There is a slight movement outside the house of the mystery man and he thinks that it's probably a brazen seagull picking at the scraps thrown onto the ground from some un-civic-minded person from the night before. But the gull is an unusual shape and making an unusual noise. Glancing around quickly, he puts his hand into the inside pocket of his uniform jacket and takes out his spectacles. But, when he slips them on, his mind still can't make sense of what he is looking at. Something pale seems to be coming out of the pavement and moving backwards and forwards, like a snake.

Mystified, he crosses the street towards the mystery man's house. When he reaches the pavement outside the house, he can hardly believe his eyes. The metal coalhole cover is lying on its back. A pale arm is waving backwards and forwards and a shrill voice is shouting out for help. He gets down on his hands and knees and peers down into the coal chute. Looking up at him is a woman, her pale face covered with coal dust, her hair a tangled mass. She gets such a fright that she slides back down the chute just out of sight. Bending down near to the ground he peers down into the semidarkness.

The young woman is scrambling her way back up the chute, looking behind her and screaming, '*He's going to kill me! He's going to kill me!*'

She reaches her arm through the opening again and he grabs it, but there's no way the woman is going to fit through.

'Steady now, steady now,' he tries to calm her. 'What's going on?'

'*Please don't let me go! There's a madman in here and he's trying to kill me!*' she sobs.

The sergeant looks up at house and notices that a light has come on in the sitting room. He's caught between two minds: should he let the woman go to slide back down the chute and knock at the door, or should he wait until somebody comes along. He looks around him for help. A horse-drawn cab passes by on the far side of the road and he waves at the cabby whose concentration is elsewhere and doesn't see him.

A bowler-hatted man is approaching from the direction of Leeson Street. When he gets close enough, McBride shouts out: '*Please, sir, assistance, over here!*'

The man approaches uncertainly, taking in the strange sight of a policeman holding somebody's arm through a hole in the pavement. He puts his briefcase and umbrella down on the ground and looks past the policeman's arm down into the blackened, tearstained face of a terrified woman.

'What's happening?'

'I don't know, but I'm going to find out. Hold this poor woman's arm and I'll try the front door,' McBride says.

'*Please don't leave, he's a madman!*' screams the woman.

'Don't worry, dear, nobody is going to leave you alone. This gentleman will hold your hand until I get to the bottom of this.'

As soon as the two men change positions, McBride walks up the steps to the front door of the house and hammers on it shouting out '*Dublin Metropolitan Police!*'. He steps back from the door and draws his baton. Remembering the appearance of the house-owner, he wishes that he were armed, but only the detectives are given firearms. On the pavement outside, another person has appeared to find out what all the commotion is about. She looks like a skivvy from one of the large houses on the square. She stands, staring down into the coalhole, talking gently to the woman trapped inside.

Sergeant McBride hammers on the door again but there is no answer.

'*You could try the back entrance!*' the skivvy shouts up at him.

'*I was just about to!*' Sergeant McBride shouts back, slightly annoyed that he hasn't thought of that.

Making his way down the street, he turns down a laneway and begins counting the houses. The back of the house has a large wall guarding it with a tall wooden double door. He tries the wicket gate and it opens to his push. Inside the gate there is a stable to one side and he can hear the gentle whinnying of a horse. He looks in through the bars into the interior and can make out the shape of a carriage. What should he do? If he goes out onto the streets again to try and get the attention of a fellow policeman, the man might escape. But if he goes on alone who is to say that the man is not armed and dangerous? He fingers the whistle in his pocket and curses himself for not using it outside. Was it pride or just stupidity?

Looking down the overgrown garden to the tall, redbrick rear of the house, he decides to press on. Nearer to the building he can make out a set of stairs leading up to the back door but set into the side is another door, probably an entrance to the basement. He thinks of his wife, Ruth, and wonders what she would say to him now. She was always a rock of sense. She would say: 'Don't you go and take unnecessary risks – you'll be out on retirement soon.' And she would be right. He looks up at the four-storey building, studying each window, but they are all shuttered and offer no clue as it what lies inside.

He goes over to the basement entrance and hammers on it with his baton, shouting '*Police!*'. It is a wooden door and some of the panels look rotten, but it is locked. Using his sizeable body, he throws his shoulder at it and it splinters inwards under his weight. He stumbles into the dark interior and shouts '*Police!*' again and listens. With all the commotion he is hoping that the man will take the opportunity to flee out through the front door, but he is surrounded by silence.

As his eyes grow more accustomed to the gloomy interior, he finds himself standing in a dim, narrow corridor. He recognises the sweet smell of death hanging in the fetid air and his stomach churns. The low-ceilinged corridor disappears away from him into darkness and seems to swallow up the light coming through the door behind him. He shouts out '*Police!*' again and the sound of his voice is swallowed up in the darkness. He contemplates going back out into the yard but remembers the pleading look on the poor, unfortunate woman's face. Taking a deep breath, he makes his way up the corridor to the front of the house. As he works his way forward, he can make out a soft, yellow light. A lone oil lamp is set on a table outside a door and burns with a steady glow. Beside the lamp there is a set of keys and leading off to the right he can see a stairway that leads up to the ground floor. As he gets closer to the door, he can see that it is secured with a padlock and chain.

Putting his ear to the door, he can hear faint voices coming from inside. One of them he recognises as that of the young woman. He grabs the keys from the table, opens the padlock and unwraps the chains. Dropping them onto the floor, he pulls open the door. The darkness inside is broken by light coming through the hatch on the far wall which must be light coming down the coal chute. He can hear the voices more clearly now, turns and grabs the oil lamp from the table. As he approaches the hatch, he puts his head through and looks up the coal chute. The young woman's hand is still being held by the people on the street outside.

'*You're all right now, miss! You can come back down!*' he shouts up into the chute.

As the young woman slides into view, he can see that she is covered in coal dust. He helps her out, feet first, and she stands in front of him, her tears cutting a path through the dust. She is no more than four feet high and for a moment thinks that he was mistaken and that she is a child but, no, she has a woman's figure. He bends his six-foot frame to console her but she draws back with fear in her eyes and screams.

The best-laid plans of mice and men, thinks Levon Mordaunt as he exerts more pressure on the garotte, pulling the two handles with all of his strength. Blood spurts out of the wound and he's banking on Sarah Murphy being so shocked that he can deal with her as well. But the little bitch is tough and she runs around the policeman who is falling to his knees, his almost-severed head hanging to one side. Levon makes a grab at her and manages to catch a handful of her hair. As he yanks hard on it, a clump comes away in his hand and she is gone through the door.

He runs after her up the stairs that lead to the front of the house. But fear is a great survival mechanism and she is already out the door and down the steps into the world outside. After locking the front door, he makes his way into the front room and peeks through the curtains. Sarah is with a small crowd of people, pointing back to the house. No doubt she is telling them about the monster who has just killed the policeman.

He opens the bookcase and the concealed section behind. On the floor there is a travelling bag. It is large and deep and he scoops up the money – large denomination notes in various currencies – and dumps them into the bag. He follows that with some of his favourite instruments of death, then shuts the bag and carries it down into the basement, leaving it outside the door. He runs back up the stairs again and over to the bookcase. Neatly lined up at the back of the concealed section is a line of glass bottles. He takes out two and opens them, scattering the contents around the room and out into the hallway. The smell of the pure alcohol is so pungent that he has to put a handkerchief over his nose and mouth. He goes back for more bottles and walks around the ground floor of the house, throwing them against the walls.

He takes the last two bottles with him, dripping them behind him as he descends the stairs into the basement. When he reaches the bottom of the stairs, he casts the bottles aside and takes out a box of matches, strikes one and throws it onto the wooden stairs. A blue flame leaps up and quickly travels up the stairs, reaching the ground floor. He hears a sudden whooshing noise and the sound of breaking glass.

Time for him to go.

Ireland, a damp little backwater European country, has been very trying for him. It took away his dignity and pride, not to mention his face. Already he is reformulating his plans as he backs the horse between the shafts of the carriage.

He rushes over to the wooden gates and opens them just in time, as some of the curious onlookers are walking up the lane towards the gates, urging each other on. Sarah Murphy has the good sense not to be with them.

He jumps up on the driver's seat and whips the horse which, after a day's rest, is only too eager to be going. Swerving into the laneway, the horse almost pulling the carriage over, he whips it again and drives straight at the people. There is some solace as he feels the right wheel bumping over the legs of one of the men who had stumbled and, as he drives onto Fitzwilliam Square, the screams of the man are left in his wake. The square is now fully awake and the traffic is steady. He guides his carriage towards Leeson Street and slows it down to a moderate speed, joining in with the morning traffic. As he goes around the final corner, he looks back towards his house. Already smoke is billowing from the ground-floor windows and traffic on the road outside the house has come to a halt as curious onlookers stop and stare.

CHAPTER 23

Christopher –
March 1920

I t's Monday night and, as arranged, Christopher waits anxiously for Anthony Caprani on O'Connell Bridge. People mill past in both directions, anxious to be home before the curfew. He turns and looks over the concrete balustrades and into the Liffey below. The turgid dark-green waters reflect his mood. The tide is out and the exposed banks on either side with their slime-covered rocks and the wail of seagulls fighting for any scraps is not the last picture of Dublin that he wants in his mind. He pats the pockets of his jacket again, making sure that he has everything he needs: passport, money, letters of introduction and a small Webley automatic tucked away into the back pocket of his trousers. An old seaman's bag he borrowed from O'Donnell leans awkwardly against his leg and a peaked cap that Nell bought for him is pulled down over his eyes.

'Sufferin' Jesus, you look the part alright! But look at me!'

Caprani stands in front of him, a large, battered suitcase at his feet. Much to the amusement of the passers-by he turns around, arms outstretched, showing off his old workmen's clothes. Although annoyed that he is late, Christopher is glad to see him. He couldn't imagine boarding the ship by himself and ending up in a country where he would struggle to find someone who spoke English.

'You took your time,' Christopher says, grabbing his bag.

'I had a lot of farewells to make.'

'I thought you're from a small family?'

'Not that kind of farewell.' Anthony smiles and winks. 'Anyway, we have a few hours.'

'You forgot about the curfew,' Christopher reminds him. 'You're not much good to anybody in jail.'

'True. Well, I suppose this is it. Speak now or forever hold your peace, as they say,' Anthony says, shivering.

The two men stand and stare across the bridge towards the Custom House, beyond which the dark shadows of ships lie moored to the quay wall. All Christopher knows is that their ship is called the *Mercure* and will be casting off before dawn. Without waiting, he makes his way between the slow-moving traffic on the bridge and towards the quays. Anthony trots beside him, trying to keep up. His suitcase is heavy and every so often he has to change hands.

Christopher finally stops to wait for him. 'What the hell have you got in there?'

'I don't know what the weather's going to be like, so I brought a choice,' Anthony pants.

They continue on down the quays, under the recently repaired Loopline railway bridge, and come to the first ship. The heady smell of the river mixed with the salty smell of the sea and the fumes from the ships bring back old memories. On Sundays he used to stroll down here with Ned, his younger brother, and they would spend the day walking up and down the quays, taking in the lines of ships. They were from all over the world in all kinds of condition, from tramp steamers held together by rust to tall cargo ships with steep gangplanks reaching up way over their heads. He'd witnessed the last of the sailing ships, long, sleek cutters crewed mainly by older men, with skin darkened under the far-off sun of the equator.

'What are we lookin' for?' Anthony says, still struggling with his suitcase and the uneven cobbles of the quay walls.

'The *Mercure*,' Christopher says, wondering how far they will have to walk.

'Mercury? Let's hope it's as speedy as the messenger of the gods.'

'Unlikely,' Christopher says.

They pass another ship, a grain cargo ship. Its portholes are level with the quay and inside he can see four sailors sitting around a table playing cards in a smoke-filled cabin. A giant crane looms up overhead. Waddling around the ground in front of the ship hundreds of pigeons compete with each other for the scattered pieces of grain.

They come to the next ship, a smaller one, the portholes below the level of the quay wall. Emblazoned on the blackened funnel is the name *Mercure*. The wooden gangway leads down onto the main deck and rises and falls with the sea.

'This is it,' Christopher says, putting his bag on the ground.

'You're joking,' Anthony says, taking in the size and the state of the ship. 'It's a fishing boat.'

'Come on, it's not that bad,' Christopher says.

A bit alarmed himself, he goes and unclips the rope placed across the gangway, a wooden structure that looks as ancient as the ship. He makes his way down the steep slope, holding onto one of the rusty metal cables with one hand, the other gripping his bag tightly. Halfway down, he has to stop as the ship rises on a passing swell. Behind him Anthony lets out a shout. When he turns his friend is looking at the palm of his hand which is streaked with blood.

'Bloody cable caught me,' Anthony groans, licking the blood and spitting it over the side of the gangway.

'Clean it up as soon as you can – you don't want to get tetanus,' Christopher says over his shoulder and continues onto the deck of the ship.

He stands on the forward deck, waiting for Anthony who is still sucking his hand and spitting into the water. Discarded around the deck are various pieces of maritime rubbish: lengths of rope and cable, an old metal bucket, a life belt and a piece of machinery he can't identify that has been taken apart and left with the parts abandoned.

Anthony joins him, takes in the cluttered deck and scratches his head.

'Is this the right ship? How is it going to get outside the harbour, never mind down to the Mediterranean?'

'Maybe it's like this for a purpose, to fool any British patrols,' Christopher says without conviction.

Making his way around the clutter, he passes by a derrick crane whose upright arm disappears into the night sky and on down a side passage with the lighted portholes.

They come to a door with a porthole and look inside but the glass is so fogged up they can't make anything out. Knocking on the glass, Christopher pushes open the door and steps over the raised step and into a steam-filled galley that smells of fish. A large cauldron is simmering on a stove which takes up most of the space. Through an open door on his left, he can see a long wooden table which is set for a meal. He hears voices coming from there and makes his way towards it.

Anthony grabs his arm. 'Are you sure about this?' He indicates their tawdry surroundings.

'What did you expect?'

'Something a bit … larger,' Anthony says.

'It's a bit cramped, I'll say that. But Collins wouldn't have sent us if he wasn't happy.'

The door on the other side of the galley opens and a group of men enter, talking and laughing. They stop when they see Christopher and Anthony but say nothing, just pass them by and on into the dining room. The door to the deck opens and two men come in. One of them is wearing a tattered captain's cap and the other is a tall, skinny man with a drooping moustache who is dressed in stained chef's whites. They have been having a heated discussion that the captain cuts short when he becomes aware of his visitors.

He takes off his cap and bows.

'You must be our two passengers,' he says in heavily accented English.

Christopher steps forward and holds out his hand.

'Christopher Flinter. And this is Anthony Caprani.'

The captain is a small man with narrow shoulders and a pot belly. He takes off his glasses and uses them like a pointing stick.

'No, no, no, this will not do. I do not need to know your names, but I can tell you mine as everybody on this scow knows it. I am Captain Richard Denot at your service.'

'Pleased to meet you,' says Christopher.

'Come, have some food.' He ushers them into the dining room.

The long wooden table is now full of sailors, smoking and talking amongst themselves. Some of them must have come through another door and Christopher is more confident as he counts over a dozen. The captain points to two chairs at the end of the table and makes his way to the head of it where he stands and addresses the crew in French as they take their seats. Christopher recognises the word *bienvenue* and *liberté* as the captain thumps the table. The men turn to Christopher and Anthony and clap politely, then the red-faced chef comes in from the galley with the large cauldron and begins to ladle out its contents. When he has filled all of the bowls he disappears back into the kitchen and struggles back in again with an enormous serving plate with large chunks of bread balanced in one hand and an earthenware jug in the other.

'*Bouillabaisse!* Fish soup. Good!' the captain calls down to them and makes a circular gesture with his hand on his stomach.

As soon as the bread is put in front of the men, the captain shouts out '*Mangez!*' and hungry hands shoot out, leaving only two small pieces of bread on the platter. They laugh at Christopher's shocked expression, but good-naturedly, and soon the volume of talk in the dining room rises as they pass the jug backwards and forwards among them, pouring wine that looks as black as ink into their glasses.

Anthony shovels a large spoonful of the thick soup into his mouth and nods his head towards the captain. The captain raises his glass and shouts out a toast. Christopher raises his glass and takes a mouthful. The wine tastes so strong that it catches in his throat and makes him cough. The men laugh again and even Anthony joins in.

'This is good stuff,' Anthony says with a full mouth. 'Just like Chianti.'

Although the ship is tied up to the quay wall there is still a slight up-and-down motion. As Christopher takes more of his soup and sips his wine, he can feel his stomach becoming uncomfortable. Around him the dining room is now quite warm from the heat of all their bodies, and the smell of fish fills the air. Anthony seems to understand some of what the sailor beside him is saying and attempts to answer him with a mixture of English and Italian. After each man finishes his bowl of soup, he takes out the makings of a cigarette and soon the dining room is full of smoke. Christopher drinks more of the wine to take his mind off his stomach, but his queasiness grows. The ship has taken on an exaggerated motion now and the sound of the men shouting from one end of the table to the other adds to his discomfort. Suddenly he can't take any more, stumbles up from the table and rushes back through the galley and out onto the deck. His stomach erupts and he barely makes it over to the rail to vomit his dinner into the dark Liffey waters below. From inside the dining-room he can hear the sound of laughter and a few cheers.

Feeling weak, he makes his way towards the stern of the ship. There is a wider space here and narrow benches on each side. He sits down on one and breathes deeply. The sea-sickness has subsided and he begins to feel embarrassed. Looking up the river towards the city, he sees a train puffing over the Loopline bridge, sending sparks off into the night sky. The curfew has started and the quays look deserted. Further on up river, past the bridge, he can make out O'Connell Bridge which is almost deserted with just a truck, probably an army tender, driving over from the south Dublin side.

'They mean no harm, *monsieur.*'

Christopher turns around. The captain is leaning against the ship's rail, blowing smoke up into the sky.

'I know,' Christopher says. 'I just had to get out and get some air.'

'You have never sailed before?'

'A few times, but I always took my father's advice and stayed on the open deck.'

'Your father is a wise man. He is a sailor?'

'No. But he went on his honeymoon with my mother to the Isle of Man and never stopped talking about it.'

The captain flicks his cigarette overboard and sits down near Christopher. He stays silent for a while. Finally, he coughs and claps his hands together, rubbing them vigorously.

'This is a cold city, my friend.'

'It is.'

'You are not one for talking, are you?'

'Don't see any reason to.'

The captain leans forward. 'The reason, *monsieur,* is that it is a bad world and people must come together. A lot of Europe was left in ruins by people not talking to each other.'

'With all due respect, Captain Denot, I don't see how it would have made any difference. It seems to me that all they were waiting for was a spark.'

'And that bloody fool Princip gave it to them with his assassination of the archduke and his wife!' The captain shook his head.

'If it wasn't that, it would have been something else.'

'Maybe you are right, young man. But it is all so depressing.' Denot stands up, facing Christopher. 'So, according to my contract, you are the man in charge, *oui*?'

'Yes.'

'Very good. *Donc*, we will cast off in the morning and head east towards Wales. We then turn south and spend some days steaming towards Gibraltar. But first we must stop in Bordeaux to drop our ballast and pick up some barrels of wine for our thirsty revolutionaries. Then, it is on to Fiume and my job is done. In all, about six days.'

'Six days at sea?' Christopher moans.

'Yes. I think that it is better to tell you. We cross the Bay of Biscay the day after tomorrow. That will be the worst.'

Christopher tries to imagine what it's going to be like spending six days in a small ship, swaying from side to side, sipping water and nibbling on some bread. He imagines Nell at home, probably in bed. Would it have been better to go on the run? At least he would be with his own people and not some feckless dreamer. But it's too late to go back. When he looks up, he sees the captain has left him alone to his thoughts and returned to his men. From the direction of the dining room the rise and fall of men's loud voices reach him. Feeling better now, he decides to go to his cabin, but realises that he doesn't know where he'll be sleeping. Reluctantly he gets to his feet and follows the captain back into the dining room.

Back in his seat in the hot, smoky dining room, he finds out that, as it is their last night in port, the captain had allowed more wine to be brought to the table. He tries to catch Anthony's attention but his friend has decided to entertain the crew with a version of an aria from some opera. Christopher has heard it before, many times, usually sung to impress the ladies. Now Anthony stands with his arm around one of the crewmen who is shouting encouragement, his toothless mouth a black maw surrounded by a scruffy beard.

Christopher waits until Anthony has finished and is back sitting beside him.

'Let's get to our cabin— I want to try and get some sleep,' Christopher mutters to him.

'Yessir, my leader,' Anthony replies, and attempts to salute but only manages to fall sideways off his chair much to the amusement to all of the men. He drags himself to his feet and sits down again.

'*You're drunk*,' Christopher hisses.

'Guilty as charged, Your Honour!' Anthony replies and breaks out in a fit of giggles.

Christopher is in no fit state to tolerate this. 'I'm commanding you to stop this foolishness and come with me to the cabin.'

Anthony stands abruptly, straightens himself up and salutes again. He pushes back his chair and marches around the table, his back erect, his face serious. The crewmen, who seem to find his antics very amusing, begin to clap in time to his footsteps. He passes around the far end of the table and returns, sitting down heavily on his chair.

'*Reporting for duty, sir!*' he says, saluting.

'Anthony, look at the men laughing at you – you're making a fool of yourself!'

Anthony, suddenly serious, puts his hand on his shoulder. 'No, Christopher, it's you they're laughing at,' he says. 'You see, we're already in our cabin. We sleep on the floor, here in the dining room.'

The rolling movement of the ship under way and the long, drawn-out sound of a foghorn awaken Christopher from a deep sleep. He is lying sprawled on the floor at one end of the dining room, a woollen blanket pulled up over his head. Beside him Anthony snores loudly, one of his arms spread across Christopher's chest. It had been after midnight by the time the sailors had their fill of wine and left the dining room. He was given a blanket and a thin mattress by the first mate and told to use his bag as a pillow. Now his back feels slightly stiff but, all in all, he feels refreshed. He moves Anthony's arm off his chest, hoping that it will waken him, but after the wine his friend has drunk, the only reaction is a loud snort.

Wondering should he get up or stay where he is, he looks at his watch, trying to see the time. But the pale early morning light that seeps through the portholes is no help. The ship's rolling motion makes the decision for him and he unwraps himself from the blanket and stands up. Although the motion is more severe than the previous evening, he finds that his seasickness is much less than before and he is even hungry.

He rolls his blanket and mattress up and leaves it beside Anthony's snoring form, then attempts to put on his clothes which he had left folded on a chair beside him. He now wonders why he bothered to get undressed. After several attempts he finally manages to get his trousers on, at one stage standing on Anthony's foot. But Anthony merely pulls the leg up to his chest and continues to snore. The rest of his clothes are easier to put on, and, getting his bearings, he makes his way out onto the deck.

Clinging onto the cold metal handrail, he watches the Pigeon

House Fort slide past. As the ship noses its way into Dublin Bay and changes direction, the whole south side of the city lies before him. A train makes its way along the coast, its smokestack belching out black smoke. Sandymount gives way to the tiny town of Blackrock and further up the grey granite of Kingstown harbour reaches out into the Irish Sea. Behind Kingstown he can make out the brooding presence of the Dublin mountains. Not that long ago he was training young men to fight there, but now the mountains seem at peace, silent and dark, not wishing to be disturbed. The ship is making good progress, its prow cutting through the low waves. A cold, invigorating spray from the sea splashes across his face, bringing with it the tangy taste of seawater.

'I see you are feeling better, *mon ami*.'

The captain is standing beside him, rolling a cigarette from a leather pouch of tobacco. He offers the pouch to Christopher when he is finished. Christopher hesitates at first but accepts it and rolls himself a cigarette. The captain cups his hands expertly around the match, creating a small, fleshy cave with his hands and they both light their cigarettes from the flame. Christopher thanks him and takes a drag which burns his throat. He coughs.

'French tobacco, all the way from Bergerac.' The captain laughs and claps him on the back.

They stand side by side, watching a ship coming out through the mouth of Kingstown Harbour.

'The mail boat,' the captain says, 'heading over to Holyhead with its precious cargo of letters.'

He has changed into a new uniform, is freshly shaven and now sports a clean captain's cap. Christopher feels self-conscious beside him, his shirt unbuttoned, his jacket open.

As if reading his mind, the captain says: 'At sea I dress to make an impression. The men need to see that their captain is capable and in control at all times. It is important, no?'

'Of course,' Christopher says.

'A ship, even a ship as small as this, is like a country. It needs a leader, just like your country, is that not so?'

Christopher laughs. 'I'm afraid most of our leaders are on the run.'

'I have heard this,' the captain says, 'but your time will come. Take it from me. Your country will no longer be ruled over by the British, if the majority of the people, in their hearts, do not wish it to be.'

'There are times when I wonder if it's all worth it. What will happen if by some miracle the British do decide to give up? Will our lot improve? Will I be able to afford to put a decent roof over my family's head?'

'That I cannot answer. Now, if you will excuse me, young man, I must go and help the bosun navigate past the Kish Bank or your adventure will be over before it begins.' The captain pats him on the back and leaves.

The ship has now turned away from shore and is heading deeper into the Irish Sea. Behind him the buildings on the coast lose some of their sharpness and he can no longer make out the morning traffic. Out of the lee of the land the breeze now finds ways through his clothing and chills his skin.

The door slams somewhere behind and Anthony Caprani appears, carrying two steaming mugs. He hands one to Christopher

'Thanks.' Christopher takes the mug, blowing on it before sipping.

'It's coffee, I'm afraid.'

'No matter,' Christopher answers, staring ahead where a lone lightvessel marking the Kish Bank is at anchor.

Anthony seems restless, walking up and down the deck sipping his coffee. His hair, usually slicked back from his forehead is now blowing into his face. He tips his mug over the rails, watching the dregs of

220

coffee drip into the sea below.

'I'm sorry about last night, Christopher. I was out of order. It's my first time away from Ireland. I got a bit carried away.'

Christopher turns and looks at his friend. Anthony's face is pale under a dark stubble and his eyes are streaming from the wind.

'You look terrible.'

'You don't look great yourself,' Anthony says with a smile.

'I don't feel it, but it's getting better. It's happened before, going over to France, to fight, but the fresh air helps,' Christopher turns to Anthony. 'About last night. I was the one out of order. I was acting like a high and mighty fool. You volunteered for this mission, you didn't have to and I appreciate that.'

'Is that what Collins told you? The fact is it was either go with you to Italy or else back to the Dublin Mountains to teach those young Volunteers how to crawl around in the wet grass. What would you choose?' Anthony grins.

'After last night, I think I'd take to the mountains.' Christopher takes a sip from his coffee.

'It could be worse, I suppose, you could be living out there.' Anthony nods at the lightvessel just off their starboard bow.

As their ship steams past, a lone sailor on board the lightvessel is emptying waste from a large cauldron into the sea. He waves over at them before disappearing back inside. The seagulls that follow their ship now change their allegiance and peel away towards the other vessel. They fight and squabble over the morsels and appear and disappear with the swell. They have now left Dublin Bay behind and their ship, clear of the Kish Bank, turns slowly and points southwards. The shift in direction has eased the side-to-side motion. Now their bow seems almost eager as it forces its way through the oncoming waves, sending up clouds of salty spray that drive the pair back inside.

✳✳✳✳

The slow-moving ship steams southwards, always within sight of land. There is great excitement on the second day out as the captain orders the bosun to steer even closer to the coast as they approach France. Most of the crew seem to be from Brittany and stand along the rails, like crows, as familiar landmarks slide past.

Unfortunately, that also means that they are heading into the Bay of Biscay. The ship slows down and the captain points the prow into the oncoming waves. Storm clouds gather and the visibility reduces suddenly. The storm drives the sailors back to their duties again. Christopher spends most of the day out on the deck, avoiding the stifling heat in the dining room which is situated over the ship's furnace. But Anthony has been adopted by the crew and has been taught to play piquet, an old French card-game for two players. He even manages to win some hands and when he comes out on deck to show Christopher the cigarettes he has won, Christopher laughs.

'What?' Anthony looks hurt.

'Have you tried them?'

'A cigarette is a cigarette,' Anthony says and lights one up.

Christopher watches as he struggles to cover up a cough, but then has to admit defeat and turn away as a spasm of coughing takes his breath away.

'I was wondering why they pocketed my Golden Flake when they won but put their own on the table when I won,' he says with disgust, but persists with the cigarette.

'Next time use theirs when you're playing,' Christopher advises.

Sometime during the early night they pass by the lighthouse that marks the entrance to La Rochelle harbour. The storm has blown itself out and the temperature has climbed. The frenetic activity of the sailors has stopped and Christopher has the deck to himself again. The wind is blowing off shore directing the smoke from the funnel out towards the sea. The air is now clear and fresh and smells of pine and sand. The stars overhead are the brightest he has even seen, like specks of light glowing unwaveringly through a black screen. He imagines what the same stars would look like to Nell. She can probably only catch an odd glance of the brighter ones through the smog of a typical Dublin night sky. He promises himself that when all this is over, he will take her on a short holiday. He has heard that the night skies in the countryside around Cork and Kerry are similar because of the clear air.

On the deck over theirs, where the bridge is located, he hears the bell signalling ten o'clock. As the final peal fades away one of the crewmen starts to play what resembles an accordion. It is some kind of slow air, and sounds not unlike Irish music. The notes are long and dragged out and another sailor joins in, singing in a deep voice. The song is in French and he cannot understand the words but there is no doubt that the song is about loss. When that song finishes there is a scattered applause and the low mumble of voices. Another song begins, a happier one, and he feels his feet tapping to the tune. At the end of that song, he hears the captain's voice and then the shuffle of feet as the impromptu session is broken up.

The temperature has dropped slightly and reluctantly he makes his way back inside and into the dining room. Under the subdued light coming from the single lamp hanging from the centre of the ceiling, he sees that Anthony has already fallen asleep and is lying on his back, both of his arms outflung.

Christopher takes off his shoes, puts his gun under his seaman's bag, wraps himself up in his woollen blanket and tries to go to sleep. But somewhere below him the ship's engines continue their relentless beat and he can feel the tremors coming up through the deck floor and into his body. He turns onto his stomach, burying his face into his seaman's bag and soon after manages to drift off to sleep.

It is the stillness and lack of movement that brings him out of a deep sleep. The dining room is empty and Anthony is nowhere to be seen. A shaft of sunlight comes through the porthole behind him and he watches the dust mites drifting up towards the ceiling and then disappearing out of the beam. The cook strolls into the dining room, carrying a tray. For once he is out of his stained chef's whites and wears an ill-fitting suit. He puts the tray on the table beside Christopher.

'Now, monsieur, I have been ashore and you can enjoy real bread *et pain au chocolat* straight from the ... *merde*, how you say... *meilleure boulangerie dans la ville* ... best bakery in Bordeaux!'

'We're in Bordeaux?' Christopher says, unwinding himself from the blanket and getting to his feet.

'*Mais oui, monsieur*,' the cook says. 'The second most beautiful city in all of France.'

'After Paris?'

The cook looks horrified. '*Non, monsieur, Rennes*,' he says and leaves the dining room, mumbling to himself.

Christopher gets up and walks over to the table, breathing in the smells. Laid out on the wooden tray there is a large ceramic bowl of steaming coffee and beside it a plate with two chunks of bread and a pastry, with little dishes of butter and jam. He realises how hungry he is and takes up the pastry, dipping it into the coffee before wolfing it down. He has seen the way the French sailors eat their bread, buttering it and tearing it apart, putting the pieces into the coffee and eating it like soup. But that's stale bread and this is so fresh it's still warm. He smothers one piece with butter and jam before eating it, then washes it down with the hot coffee. After barely letting any food past his lips for several days, the simple breakfast tastes like a feast. He takes up the bowl of coffee and makes his way out onto the deck to get his first look at Bordeaux.

The pale sun is shining directly into his face and he has to squint for several seconds. When he can open them properly again, he sees they are on a river. The ship is moored to a quay wall opposite a redbrick warehouse. Along the length of the quay in either direction, what looks like thousands of wooden barrels of wine are stacked, waiting to be loaded onto ships of all shapes and sizes. Next to the *Mercure*, stevedores are rolling wooden barrels into a net, which they then fasten. The crane on their ship lowers a cable and the stevedores attach the hook at the end onto the net then whistle to the crane operator. Slowly the cargo rises into the air and the arm of the crane swings it around over the hold and lowers it into the darkness. Then the empty net appears out of the hold and is swung over onto the quay wall.

As the stevedores roll more barrels onto the net for the next load, Christopher takes his chances during the lull and makes his way past the hold and up to the bow of the ship to get a better view of the port. Their tiny ship is lost among a long line of ships that stretch out all the way down to a bend in the river. Behind the warehouses on the quay, he can see the roofs of buildings stretching away from the river. There seems to be frenetic activity everywhere he looks. A ship's horn sounds out a mournful cry and, several vessels away, a bow swings out into the river. The dark bulk of a ship slowly slips away from the quay wall, pivots slowly around and steams downriver towards the sea. He drinks his coffee as he watches another ship slipping into the vacant berth left by the departing vessel.

The sun shines down from a blue sky directly overhead and he reckons it must be almost midday. He makes his way back towards the dining room and on to the stern of the ship but there is no sign of Anthony anywhere. He asks one of the sailors, using sign language, but the man shrugs and continues scrubbing the deck. Back in the dining room his tray has been taken away. He can hear the cook talking to somebody inside the galley but when he goes in there is nobody else there. The cook is back in his stained uniform and is chopping up a chicken and putting the bits into a large, steaming cauldron.

'Do you know where my friend is?' he asks.

The cook turns to him, winks and points to the floor. 'Below deck. He play cards.'

Christopher goes outside again and makes his way down the gangplank. He looks up to the bridge of the *Mercure* and the captain waves down to him. Out on the river smaller boats crisscross backwards and forwards, carrying smaller loads of cargo from one warehouse to another. The scale of the port is daunting and reminds him of just how small and insignificant his own country is and how hopeless his task. Collins has given him what he calls a 'float' of a hundred and fifty pounds. What if he was to jump ship, find a hotel and write home to Nell? She could join him in Bordeaux with their small savings and together they could take a ship to America and begin a new life.

He hears his name being shouted out. Anthony is standing at the top of the gangplank, his face a picture of sadness. No doubt the games of cards had progressed from cigarettes to money and Anthony has lost.

'*How much?*' he shouts up at him.

Anthony holds out his arms. Everything.

Anthony is a hopeless case. But Christopher too feels hopeless. What if this mad fight for liberty doesn't succeed and there's another hundred years of being ruled over by a disinterested government based in London – what then? Then again, he believes that since the British made that terrible mistake of executing the leaders of the 1916 Rising more and more of the people share the same yearning for freedom.

The thought of what his wife is doing hits him in the stomach and almost takes his breath away. Who is he fooling? He knows Nell. She would never leave Ireland.

Turning his back on the warehouses, he makes his way back up the gangplank.

CHAPTER 24

Byatt and Irvine

Robert Byatt and Harry Irvine make their way down Talbot Street again. Over the past several weeks they have been tuning into the life cycle of the Monto. Now they dress accordingly, both in casual attire, their hats pushed to the back of their heads, their countenance merry, just two men out for an evening's enjoyment. Most of their time has been spent drinking in Shanahan's pub, a rough establishment that serves the most diverse collection of customers that Robert has ever laid his eyes on: businessmen, sailors, students, local workers, some bohemian types and a sprinkling of prostitutes. One of the barmen bemoaned the missing soldiers who used to come there to drink until they passed out. But the increasing attacks on soldiers on the streets has ended that. However, Robert suspects that there are some present dressed in civilian clothes. But nobody seems to care.

On occasional evenings they have visited some of the better brothels, Harry playing too drunk to avail of their services and Robert feigning fussiness, turning down the unfortunate prostitute when he is brought up to the room. Some of the girls seem to be from the country, naive farmers' daughters or poverty-stricken women from the bigger Irish cities, but the rest are street-hardened and alert to any of the questions that Robert asks, and so they decide to concentrate on Shanahan's pub as the best source of local gossip. Robert, with his British accent, usually takes a back seat and looks on as Harry buys drinks all around him, disguising his sexual preferences with loud conversations about the beauties of womanhood.

It is Friday evening and Shanahan's is packed with all of humanity who seem intent on starting their weekends well and drinking as much as they can before the curfew. Enveloped in a cloud of smoke, Harry Irvine is holding court. Now he is becoming a familiar figure. Robert sits beside him, occasionally nodding his head in agreement to some comment Harry has made. Harry, he thinks, is a natural actor. Compared to the man he met several weeks earlier in that dark, seedy restaurant, there is a big difference. Gone is the effeminate, unsure figure who approached him. Now Harry is one of the loudest in the bar and seems to be enjoying his new role as a character about town.

Robert turns his back on Harry and his companions and looks up and down the bar. They have not laid eyes on Phil Shanahan, the owner, yet. Time is running out. Shanahan is their last hope of discovering what happened to Jonathan. As the owner of the bar and a known republican, they hope that he can impart some valuable information. But Shanahan seems to be away a lot of the time. Harry had risked some gentle probing about the owner and found out that Shanahan is becoming more deeply involved in politics.

Staring up at the door marked private, to what must be Shanahan's living quarters, he almost wills the brass door handle to turn, but his wishes are in vain. Curfew is approaching but the pub is packed with customers still.

Harry runs out of the money that Robert gave him that evening and they now sit alone at the bar, their companions having drifted away. A bell sounds, a ship's bell that clangs with urgency. The familiar cry of: '*Have you no homes to go to?*' and '*Curfew time, gentlemen!*' is having no effect. The crowds have stocked up on their drinks and one of them, a musician from a nearby theatre, has commandeered the old piano in the corner. He starts a popular street ballad, 'Sweet Rosie O'Grady', and dozens of lusty men's voices join in the chorus.

The barmen finally give up. They hold a discussion between themselves and one of them approaches the door marked private and raps on it with his knuckles.

Robert grabs Harry's sleeve and nods discreetly towards the door. After several minutes it opens, and there stands Phil Shanahan, at last. He is a tall man and broad, with a handlebar moustache. Taking in the crowd of rowdy customers on the other side of the bar, he makes his way towards the bell. Grabbing the rope in one, brawny hand, he beats the knocker as hard as he can against the bell. But still he is being ignored.

Finally, standing up on the counter, he lets out a bellowing roar: '*Everybody out or I'm calling the police!*'

The singing peters out and Robert can see why. Shanahan is glaring down at his customers. Held casually in his right hand, which is hanging at his side, is a large revolver. The pianist gets up from the piano and bows over to Phil. The rest of the customers begin to finish off their drinks and one by one drift towards the door and out onto the streets. Shanahan jumps down from the bar and has some words with his barmen before heading back towards his living quarters.

Robert strides through the thinning crowd. '*Mr Shanahan! May I have a word?*' he says loudly enough to attract the bar owner's attention.

Shanahan turns and looks Robert up and down, taking his measure. 'What about?' he says.

'Christopher Flinter.' Robert blurts out the name in desperation, hoping that it will bring some recognition.

Shanahan rubs his chin. 'Flinter, you say? Now where did I hear that name before?' He scratches his head. 'You're looking for him?'

'I would like a word with him, yes. It's a long, complicated story. But I would appreciate any help.'

Harry has joined him now, swaying slightly beside him and smiling up into Shanahan's face. It strikes Robert that they must seem a peculiar sight to the bar owner. A sober man accompanied by a drunk. Robert puts his hand on Harry's shoulder:

'Why don't you wait for me here?' he says, hoping the look he has given him will sink through the haze of alcohol.

'Of course!'

Harry hiccups and walks back to the bar.

Shanahan watches him go and turns to Robert again.

'Now that I think about it, there was a young gentleman here a while ago. I think I might have some information inside.' He nods towards his private quarters and, lifting up the bar flap, says, 'Come in.'

Robert stares at the gun which is still hanging from his hand and Shanahan puts it into his pocket.

'Don't worry, tricks of the trade, it's not loaded.'

Robert follows his broad back up a dark hallway. At the end of the hallway a light filters out through a half-open door. Shanahan goes through the doorway and holds it open for Robert to precede him. He closes over the door, then swivels quickly around, the gun back in his hand.

But as he raises the weapon he is stopped in his tracks. The sharp end of a metal blade is held inches from his throat. He hesitates for a split second, weighing up Robert's resolve, but the determined look in his eyes tells him all he wants to know. He drops the gun and it clatters onto the wooden floor. Robert kicks it away and points to one of the armchairs with his sword.

'Sit.'

Shanahan, head shaking but with a smile on his face, goes over to the chair and sits down.

'You don't know what you're doing – you'll never get out of here alive,' he says.

'Then both of us are in the same boat,' Robert says and picks up the heavy revolver.

'Good point.'

Shanahan reaches up to the mantelpiece and picks up a pipe. As Robert watches as he lights it, dragging on it until the tobacco begins to smoulder. When he is happy with the glow, he takes a pull and looks up at Robert.

Keeping the blade pointed at Shanahan, Robert sits facing him. His eyes flick around the room, taking in the dying embers in the fireplace and the old clock on the mantelpiece. There is a window that looks out onto the blackness outside and two other doors leading into the sitting room.

'What's in there?' Robert points.

'That's the bedroom, the other one's the kitchen. Don't worry, I live alone.'

'The way you treat your guests, I'm not surprised,' Robert says, holding up the gun.

Shanahan laughs, then begins to cough. He puts the pipe back onto the mantelpiece and spits into the ashes of the fire.

'Strangers who turn up enquiring about my friends tend to have that effect of me,' he says, wiping spittle off his chin with a handkerchief.

'Christopher Flinter is your friend?'

'I would like to think so. Why are you looking for him? I thought he had earned his pardon from you bastards in the Castle. But it seems not.'

Robert lowers the blade of his swordstick. 'I've nothing to do with Dublin Castle. I'm here on … other business.'

'And what would that be?'

Robert considers the question. What is he really doing here? His brother is dead, but he has already been informed of that. Is it the ignominy of his final resting place, abandoned and forgotten among the grass and weeds in a graveyard far from home, or something more? What would happen after he finds out about Christopher Flinter? Would he find himself chasing another ghost around the streets and laneways of this broken city? But he knows the answer to his own questions: he could never live with himself if he didn't do his best to find out what happened to his brother.

He fishes out the notebook from his pocket and waves it in front of Shanahan.

'This is why I'm here. This is my murdered brother's notebook, and Christopher Flinter's name is one of the few mentioned.'

Shanahan looks at the notebook, then back at Robert.

'What was your brother's name?'

'Jonathan Byatt. Major Jonathan Byatt.'

Shanahan nods and puts the pipe to his mouth, drawing on it, as if contemplating his answer.

'You might be surprised to know that Christopher Flinter was one of only two people at your brother's funeral. The other one was his now wife, Nell Claffey.'

'So, it's true. He was treated differently.'

'I'd go as far to say that his superiors treated him like an animal. If they had their way his murdered body would have been abandoned where he died. As a matter of fact, that was probably not too far from where we're sitting now – in the rat-infested tunnels of the Monto.'

Robert flops back into his chair. It is worse than he had thought.

'Tell me what happened, please,' he says, sliding his blade back into his walking stick.

'Your brother offered Christopher a pardon if he found out the whereabouts of a man with the codename Janus. Janus, among other things, was a serial killer, mostly of prostitutes who lived here in the Monto.'

Robert's face grew pale when he heard the name.

'Go on.'

'Unfortunately, Janus got to your brother before Christopher got to Janus. In the end it was Nell Claffey who saved the day. She shot Janus and rescued Christopher.'

'Janus is dead?'

Shanahan looks uncomfortable and shrugs.

'I thought he was. I was there. He took the shot full in the face. No man – no normal man would have survived the wound. Now, we're not too sure. And that was down to me. I should have gone back down there and made sure. He was the devil himself. When at last I sent some people down the body was gone – but, if he did survive, he could have crawled off and died elsewhere – or the rats could have got him.'

'I still don't fully understand why my brother was buried without any ceremony, in a civilian graveyard. There's not even a gravestone over him.'

'That's the strange part. You'd have thought that the police or the army would have been happy to catch a serial killer. But Christopher thinks that Janus was a double, maybe even a triple agent. And the powers that be over in London weren't happy to lose him.'

Robert looks at him helplessly. 'Where does this leave me now?' he asks, half to himself.

'Christopher's away, I can't say where and I'm not sure when he'll be back.'

'What about this Nell person?'

Shanahan looks uncomfortable. 'You should forget about Nell.'

'I'm afraid it's too late for that, Mr Shanahan – she seems to be the only link to my brother available.'

Shanahan scratches his head. 'I'll be honest, Mr Byatt. I too have a brother and I wouldn't like to be in your position. You haven't heard it from me, but Nell was brought up around here. You could do worse than to keep an eye on Anna Macken's brothel. That's all I'll say.' Shanahan begins to poke at the dying ashes of the fire.

Robert stares at the sparks flying up the chimney as the fire catches light again. Shanahan throws on some loose pieces of turf to keep it going. Maybe it's a metaphor, he thinks. From almost dead ashes a new fire can be started. He takes out his pen and opens up his brother's old notebook. Under the last entry, he writes in the names of Nell and Anna.

'You know, this notebook is like my brother's voice coming back from the grave.'

He snaps the notebook shut and puts it back inside his pocket. Taking the revolver up in his hand, with an expert flick he flips open the chamber and empties the bullets out onto the ground. He hands the gun to Shanahan and prepares to leave. He makes his way over the door and opens it a fraction, looking out into the hall, but it's empty and the voices coming from the bar at the end are reduced to the low mumbling as the last few reluctant customers get ready to depart.

Before he leaves, he turns to Shanahan.

'I want to thank you. You've told me more than you had to.'

Shanahan barks a laugh that leads into another fit of coughing, but when he stops he becomes more serious.

'I hope you have enough sense not to tell anybody of our conversation.'

'Of course not.'

'You never know, Mr Byatt, we might meet again. But the next time I'll be better prepared, mark my words,' Shanahan says with a twinkle in his eyes.

Robert bows his head in acknowledgement and makes his way back down the hallway. When he pushes open the door, it's onto an almost empty barroom. The gas lights are turned up full and two barmen in aprons are trying to make inroads into a counter full of empty glasses, washing and rinsing as quickly as they can so that they can go home. A young helper races around the bar, wiping down tables and emptying ashtrays into a bucket. The barmen look up as he emerges from the private quarters, but go back to their task. They have probably seen stranger people emerging from Phil Shanahan's private quarters.

Robert goes around the bar where his friend Harry Irvine is one of the last customers and is draped across the counter, snoring. Gripping him under the arms, he shakes him gently.

'Come on, Harry boy, we have things to do.

CHAPTER 25

Anna

Anna Macken is woken from her sleep by the loud knocking on her front door. She looks at her watch: half past eight. Probably one of last night's customers with a complaint.

The banging continues. She curses the kitchen maids who are probably too busy gossiping to hear the racket. Reluctantly she gets out of bed, puts on her dressing gown and stumbles over to the window and opens it. She thrusts her head out, ready to hurl a tirade of abuse at the man below, but the sight of an almost unrecognisable Sarah below makes her catch her breath.

'*Sarah, I'll be down in a minute!*' she shouts.

Racing down the stairs, she almost collides with one of the scullery maids and pushes her aside. When she opens the front door Sarah almost falls into the hall. Her dress is torn and covered with black dust and her hair is a mess. Her face is smeared with dirt.

Anna half carries Sarah over to a chair in the hall and shouts over her shoulder at the maid. '*Bring me a shot of whiskey first, then a basin of hot water and a blanket!*'

Sarah's body is shaking as if in great shock. Anna has never seen her like this and she has seen her in ugly situations. Especially after her lover, Moussa, was killed. Moussa, a giant of a man, was not alone her lover but also her protector. Without him she had to put up with the usual disgusting suggestions of some of the drunken men. Now she sits like a tiny broken doll, breathing heavily, her head bent.

The maid comes back with a large glass of whiskey which Anna takes from her and drinks some herself. 'I don't want to kill her with too much!' she snaps at the maid, then tips Sarah's chin up and looks into her tear-stained eyes. 'Here, love, take a few sips of this.'

Sarah accepts the glass and takes a gulp of whiskey, shivering as she swallows. 'Thanks,' she whispers.

'What in God's name happened to you?' Anna demands.

'It's all very hazy. I was doing some shopping and was walking down Mabbot Street on the way back here. Then something was put over my face and I woke up in a cellar of a house.'

'Jesus, Mary and Joseph! What's goin' on? First Kevin, then you!' Anna blesses herself.

'I managed to free myself and crawled up the coal chute. A policeman came into the cellar to rescue me …' Sarah breaks down in tears again.

'What's the matter, child?'

'That monster killed him! Cut his throat like a pig! There was blood everywhere!' Sarah shudders.

'*What?* Who did such a thing?'

Sarah takes another gulp of whiskey and looks at Anna. 'It was Moussa's killer. The man who was killing all of those women.'

'But he's dead, child,' Anna says, patting her hands.

'No. He's not dead. I know what I saw. He was wearing a mask, but I'll never forget those eyes. And he got away!'

Anna feels a chill in her stomach. If what Sarah says is true, then nobody is safe. But is it true? She remembers only too well Phil Shanahan's description of what had occurred that night when Phil, Sarah and Nell had gone down into the tunnels under the Monto. Phil was all praise for Nell, boasting that she had shot the man's head off with her first shot and saved Christopher's life. Then, in subsequent tellings, when Phil was behind his bar, it had gradually turned into 'shot the man's jaw off'. Then there was Kevin's disappearance …

She turns to the maid. 'Get yourself around to Phil Shanahan's pub. Tell him I want to see him immediately, and don't take no for an answer.'

Phil Shanahan stands waiting in front of Anna's desk which sits at one end of her bedroom, the largest room in the house. He has never been asked up here before and so knows that it's serious. Phil supplies all of the drink to Anna's brothel and if he were to lose that he might as well close his doors. Sitting in a chair looking out through the window is Sarah Murphy. He tries to attract her attention to find out what's happened but she just stares resolutely out over the rooftops opposite, refusing to look at him. Behind the screen at the end of the room, he can hear Anna grunting and moaning as she dresses herself, complaining to the maid that it was the wrong dress she had brought her and sending her back to the wardrobe. She finally appears from behind the screen, dismissing the maid who disappears gladly through the door.

'Well, Anna, you're looking well,' Phil lies, with his widest smile. It's the first time he has seen Anna without make-up on and she looks twenty years older.

'Keep it for another time, Phil.'

Phil's heart sinks and he wonders what has happened. With little Sarah present he thinks that one of his customers, or worse, one of his barmen, has interfered with her in some way and he's being held responsible.

'Of course, Anna. What can I do for you?'

Anna takes her place behind the desk, puts on her spectacles and looks up at him.

'Sarah here was drugged and kidnapped from the street, but managed to escape. She tells me that the person responsible was the man from the tunnels, the one responsible for the death of those poor girls. The dead man, according to you.'

Phil's nightmares are coming true, but he's not going to give up yet.

'She's mistaken, Anna. Sure, wasn't I there myself? The man's face was blown clear away – you can ask Sarah.' He looks over at Sarah for support. 'No-one could survive that.'

Sarah shrugs her shoulders and takes a sip of what looks like whiskey.

'That's good to hear, Phil,' says Anna. 'By the way, where's the body buried?'

Phil's mind scrambles for an answer as Anna's eyes bore into his. Why didn't he go back and make sure? 'I hate to say it, Anna, but the man, monster that he was, didn't get a Christian burial. As we speak his skeleton is probably not too far away from where we are. Rats, you know.'

Anna puts her head into her hands and shakes it from side to side then looks up at him.

'In other words, the body was never found, was it, Phil?'

Phil's strained smile is beginning to hurt and the palms of his hands are sweating. This is only the beginning. Sarah will tell Nell and there will be hell to pay. Not to mention how Christopher Flinter will react.

'No, Anna, the body was never found … I'm sorry,' he admits.

'Your apology is a bit late for Kevin, isn't it?'

Anna jumps up from her chair and turns to Sarah. 'You're coming with me.'

'Do I have to? Can't I stay here?'

'No. I need you to tell Nell exactly what you told me.'

'But Nell warned us that we weren't to come near her at work!' Sarah protests in alarm. 'She – she said she might get fired if –'

'If what? If we're not respectable enough for a posh shop?' Anna glowers.

'No, but …'

'Well, she might have a point – but no matter – this is an emergency.'

Anna's car brakes to a sudden stop outside Healy's Department store on Dame Street. The engine splutters a few times, backfires and cuts out. Some passersby duck their heads when they hear the loud backfire, thinking that there may have been another shooting. A man with a walrus moustache glares at Anna as she gets out of the car but Anna ignores him and marches straight ahead.

As Anna pushes through the doors into Healy's, she realises that she doesn't know what department Nell works in. She walks through the ground floor, past the men's clothing section, through the women's and then onto the shoe section, but there is no sign of her daughter. She goes up to the first floor. On this floor are the more esoteric wares: perfumes, lingerie and a large section of home furnishings, but there is still no sign of Nell. She remembers then that Nell had mentioned a secretarial course so she goes up another flight to the offices, knocking on the first door she comes to which is marked private.

A bespectacled man in a waistcoat emerges and takes off his glasses. 'May I help you?' he says, looking Anna up and down, taking in her flamboyant clothes, wrinkling his nose at her perfume.

'Have you never seen a lady before?' Anna snaps.

The man's face reddens. 'I apologise – we don't normally have ladies on this floor.'

'I'm looking for my daughter. She works somewhere in the store, possibly in the offices,' Anna says.

'I see. Her name?'

'Nell Flinter, but I wouldn't put it past her to use her maiden name, Claffey.'

The man looks up and studies the ceiling, mouthing the two names to himself.

'No. I'm afraid neither of those names are familiar,' he says finally.

'But she does work here!'

'Madam, I am the general manager. I make it my business to know everyone who works in the store and I am sure that I have never heard either of those names before.'

'Thank you,' Anna says. 'I'm sorry to disturb you.'

She marches down the stairs and out to her car. She gets in, slamming the door behind her and takes off her hat. She turns to Sarah who is staring straight ahead, avoiding her gaze.

'Well, well, well, I should've known,' Anna says, gripping the steering wheel. 'Why didn't you at least stop me making a fool of myself. Nell doesn't work in there, does she?'

Sarah avoids her gaze and begins to fidget.

'What do you have to say for yourself, young lady?' Anna says, prodding her arm with an accusing finger.

'Nell told me not to tell you. She said you would be upset,' Sarah admits, hanging her head down.

'Of course I'm upset! She lied to me, her mother!'

Anna opens her handbag and takes out her cigarettes. She lights one up, inhaling deeply. Then she turns on Sarah again.

'Why did she tell me she had a job at Healy's? Is she working in the fish market and too ashamed of it?'

'I'll let Nell tell you. I don't want to break a promise,' Sarah says, looking away.

'You girls!' Anna says, shaking her head and picking a stray piece of tobacco from her lip.

A policeman passes by, staring in at the two women but Anna just returns his stare and he continues on his way towards Trinity College.

Anna smokes her cigarette for a while, thinking.

Then she stubs her cigarette out and prepares the car for starting. She gets out and stands at the bonnet, looking around. Eventually a young man approaches and she asks for help to crank the engine. When the car comes to life, Anna puts some coins in his hand and sits in again beside Sarah.

'There's only one way to find out, isn't there?' she says, then pulls away from the pavement. She strains at the steering wheel to turn the car in the opposite direction and swings around across Dame Street. Sarah bends her head down in discomfort as the sudden moves frighten the horses of a passing carriage. The shouts of protest from other drivers fill the air but Anna ignores them and continues towards the Liberties.

It's early evening and Nell is cooking her dinner when she hears the banging on her door. She takes the pot off the flame and switches off the gas, hoping that the caller may go away, but the banging continues. The last thing she wants is Mary Sherry coming down to investigate Christopher's continued absence. She can normally tell by the volume and the pattern of the knocking who it is. Mary Sherry's is gentle but insistent while her husband's knock is louder but more spaced apart as if he almost apologising. But this is neither of these and when she opens the door her mother barges past her into the room with Sarah following behind, her head bent, avoiding her gaze.

'Well, come in, why don't ye?' Nell says to her mother and slams the door shut.

'You have some nerve!' Anna says, hands on her hips, ready for a fight.

Nell faces her mother and by the look on Sarah's face can almost guess what's coming next. Her mother's face, without any make-up, looks old and tired. To try and put off the inevitable, she goes back to the stove and begins stirring the stew. Her mother pulls out a chair at the table and lowers herself into it, Sarah taking the one beside her. If her mother looks older, Sarah looks younger, like a little girl who's just lost her doll. Her face, small and pretty, is also free of make-up, but unlike Anna's still has a look of innocence, even after everything she has seen in her life: the boisterous life of a brothel, the loss of her lover and her new-found spirit of revolution.

Nell eventually gives in and joins the two women at the table, ready for an argument.

'We've just come from Healy's,' her mother says, 'and nobody there has ever heard of Nell Claffey *or* Nell Flinter. I've never been so embarrassed in all my life. What's going on, Nell?'

Nell composes herself, her alibi already well-rehearsed.

'That's because I don't work there. I work in Dublin Castle.'

'Dublin Castle! Working for the British?' Anna says, looking from Nell to Sarah.

'Yes. A job is a job, so I took it when I was offered it. I knew you'd be annoyed so I pretended I was working in Healy's.'

Anna looks from Sarah to Nell. Nell is looking straight into her eyes but Sarah still has her head bowed.

'You took a job in Dublin Castle after what they did to Christopher? I don't believe you.' Anna turns to Sarah. 'Look at me and say she's telling the truth.'

Sarah shakes her head: 'Leave me out of this.'

'Very well, Miss High and Mighty, if you're really working in the Castle, you might be able to help your friend here. She was kidnapped and assaulted last night and witnessed the murder of a policeman.'

Nell puts her hand on Sarah's arm. 'No!'

Sarah begins to cry.

'And guess who's behind it?' Anna says triumphantly.

'Don't be gloating, just spit it out!' Nell snaps.

'The man you shot down in those tunnels. It seems he's not quite as dead as you thought and is creeping around Dublin, wearing a mask!'

Nell's blood runs cold. 'But Phil Shanahan ...'

'Phil Shanahan is a liar, just like the rest of them. I've just talked to him. Says the rats probably got him. A full-grown man. Who does he think he's talking to? He should have gone back to make sure.'

Anna gets up from her chair and begins to pace the room, thinking and mumbling to herself as she sometimes does before coming to a decision. She likes to portray a world-wise and tough woman, but underneath all of her bravado she's frightened.

'You've got to tell Christopher, he'll know what to do,' she says. 'This is turning into a nightmare. First, I lose Kevin, then Sarah is assaulted in broad daylight.' She stops her pacing and looks at Nell. 'We have to talk to Christopher immediately. He's at work, I take it?'

A guilty silence descends on the room. From somewhere outside the sound of Anna's car horn sounds and they can hear the laughter of children gradually growing fainter as they run away. Anna takes her place back at the table and takes out a packet of cigarettes, taking one out with trembling fingers and putting it to her lips. She offers them to Sarah and Nell who shake their heads. After lighting a cigarette, she looks at them.

'Don't take me for an old fool. There's something you two aren't telling me. I know you're involved with Cumann na mBan, Sarah. And you, Nell, you've no love for the British, yet here you are, working for them. And you haven't answered my question. Is Christopher at work?' Anna looks from one to the other.

Nell gets up from the table, sighing. Taking a small bottle of whiskey from the sideboard she pours Anna a large measure.

'Drink this, you'll need it,' Nell says, and over the next half an hour she tells a shocked Anna everything.

When Nell has finished her story, Anna puts her head into her hands. Nell goes to comfort her but she holds her hand up.

'Stop, just let me think for a while.'

Nell and Sarah exchange glances and wait. Anna is mumbling to herself again but the sounds are as unintelligible as before. She seems to be arguing back and forwards almost as if she is in a trance. Finally, she stops mumbling, sits up straight and looks over at them.

'I've come to a decision,' she says, and begins to put on her gloves. 'You will both come with me now. Christopher is no longer around to protect you but I am. You're both coming back with me, to the Monto. The Castle is too near to where you live and you have to get there and back every day. It'll not take that monster long to find you. I have a new doorman, Brendan – he'll be your bodyguard and travel in with you, there and back. He does nothing all day anyway so at least he'll earn his money.'

'I think your mother is right, Nell,' says Sarah. 'This man isn't going to stop until he finds you. Why don't you do as she asks, at least until Christopher comes home?'

'I don't know, it feels like I'm running away, and I've never done that before.'

'Don't talk like a fool, Nell,' says Anna. 'You're just taking reasonable precautions. You can have the old mews out the back – you and Christopher will be snug in there when he gets back.'

'You have it all worked out. It's what you've wanted all along, isn't it?' Nell says.

'That's not true, Nell. Yes, I admit I hate this place and despair every time I visit, but it's your home and I would never ask you to leave it except that now you're in danger and need protection. Anyway, it'll only be until Christopher comes back – then you can make other arrangements if it doesn't suit.'

Nell looks around the flat, taking in her little kingdom. At the sideboard with the photographs and the ornaments she has collected. At the pieces of furniture that she and Christopher have furnished the place with. How could she allow some spectre from her past force her from the place she now calls home? A place where she and Christopher, even though they've had their share of problems, have had so many happy times. Then she thinks of Janus and what has just happened to Sarah.

She turns to her mother.

'Alright. You win.'

CHAPTER 26

Burns

John Charles Burns begins to pack his jewellery sample case and prepare for another day on the streets of Dublin. Under the velvet-lined tray of engagement rings he places his Webley revolver and a box of ammunition. He places another tray of necklaces over this and closes over the sample case, locks it carefully and puts the tiny key under the band inside his homburg. A sudden knock on the door makes his heart race and he makes a grab for his homburg to get the key, but then he remembers that he has ordered breakfast in his room the night before.

The hotel he is staying in, the Granville Hotel, is perfect. There is a fire escape at the end of his corridor and his room has a window overlooking the main street of the capital, Sackville Street. The hotel is filled mainly with salesmen, like himself, and the banter in the evening is usually about everything under the sun, except the sporadic gun battles on the streets outside, which suits him. The staff in the hotel are diplomatic to a fault and not one has mentioned the occasional prostitute he brings up to his room to ease his loneliness. On one occasion he had left his Webley revolver behind on the bed and was convinced he had lost it and was ready for a bawling out in Dublin Castle when he went up there for a replacement. But when he returned that evening, it lay in the middle of the newly made-up bed and nothing was mentioned of it since.

Burns is one of the many new British agents in Dublin, so many now that it's almost a competition to see who can kill or capture the leaders of the rebellion. The killings in the capital are escalating on both sides as the British forces and the Irish rebels attempt to get the upper hand. Burns, a British army veteran from Manchester with Irish parents, is not afraid of danger. An ex-sergeant from the Royal Field Artillery, he looks on this as a golden opportunity and is intent on making a name for himself in this backwater of the British Empire. Already he has infiltrated the Gaelic League in London for British army intelligence and has the names of several Sinn Féin contacts.

Burns, at thirty-seven, is desperate for promotion. Made an NCO at the height of the Great War, he was convinced that he would be made an officer in the field, but even though his service was exemplary, the promotion never came. But if he can prove himself a loyal British subject by helping rid the capital of the hard core of Irish rebels, he thinks that all will change and his dream will be fulfilled: he can return to England a lieutenant, or even a captain.

Today he is hoping to meet the man who can make that dream come true, a man who claims to be able to identify and locate the biggest bogeyman in Ireland: Michael Collins. And there is another bonus: he had heard that Winston Churchill had put a £5,000 bounty on Collins' head. In one swoop he would get the recognition he needs and enough money to return home in style. Not that he holds out too much hope as Collins has eluded the best brains in Dublin Castle. The note had been hand-delivered the previous evening while he was at supper. He had raced outside but the streets, due to the curfew, were empty. Whoever it was must either have been very lucky not to be picked up by an army patrol or else he knew his way around the streets and side streets of Dublin.

After his breakfast, he makes his way down to the reception desk at the same time as usual and asks if there is any post for him. The receptionist reaches behind and takes out three letters and hands them to him. He examines the postmarks of each: two are from the Dublin sorting office and the other has a Manchester postmark. The Dublin letters he sent himself the day before to reinforce the lie that he is a working salesman. Tipping his hat to the receptionist he makes his way outside, tears up the letters he had sent to himself and puts them into a rubbish bin. He opens the other one. It is his mother, and, as he suspected, she is asking for more money. His father has once again lost their monthly rent after a visit to Chester racecourse. This letter he tears up into tiny pieces and throws it into the air, watching the tiny pieces of paper floating in the direction of the Liffey.

Besides his living expenses and a few extra pounds for spending, his finances are in a dire state and every letter he receives from his mother reminds him of this and puts him into a worse humour. Each letter is like a reminder of his failure. But he is not a quitter and, tightening his grip on his sample bag and pulling down the rim of his homburg, he heads down Sackville Street towards his rendezvous and what he hopes is a worthwhile source of information.

As he makes his way across O'Connell Bridge towards the south of the city, he fingers the envelope he received the night before. The whole episode is a mystery. Obviously, the letter writer is male, rich and sophisticated, unlike some of the characters he had approached in Dublin so far. The writing paper and the envelope are of superior quality which indicate that the person is also not without means. But the syntax of the letter is unusual. In one or two places, words lapse into American English: *defense* not *defence*. It's as if the person was trying to hide his background but at times it had slipped his mind.

Bewleys Oriental Café is a step up for him. The venue is a welcome change to the furtive meetings in dark doorways or back alleys where he normally plies his trade. It is expensive and exclusive to the Dublin middle classes, but the letter writer will be paying. The other positive is its location: just around the corner from Dublin Castle, so he needn't be looking over his shoulder all of the time.

The café, after the morning rush hour, has few customers. As soon as he walks through the door, he becomes aware of a man waving to him from a booth towards the back. He makes his way through the tables and takes a seat opposite the mystery man, placing his sample case under the table. The man, who is wearing a heavy topcoat with the collar pulled up, nods. Sitting directly across from him, he can now see that the man is wearing a mask over the bottom half of his face. He had seen quite a few of the maimed and injured after the war. He extends his hand.

'John Burns, at your service.' He smiles, noticing the strong grip of the man opposite.

The man replies with what sounds like a single word that seems to have almost a gasp in the middle but he realises that he is telling him his name: 'Levonmordaunt.'

Levon Mordaunt's voice has a strange liquid-sounding lisp but is just about understandable. It comes through the slit in the mask that has been painted as an unsmiling mouth. But he has seen worse in the many hospitals he visited after the war to commiserate with old comrades. The man puts his hand up for service and a young woman dressed in the black-and-white uniform comes over to the table. She seems nervous and he notices that she stands away from Mordaunt, probably due to his disfigurement. Or maybe it's something else, something more primeval. Mordaunt is a large man and his presence is formidable. He looms over the table and probably looks like a monster to the poor girl.

'Coffee, please. And some of those fancy cream cakes from the display,' Burns says.

The waitress writes down his order and leaves.

'I received your letter last night and I must say I was a bit puzzled. Something about information you wish to pass on?' Burns says, trying to sound casual. He takes his hat off and puts it on the chair beside him.

'Yes.'

'But why would a travelling salesman –'

'Don't waste my time,' Mordaunt says, each distorted word dragged out from the depths of his chest and sounding painful. 'You're here, like all the rest of your kind, to gain grace and glory.'

'That information, Mr Mordaunt, could get you arrested.'

'If I know who you are, who else knows?'

Burns raises his hands up in surrender and smiles. 'Very well, but I had to be careful. I admit to being an agent of the Crown. Now what can you tell me?'

'It is what we can do for each other,' Mordaunt says.

Burns is disappointed. Just another snitch, even if a well-dressed one, trying to sell him information which is probably useless. He has wasted tens of pounds on snitches already and all he has to show for it are the identities of some low-level couriers. Now his cupboard is bare.

The waitress comes back to the table carrying a three-tier silver cake stand, each tier with a selection of dainty cakes, and puts it down beside him. Burns selects three of the cakes from the stand and puts them on the plate in front of him. He takes one in his hand, the largest, a pastry bursting with cream and topped with chocolate, and bites into it. The taste of the fresh cream combined with the chocolate is incredible. When he has finished that cake, he chooses another one as the waitress puts his coffee on the table beside him.

'If you're here to sell information, you've come to the wrong man,' he says, and starts on the second cake, a sponge covered in icing with a tiny piece of candied fruit on top.

Mordaunt leans over the table. 'I know that is not true.'

Burns looks at his watch. 'Very well. I'll give you ten minutes.' He dabs at his moustache with his napkin. 'Tell me what you've got.' He runs his tongue around his teeth, picking out crumbs.

'What I've got, John ... is it alright if I call you John?'

'You can call me whatever you like – just get on with it.'

'What if I was to tell you that I know the identity and whereabouts of most of the leaders of Sinn Féin: Mulcahy, Collins, McKee, Thornton –

"Stop, stop, stop!' Burns holds up his hand. 'What makes you think I don't know where any of these men are? I can walk over to Abbey Street right now and arrest McKee.'

'On your own?'

'Are you calling me a coward?'

'No. But he has already moved to a safe house in Phibsborough.'

'Says who?'

'I know where you get your information and I know it's already out of date. You pay pennies to your informants, who are mostly IRA plants. The rest of the time you struggle around the streets of Dublin picking up bits of information here and there. If not on the streets you meet up with your fellow spies in the Cairo Café and spin yarns about your exploits. Am I right?'

Burns, a proud man, struggles with Mordaunt's painfully slow but accurate description of his endeavours. He seems to know what he's talking about and he wishes he had met him earlier. And that about summed up his life: always just about reaching his destination but never arriving. If he makes another trip to Dublin Castle and asks for more money, he knows he will be refused. Mordaunt is like a mirror, reflecting back all of his failures, and there is nowhere to hide.

'If I'm so useless, what am I doing here?' Burns holds out his arms and looks around him.

'Nobody said useless, John. Just misguided.'

'Let's cut to the chase. What do you want?'

'Do you know of a Captain Benjamin Stern?'

The question catches Burns off guard. He knows of Stern. Has seen him a few times in the Castle Yard coming or going to his office. Rumour has it that he is in Dublin against his will and is waiting for a transfer. But he is a man who keeps to himself.

'The Jew? I've seen him around and about. Seldom see him doing anything useful. Waiting around for a transfer. Bit of a playboy, if you ask me.'

'Tell me more,' Mordaunt stiffens, like a hunting dog on the scent.

'He's been seen sniffing around one of the secretaries. Not very officer class, if you see what I mean. Why do you ask?'

'Let's just say that I had dealings with him but he seems to be avoiding me. And the transfer?'

Burns takes up his coffee cup and sips the cold coffee to give himself time to think. If he didn't know better, he would have said that Mordaunt might have been sweet on the good captain. But that didn't make sense as Stern is a career soldier and even if his flirtation with the secretary was a ploy, he would have been found out by now and in any case at least someone in the Castle would know it.

'Wants to go to the Holy Land. There are rumours of some kind of disturbances.'

'Captain Benjamin Stern is a Zionist?'

'Whatever that means,' Burns says. 'I just know he shows sweet Fanny Adams interest in his job.'

'That would explain some things,' Mordaunt says, half to himself.

Burns looks at his watch. It's approaching midday and there are more customers coming into the café, some of them glancing at the strange man sitting opposite him. A part of him wants to leave and get away from Mordaunt, but another part, the part that got him through the war and onto the payroll of the army secret service keeps him seated. But then a thought occurs to him: what if Mordaunt needs him more than he is letting on? With a face like that it's a wonder he's even going out in full daylight. He senses a voice at the back of his mind, and it's telling him to test Mordaunt's mettle.

'Well,' he says, standing up and putting his hat on, 'it's been wonderful to meet you and I'm sorry if I didn't come up to your expectations.'

Mordaunt points at the chair. 'Sit. I'm not finished.'

'I'm afraid I have to be somewhere else,' Burns says, and reaches under the table for his sample case. When he straightens up again Mordaunt has his wallet out and is flicking through the notes inside. Burns can see a thick wad of five-pound notes, more than he has ever seen together in his life. He takes his seat again and waits. Mordaunt takes out some of the notes and fans them out on the table. Burns counts eight five-pound notes, forty pounds: a small fortune. He can feel his mouth salivate and reaches over for them. But Mordaunt is faster and slams his hand over the notes.

'Don't be so quick to take the money – you don't know what I want yet.'

'That's true,' Burns says, leaning back in his chair.

Mordaunt tries to laugh. It's the strangest noise Burns has ever heard, a liquid cackle that ends in a fit of coughing. More people are looking at them and he is beginning to feel embarrassed but Mordaunt doesn't seem to notice them. When the fit of coughing is over, he pushes the notes over the table to him.

Burns gathers up the notes, which are brand new, folds them and puts them into his pocket.

'They say fools jump in … where angels fear to tread,' Mordaunt says.

'They also say a fool and his money are easily parted,' Burns replies.

'*Touché.*'

Burns is already spending the money. He will send five pounds over to his mother to help with the rent, but telling her that will be the last she'll get from him. Then tonight he will make a trip to the Monto and pick up one of the better prostitutes, or maybe even visit one of the bigger brothels. It would tickle him to rub shoulders with the higher-ups. After that, who knows? No contract had been signed – if he didn't like what he was asked to do he would just play Mordaunt along for a while, until the money is gone. Then, if there is trouble, some of his fellow agents would help. One or two of them owe him.

'Well, let's see what you have for me?' Burns sits back in his chair.

'I'm looking for the whereabouts of a man.'

Burns is confused. First by the mention of Stern's name, and now a mystery man. Maybe he was right the first time. Maybe it is some sort of a secret perverts' club.

'Have you tried any of the parks in Dublin?' he says with distaste.

'No, you fool! It's not for that. I need to know the whereabouts of a Christopher Flinter, possibly living or used to live in the Liberties.'

Burns doesn't know the Liberties but has passed it by and heard the district being mentioned a few times by the other agents.

'It just so happens that I know that particular area very well,' he says with a confident smile, 'but it's large and overpopulated. Mostly tenements. Home to several thousand close-knit people. It will be a hard task to get any information from them.'

Mordaunt takes out his wallet again and counts out some more five-pound notes. He holds them up for Burns to see and, just when he is reaching out to grab the notes, tears them across the middle, handing the man opposite one half of the torn notes and putting the other halves back into his wallet.

'That might encourage you to try harder,' Mordaunt says.

'Very clever, Mr Mordaunt. And what if I find him, what do I do then?'

Mordaunt reaches out and grabs his hand, squeezing it with such force that he can feel the bones rubbing up against each other.

'Nothing. You come to me and me only, is that understood?'

'Of course!' Burns cries out.

The background conversation in the café drops and the two men are becoming a source of attention. Mordaunt releases his hand and sits back. The grip had been so strong that the back of Burns' hand is bruised and he suspects that his little finger might even be dislocated.

'And don't take me for a fool. If you don't find Flinter, I'll take a trip down to the Granville Hotel and demand my money back. Are we clear?' Mordaunt says, locking his eyes into Burns with such an intense look that the café around them seems to disappear and all that's left are Mordaunt's eyes which burn into his very being.

'Don't you worry, you're in good hands,' Burns says, already thinking of changing his address.

CHAPTER 27

Nell and Stern

Nell changes her daily routine and takes a different route every weekday morning from Anna's house in the Monto to Dublin Castle. Sometimes she takes the northern route, crossing Sackville Street and going as far as Little Mary Street and then turns down Capel Street, all the time being shadowed by Anna's doorman. At other times it's more direct, cutting up one or other of the quays and joining the bustle of other workers who are trying keep a semblance of normality in their lives after the arrival of the Auxiliaries and the so-called 'Black and Tans' who seem more uncouth than the regular soldiers. Small platoons of them, dressed in the mismatched uniforms that has earned them their nickname, roam the streets looking for any excuse to search a person, man or woman. The only people who seem to be happy with their arrival in Dublin are the bar owners as they have become their best customers. Dublin Castle has also changed. Now all of the entrances are guarded by soldiers squatting behind sandbags and barbed wire.

When the weather is fine, Nell often finds herself taking the longer route, wandering across the Liffey to the south side to follow the banks of the canal, cutting off down Baggot Street and on past the Shelbourne Hotel. She finds her thoughts drifting back to her lunch with Benjamin Stern and wonders if it's Christopher's absence that has caused this. Her life in the Liberties since their marriage, she has come to realise, has not been an easy one. But now that she is back in the Monto and living under Anna's roof again, she has the time to contrast and compare her old life with the new.

In the evenings everything has changed for the better. Sarah has taken her old room in the basement of the house and Anna has kept to her word and insisted on bringing in a builder to convert the old stables into a small but comfortable mews house. The only sounds are from the occasional carriage passing up the laneway to the rear or the faint sounds coming from Amiens Street train station. She doesn't have to cook anymore and she finds herself having more time to read again.

Anna has organised it that the brothel's nightly buffet is laid out earlier and Nell has the pick of it for her dinner. Without the custom of the soldiers the brothel has become less busy. Now most of the customers are businessmen or higher-paid civil servants with the odd sprinkling of students from rich families who have money to spare. Her daily meetings with Crotty are on hold after she told him why she was moving and they only meet now when she has important intelligence to pass on.

As late April gives way to May she finds herself thinking less and less of Christopher and feels guilty. The one letter she had received from him was through Crotty and had just mentioned his arrival in Fiume. It was dated several weeks earlier and was the first letter she had ever received from him. Although his handwriting was neat and readable, the language was awkward and the spelling not much better. When she should have been thrilled about its arrival, all she felt, after the initial excitement, was a growing sense of loneliness. But she hasn't time to dwell on her feelings as the gun battles in the streets are growing more frequent and more savage and the atmosphere in and around Dublin Castle is tense. Michael Collins' squad of men is proving lethal. They carry out brutal assassinations during the daylight hours and melt away into the surroundings crowds. That leads to retaliation, mainly from the Auxiliaries, who arrest suspects and burn their homes. And so, the vicious cycle begins again.

Nell skips her normal lunchtime routine. Instead, she finishes off the last of the typing and stacks the sheets neatly in the out-tray. It's past three o'clock and the office is quiet. Looking through the window she can see that the rain has eased off and the sunlight is struggling to find a way through the low clouds. She puts on her coat and takes her lunch from the drawer. The one benefit of working through her lunch hour is that she's sure that her favourite bench in the yard outside will be free.

By the time she makes her way outside and reaches the bench, the clouds have completely passed. Taking out her handkerchief she wipes the rain from the bench and sits down. A convoy of vehicles is coming through the gates of the castle yard from Dame Street and trundle past her, black smoke pouring from their exhausts. She waits until the air has cleared and unwraps her lunch. Sarah has made her cheese sandwiches with pickles. She's halfway through her first sandwich when there's a commotion coming from the direction of the Ship Street gates.

A platoon of troops runs into the yard, their rifles unslung. From somewhere outside she hears sporadic shooting. A bullet ricochets off a wall quite near to where she sits, knocking chips of granite from the wall.

'*Nell, get down!*'

One of the soldiers is Captain Benjamin Stern and he's shouting across to her and gesturing with his arms. She has never seen him like this before. Normally he is a quiet presence in the office and seems to spend most of his time smoking a pipe and staring out through the window. Now he is a changed man, issuing orders to the soldiers in a controlled voice, running backwards and forwards as he organises an orderly retreat from the gate. Nell gets up from the bench and stumbles towards the entrance to the offices. Once inside she looks back into the yard, anxious for the life of the captain and yet, at the time, feeling that same haunting guilt.

One of the soldiers staggers forward and falls onto the ground. Benjamin turns back and directs two of the other men to pick him up. While they are helping the wounded man limp into the shelter of the main building, Benjamin has taken his rifle and is aiming and firing towards the Ship Street gate. The firing from outside the Castle becomes even more sporadic and stops altogether. One of the two trucks that had come into the yard earlier races back out into the street in pursuit, hoping to catch the rebels. But Nell knows the assailants will have already disappeared, melted into the city.

As the street battles have been escalating in Dublin, Nell isn't completely shocked by what has occurred, but is still surprised that Collins had ordered an attack, even on such a small scale, on Dublin Castle itself. The arrival of the Auxiliaries and Black and Tans in Dublin and the constant British army raids and arrests happening across the city had quietened the IRA. But knowing what she did about Collins, Nell had an idea that it was the very time that Collins would strike back, but not on such a target. The shooting has now completely stopped and medics are running towards the small band of soldiers who had been under attack. It seems that one of the soldiers is hit, but not badly, and after a few minutes he is able to make his way back towards the dispensary with the help of the medical orderlies. But then she realises that there is another body on the cobblestones. It lies, sprawled, in an unnatural pose. There is no movement from the soldier and he's too far away to identify. Some of the men have taken off their helmets while another medical orderly struggles with a wound. More of the stricken soldier's comrades pour out of the barracks and sprint towards him.

Without thinking she runs towards the growing group of soldiers in the yard, her heart pounding. The thought foremost in her mind is that the soldier lying on the ground might be that of Captain Benjamin Stern and it is almost too horrible to imagine. She pushes her way through the gathering crowd of men until she is looking down on the injured soldier. She realises straight away that it isn't Benjamin. Then her eyes drifts down to the wound. He has been shot through the back and the bullet has erupted out through his stomach. Now his intestines lie exposed and quivering outside of his uniform. The sight of the gaping wound and the visceral anger coming from the man's comrades, some of it directed at her, make her feel lightheaded. The wounded soldier on the ground is shouting out for his mother and gasping for breath. As the medic works furiously on his wound, he tries to sit up. His right arm reaches out, hand extended, as if greeting somebody and then suddenly, as if somebody had switched out a light, his body goes slack and he is gone.

Nell turns away from the scene and begins to push her way through the tightly packed soldiers. Soon she is in their midst. Word passes through them like an invisible thread that their comrade is dead. Their anger is palpable and they ignore her pleas to get through. She feels constricted and short of breath and her heart begins to pound. Her breath comes in short bursts and she lifts her head towards the sky looking for respite, anything to avoid the angry faces around her. But the surge of bodies continues and she imagines that there is no way out and that she is trapped by hundreds, possibly thousands of men. The faces are now spinning around her, over her, and she feels that she can no longer breathe. She feels faint and falls to the ground. As the darkness descends the tiny piece of sky that represents survival to her begins to recede until it is just a bright dot in the distance.

When she wakes up, at first she doesn't recognise her surroundings. The bed she is stretched out on is a single bed with a hard mattress. Somebody has covered her with a blanket. Across from the bed her coat is draped over a chair and her hat is on a small wooden chest of drawers beside it. There is one small window in the room which is slightly open. Through it she can hear the faint shouts of commands from outside.

It all slowly comes back to her. She remembers the soldier dying in the yard and her attempt to push her way through the crowd. She remembers the horrible sensation of fainting … and after that nothing … until she came to her senses as she was being carried by Benjamin to this room. As she was still in shock he gave her a hefty measure of whiskey and made her lie down. So she fell asleep.

She looks around the sparsely furnished room more closely. It is long and narrow. Apart from the bed and the chest of drawers and chair across from it, there is a tall, wooden locker at the end furthest from the door and beside this an army chest. Other than a picture of King George which hangs on the wall over the chest of drawers, the room is bare.

Benjamin has left a glass of water on the chair and she suddenly realises how dry her mouth is. She pushes down the blanket and sits on the side of the bed. Other than the occasional shouts coming from outside there are no other noises. She gets up quickly, takes up the glass of water and drinks it back in one, long, drink. She is sitting on the side of the bed, lacing up her boots when she hears the sound of tapping on the door.

'Yes?' She stands up, and faces the door.

The door opens and Captain Benjamin Stern's head appears. He steps inside. He is, once again, the person that she has come to know, and not the man of action that she had witnessed during the attack. He has a sheepish smile on his face. She remembers her feelings of distress when she had thought he was injured and lying in the yard and blushes.

'You've found your things, I see,' he says, looking around the room, avoiding her eyes.

'I did, thank you, Captain.'

'I told you before, it's Benjamin.'

'Thank you, Benjamin. I'm sorry – I fell asleep.'

'Blame the whiskey I dosed you with!'

'How long did I sleep?'

'Just an hour.'

'I have to get back to work.' Nell reaches out and picks up her coat and hat.

'It's too late for that now. But don't worry – tomorrow I can vouch for the fact you were ill.'

Nell feels slightly disoriented and sits back down on the bed, clutching her coat and hat in her hands.

'Can I get you anything, Nell? You're very pale. A little more whiskey?'

She shakes her head.

'Let me get you some tea from the mess.'

Before she can reply, he goes out, leaving the door ajar.

Through the open door she can see another room, a sitting room. She gets up and wanders inside, carrying her coat and hat. She is curious to see where Benjamin spends his time when he is not on duty. The room is smaller than she had expected, not much larger than the bedroom. But there is a more homely feeling to it as there is a small fire burning in the fireplace with armchairs on either side. Hanging over the fireplace there is a wooden wall clock that ticks away with a steady reassurance. In the centre of the room a small table with one chair takes up most of the available floor space. A wooden writing bureau sits against one wall. Along the top there is a collection of photographs. She goes over to the bureau and studies them. They are typical family photographs mixed in with more military type with Benjamin posing in various different scenes, some of which look exotic with a tall palm three in the background of one and a stone fort, somewhere in a desert, in the background of another. She studies the family portraits looking for a Mrs Stern but doesn't find any and a feeling of relief is quickly followed by feelings of guilt.

'I see you've already met my family.'

Startled at the sudden sound, she turns and Benjamin stands in the doorway with a tray in his hands. He comes in and kicks the door closed with his heel.

Nell sees that there is a teapot with two cups on the tray and a large plate of sandwiches.

'That really wasn't necessary,' she says.

'Rubbish – if I had a mirror, I could show you how pale you are.' He puts the tray onto the table. 'Let's have it beside the fire.'

'That would be nice.'

'Let me take your coat and hat.'

Nell hands him her coat and hat which he hangs up on a hook on the door. He takes off his own uniform jacket and hangs it beside hers.

'We have sugar but I'm afraid there's no fresh milk,' he apologises.

'I drink it either way.'

'A girl after my own heart,' he says, pouring a cup of tea for her. 'Help yourself to sugar.'

She puts sugar in her tea and goes to sit on one of the armchairs beside the fire, wrapping her hands around the warm cup.

Benjamin puts the plate of sandwiches on a coffee table between the two armchairs, then pours himself a cup of tea and sits opposite Nell.

It all feels very intimate and Nell has to keep reminding herself that in Benjamin's mind she is a single woman and that any hint of attraction might be taken up the wrong way. She sips her tea which is strong, almost bitter, and accepts one of the sandwiches from the plate on the tray.

'We call it army meat,' Benjamin jokes as he takes one himself, 'I'm afraid that it's out of a tin.'

Nell takes a bite from the sandwich. 'That's not bad,' she says even though the gelatinous meat tastes over-salty and the texture is unpleasant.

'You needn't lie, they're terrible,' Benjamin admits, laughing, 'but you get used to it.'

'Life in the army can be terrible – why do you do it?'

'It's not all bad, and you get to see the world,' Benjamin says, taking another sandwich.

'But what happened out in the yard, how can you live with that?'

Benjamin takes up a poker that's lying in the fireplace and begins to poke some more life into the fire. Sparks fly up the chimney and when there are more flames, he uses a tongs and puts more coal into the flames.

Nell can see that he is grappling with her question and playing for time, then feels that she had gone too far. After all, Benjamin was part of an army that was subjugating her fellow countrymen and women.

But then he runs his fingers through his hair and looks her in the eyes.

'It's hard for you to understand, Nell, but the army has been my life for over ten years. It's more like a family to me.'

'And you do what your generals say all the time, I suppose?' Nell can feel her sense of injustice rising.

'That's the way it is. We obey the generals and the generals obey the government. So, we follow orders.'

'Even though they can be wrong?'

'Nell, believe me, I'd rather not be here in Ireland. But I have no choice in the matter. I was ordered back on the whim of one of my superiors. And here I am.'

'And where else would you rather be?'

Benjamin gets up from his chair and walks over to the bureau. He takes one of the photographs off and brings it back, showing it to Nell. A man and a woman pose outside a squat, flat-roofed house. It is painted a brilliant white colour and a dog lies sleeping across the porch in front of the entrance. In the background there are palm trees. Both the man and the woman have their hands up to their faces, shielding their eyes from the sun.

'There. That's where I'd rather be,' Benjamin says and takes the photograph back, studying it himself.

'Who are they?'

'My parents. They moved to Palestine last year, to a town called Jaffa. We, I mean the British, have the mandate down there. That's where I'd rather be, not here. And one day, mark my words, I will.'

'The Holy Land?'

Benjamin laughs and goes back to the bureau, placing the photograph back to where it belongs. It amuses Nell to see him taking great care in placing the photograph just so. When he comes back, he turns his back on the fire and clasps his hands behind him.

'Well, it is called the Holy Land, but we prefer to call it home. I mean our people, the Jews.'

'And who lives there now?'

He takes his seat again and seems more animated than he has ever been, like a schoolboy rushing to explain some new discovery.

'That's the wonderful thing, Nell. There are Jews, Arabs, Muslims, Christians, all faiths and none. It's a wonderful place, a giant melting pot of humanity.'

'Unlike Ireland?'

'In some ways we are alike, the Jews and the Irish. For hundreds, even thousands, of years the Jews have been victims. But it's more complicated. The Irish have only one enemy, Great Britain, the Jews had many enemies over the ages.'

'What makes our fight different from yours?'

'That's difficult to answer, Nell. And I think we need something stronger than tea to discuss it.' Benjamin jumps up again and goes back into his bedroom.

It's the most animated Nell has ever seen him. Almost a different person, a younger version of himself. She had seen some of it peeking out when they had lunch in the Shelbourne but after that he seemed to go back into his shell.

She hears him rummaging around in his bedroom and when he returns he is carrying a strange-looking bottle. He fetches two glasses from a shelf and places them on the table. Then he sits again, pulls out the cork of the bottle and pours some of its contents into the glasses.

'Please, try this.' He pushes one glass towards her. 'My father sent it over to me a year ago but I haven't had the chance to share it. My fellow officers are more the brandy type.' He sips from his glass, encouraging Nell.

Tentatively she takes a sip. It has a strange taste which she recognises as aniseed but, after she swallows it, she can feel her throat burning and coughs.

'Oh my God!' she gasps. 'What *is* that?'

'That, Nell, is arak, all the way from Palestine,' Benjamin says with pride and takes another sip.

Nell puts the cup to her mouth, more cautiously this time, and finds that the taste is growing on her.

They sit in silence as they drink, Benjamin with a faraway look in his eyes. She realises that at this moment she feels more comfortable with Benjamin than with anyone else she can think of, except Christopher of course. She finds herself comparing the two men. Where Christopher always seems to be seeking something he can't put into words, Benjamin seems certain of what he wants.

'What do you think?' Benjamin nods at her cup.

'It's very nice,' admits Nell.

The heat from the fire and the arak are having their effect, and she's beginning to feel slightly woozy. The arak is strong. She'd better not drink any more.

He rises and comes to pour some more for her.

'No, no,' she says. 'In fact, I think that I'd better be going home. My aunt will be worried about me if I'm late.'

'Oh,' Benjamin says, a look of disappointment on his face.

He reminds Nell of a child who has just lost a favourite toy.

'I was enjoying our little discussion,' he says.

'Me too,' she says, 'but I must go.' She stands up and puts her glass on the table.

The effects of the arak are even stronger than she had thought and she staggers slightly.

Benjamin jumps up and puts his hands on her shoulders, looking into her eyes.

'Are you sure you're alright?'

'I think so,' Nell says.

Benjamin's hands run down her arms and then around her back. He pulls her towards him.

Nell wants to resist, to pull away from him, but she finds herself falling forward and puts her head on his chest. They stand like that for a while and she can hear the beating of his heart through his shirt. He pulls back slightly and looks down at her, lifting her chin up. She closes her eyes, waiting. The kiss, when it happens, is gentle. She puts her arms around his waist and returns the kiss, but then pulls back when she realises what's happening to her.

'I shouldn't, Benjamin.'

A look of confusion crosses Benjamin's face, then embarrassment. He steps away from her, head bowed.

'I apologise, Nell, I had no right to do that. I assumed ...'

'Don't apologise, Benjamin. Let's blame it on the arak,' Nell says, trying to lighten the mood.

She takes her coat and hat off the back of the door and puts them on. Her fingers feel large and clumsy and she finds it hard to fasten the coat. Benjamin comes over and helps her with the buttons, then puts on his own uniform jacket, places his cap on his head and salutes.

'Captain Stern ready to escort my lady home,' he says, standing erect and opening the door.

'Home?'

'Of course. I can't see you walking home in the evening when all of this is going on. It's only a short distance to the Liberties, but still, anything could happen.'

Nell's mind freezes for a second. At this moment she should be on her way back to the Monto.

'It's not necessary, Benjamin. I know the streets around here better than you. And you're in uniform. I couldn't have that on my conscience if you were caught up in –'

'Listen. I've been around the Liberties before and nobody took any heed. We can use the side gate. Now, let's be on our way.'

He holds the door open for her to leave the room.

'Wait, Benjamin. Close the door. I have a confession to make,' she says.

Benjamin looks apprehensive as he closes the door and turns to her.

'Well? What's this big confession,' he says, reaching out for her hand.

'It's not that big, Benjamin. It's just that it wouldn't do for me to be seen with a British solider in the Liberties,' Nell says, lowering her head.

'I'm so, so sorry, Nell. How stupid of me. Of course … I don't know what to say …'

'Don't worry, Benjamin. But if you want you can accompany me to the gates …' Nell says.

'Of course.'

They make their way down the flights of stairs and through the offices. Outside, thankfully, dusk is approaching. As they make their way across the cobbled yard together very few people pay them any attention. Small patrols are coming and going through the main gate and most of the people working in the offices have already gone home. Before they part at the tall iron gates Benjamin reaches out for her hand and squeezes it before she turns away, stopping to wave back at him.

❋❋❋❋

Unnoticed to either of them a tall man stands in the shadow of the guard's hut outside the gate. He is lighting a cigarette but his hand with the lighted match pauses as he watches.

When Stern disappears back towards the barracks, John Charles Burns considers what he has seen. After a moment he takes out his well-used notebook and writes something into it, then puts it away before he makes his way towards Dame Street in pursuit of the young woman.

As she makes her way towards Christ Church cathedral her manner is unusual. She seems to spend a lot of time looking over her shoulder as if she knows someone is following her. But when she gets past the cathedral she seems to relax. He is in two minds whether to continue. Back at the hotel the serving of dinner will be already underway and he risks missing his evening meal, but there is something about the bearing of the woman that doesn't sit well with him. She enters the warren of streets that is the Liberties. Following her is easy as the streets are teeming with life, mostly poor people who would rather be out in the fresh air than trapped in a tenement.

Eventually she comes to a large, squat, two-storey tenement building and lets herself inside. He takes out his notebook, writes the address and prepares to leave but, just as he turns to go, she emerges again with some post in one hand. He has to turn away and pretend he is lighting a cigarette as she makes her way past him and retraces her steps back towards Dame Street. He follows as she crosses over the city quays and makes her way down towards O'Connell Bridge. He is tempted to turn off towards his hotel on Sackville Street but something keeps him doggedly on her trail. She turns off the quays and makes her way towards Amiens Street train station and he is slightly disappointed. Perhaps she was just taking a train. But no, he follows her all the way to Mabbot Street, the entrance to the Monto. She takes another turn and goes into one of the classier brothels, one that he couldn't afford, and closes the door behind her. He waits for another half hour but there is no sign of her emerging from the building.

Sensing that he has uncovered valuable information for his new employer, Burns emerges from the shadows, smiling, and walks away.

CHAPTER 28

Towards Fiume

The *Mercure* passes the Rock of Gibraltar during the night. Christopher stands leaning against the ship's rails and watches as the pale edifice drifts past. For a moment it seems that their ship is stationary in the water and that the mighty rock, a paler presence in the darkness, is slowly moving to their stern. Anthony Caprani, quieter than usual, stands beside him smoking one of the French cigarettes that he has begged from one of the crew. The pungent smell of the French tobacco drives Christopher upwind of his friend. As Anthony's cigarette glows in the darkness, Christopher considers what he is going to do about him.

The *Mercure*, according to the captain, is going to turn to starboard and hug the shores of North Africa, pass Morocco, Algeria and Tunisia and then swing over towards Sicily, taking on fuel in Palermo. 'There are British warships,' he had told them, 'and I do not want to be boarded.'

'What're you thinking about?' Anthony asks.

'This and that.'

'About Bordeaux ... that won't happen again,' Anthony flicks his glowing cigarette out into the night and watches it all the way down into the sea below.

'How can it? You're broke.' Christopher looks at Anthony but it is too dark to see his eyes.

'You're right, I am. But I've learnt my lesson.'

'It was an expensive lesson, Anthony. You lost everything in that game – what are you going to do now?'

Anthony considers the question. 'I suppose you could sub me a few bob?'

'With what?'

'I know you were given some money, Christopher. How about a loan? I'll pay you when I get back.'

'I'm afraid I can't, Anthony. The money is for our board and keep in Fiume. Who knows how much it's going to cost us and how long we're going have to stay?'

Anthony sighs loudly. 'You win, Christopher. What if you loan me a few quid? That's not going to break the bank of your precious stash.'

Christopher walks across the deck to the illuminated porthole. Facing away from Anthony he unbuttons a fastener and takes the envelope from his inside pocket. He opens it and flicks through the money, taking out two pound notes. He puts the envelope back carefully into his inside pocket and refastens it, then goes back to the rails and hands the notes to Anthony.

'There you are, but I'm making a note of it. And, if you get involved in another card game, you can go back home with the ship and I'll make my own way in Fiume.'

'Thanks, Christopher, I won't let you down,' Anthony says and the two notes disappear into the pocket of his jacket.

The two men stand side by side looking out at the sparkling green sheet of phosphorescence as the ship makes its leisurely way through the sea. They feel the ship changing course and Europe falls away. Although there is a slight breeze on the deck, the air has become warmer since they left the Atlantic behind. One of the sailors appears from the darkness and indicates that they should follow him. They make their way down the deck and around to the starboard side of the ship. The sailor points to a line of lights in the distance.

'Maroc,' he says, pointing across the water.

'Morocco?'

'*Oui.*'

Although they are several miles from land, the smell of the African continent comes across to welcome them. Under the tangy smell of the sea Christopher can get hints of sand and vegetation and wood fires. A bell sounds from somewhere along the coast and the lanterns from fishing boats further in towards the shore can be seen bobbing in the night. The string of lights disappear behind them and only the occasional pinpoint of light disturbs the horizon. Christopher turns to the sailor.

'How far to Algeria?'

'Algerie? Maybe five hours, maybe more.'

Christopher had wanted to catch a glimpse of the Algerian coast. Moussa, the friend who had eventually betrayed him, had encouraged him and Nell to go there with him. They were supposed to buy a house on the beach, Moussa and Sarah and Nell and himself. But, in the end, Christopher had turned the offer down, a decision that lead to Moussa's death and his own injury. He sometimes wondered if he had made the right decision? If he had gone along with the plan, Moussa might still be alive. But then again Janus would also be alive and who knew what damage he would have done. On balance, he thinks that perhaps he did the right thing.

He pulls his jacket tighter against the wind which is now becoming colder.

'I don't think I'll wait up to see it,' he says to the sailor.

'Nothing to see. Tomorrow you will see Tunisie and after, we arrive in Palermo.'

'Palermo? Great!' Anthony says rubbing his hands together in anticipation.

'Maybe we should get some sleep,' Christopher suggests.

As they walk back towards their sleeping space in the dining room, he can almost feel Anthony's excitement at the prospect of landing on Italian soil at last, but he is not looking forward to their arrival. The captain had already told him in confidence that nobody would be let ashore in Palermo as the port was full of tricksters and thieves, not to mention the ladies who plied their trade along the wharf. Christopher was learning a lot from the captain. Although he was one of the crew and mixed freely with them, all of the sailors respected him and followed his orders without question. It was something, he knew, he would have to perfect himself if he was to complete his mission and return home.

'*Palermo!*'

The shout brings Christopher out of a deep sleep. When he wakes and looks around, he finds that he is alone. The movement of the ship, which has been part of his daily life, has stopped.

Outside on the deck the sunshine is intense. The *Mercure* is moored to a concrete pier that juts out from a harbour wall. Already the crane is at work. Below him on the pier two men with a donkey-drawn cart wait for it to be lowered. When the metal bucket lands on the pier they begin to shovel the coal into it, shouting up to the sailors who are lined up along the deck. Some of them are stripped to the waist and enjoying the sunshine and some of them are looking out over the town.

A peculiarly shaped mountain guards one side of the harbour. It reminds Christopher of a monstrous sleeping whale lying in the sun. Surrounding the town, a low range of hills meet up with the mountain which makes it look even more incongruous. He points it out to a nearby member of the crew and asks him in broken French what it is called.

'*Monte Pelligrino!*' the man shouts back.

The two men on the pier have already filled the bucket that had been lowered down by the *Mercure* and the crane swings up and across, depositing the bucket on the deck at the aft of the ship. The coal tumbles out of the bottom of the bucket making a loud, hollow noise as it hits the deck below, then the crane operator lifts the bucket again and swings it over the side to the waiting men.

Behind the harbour the town is spread out along the coast, with a lot of horse-drawn traffic moving up and down the seafront road. The buildings, three and four-storey, are built with sandstone and reflect the morning sun back into Christopher's eyes. To him it is a peaceful scene. He can even see the roof of a church just over the buildings.

'It looks pretty tame to me, but then I suppose I've never been here,' says a voice.

Anthony is standing beside him. He looks smart and had obviously dressed expecting to go ashore – but that was not to be. With the increasing heat of the morning, he has opened his shirt and taken off his tie which hangs listlessly from his hands.

Christopher nods in agreement as they watch the slow pace of the loading. Another cart has come down the pier and has stopped beside the original one. This one is drawn by a horse and is freshly painted. The two men sit up on the seat and smoke their cigarettes, waiting.

The bucket swings over the rails of the ship again and lands gently beside the lead cart. As the two men shovel more coal into it a shouting match develops between the two teams. The sailors drift over to the rails of the *Mercure* to see what is happening and the shouting turns to something else. The four men are now squaring up on the pier. Christopher watches as they begin to push each other, pointing to the *Mercure*, and then he sees the flash of a blade in one of the men's hands. Other people converge on the altercation and it ends quickly, but not before there has been an injury. Some men emerge from the crowd, carrying the victim. They make their way onto the harbour wall and continue towards the town. As quickly as it had begun all now seems to be quiet again. The newly arrived cart pulls up to the metal bucket and the two men begin to shovel the coal from their cart into the bucket. One of them starts to sing something in Italian and the morning returns to its former serenity.

'Jesus, no wonder the captain doesn't want us to go ashore,' Anthony says, scratching his head.

Christopher laughs. 'Always take the advice of an old sea dog,' he says, clapping him on the back. 'I'm off to the bathroom to finish waking up.'

The *Mercure* finishes taking on coal in the early afternoon and edges out of the harbour and into the Mediterranean again. Hugging the coast, it passes through the Messina Strait that evening and sets its course for the Adriatic Sea. Some of the crew have decided to pitch their hammocks under the lee of the bridge. Christopher and Anthony are given accommodation in the crew's quarters, two hammocks in the far end of the cabin nearest to the engine room. After dinner, the crew watch as they clamber up into the canvas beds. Christopher, the taller of the two, climbs in, one leg at a time, and is given a round of applause and a few whistles. Anthony struggles and tips over onto the deck a few times but when he eventually gets the knack is given an even more rowdy round of applause. As the two men get comfortable, the rest of the men finally go to their own hammocks. The comfort of the hammock and the slight motion of the ship lulls Christopher into a deep, dreamless sleep.

The recently declared republic of Fiume is bordered on one side by Italy and Croatia on the other, but most of the population seem to be Italian which suits Anthony particularly. Without any difficulty he finds a *pensione* for them near the harbour. The rate, to Christopher, seems high but after he exchanges twenty pounds in a nearby bank, he receives a small bundle of high-denomination colourful notes, which they celebrate in a restaurant near the *pensione*.

Christopher's first glimpse of Gabriel d'Annunzio, the so-called king of Fiume, is on the morning of their second day in the city. The faraway figure reads aloud from a sheet of paper which he holds in his right hand. The morning sun seems to pick out his small figure as he makes extravagant gestures to emphasise the speech. The crowd around them seem in a good humour. Soldiers mix with civilian men and women. Anthony can't keep his eyes off the brightly dressed women who talk and laugh with the soldiers.

D'Annunzio is standing on the balcony of a baroque building, the old presidential palace, according to Anthony. He is flanked on either side by soldiers and is just about up to their shoulders. Christopher and Anthony push their way through the crowd until they are standing almost underneath the balcony. From this vantage they finally get a close-up view of the general.

D'Annunzio looks to be in his fifties with bulging eyes and a round, bald head. His moustache points upwards and seems to vibrate with his voice. The uniform he is wearing is the most decorated that Christopher has ever seen. A long line of dangling medals runs across his chest and shine in the morning sun. The crowd seem to hang on to his every word and shout their approval in places. The atmosphere in the streets is carnival and street hawkers walk among the people, selling everything from sweets to coloured fans.

A loud cheer goes up when d'Annunzio finishes and Christopher turns to Anthony.

'What was that about?'

'The great leader, apparently, is a poet. He was reading out one of his poems.'

'I thought it was a speech or something,' Christopher says, taking in his surreal surroundings.

The crowd begins to drift away after d'Annunzio disappears through the doors behind him. It is noon and the waiters from various restaurants are setting up tables on the pavement outside their restaurants. The two men head down the street and back to Porto Baross where the *Mercure* is preparing to set sail for Ireland. Anthony is paying more attention to the gaily dressed young women than he is to the pavement and almost walks into a lamppost. They cut across the Corso, the main street in Fiume, and here too the crowds are leaving their places of work. Overhead the sun is at its height and the elegant sandstone buildings lend them some shade until they arrive back at the harbour.

The *Mercure* looks deserted and they walk up the gangplank without meeting any of the sailors. They make their way to the dining room, the centre of the ship, but it too is deserted. They go outside again and walk forward to the bridge.

When they get to the top of the stairs, they bump into Captain

Denot who is emerging from his cabin. He looks embarrassed. Behind him Christopher can see a woman who is putting on her hat. She walks around the captain, kisses him on the cheek and says '*Ciao!*' before disappearing down the stairs in a waft of perfume to the deck below. The three men watch as she walks carefully down the gangplank, impeded by her high heels and the tight skirt she is wearing.

The captain turns to Anthony and shrugs. 'What can I say? You must know the old adage: a sailor has a wife in every port. In my defence, I have only one. But, excuse me, I should have introduced you.'

They follow the captain onto the bridge and he takes his usual high captain's chair. The bridge is quieter than they have ever seen it. No noise or bustle or shouting of commands. The only sound is the cry of the gulls who hover around the sky, squawking and swooping down towards the water. A ship is manoeuvring into the harbour, its propellers churning up tasty morsels for the waiting birds.

The captain is dressed in his civilian clothes and fishes around in his pocket. He takes out his cigarettes and offers them to Christopher and Anthony.

'Where are the rest of the men?' Christopher asks, taking a cigarette.

'Some are helping with the reprovisioning of the ship. The food is very good down here, lots of fresh vegetables and cheap wine. The rest are, how do you say, at play!' He raises an eyebrow and drags on his cigarette.

'We've seen the general this morning,' Anthony says.

'Congratulations! That was very quick.'

'What he means,' says Christopher, 'is that we saw him on a balcony in the town giving a poetry recitation.'

Captain Denot laughs. 'There is poetry every morning and concerts in the evening along with wonderful fireworks to keep the people happy. Welcome to the new post-war world!'

'I think I'm going to move down here,' Anthony says.

'Not before we meet the general and get the arms,' Christopher answers.

'Ah, the arms!' The captain sighs, leaning back in his chair.

'What about them?' Christopher says.

'Well, they do exist. I was talking to a member of the sailor's union yesterday evening. He came down to talk to me about the harbour dues. Apparently, late last year they were taken from a ship heading to Russia for the revolution. Giuseppe Giulietti is the militant leader of the Italian Maritime Workers' Union. He took over an Italian cargo ship called the *Persia*. It was en route to Vladivostok in Russia, where she was to resupply the White Armies then fighting Lenin and the Bolsheviks.'

'Is that a problem?' Christopher asks.

'Unfortunately, the Italian government did not like it and they are now blockading the harbour.' The captain points towards the window.

A long, dark shape sits at anchor on the horizon. It's too far away to make out any details but there is no mistaking the large guns fore and aft.

'*Damn!*' says Christopher.

'*Oui.* Damn indeed,' the captain notes, 'but it is not a very tight blockade. In fact, a lot of the officers, according to my source, come into the city in the evening and enjoy, the, how do you say, amenities.' The captain smiles.

'Well, is it a problem or isn't it?' Christopher demands.

'The problem, if there is one, is with the Americans. They do not like the idea of arms going back to Ireland to use against their allies, the British.'

'Did you know this would happen before we left Ireland?'

'I worked it out myself, Christopher. And your leaders should have worked it out too.'

'But you still set sail when you knew all of this?'

'Of course. This is a commercial ship – it makes money wherever it can. I was asked to bring you here, and here you are.'

'But you will transport the arms back if I can buy them?'

'Depending on the situation, *n'est-ce pas?* I will be back here in about three weeks' time. All should be apparent by then.'

'*Three weeks!* I thought you were returning next week, on the way back from Trieste!'

'That was the plan. But I received a telegram yesterday. Trieste is off. Instead, we sail to Athens.'

'What are we to do?'

'Do? You are young, you have money, what do you think?'

'I also have a wife,' Christopher replies, the colour rising in his face.

'*Bien.* Good for you. In that case I advise you to become a tourist. Remember, you still have to meet the good general and discuss the purchase of the arms. Anything could happen. In three weeks' time, those arms could be anywhere.'

'This is a disaster,' Christopher says to Anthony, who seems to be trying to suppress a smile.

'Look at it this way,' says the captain. 'You have done your duty and now can concentrate on the delights of Fiume.' He claps his hands and stands up.

'That sounds very sensible to me, Christopher,' Anthony says.

'I thought you'd say that.'

'Anyway, gentlemen. I must put on my uniform and prepare for sea,' The captain holds out his hand, anxious to be away.

Christopher and Anthony make their way back to their *pensione*. The room, which seemed large enough for a short stay, now feels cramped. The news from the captain is depressing to Christopher but Anthony, by contrast, cheerfully decides to take a bath. Strains of badly sung opera come from the bathroom as Christopher begins to write his first letter to Nell. After a few false starts he finally tells her the bad news. He can imagine her reading the letter in the light of the dining-room lamp. When he has finished the letter, he begins to compose a telegram, addressed to a safe-house in Harcourt Street, saying: 'Arrived safely stop might have to stay longer than agreed stop please advise.' When he is finished writing he puts down his pen. Tomorrow he will go with Anthony to the post office. Outside the window the lights that ring the harbour come to life. A string of pearls stretches around the dark waters – he has done as much as he can do.

More and more people pour into Fiume in the following weeks. The area has now been declared an independent state. It doesn't take long for the news to travel across Italy and the town has a carnival atmosphere. The poetry readings by the eccentric leader continue and the concerts still take place on most evenings and include spectacular firework displays. It is a surreal atmosphere as tenders crisscross the bay, dropping the officers of the Italian warships who are supposed to be blockading the port into the city. Artists, bohemians, adventurers, fugitives, refugees and cranks began to show up at Fiume in droves. A new phenomenon occurs. Married couples come to the city so that they can get officially divorced and Anthony, with his knowledge of Italian, takes advantage of this and most nights his bed in the *pensione* is not slept in.

In secluded coves, beyond the harbour, there are rumours of orgies. It's as if the pent-up frustration after the Great War has exploded and people want to taste as much life as they can. The carnival atmosphere is helped along by the weather. The end of spring sees blue skies most days and Christopher and Anthony have to go out and buy lighter clothes. The cold dark streets they had left behind in Dublin seem to belong to another world.

News from Ireland is infrequent and Christopher begins to think that they have been forgotten about. He spends St Patrick's Day alone, sitting in a café on the waterfront watching the comings and goings of the ships while Anthony is off cavorting again with a rich divorcee.

Days drift by effortlessly and Anthony gets a job working in a small bar near the palace. Christopher wants to order him to give it up, but can't, as they need the money now.

It's early evening. Christopher leaves their *pensione* and takes his daily stroll up to the trattoria where Anthony works. After weeks of silence, a letter has arrived from Ireland that afternoon addressed to them both. The streets are full of life. As the days grow longer the crowds grow larger. Now he has to navigate his way through the sidewalk tables and the smoke and chatter of the diners. Where one café or bar starts or ends is a mystery. You can take a seat at one of the seemingly random tables and a waiter appears from several doors up to serve you and it all adds to the general confusion and hilarity on the streets. He approaches the trattoria from the far side of the street to make sure that there is a free table available outside and away from the entrance.

They pretend not to know each other as Anthony comes out of the trattoria to take his order. Christopher can't work out how he gets away with it, but he has never had to pay for anything. What he looks forwards to mostly are the titbits, or stuzzichini, Anthony smuggles out from the kitchen on little saucers before the meal.

'Prego,' Anthony says as he bends over the table, takes his towel from over his shoulder and wipes the surface.

'We got a letter today.'

'What does it say?' Anthony takes out his notebook and pretends to write.

'I didn't open it. The letter's addressed to both of us.'

'Orders from the top, no doubt.' Anthony pockets the notebook. 'Why don't you read it and tell me when I come back.'

As soon as he leaves Christopher rips the envelope open. The news is good: they have to return home. He scans the rest of it quickly as Anthony comes back with a tray of small dishes and places them in front of him with a glass of chilled white wine.

'Well?'

'We're going home, Anthony, at last.'

'What's happened?' Anthony flops down on the chair opposite.

'Apparently De Valera has ruled out buying the arms.'

'And what De Valera says goes.'

Éamon de Valera is now President of the Dáil, the self-elected Irish government. Prior to his political career, he was a commandant of the Volunteers at Boland's Mill during the 1916 Easter Rising and sentenced to death but released for a number of reasons, including his American citizenship having been born in New York.

'Here, let me see that,' Anthony grabs the letter and reads through it, then reads it again.

'Why do you think that happened?' Christopher takes up a piece of toasted bread and dips it into a dish of olive oil with piece of garlic floating on the top.

Anthony throws the letter onto the table in disgust. 'De Valera is a long streak of water. He's afraid of upsetting the Americans.'

'I don't understand – what's it got to do with them?'

'Christopher, you're a good soldier, but a lousy diplomat. De Valera's over there selling Irish government bonds and he doesn't want to upset the Americans. The British are their allies now.'

'Well, let's drink to that! You can give up your job now.'

Anthony looks at the passing crowds, all dressed up for the evening. His sallow skin has darkened in the sun and now he could be mistaken for one of them. The first fireworks of the night explode in the darkening sky, scattering tiny sparks that descend like a shower of golden rain and then quickly fizzle out. From the municipal park they can hear the sounds of the orchestra tuning up. One of Anthony's girlfriends waves over at him and passes by.

Christopher can see a look of sadness on his face.

'You don't want to come home, do you?' he says.

'What for? You know I'm no good to Collins. I'm only here because I speak Italian.'

'That's not true. You've a better brain than most of them.'

'It's not brains Collins needs now – he has the brains – what he needs from us is courage and heart. And my heart's not in it.'

'What if I order you to come with me?' Christopher says without conviction.

'What're you going to do, court-martial me?'

Christopher sips his wine and takes up a small piece of bread with black-olive tapenade spread across it. The bar owner has appeared at the door and is looking around for Anthony.

'I think your boss wants you,' Christopher whispers.

Anthony looks around and waves up at him then turns back and shrugs.

'Giovanni doesn't mind, I pay for it anyway.'

'You've been paying him for my meals? What with?'

'Tips. And I'm teaching his daughter English. Everybody wants to speak English. I think most of them want to emigrate to America.'

'You should've told me you were paying.'

'Then you wouldn't have come. What then? Starve yourself for the cause?'

Christopher straightens out the letter on the table again and reads it.

'The *Mercure* docks in two days' time. In a week you could be back home.'

'I am home, Christopher. I'm staying here, that's final,' Anthony says, raising his voice.

A young couple at a nearby table look over at them, then go back to their meal.

'Very well. I'll tell them you decided to stay, in case other arms appear. I've never seen as many uniforms from different countries – maybe you'll be able to pick some up.'

'Thanks,' Anthony says. 'I won't forget it. And in appreciation I'm going to take you out for a '*celebrazione*' tomorrow. To show you all you've missed.'

Anthony gets up and, flicking his towel through the air, dances around in a circle.

They start drinking the next day in their favourite café down in the port where they had spent many days. Anthony explains to the owner that Christopher is leaving and he sweeps their beer glasses aside with a dramatic gesture and brings over a bottle with a dark liquid to the table. He produces three small glasses, tops them up and holds his glass up, shouting '*Saluti!*' before drinking it back in one go.

Christopher and Anthony pick their glasses up and follow his example. The highly flavoured liqueur goes down easily. The owner pours another three glasses and together they drink them back. Then the owner comes around to Christopher, almost lifts him from the chair and kisses both his cheeks.

Another local comes into the bar. He's shabbily dressed and senses that there might be a free drink going so shuffles over. As he joins in the celebration another glass is produced and the four glasses are filled again.

Christopher turns to Anthony: 'What is this? Is tastes nice.'

'That's amaro – from the owner's local village. And it's lethal.'

'Too late now,' Christopher says, laughing.

'Come on, this is only the first bar. We've a few more to go to,' Anthony says, grabs him by the shoulders and hauls him to his feet.

They make their way towards the centre of the town, stopping here and there, Anthony explaining to the bar and café owners that it's his friends Christopher's last few days. More drinks are produced and more stuzzichini. By the time they've reached the town centre Christopher's vision has become unfocused. They end up in Anthony's bar and the proprietor comes out and kisses him on both cheeks, then brings them into the restaurant. Inside there is a long table already set out for them. They take a seat and almost immediately large platefuls of pasta are produced and bottles of wine wrapped in straw. Before long, their table is full of the proprietor's family members and their friends.

At some point in the evening Christopher turns to talk to Anthony but his friend has disappeared. In his place there is a young woman. She says she wants to practise her English on Christopher and he says yes. Her name is Emilia and as the night wears on they are pushed closer and closer together, forming a little huddle against what is now a noisy party. As she leans in closer to him, turning her head to catch a word, Christopher kisses her cheek gently, then regrets it and apologises. Emilia puts her finger up to his lips and takes him by the arm, leading him out of the café.

Emilia lives one floor up, over a pharmacy. Her door is at the end of a long dark hallway that leads towards the back of the building. The more they move down the hallway the worse the smell: a mixture of cooking and of vegetables gone off. He stands behind her as her hand with the key tries to find the lock in the dark. After she finds the lock and pushes open the door the streetlights cast a glow over her face. For a split second he stands on the threshold. A blurred image of Nell flits through his mind and then disappears as he steps inside her room and kicks the door closed behind him.

'You like?'

She turns towards him and sweeps her arms around the room proudly. From what he can see her living quarters it is nothing to be proud of. The light from the street lamps outside cast an orange glow into the interior of the tiny room. The feeling that hits him is sadness. Everything that she possesses is within these four walls. On one side there is a tiny kitchen with a gas stove and sink, on the other there is a large double bed and scattered around the room are mismatched pieces of furniture and one armchair with a sunken cushion; and that's it.

'It's really nice,' he says, looking around again in case he has missed a door.

'For me, it is heaven,' she says and approaches him, an uncertain look on her face.

He reaches out and enfolds her in his arms. Her tiny, perfect face looks up at his and they kiss, gently at first, and then more passionately. She breaks away from him and stands in the light of the streetlamp outside. With a few twists and turns, she sheds her clothes and stands before him, naked and smiling.

'Now you,' she says, pulls the blanket back and gets into bed.

Christopher almost stumbles over her clothes hidden by the shadows on the floor and feels awkward. He sits on the side of the bed to take off his boots and struggles with the laces. She watches him intently as he takes off the rest of his clothes. When he is finished, he hesitates for a moment. She lies on her side, propped up on one elbow, that enigmatic smile playing across her face. With a quick flick she pulls the blanket back and pats the sheet beside her. When he joins her, he can feel himself sinking down into the bumpy mattress and the look of surprise on his face makes her smile.

But the hollows in the mattress brings them together. As if caught in a trap they roll into each other. Her body, when he touches it, is cool, which surprises him. Unlike Nell in the early days of their marriage, Emilia seems curious about his body, tracing her fingers down his arms and his back. It is Emilia who finally takes the initiative and pushes him on his back. He closes his eyes and lets her body guide his. Outside it has started to rain. The noise of the heavy drops against the window grow in volume, almost drowning out her cries as she joins her body with his until they are as one being, seeking a release in each other.

When he wakes up the following morning, his mind struggles out of a dream about a bizarre version of his ocean voyage which fades almost immediately. He looks around in panic, wondering where he is. The memories of the previous night bring with them a sense of shame. His first sensation is of the smell of coffee. Emilia is boiling a metal cafetiere over a single ring of gas. She is wrapped up in a blanket and her hair is loose and falls over her face as she bends forward. The rain has stopped and a beam of sunlight crosses the room, landing on the door. In the light of day, the inside of the flat is drearier than he remembers.

Emilia becomes aware of his movement on the bed and turns.

'Good morning, Christopher,' she says slowly, pronouncing each word. 'How are you?'

'My head is throbbing,' Christopher answers, waiting for the pain to subside.

'I do not know that word.'

When she turns back to the stove to check on the coffee, he jumps out of the bed and grabs up his clothes from the floor.

'Toilet?' he asks.

Without turning around, she waves her hand in the direction of the door. Remembering the length of the hallway and the number of doors off it, he decides to put his clothes on in the room before he goes outside. Unlike the previous night it is a hive of activity. Children come and go through various doorways and stare at the stranger in their midst. There seems to be no logic among the tenants of the building. Most of the doors are left unselfconsciously ajar and inside mothers are struggling with reluctant children as they get them ready for school. When they see him passing by, barefooted, they pull their children closer to them and give him a dirty look.

The bathroom, when he finds it, is almost at the end of the hallway. Inside there is a small, stained sink and the toilet is a white ceramic hole in the floor with places for your feet on either side. He relieves himself awkwardly, his steady stream missing the hole occasionally and splashing his feet. When he is finished, he tries to wash himself as best as he can in the sink but it is almost impossible in the cramped space. When he leaves the bathroom the stairs to the ground floor are directly to his right. He glances up the corridor towards Emilia's apartment. For an instant he imagines himself walking up to the door and going inside, finishing his breakfast and spending the day with her. And then maybe the next day, and the day after that. Beginning a new life in fact, away from his life in the Liberties and the uncertainty of the war against the British. But then he remembers what had brought him here in the first place. An image of Nell appears through the fog of his hangover along with the country he has left. His responsibility and love towards both bring a sudden lump to his throat and he takes the stairs quickly, his boots under his arm, in case he changes his mind.

CHAPTER 29

Levon

John Charles Burns is in good humour as he steps through the door into his hotel room. It has been a good week with two successful raids on IRA safe houses and nobody lost due to the element of surprise. Although none of the higher-ups in Dublin Castle have said anything to him, he can feel that his progress is in the right direction. More people know his name now and he has caught one or two of the soldiers in the Castle yard pointing to him as he went past. Weeks have gone since the meeting with his mysterious benefactor. Now there is no trouble getting extra cash from the Castle. In that time, he has moved to a better room, a suite in fact, sent some money home and worked his way down the list of addresses that were handed to him. Now he needs more information to boost his profile in the Castle and also to retrieve the rest of the torn five-pound notes.

As soon as he closes over the door, he senses he is not alone. He switches on the light waiting for it to glow to its full intensity. Sitting in the armchair beside the fireplace is the very man he had been thinking about, Mordaunt. Although not looking forward to dealing with him, the timing is perfect. The notebook in his inside pocket contains more than enough information about Christopher Flinter to trade for more money and another list of names. His head is giddy with the possibilities, both to his financial status and his status within the Cairo gang. He would show them what a real agent was capable of.

'Mr Burns,' Mordaunt says, without turning around from the fire.

'How did you manage to get into my room?' Burns asks.

Mordaunt doesn't answer him.

'I'll just go and hang up my jacket,' Burns says.

In the bedroom he takes off his jacket and hangs it up in the wardrobe then takes out his precious notebook and slips it into his pocket. At the bottom of the wardrobe there is a small, metal strongbox with a lock. He unlocks it with a key from his keyring and takes out the tiny revolver, putting it down the waistband of his trousers, then pulls his waistcoat over it and brushes it down to conceal the slight bulge. He looks at himself in the mirror of the dressing table, adjusts his tie, then goes back into the room.

'Have you anything for me?' Mordaunt asks in that slow, sibilant whisper that seems to have got worse, as if his voice hasn't been used for a while.

Burns takes the chair across from him and reaches into his pocket, taking out the torn five-pound notes and placing them onto the mantelpiece.

'I do. Did you bring the matching pieces?' he says.

Mordaunt takes out his portion of the bank notes from his wallet and places them also onto the mantelpiece. Burns feels a stab of disappointment. A quick glance into the wallet seems to reveal that it is almost empty. Now that his eyes have adjusted to the light in the room, he can study Mordaunt a bit more closely. He is wearing the same jacket as the last time they met but it is looking slightly the worse for wear. His white starched collar also shows signs of wear and discolouration along the fold and he can detect a faint odour coming from the man opposite. His trousers seem alright but his shoes look unpolished and scuffed.

Burns reaches up to the mantelpiece and gathers all of the notes together.

'You'll get more than your money's worth today,' he says, folding the pieces and putting them into his waistcoat pocket.

'We shall see.'

Burns takes the notebook out of his pocket and holds it up in front of Mordaunt who reaches out for it. But he whips it away, shaking his head.

'I think that I've done you a great service. In fact, I've risked my life getting this information. Under the circumstances I think we should renegotiate.'

'Really?'

'The streets are very dangerous out there now,' Burns says. 'Roving squads of assassins killing people in broad daylight.'

'What do you suggest?'

'How about another forty pounds and another list of suspects. But this time I want the leaders, not the foot soldiers.'

'I have that very information here.' Mordaunt pats his jacket.

'And the money?'

'I need to go to my bank for that.'

Burns thinks for a while, then smiles. 'I know. Why don't you give me a deposit, let's say that list in your pocket. And I'll give you a glimpse of my investigations to whet your appetite.'

Mordaunt takes out a handkerchief from his pocket and mops his brow. Then he lifts the mask somewhat to wipe his face. The shock of even that glance at his injuries turns Burns stomach and he has to avert his eyes. He had seen injuries during the war but they had been wounds covered in gore and blood and in the heat of battle he accepted them. But to see a portion of a man's face so hideously exposed brings it all back to him.

He waves a hand at Mordaunt. 'Please, please put it back.'

Mordaunt chuckles, the sound coming from somewhere deep in his chest.

'Why don't you tell me what you have and I will see?' he says.

Burns debates with himself if it's worth negotiating, but now all he wants is this man out of his life. There has been a slippage in Mordaunt. In the few weeks since he has seen him there has been a change in his demeanour and he doesn't like it. He opens the notebook out and reads back on his notes.

'I followed the woman, Stern's lady-friend. She went into a tenement house in the Liberties, but didn't stay long. Then she came out with something like envelopes in her hand and made her way back into the city and on into the Monto. In the Monto she went into one of the more upmarket brothels and didn't come out that evening.'

'The Monto,' Mordaunt whispers. 'Is this woman a whore?'

'Definitely not. I know a whore when I see one. But that's not the best!' Burns is excited, unable to help himself.

'Well, hurry, tell me.'

'I went back to the house in the Liberties the next day and knocked at the door. Said I was looking for a Miss Claffey.'

'Why Claffey?'

'That's the name she uses in Dublin Castle.'

'Uses?'

'Wait till you hear this,' Burns says, almost beside himself, 'the woman who answered the door said: there is no Nell Claffey here but there is a Nell Flinter.'

'Flinter?'

'Nell Flinter,' Burns says. 'Wife of Christopher Flinter, who hasn't been seen for weeks.'

On hearing the news Mordaunt sits back into his chair. His breathing has increased and a liquid rattle sounds behind the mask.

Burns is disgusted when he sees the spittle dripping onto his jacket.

'Tell me everything,' Mordaunt wheezes.

'That's it. It's obvious, she works in Dublin Castle under an assumed name, lives a double life between the Liberties and the Monto, goes into Shanahan's, well known visiting place of the IRA, and passes on information. That last part I'm not trading by the way – when I reveal her true identity in the castle it will be a mighty feather in my cap.'

'Of course,' Mordaunt says. 'I understand.'

Mordaunt stands up and takes a sheet from his pocket. He hands it to Burns who opens it out to read it, but the page is blank. He looks up at his visitor but Mordaunt has walked behind his chair and has looped something around his neck. Just in time he manages to push his fingers between the thin wire and his neck and tries to grab hold of it. But the pressure of the wire is relentless. From the corner of his eye, he can see Mordaunt's right hand as it tightens its grip over the piece of wood, one end of the garrotte. Burns has never seen a garrotte but knows how it works. He struggles become more violent as he tries to shake his head to dislodge the wire, but it only makes it worse and the thin strand bites even more. It cuts into his fingers, severing them, and on into his neck, cutting deeper and deeper into the skin, and then deeper, beyond the skin, into the muscle and tendons and on into his throat which fills with blood that pours down into his lungs. He tries to plead for mercy, looking up into Mordaunt's eyes in his last fleeting moments, but all he sees is a terrible blankness.

✳✳✳✳

The meagre light thrown out by the street lamp on Francis Street isn't enough to illuminate the narrow laneway properly. The tenement is in darkness and the number on the door is impossible to make out. Captain Benjamin Stern strikes a match and checks the address again against the address that had been left on his desk. It's the right number on the door but surely there must be a mistake, he thinks. How could a woman such as Nell live in a place like this? His heart sinks with sadness. Before the match flickers out he can see that the door to the tenement is slightly ajar.

Unable to help himself, he pushes open the door and slips inside. The lobby is unlit except for one flickering oil-lamp and there is a stale smell of cabbage. At the top of the stairs on his right he can make out a landing with a door off it. From behind the door come the sounds of voices, children's voices, and he recalls that Nell had told him that she lived on the ground floor with her aunt. In a way this all helps his cause. In some part of his mind, he imagines himself rescuing Nell from this foul-smelling place and giving her the life she deserves.

Across from the entrance is the doorway to what must be Nell's flat. The door, he is surprised to see, is also partially open. Perhaps the note on his desk was from Nell herself? But he discounts that immediately as he considers himself a good judge of character and the woman that he admires so much would never stoop to this. Still, he is fascinated. He creeps over to the door and looks through the chink. Inside there is a sitting room with a table in the middle and four chairs placed around it. He can make out other bits of furniture, most of them worn with use, but well-kept.

'You can go inside, Captain Stern,' a male voice whispers directly behind him.

He knows straight away who the voice belongs to and turns quickly. Detaching himself from the shadows is the unmistakable figure of Levon Mordaunt.

'What in the name of hell are you doing here?' Stern whispers.

'I might ask you the same question.'

Stern realises who was responsible for the note on his desk. But how did he get inside Dublin Castle to deliver it?

As if in answer to his question, Mordaunt says: 'You got my note, I see. Cost me a shilling or two, but your soldiers aren't very well paid so don't blame them.'

Mordaunt's speech, although unnatural, isn't as bad as their last meeting and he suspects that he has been deliberately using it as a ruse to stop him asking any probing questions. He immediately regrets underestimating the man and decides, no matter what happens, he will take him in for closer questioning.

Mordaunt walks around the captain and pushes open the door, urging him into the room. Confused, Stern steps over the threshold. The room is neat and tidy. A curtain hangs from the ceiling down one end and is pulled back to reveal a kitchenette. Through the open doorway of what he believes is the bedroom he can see a large double bed.

'Take a peek at the family pictures,' Mordaunt says beside him. 'They're charming.'

Unable to resist, Stern goes over to a dresser. Several framed photographs are lined up, facing out into the room. It is the largest of them that attracts his attention. Nell is standing beside a young man dressed in a dark suit with a flower in his lapel, and she is wearing a wedding dress. He picks it up, trying to make sense of it. Beside it there is another photograph, this one with Nell sitting on a bench in a park with the same man.

'Let me introduce Mr and Mrs Christopher Flinter,' Mordaunt says.

'This can't be, I refuse to believe it.'

'It is,' Mordaunt says impatiently. 'Can't you recognise what's in front of you?'

'But where is she now? I want to hear it directly from her own mouth. This man could be dead. Nell could be a widow.'

'Nell is an agent. You and I know that. You'll have to arrest her. She's an enemy of the Crown and the punishment for spying is death.'

'Who have you told this to?'

'You're the first to know. Don't worry, I won't tell anyone you're sweet on the young lady.'

'Why me? Why should I do this?'

'Who cares? Just arrest her.'

Stern rubs his forehead where a pain is beginning to develop. He looks at Mordaunt with hate in his eyes.

'Why are you doing this? I thought it was just Christopher Flinter you were looking for?'

Stern can see that Mordaunt is beginning to lose patience and it gives him a certain amount of satisfaction.

'It was. Is. She is a bonus. Get on with it, I will even give you the address where she is staying. In the Monto.'

'The Monto? Isn't that where Major Byatt met his end? In the tunnels underneath? I seem to remember reading in the files that he had been killed by a person or persons unknown? And in those same files it states that Christopher Flinter was given a pardon by Major Byatt. There is something rotten going on here. I think we should both go back to the Castle where we can discuss it.'

Mordaunt begins to pace around the room, like a caged animal, muttering to himself. Walking under the full glow of the oil lamp Stern can see that Mordaunt looks dishevelled, almost wild, his clothes a far cry from the ones he wore at their last meeting. Something seems to have changed in him.

He walks over to the dresser with the photographs and looks at them, then turns. 'You don't understand. *Christopher Flinter has to suffer! He is responsible for ruining my life – and for this!*' He howls in desperation and lifts the mask from his face.

Stern looks at the terrifying visage in front of him, but he has seen worse gunshot and shrapnel wounds before. It is evident that Mordaunt has taken leave of his senses and that the motivation driving him is a powerful one: revenge.

'I'm sorry you feel that way but I've made my mind up. Until I get all the facts I will keep Mrs Flinter, if that's who she truly is, under observation.'

'All because the little Jew can have his way with the pretty lady!' sneers Mordaunt. 'My only mistake was in coming to you with this information. I should have known that your lust would cloud your sense.'

'That's disgusting,' Stern says and turns to leave.

'Stop, or I'll shoot,' Mordaunt says.

Stern turns. Mordaunt is pointing a revolver directly into his face. 'You wouldn't dare.'

'Now that I think about it, I've been a fool. I don't really need you at all – alive, that is. After they discover your body outside her door, the evidence will speak for itself.'

Stern looks down into the dark tunnel of the revolver and sees the cylinder begin to rotate as Mordaunt puts pressure on the trigger. He jumps to one side but Mordaunt allows for this. The roar of the gun is deafening. He feels himself thrown backwards as his head is struck by the bullet and he falls onto his back. Why? he wonders. He looks up at the ceiling and Mordaunt's face slips into view, his eyes staring down at him, then it disappears and he is aware of the door closing. Perhaps all is not lost, he thinks, as he tries to focus on a dark stain on the ceiling. It is in the rough shape of a dog, a dog he once owned. He is back in a park somewhere in London with his father and he is throwing a stick through the air. The stick rises upwards towards the sun and the park is bathed in a brilliant white light.

Mordaunt places the mask back over his face and ties it securely. In the flat above he can hear feet moving around and distorted voices, arguing. Closing the door to Flinter's flat behind him, he makes his way to the front door. As he closes the door gently behind him, he can hear tentative footsteps coming down the stairs. Outside one or two curtains twitch in the houses opposite and heads appear, gazing out into the semi-darkness of the lane. As he makes his way towards Dublin Castle, he wonders why Stern would have ignored all of the evidence he had presented to him and given Flinter's whore the benefit of the doubt. What makes a sane man act that way? It is beyond him, he has no answer.

Outside the gates of Dublin Castle two sentries huddle together, smoking. They stare at him as he tries to explain that he believes that a soldier, in fact an officer, had been shot. A Captain Stern, according to the small crowd who had gathered outside. As one of them goes into the yard to tell his superior, the other begins to write down the details. He gives the soldier his old address in Fitzwilliam Square and assures him that if he can be of any assistance he will be, but he needed to be off.

Back through the dark streets, to the dark tunnels, his new kingdom – his home. Down there nobody points at his face or pulls back in horror. His only company are the rats that skitter away as he approaches. His eyes are becoming used to the dark. He can feel them grow and dilate. The map of the subterranean city is becoming etched on his mind. This side branch brings him away from the centre of the city, the next brings him to the Monto. Another turn brings him back to the convent where he emerged as a half-dead man sometime in the past. Now he uses the convent for provisions, rooting around the bins in the basement of the kitchen. He doesn't need much to survive and wonders why he had bothered to accumulate all that wealth.

Since moving into the darkness his cunning has grown. It talks to him now. He would never have figured out such a simple solution in such a short space of time and taken such decisive action. Usually, his plans are elaborate and he's proud of them, but he is now convinced that this is, in fact, a weakness. Stern's corpse in that woman's house will be sufficient to get Flinter's wife arrested and probably executed for treason. After that Flinter has nobody and he will remind him of this. A nice piece of bait to get him down into his kingdom, the last piece in the jigsaw puzzle. Does this make him evil? What is evil? Are rats evil? No. Rats have no morals. They devour and in their turn are devoured. That is the way of all flesh.

And what happens when this is all over? What then? He has given this more thought. Everything he needs is down here, in the tunnels. Food, water, freedom to roam wherever he wants, and, of course, the darkness. In time he might allow other people to join him, probably some waifs from the streets above. It will be a proper kingdom, with proper subjects. Why did Stern call him mad?

CHAPTER 30

Nell

Nell drifts with the morning rush-hour workers making their way along Capel Street. Crossing the bridge, she has her first glimpse of City Hall. From this distance the classical building looks as if it doesn't belong. The shops on either side of Parliament Street, which leads up to Dame Street, look dowdy and tired compared to it. As is happening more often, with her first glimpse of City Hall which nestles beside Dublin Castle, her thoughts turn to Benjamin. She has been careful not to be left alone with him and now takes her lunch with the other office workers in the canteen. When he approaches her in the office the wounded look in his eyes when she acts as if nothing had happened between them, makes her feel conflicted and confused.

'Nell.'

Crotty is standing in the doorway of Read's knife shop and is beckoning to her. He looks tired and he is pulling nervously on a cigarette, his cap pulled down over his eyes. For a split second her heart skips a beat. Is this about Christopher? As she approaches him, he nods to her to follow him and turns down Parliament Street towards the quays. Keeping up with him is difficult as they are now making their way against the flow of people. He crosses the road towards Capel Street Bridge and she knows where he is heading: their usual rendezvous, Gogarty's tearooms. But this time there is no complicated secret rituals as he throws his cigarette onto the ground and ushers her inside. She goes to their usual table at the back and waits while Crotty orders at the counter. Before he joins her, he looks out through the window in the direction from which they came and seems, at last, to relax.

'What's the matter?' Nell grabs his sleeve as soon as she sits down. 'Is it Christopher?'

'No, not Christopher. It's you.'

'Me?'

'What the hell have you been up to?'

'I don't know what you're talking about.'

The waitress comes down and leaves their tea with some toast in front of them then leaves.

'We've just got word from one of our agents in Dublin Castle,' Crotty says. 'They're looking to take you in for questioning.'

'*Me?* I don't understand. It must be a mistake!'

'They found the body of one of their officers at your house in the Liberties. He was shot.'

'I don't know anything about that. Why should I?'

Crotty took his cap off and left it on the chair beside him.

'Our contact said that you ... knew this particular officer,' Crotty says and now he seems uncomfortable.

Nell feels her body contract as if someone is about to attack her. Her breath comes in short, ragged gulps and her stomach is threatening to throw up her breakfast.

She braces herself. 'Was it a Captain Stern?'

'Yes.'

Nell closes her eyes. She pictures him the last time they had been alone in his quarters. The crackling fire. The photographs. His ambition to go to the Holy Land and spend time with his parents. All gone. She asks the question she is dreading to ask but has to.

'Was it Christopher who did this?'

Crotty looks confused for a moment but then shakes his head.

'No. It couldn't have been Christopher. He's on his way back but won't arrive for days yet. I was going to tell you the good news today. But now ...' He shrugs and sips his tea.

'Do they think I did it?'

'We don't know. But it doesn't look good. A British army officer shot dead in the same house where a clerical officer from Dublin Castle lives.' Crotty shakes his head. 'This is all very bad. I'll have to tell the boss. And he has enough on his plate.'

'What am I supposed to do now? I can't go back there.'

'Is there any chance that they know where you're living now?'

'No. I've been extra careful when I leave my mother's house. I use the back entrance and go a different route every day.'

'Good girl. I suppose that's something. Let me think about it.' Crotty takes a half-smoked cigarette from behind his ear. He lights it up and blows smoke towards the ceiling. When he is finished, he stubs it out in the ashtray.

'I suppose it's not a disaster. We lose you, that's true, but we have other people to take your place inside. And it's not as if you've been passing on any useful information lately. In any case, Stern was a British officer so that's one less to deal with.'

Nell leaps up from her chair, leans across and slaps Crotty across the face. The sound of the slap is hard and clear. The few other customers glance over at their table, then decide it's a lover's tiff and turn back to their food.

Crotty, stunned, rubs his face and stares up at Nell who is glowering down at him.

'*You didn't know him. He was a better man than you'll ever be!*' Nell hisses.

A knowing smile spreads across Crotty's face. 'Goin' back to your old trade, are you?' he sneers.

Nell reaches for the teapot but Crotty gets there first and grabs her by the wrist. The waitress, who had been looking over at them, rushes behind the counter and into a back room. She returns straight away with the owner, a tall, well-built man. The waitress must have disturbed him as he is pulling up the braces of his trousers and looks angry. He walks out from behind the counter and straight over to their table.

'What's going on here?' he says, looking at Crotty who still has Nell's wrist in his hand.

He lets it go and sits back in his chair, smiling up at the owner. 'We had a little bit of a tiff, you know how it is with newlyweds.'

The owner turns to Nell who is rubbing her wrist.

'Is that right, ma'am?'

'Yes, just a tiff,' Nell agrees.

'This is a respectable business. Why don't you take it outside?' the owner says, and begins to clear off the table.

Outside Crotty makes a show of putting his cap on and checking his reflection in the window.

'I'm sorry, Nell. That wasn't called for. We're under a lot of pressure at the moment. I'm ducking and dodging every day. I think it's getting to me.'

'I'll accept your apology. This time.'

'You won't mention this to Christopher, will you?'

Nell takes in the figure of Crotty standing in front of her. Not much more than a teenager really, and already immersed in the bloody business of a revolution which is creeping steadily to a full-scale war.

'No, I won't mention it to Christopher. Anyway, I fight my own battles,' Nell says, turns, and walks away.

She takes the long way back to the Monto, avoiding any patrols she comes across, and keeps clear of the main thoroughfare. She walks slowly, absorbing the news of Stern's death. Who could have done such a thing? Obviously it wasn't the IRA as Crotty, part of Collins' inner circle, would have just told her, unabashedly, that they had assassinated a British army agent and that would be that. The only other person she can think of is their tormentor, the monster she had shot in the tunnels. If only Christopher had been conscious at the time, he would have taken the right steps to make sure that he was dead. It felt like he was tightening his grip on them. First, he kidnapped Anna's doorman, then Sarah, who was lucky to escape. Then he killed Stern because he must have known, somehow, that they had met. But how did he know that? It was all very confusing. Now the news of Christopher's arrival back home. She was making her way across Sackville Street when it hit her. The monster's next target might be her mother. A loud horn brings her back to the present and an irate driver shouts out of the door of a goods lorry. Barely acknowledging him, she begins to run as fast as she can back towards the Monto.

CHAPTER 31

The return

The *Mercure* noses its way carefully around the south wall of Dublin Docks and up through the mouth of the River Liffey. Unlike the night of his departure from Dublin port, Christopher can now take in the full spectacle of the dramatic landscape. Off to the port bow lies the old Pigeon House Fort. Beyond the new power station is the city and beyond that the low dark shape of the Dublin mountains. As the engine of the ship slows down further to navigate through the busy waterway of the port, he finds himself becoming more impatient and as the ship edges closer to the docks he has to stop himself from leaping over the rails and onto Irish soil.

As it turns out, he is disappointed to find that only Crotty is standing at the end of the gangway waiting for him to disembark. He looks more dishevelled than when they had first met and paces around the quay wall impatiently.

Captain Denot, who is standing beside him wishing him well, looks down at the waiting figure and smiles sadly at Christopher.

'You were expecting somebody else? Maybe your wife?'

'Hoping more than expecting. I knew they wouldn't have told Nell exactly when I was arriving,' Christopher says, then embraces the captain.

The two men hold each other for a while, then Christopher walks down the gangplank, his legs still unstable after the sea voyage. At the end of the gangplank, he turns and waves farewell to the captain who is already making his way to the ship's derrick to organise the unloading of the cargo.

Crotty comes over, takes his seaman's bag from him and nods towards a car which is parked but ticking over just up from the ship.

'Are you dropping me home?' Christopher asks, already guessing the answer.

'Not yet – we've got to go to see the Big Fella. Where's Caprani?' Crotty says, and throws the sea-bag into the back of the car.

'It's a long story.' Christopher avoids the question.

The car pulls away from the docks and heads towards the city. It crawls through the morning traffic then turns right onto Amiens Street, stopping outside a small, nondescript café. Crotty points to it but remains in front with the driver. The street around them is busier than Christopher had remembered. Platoons of British soldiers make their way along the far side, heads turning nervously as they scan the crowds for trouble. An army convoy patrol makes its way towards them, a Crossley tender led by one of the new armoured troop carriers.

'What's been happening? There seems to be a lot of soldiers around,' Christopher says.

'Things are hotting up, but the Big Fella'll fill you in.' Crotty leans over and opens the door, signalling the end of the conversation. 'We'll come back in a quarter of an hour.'

Christopher gets out and, as soon as he takes his bag from the back of the car, it pulls off into the traffic. Inside the café there are a handful of people but Michael Collins isn't among them. He orders a pot of tea for two and heads for a table near the back. As soon as he sits down the door opens and Michael Collins, wearing a business suit and carrying a briefcase, enters. He waves down at Christopher and makes his way towards the table. Christopher still finds it hard to take in how the man walks around the streets of Dublin so openly. It takes a special kind of person to carry it off. Collins' sheer magnetism should give him away, but he seems to be able to merge in with the other customers, his height disguised by a slight stoop and his hat pulled low over his face.

'I'm glad to see you safe and sound, Christopher,' he says, taking the seat across the table.

'You were right, it was more of a holiday.'

'Where's Caprani? I told Crotty I wanted to meet the two of you.'

'He decided to stay on for bit,' Christopher says.

'Did he now? And you allowed him to?'

'There wasn't a lot I could do.' Christopher takes out a cigarette to cover his uneasiness.

'Well, I suppose he's not a great loss,' Collins says after a while.

'And you know about the weapons,' Christopher says. 'All in all, it wasn't a very successful mission.'

'Don't let it worry you. We had an idea you wouldn't get to meet the general, but we had to try. It's all politics. The Americans let it be known that they didn't approve and they're the source of a lot of our funds.'

'I understand. How are things in Dublin?' Christopher murmurs, leaning over.

'The city is turning into a battleground. They hit us, we hit them. Nobody's flinching so far. That's why we need that American money, to keep going.'

The waitress puts the teapot and the two cups on the table and leaves them be. Christopher notices that there had been no repartee exchanged between her and Collins and wonders if she's one of Collins' operatives. He pours himself and Collins some tea and sits back.

'Why are we meeting here?'

'It's a long story. Nell is not that far away from here, so it's easier to have our little chat and then you can be on your way.'

'Where is she?' Christopher asks, but already knows the answer.

'Safe and well in the Monto,' Collins says, but looks uneasy.

'What's happened?'

'Several nights ago, a British agent, Captain Benjamin Stern, was found shot dead in your flat. Did you know him?' Collins asks, watching Christopher's reaction.

'Never heard of him.'

'It seems Nell did.'

'Did they work together?'

'They worked in the same section, that's all we know. Stern wasn't a very active agent. Supposedly biding his time. In any case, we got a message to Nell just in time.'

'Thank you,' Christopher says, relaxing back into his chair.

'Don't be so quick with your thanks. She'd already moved back to the Monto.'

'I didn't know that – the postal service in Fiume was hopeless.'

Collins starts to fiddle with his hat, pushing it backwards and forwards between each hand.

'I had words with Phil Shanahan as soon as I found out she moved. I don't like it when I'm kept in the dark.'

'What had Phil got to say?'

'He told me everything. About the reason you earned your pardon from the British.'

'So what? I never hid that from you. It's all in the past anyway.'

'Take it easy, Christopher,' Collins says, glancing over his shoulder at the other customers. 'That's the problem – it's not all in the past.'

'What?'

'The man shot in the tunnel back in '16 – Janus you called him – survived. We think he's out to get you and Nell. He's already killed at least three people and attempted to kill another. We don't have time for personal vendettas, Christopher, there's a war going on.'

'Jesus Christ. His name is Levon Mordaunt. But how can you be sure it's him?' Christopher says, all of his elation at arriving home slowly ebbing away and in its place is a cold sensation of horror that begins in his stomach and spreads out through his very being.

'The body of an RIC officer was found in the basement of a house in Fitzwilliam Square. The house was torched but the flames didn't reach the basement. He was garrotted. In the same cellar we found your mother-in-law's doorman, tortured and killed in the same way.'

'You said three.'

'A British agent, John Burns, was found in his hotel room: dead.'

'Garrotted?'

'The same way.'

'And the attempted murder?'

'Sarah Murphy – I believe you know her.'

'*Sarah!* Is she alright?'

'Yes – she was kidnapped but rescued by the RIC man who was then murdered himself. We've been out searching for this madman, but he seems to have disappeared. For now. Although it's hard to believe with his disfigurement.'

'We thought he was dead,' Christopher says, shaking his head.

'Even Phil believed he was dead. But don't worry, we'll get him. He's a conniving bastard but he won't get away with it, Dublin is too small a city for him to survive after I put out the word.'

'What do I do now?'

'There's not a lot you can do, for now. Go and be with Nell, I'm sure the poor girl needs you, and tell her not to worry, we won't let her down. The British aren't sure she had anything to do with Stern's murder but she'll have to stay put until this mess is sorted out. By the way, Crotty will be on guard at night. I don't think our friend comes out in the daytime. When all this is over, we can talk.'

Collins reaches into his pocket and puts some coins on the table, turns, and leaves the café. Even for such a busy man he had guessed that Christopher had probably used up the money he had been given and hadn't enough for the tea.

In a way he should be thankful to Nell's mother that he had somewhere to go as their flat in the Liberties would be under observation by the British. He scoops the coins up from the table and leaves just the bare amount for the tea. Taking hold of his seabag, he leaves the café and turns towards the Monto.

CHAPTER 32

Robert and Harry

The bells of the Magdalen laundry chime out the start of a new day in the Monto. Outside, Mecklinberg Street puts on its daytime face. Shoppers pass by the lampposts where, the night before, prostitutes plied their trade.

Robert Byatt rises from his uncomfortable bed and stares out through the window. Across from his lodgings, Anna Macken's brothel looks sad and neglected, the interior window shutters closed over keeping the daylight at bay from whatever lies inside. He has been lodging here for several weeks, taking in the comings and goings of the brothel. Harry Irvine joins him whenever he can, but he is losing hope.

Almost on cue, a young woman, tiny and delicate, comes out through the doorway and, as she does every morning, looks up and down the street before disappearing back inside and returning with a bucket of water. She sluices down the granite steps and uses a yard brush to get rid of any of the previous night's detritus. Strangely enough she sweeps everything down the steps onto the pavement but doesn't, as he would have expected, continue on sweeping into the gutter. Instead, she looks up and down the street again, and disappears back inside the building. Robert takes a note of the time in his notebook and places it on the table beside the window.

After he washes and has breakfast it's almost ten o'clock. The landlady, a Mrs Sweeney, insists that breakfast begins at eight o'clock and ends at nine but she has made an exception for her 'English gentleman' and lets him sip his tea while she cleans up after the other lodgers.

Harry Irvine has lectures in the afternoon and he expects a visit from him soon. While he waits in his room, he reads through Jonathan's notebook again to see if there is anything he has missed. The doorbell sounds downstairs and he can hear the sound of Harry's voice loudly greeting Mrs Sweeney and commenting on the latest news from the streets of Dublin as he makes his way upstairs. He opens the door just as Harry is about to knock.

'Good morning, Robert.' Harry makes his way into the room, a paper bag held out in greeting.

Robert takes the bag and looks inside: cakes.

'I'll make the tea,' Robert says and puts the cakes down on the small bureau beside the window.

'I see you've been revisiting Jonathan's notebook,' Harry says and picks it up, flicking through it.

'A waste of time. I can almost recite it at this stage,' Robert says, preparing a tray.

'I know it seems disheartening, but look where we are,' Harry says, counting off on this fingers. 'We know that Jonathan was murdered and buried anonymously for some reason, we know that Christopher Flinter is involved, we can hazard a guess that this Mordaunt person probably had something to do with Jonathan's murder –'

'I know, I know,' Robert said with irritation, 'but it all feels so useless. Where is Christopher Flinter? Where is Mordaunt? We have no idea and without them it's useless. I've seen people going from obsession to madness and it's not a pretty sight, Harry.'

'I don't think you're obsessed, Robert. I think what you have is a mixture of guilt at not being able to be with your brother in his hour of need and a sense of outrage at how he was treated. It's perfectly normal. I feel it too.'

Robert pours Harry a cup of tea and sits on the bed.

'I suppose you're right – we have made good progress in a way. And at least I can say I did my best.' Robert sips his tea.

'Aren't you having a cake?' Harry smiles and goes over to the bag of cakes.

'You're always in such a great humour, Harry – how do you do it?'

But Harry does not reply and is staring out through the window, his gaze fixed on Anna Macken's house. When he turns to Robert his expression is a mixture of happiness and wonder.

'I've just spotted Christopher Flinter.'

Robert jumps up from the bed and looks over towards the brothel. But the front door is closing over and all he sees is the back of a man disappearing inside.

'Are you sure it's him? It's been a long time,' he says to Harry who is already buttoning his jacket.

'I wasn't certain at first, but then I remembered he has a slight limp. Let's go.'

'Wait a minute, what do we say? Let's talk this through,' Robert says, putting a hand on Harry's shoulder.

'Why wait? You said it was useless, and now this? Let's just go over there and find out. It could be that there is a more mundane explanation for your brother's death. If that's the case, you can be released. Don't you want that?'

Robert turns away and looks out at Anna Macken's house, trying to imagine what might lie beyond that gaudily painted door.

'Maybe I'm afraid to find out either way, Harry.'

He feels Harry's hand on his arm.

'Whatever happens I'm here for you, Robert. Forgive me, perhaps you're right. Let's finish our tea and take stock.'

CHAPTER 33

Homecoming

Christopher barely has time to put his seaman's bag onto the floor when Sarah Murphy runs across the hall and jumps up into his arms. She grabs his shoulders and squeezes him, tears coming into her eyes. Christopher puts his arms around her and pats her on the back.

'There, there, Sarah. What's all this? I haven't been gone that long,' he says, trying to comfort her.

'You don't know how happy I am to see you. It's been a terrible few weeks,' she says, weeping.

Christopher stands back from her and places a finger under her chin, lifting her face to his.

'What's happened? Is it Nell?'

'No, no, she's fine. She'll explain herself.' Sarah takes a hanky from her sleeve and dabs at her eyes, then blows her nose.

'Where is she?'

'Anna has given her the coach house at the back. I'm sure you're dying to see her.'

'I am, Sarah. But I want to know what's happening and why she's here.' Christopher takes her by the arm and leads her into the main parlour.

The room hasn't been tidied up yet from the previous night's revelries and the chairs are scattered about, some with empty bottles and glasses in front of them. The odour of tobacco and cheap perfume permeates the air and he is glad that he had made the decision to have nothing to do with Anna Macken's brothel. He finds a chair that is fairly clean and sits Sarah down. She begins to fiddle with her handkerchief.

'That monster from the tunnels has come back from the dead, that's what's happened.'

'So I've heard, but are you really positive it's him?'

'*Whatever his name is! He wants revenge, he keeps on coming and coming and nothing can stop him!*' Sarah cries out hysterically.

'Sarah, calm down and tell me exactly what's happened before Anna comes down. I presume she's still in bed?'

Sarah nods and composes herself. 'Anna's doorman was kidnapped. That's when it all started. Then he kidnapped me. It was horrible.'

'Now think carefully, are you absolutely certain it was him?'

'I told you! I'm positive. His face is almost covered with a mask. But it was his eyes. They look dead, like a fish, but they stare into you, like they're looking right through you as if you're nothing, like you're an insect.'

'But you got free?'

'By the grace of God. But the poor policeman who came to my rescue wasn't so lucky. And he used that wire thing on him, just like before.'

Christopher feels a coldness creeping up his body. Collins giving him the cold information is one thing, but talking to somebody who has lived through it is another.

'The garrotte?'

'Whatever it's called. But I got away. We read in the newspaper on the following day that the house I was in was burned to the ground.'

'So, it is him. But why …'

Sarah grabs his arm. 'Because he's insane, Christopher, it's in his eyes. And he won't stop until he gets what he wants. We're taking as much care as we can, but we need you more than ever.'

'Don't worry, I'm here now,' he says, patting the back of her hand.

'Thank God for that. Now, go on and see Nell – I must get down to the kitchen.'

Christopher makes his way through the silent kitchen at the back of the house and out into the back garden. It feels strange to be walking through the familiar yard with the sheets blowing in the wind. Down further the old stables look the same, except that this time it is Nell inside, and not Sarah and Moussa. He tries the handle of the door but it's locked. Creeping up to one of the windows he looks inside. Nell is stretched out on a long sofa, asleep. Looking in at her like that, alone and unprotected, a lump comes to his throat. All of the foolish thoughts and uncertainties that had sprung into his mind when he was away disappear and he murmurs a silent prayer for forgiveness for his betrayal.

As if hearing his thoughts, Nell pushes herself upright from the sofa and rubs her eyes. She looks towards the window and sees what she thinks is an apparition. Still half asleep she struggles to her feet, coming over to the window. When she looks out and sees it is really him, tears of joy pour down her cheek and she runs to the door and unlocks it, pulling back the metal bolt. Christopher almost jumps through, encircling his arms around her, soaking in her warmth.

'Don't you ever go away again,' Nell mumbles into his shoulder.

'I promise,' Christopher says, breathing in the smell of her hair.

They separate, looking at each other in an almost shy manner. Christopher looks around Moussa and Sarah's old place.

'You've made a nice home of this,' he says

'It's all down to my mother. I didn't want to leave the Liberties, our first home.'

'I know, I met Collins earlier, he told me what's been happening. And I spoke to Sarah just now.'

'We're all frightened, Christopher. What's going to become of us?'

'Nothing, while I'm around. It's only one man, Nell, I'll be here now and Collins has promised to put a guard outside during the night.'

Nell smiles up at him in relief.

'I'm so glad you're back. The daylight hours are the worst. At least at night there's a crowd, although that seems to be getting smaller by the day.'

'We could just leave, go down the country if you like.'

'No. And leave Anna and Sarah at the mercy of that monster? Why should we let him win?' Nell says, her temper rising.

Christopher smiles at the old Nell, the woman he fell in love with. 'You're right. What was I thinking?'

Nell reaches up and pinches his cheek. 'You've lost weight. What were they feeding you?'

'The food in Fiume was wonderful, but the food on the ship on the way back wasn't great.'

'Let's go up to the house,' Nell says, taking him by the hand.

By the time they get back into the house Anna, still dressed in her nightgown, is out of bed and organising the clean-up from the night before. She nods at Christopher when she sees the couple.

'Hello, Christopher, good of you to drop in,' she says with sarcasm.

'He's here, isn't he?' Nell snaps. 'I'm going into the kitchen to fix him something to eat.'

Christopher pulls out a chair from the large banqueting table and sits down.

'Is that your bag in the hall?' Anna asks him

'It is.'

'I'll get one of the girls to drop it down into the mews. I presume you'll be staying here?'

'Until this is all over, yes,' Christopher says, taking in the sight of Nell's mother who has aged since he had last seen her. 'Listen, Anna, I didn't want any of this to happen. We'll have a man outside during the night and I'll be here during the day –'

Christopher is interrupted by loud knocking on the front door. He goes out into the hallway and sees two blurred shapes through the side window: two men. He looks at Anna, who had joined him, but she shrugs her shoulders.

'It's a bit early for customers,' she says.

'Go into the kitchen with Nell, I'll see who it is.'

As soon as Anna disappears, he takes out his revolver, holds it behind his back and opens the door. Standing outside are two men, strangers. If it was in the evening, he would have no doubt who they were: customers. But at this time of the day the only people he could think of were the police, the British army or travelling salesmen trying to win some orders from Anna. But they resemble none of these. One of them is about his age and the other is older, but straight-backed with a military air. He looks at his face and something stirs in the back of his mind; but is gone. Both are dressed well, the younger one sporting a silk cravat, the older one with a sombre suit and carrying a cane.

'Can I help you?'

The older one steps forward.

'Are you Christopher Flinter?'

Christopher opens the door further, at the same producing the revolver. The younger man shies away but the older one ignores the weapon and looks him unflinchingly straight in the eye.

'I believe you knew my brother, Jonathan Byatt. My name is Robert Byatt. And this is my friend, Harry Irvine.'

Christopher sees the resemblance. Robert Byatt is an older but more formidable version of his younger brother, who always seemed to Christopher to have a slightly hesitant air about him. He lowers the gun to his side.

'I would have guessed.' He stands back. 'Come inside, we have a lot to talk about.'

Christopher leads them into the large parlour at the front of the house which is now almost back to the way it should be. He closes over both the hall door and the connecting door to the back room and nods towards the table. When they are seated Robert takes out a notebook and puts it on the table. It had been over three years since Christopher has seen it, but he recognises it right away. It was Jonathan's notebook. The presence of his brother and the notebook bring him back to that fateful night in the bowels of the city and all that led up to it. It brings a lump to his throat and he reaches out for it, picking it up and turning it over in his hand.

'Your brother was a special person,' he says, handing it back. 'I owe him my life.'

'Now you can pay him back,' Robert says, putting the notebook back into his pocket, 'by telling me everything that happened. From when you first met, until he ended up, forgotten, in that abandoned grave.'

Christopher feels uncomfortable under Robert's gaze. Perhaps he should have made the effort to find out where Jonathan was buried and visited it – he realises that now. But when you've been through a war where so many of your fellow-soldiers are killed and sometimes buried where they fall only to be dug up later and taken away, graves

326

gradually lose their importance.

'I didn't know,' he says, almost in a whisper. 'I thought that they would have shown some respect for what he achieved, not for who he was.'

Harry stands up quickly, his face contorted in anger.

'And what would that have been, exactly? Do you think he lived a sinful life? A great Irishman, Oscar Wilde, who lived not far from here once said the only sin is stupidity.'

Robert reaches out and takes his arm, encouraging him to sit back down.

'Let's all keep cool heads here, Harry,' Robert says.

Christopher holds up his hands. 'I'm sorry. I didn't mean it to sound that way. Jonathan was one of the bravest men I've ever met and it broke my heart to see the way he was treated by his fellow countrymen at the end.'

'Then honour his memory,' Robert says. 'Tell us exactly what happened.'

Christopher recounts everything that he can recall, from their first meeting in Jonathan's tiny office in Dublin Castle, right up to his last lonely journey in the plain wooden coffin up to the British barracks in Arbour Hill. He had thought that he had exorcised those terrible days in May 1916 from his memory, but with Jonathan's brother gently encouraging him, he realises that they still lurk somewhere just below the surface of his mind. When he finishes the story, he realises that it's early afternoon and he's beginning to feel mentally and physically fatigued after reliving those dreadful days. The two visitors look at each other in horror.

There is a soft knock on the door and Nell, who must have been listening outside, comes into the room. The three men get to their feet as one but she tells them to remain seated. After Christopher has introduced her, she looks at Robert and Harry.

'Would you like a cup of tea?'

Harry rises to his feet. 'Thank you very much, Nell, but I have a prior engagement with some students,' he says, bowing.

'Thank you, Nell. I'll have a cup, if you don't mind,' Robert says.

After Harry leaves with the promise of returning that evening, Nell leads the two men down into the large kitchen at the rear of the house. Sarah and another maid are working away, stirring and checking the contents of the multiple steaming pots that sit on a long cooking range that runs the length of one wall.

When Sarah sees the two men standing in the doorway, she clears off a wooden table at one end of the kitchen and pulls out two chairs.

'Sit here, I have something prepared for you.'

'I'll leave you to it, I'm sure you have a lot to discuss,' Nell says and departs.

As soon as the two men sit down Sarah puts a tray with a large plate full of sandwiches, a teapot and some cups in front of them. When she is finished setting the table, she comes back with a large jug of milk and two empty glasses, standing back from the table to see if she has remembered everything.

'I think that's enough, Sarah,' Christopher jokes, loading sandwiches onto his plate.

'Just leave some room for dessert,' Sarah says, and goes back to her pots.

The two men eat in silence, Christopher eating with fierce concentration, and Robert sipping his tea. As soon as they are finished, Sarah comes and whisks all of the plates away and puts two bowls of apple tart covered in cream in front of them. When the dessert is finished, Robert takes out a leather cigar case and offers Christopher a cigar.

'They're from Cuba,' he says, takes one himself, snipping off the end and rolling it between his fingers.

They sit together, smoking their cigars, the pace of activity in the kitchen increasing as the evening draws nearer. There are four women in the kitchen now, casting glances in their direction.

'I think they want us out,' Christopher says. 'Let me grab my jacket and we can take a walk while we finish our cigars.'

'Where are you staying?' Christopher asks Robert, who points across the road to his lodgings.

'Been there for several weeks. It's not the Ritz, but its location makes up for that.'

'That's how you knew I was home?'

'Not me. Harry. He remembers you from before, with Jonathan in that strange little restaurant.'

'If he's the same person I think he is, his appearance is … different.'

'They all look different in the daytime, they have to,' Robert says.

The two men walk in silence together. After about ten minutes they end up outside the walls of the Magdalen Asylum for Penitent Females. The sombre brick building looks out over Gloucester Street, its closed doors and high walls disguising its true activity: a giant, industrial laundry. Christopher stops and looks up at the structure.

'Nell spent her childhood in there, before Anna rescued her.'

'Looks more like a prison,' Robert comments.

'She never talks about it. She was too young to remember what life was like inside those walls.'

'What do you intend to do? I mean, while this murderous madman is running around?'

'I've given that some thought,' Christopher says, dropping the rest of his cigar onto the ground and stamping it out, 'and decided that it's no use running from someone like him. I'm going to stay and wait for Mordaunt here, in the Monto. He's bound to try and get to me, he's that kind of man. But it ends here.'

'Mordaunt. Now that you've told me his name, he feels like a real person. But you're alone in all this?'

'Not completely. Anna's house is being watched during the night and I'm here during the daytime. Anyway, he's only one man, and he bleeds like any other.'

'I think I can see now what Jonathan saw in you,' Robert says.

'Jonathan was a good man.'

'I agree and that's why I'm going to stay,' Robert says. 'He deserves no less.'

CHAPTER 34

Crotty

C rotty slumps in the car, knees propped on the dashboard, head almost below window level. Shadows stagger by, remnants of the night's carousing around the streets and laneways of the Monto. Anna Macken's house, which is further down Meckleburgh Street, is discharging its clients in ones and twos as its night of entertainment and debauchery is drawing to a close. Crotty wonders to himself if his father ever visited the Monto, but doubts it. He has no recollection of his father, a staunch Catholic and family man, ever staying out of the house past seven o'clock.

The memories of his father, dead the year before from TB, brings his own, conflicted part in the struggle against the British into focus. The commandment, 'Thou shalt not kill', although fading, is still branded in his brain, a permanent lesson from childhood. But Collins has lectured him on St Augustine's *jus ad bellum*, and reassures him that what they are doing is not alone a good cause, but a just cause. But he still has to wrestle with his conscience and he knows that Collins has recognised this in him and he has never, yet, been asked to take part in any assassinations. But somewhere, deep in his heart of hearts, that part of him from childhood when he knelt on the hard floor of the kitchen reciting the rosary, tells him that what he is doing now is wrong.

The presence that materialises in the darkness behind him is expected, but still a slight shock. The extra weight that tilts the car back, the slight breeze that enters, the strange sound of his breathing and the smell all coalesce together in his mind as the very incarnation of evil his father had lectured him about again and again. And here he was, dealing with the devil himself. He sits up upright, expecting the sheet of paper handed to him from the darkness. He lights a match and looks down the list of names and addresses of the British agents. Each one will meet their death at the hands of the Squad, hopefully saving many Irish lives in the future. He folds the sheet carefully and puts it into an inside pocket.

'You know what you have to say?' the voice whispers.

'Of course I do!' Crotty almost spits out.

'But you are unsure, I can sense it.'

'So what? I'm here and I'm going to do it, the rest is none of your concern.'

'I don't trust people like you. I've made that mistake before and I've paid for it.'

'Don't worry, I'm not doing this for you, I'm doing it for the cause.'

'Don't delude yourself, you're doing it because your superior ordered you. A fascinating man, Collins … a true survivor … a new man. Causes need people like that to lead them, otherwise it's just a ragged rabble that could come apart and drift away in search of a new leader.'

'Whatever you say, now get out of the car.'

Crotty can almost feel the menace emanating from the dark shape behind him and for the first time since he can remember he is truly frightened. But some innate sense in him has warned him not to show it. For the briefest of moments, he reconsiders what he has to do. He doesn't particularly like Christopher Flinter, but Nell is a different matter. In any case, it's not as if Flinter can't take care of himself. Maybe he can come out on top. Maybe. He waits for several minutes, the sound of his quickening pulses beating in his ears.

He turns.

'I said get out of the …'

But the back seat is empty.

Crotty gets out of the car and makes his way towards Mabbot Street, joining in with the thin crowd that are making their way towards Talbot Street and home. But he turns down Talbot Street and begins a slow jog until he reaches Buckingham Street then does a complete circuit until he is back on Meckleburgh Street, sweating and out of breath. Through the windows in Anna Macken's house he can see that the downstairs salon is almost empty of clients. He makes his way up the steps and raps loudly on the door. An older woman, overdressed in a full-length deep-red velvet skirt, opens the door. He presumes that this is the madam herself, Anna Macken, a formidable woman with a heavily made-up face and hard eyes.

'I'm sorry, but we're finished for the night,' she says with a smile.

'I have to see Flinter, it's an emergency,' he gasps.

She hesitates for a moment, then stands back to let him in.

'You must be Crotty – he said there would be somebody guarding us,' she says, and leads him into a parlour. 'Wait here.'

The room, although well appointed, looks like a fight has taken place recently. The armchairs are lying about in random fashion and half-empty empty bottles and glasses are scattered around the carpeted floor in a haphazard way. The air reeks of perfume, sweat and cigarette smoke. From upstairs he can hear the faint sound of female laughter.

Christopher Flinter comes through the parlour door and closes it behind him. He looks bleary-eyed and half asleep, his shirt half done up and his boots unlaced. He motions to one of the chairs and drags one over beside it for himself. The door opens behind him and Nell's head appears around it, but relieved on seeing who it is, she closes over the door and he can hear her footsteps going back down the hall.

After seeing Nell, sleepy-eyed and vulnerable, Crotty feels a surge of guilt. He takes off his cap and plays with it.

'You look like you've seen a ghost,' Christopher says.

'Maybe I have.' Crotty shrugs.

'Did you chase him too? You look winded.'

'I might've been mistaken, it was just a dark shadow.'

'We all make mistakes.' Christopher pats him on the knee. 'Where did the shadow lead?'

Crotty bowed his head and mumbles: 'I think it's called … Faithful Place.'

Christopher stiffens.

'Are you sure?'

Crotty nods. 'Almost certain.'

'Almost? Think, it's important, because that's where we found the murdered bodies of two women.'

'I'm certain.'

Christopher stands up and begins to paces the room, kicking aside bottles. He takes a seat beside the fireplace and pokes through the dying embers of last night's fire, lost in some distant place. Outside the door there are more giggles and a man's harsh laughter, then the sound of the door opening and closing, then silence again.

Crotty puts his cap back on and gets up to go. Before he leaves, he takes a Mauser semi-automatic from its shoulder holster and leaves it on the chair.

'I heard you prefer these.'

Christopher picks up the pistol and balances it in his hand. The wooden handle has the familiar '9' carved into it, denoting that it takes 9mm bullets. He makes sure the safety catch is on before he slides back the retaining clip and checks that it's loaded then slides the clip back into position. Nine bullets in the magazine and one in the chamber: more than enough for what he intends to do.

Robert Byatt wakes up to the sound of insistent knocking on his door. When he opens it, Mrs Sweeney is standing outside in the corridor with a young boy. Her fingers have a grip on one of his ears and his face is scrunched up in pain. She marches past Byatt into the room and stands beside the window.

'This urchin says he has a message for you,' Mrs Sweeney says, 'from over there.' She nods in the direction of Anna Macken's.

'Thank you, Mrs Sweeney,' Byatt says. 'You can release the boy now.'

Mrs Sweeney seems disappointed but lets go of the boy's ear.

'This is a God-fearing household, Mr Byatt, I must say I am disappointed in you.'

'Let those who are without sin cast the first stone, Mrs Sweeney,' Byatt says, putting a hand on the boy's shoulder.

Mrs Sweeney's face reddens and she marches out of the room. Byatt waits until he can hear her footsteps going down the stairs before turning his attention to the boy. He is a product of the city, malnourished and small for his age. Under his fingers he can feel the shape of the boy's collarbone and it feels as if it could snap with the slightest pressure. He puts his hand into his pocket and takes out a silver shilling, leans over and holds it out to the boy, who grabs it and keeps it clenched in his tiny fist.

'Well, earn your money – what important message have you for me,' he says in mock seriousness,

'The man over there,' the boy turns and points to Anna Macken's, 'said that you should read this at your earliest ... earliest ...'

'Convenience?'

'Yes, sir, that's what he said.'

'Very well. I shall go to him directly and report to him that you have done a splendid job.' Byatt stands to attention and salutes the boy.

The boy puts the shilling coin carefully into his trousers pocket and returns Byatt's salute before running from the room. Byatt watches from the window as he runs down the steps of Mrs Sweeney's and takes off down the street towards a sweet shop. The boy reminds him of his brother: his youthful eagerness to please. The picture of Jonathan's last resting place springs into his mind: the weed-covered grave in the forgotten corner of the cemetery. He opens the note with a trembling hand. Written in awkward capitals is the sentence: *I KNOW WHERE HE IS. MEET ME IN SHANAHAN'S – CHRISTOPHER.* He goes over to the wardrobe and takes out a jacket, buttoning it up as he looks at his reflection in the mirror, then puts on his hat and grabs his cane. Before he leaves Mrs Sweeney's, he phones the number that Harry Irvine has given to him.

CHAPTER 35

The chase

Shanahan's pub, mid-morning, is virtually empty. Two men, farmers on their way back from the Smithfield market, sit at the bar comparing the prices they got for their livestock and bemoaning them to each other. Christopher Flinter sits at a small table nursing a pint of porter. Across from him Robert Byatt and Harry Irvine digest what they have been told.

'And this house, where the two women were found, slain, is the same one where our mysterious friend disappeared?'

'Yes. It was a house belonging to a friend of Nell's, Connie Noble. We found their bodies there and discovered the entrance to a tunnel.'

'I can vouch for that,' interrupts Irvine. 'There's a whole system of tunnels under Dublin. More like a catacomb really, a city under a city.'

'So now we know where he's been hiding,' Robert says.

'I just don't understand why Crotty came to me. He should have gone to Collins first,' Christopher says, taking a sip from his pint.

'Maybe he was in shock,' Robert suggests.

'Either way, I'm going down after him,' Christopher says.

'Don't do anything rash, Christopher,' Harry says. 'This man is obviously insane and a cold-blooded ruthless killer.'

'I have no other choice, I can't have this hanging over my family's head for the rest of our lives.'

'You do have one advantage,' Robert says. 'You have us. He won't be expecting that.'

'I'd feel better if you stayed with Nell and Sarah. If this ends badly, he will come for them.'

'Out of the question. Jonathan was my brother. Harry can stay in Anna Macken's until we get back. It's settled.' Robert stands up. 'Let's be off.'

Faithful Place is very much as Christopher remembers it: ragged children, prostitutes at the end of their days and idle men standing on the corners, smoking. But Connie Noble's house now looks abandoned. Some of the windows are broken and the shattered front door opens with a push. Inside the house it's darker than he remembers and there is a smell of abandon. The gas has been switched off. In the front room where Connie kept her gentlemen callers waiting, there is no furniture left and the old grandfather clock that Connie was so proud of is long gone.

'Are you sure this is the house?' Robert says, prodding his cane into a pile of rubbish in the middle of the floor.

'It looks different than the last time I was here, but this is it alright.'

'It would seem to me that the entrance to his lair would be better disguised.'

'You won't find many people from around here going down into the cellar, never mind the tunnels,' Christopher says, and goes back into the hall.

In the gap under the stairs the door that has appeared in his nightmares is slightly ajar. He lights the oil lamp he brought with them and adjusts the wick to its highest point. As soon as he pulls back the entrance to the cellar, he can smell something unclean on the air that wafts from down below. Before he makes his way down the stairs, he takes out the Mauser Crotty had given him and holds it firmly in his right hand.

Taking his time, he goes down into the darkness with Robert coming up close behind.

Down in the cellar there is no difficulty in seeing the entrance to the tunnel as the old curtain that once covered it is now gone.

'That's it, over there.' He raises the lamp so that Robert can see.

'This is all too easy, Christopher – I don't like it,' Robert whispers.

'If you knew the man, you'd know that his arrogance knows no bounds. I can almost bet that I know where we'll find him.'

'Well, I'm not taking any chances. I want this man alive and I want to question him.'

'I can't promise you that,' Christopher says, and goes through the entrance to the tunnels.

When Robert catches up on him, he puts his hand on his shoulder.

'He might be armed, Christopher. And we're just walking targets.'

'Mordaunt won't kill me right away, he's not that kind of man. He'll take his time and play with me like a cat.'

'Still, at least lower the lamp. I'll stay back in the shadows, just in case.'

'Alright. But don't let him get inside your head – ignore whatever he says.'

'What do you mean?'

Christopher hesitates, then turns to Robert, holding up the lamp so that he can see any reactions on his face.

'It's true that Mordaunt killed your brother, but I don't think it happened … right away.'

'I'm confused … I thought that Jonathan was shot?'

'No, that might be what the records say. But he used your brother to get to me. He wanted to find out where I was. I was the only thing that stood between him and what he thought of as a flawless plan,' Christopher says. 'So he tortured Jonathan.'

Robert's jaws clench and his face hardens. 'I see.'

'I'm sorry I had to tell you, but it's something he would use against both of us. At least I was prepared. Now you are too.'

Christopher lowers the flame on the lamp and enters the tunnel. The mixture of smells inside – mould, decay and something else that reminds him of the trenches – brought back the memories of the last time he had walked into this underground place.

Behind him he heard Robert gasp at the stench. He turns. 'Use your handkerchief.'

But Robert shakes his head and urges him on.

Christopher hands him the lamp and pulls back the safety catch on the Mauser before he leads the way again. As they walk through some ancient rubbish, they disturb some rats who flee before the light from the lamp. On their left Christopher can hear the gurgle of water making its way down towards the sea. They walk on in silence for another twenty minutes. Ahead, he remembers, there is a slight bend and it was just beyond this where Mordaunt had set up his torture chamber.

He turns to Robert.

'If I'm not mistaken, we're nearly there. If you want to stay behind me in the shadows, now's the time.'

Robert nods and lets Christopher walk on.

Even though Christopher is armed and knows that Robert is behind him, he still feels as if he's walking into a trap. What if Robert betrays him, as Moussa did all those years ago? But he knows he's making Mordaunt into a more formidable adversary than he really is, making him an almost omnipotent being, instead of what he truly is: a madman with delusions of greatness. But still, he finds his feet dragging as he approaches the bend in the tunnel and the pistol handle is becoming slippery with his sweat.

As he rounds the bend, Mauser extended, he sees a figure just yards away. Sitting behind an old and battered table is Levon Mordaunt. The sight of the man who has brought so much terror and destruction into everybody's life almost seems like a mirage thrown up by his imagination. But he's a different Mordaunt to the one he remembers. Illuminated by several candles that flicker in the slight draught, his clothes appear shabby and worn. His hair looks over-long and unkempt. But it is his face that fascinates him. The once-white mask that covers his wound looks filthy with grime.

Walking stealthily forward, Christopher stares, hardly blinking, at the figure in front of him but occasionally flicks his eyes around and beyond the solitary man.

But Mordaunt seems to be just writing on a sheet of paper, possibly another odious scheme, his concentration absolutely rivetted on his task. Maybe he has taken that final step into madness.

Mordaunt puts the pencil down and looks towards him.

'Welcome, Christopher, to my new kingdom,' he says, and extends his hands on either side. The voice is different but the confidence is still there.

'I see you've lost none of your bluster,' Christopher says, and puts the lamp onto the ground, moving his left hand to steady the barrel of the Mauser.

'That's very rude, Christopher – did you learn those manners in Fiume?'

Christopher tries to hide his surprise and instead aims down the sight on the barrel, pointing it directly at Mordaunt's heart.

'No, in the trenches.'

'Are you going to arrest me?'

'And let you talk your way out of prison? No, it ends here and now.'

'Then that makes you worse than me and –'

'Shut up. No more talk.'

'At least your friend, Jonathan Byatt, was going to do the right thing.'

'And he paid for it.'

'Well, he did goad me. Having to drill through a kneecap is no easy matter.'

Christopher hears a strangled cry and Robert rushes out of the darkness and into the light. But before he can reach him Mordaunt is already on his feet and a revolver appears in his hand. Christopher adjusts his aim and pulls the trigger of the Mauser, twice in quick succession. The sound of a loud click reverberates off the roof of the tunnel and seems to have a bigger effect than if the gun had gone off. Robert stops mid-stride and looks at Christopher who pulls the trigger again. But still the sound is of a hammer falling on dummy round.

'*Tut, tut*, Christopher. No back-up plan?' Mordaunt taunts.

'How …?' Christopher stutters.

'A new ally, for now. What I was able to offer far exceeded your puny life and the life of your accomplice: *quid pro quo*. Don't you ever learn? There are no such things as friend or foe, just winners or losers. And you are a loser.'

Christopher lets the gun drop onto the ground and waits for the inevitable to happen.

'You bastard,' he says with tired resignation.

Mordaunt backs up against the wall and points the gun at Robert.

'Don't be so eager to die, Christopher. Aren't you going to introduce me to your friend? Although he does look vaguely familiar.'

Robert stands erect.

'My name is Robert Byatt. The man you tortured and murdered, Jonathan Byatt, was my brother.'

Mordaunt's eyes almost dance with glee.

'How extraordinary!' he says, staring at Robert's face. 'I couldn't have planned it better. Oh, I wish I had more time to spend with you gentlemen, but I've other things to attend to.'

A voice shouts out from the darkness.

'Put down that gun, we have you surrounded!'

Mordaunt swivels, points the gun in the direction of the voice and lets off several booming shots into the darkness. In the spilt second that his attention is elsewhere Christopher kicks over the table with the candles. The only light now comes from his lamp which is on the ground. He dives to his left as another bullet grazes his side. In the flash from the muzzle of Mordaunt's gun, he sees that Robert has withdrawn a blade from his walking stick and with lightning speed chops down on Levon's hand that holds the gun. A sharp scream rends the air followed by the clatter of the gun falling onto the ground and the sound of footsteps running away down the tunnel.

Christopher takes hold of the lamp and turns it up. Robert stands, his blade dripping with blood and beside him is the grinning figure of Harry Irvine. He bends down and picks up Mordaunt's revolver, intending to take after the fugitive, but Robert steps forward and puts his blade across his chest.

'Leave this to me. I've hunted far more dangerous game than this.'

'We should all go – tell him Harry,' Christopher says, brandishing the gun and turning to Harry who nods in agreement.

'I agree with Christopher – the man has proved to have too many tricks. We should all go. But,' he adds, 'on the other hand, I think that Robert has the right to decide his fate and avenge his brother if that's what he wants to do. It shouldn't take too long – he's not going to get that far, look at the ground.'

Christopher looks at the floor of the tunnel. Leading away from where they stand there is a dark streak of blood that disappears in the darkness.

'Very well, but take the lamp, Robert. Harry and I will follow you close behind.' Christopher picks up one of the candles, lighting it off the lamp.

Robert makes his way after Mordaunt, following the trail of blood that glistens along the floor of the tunnel. The light from the lamp extends several yards ahead and he can see that the blood trail is becoming less and less obvious. Mordaunt has probably put pressure on it, he knows, but not enough to lessen the flow completely. The smell of the blood has brought other hunters out: rats. A line of them follow the trail, whiskers twitching, tiny tongues lapping at the new source of food. As they become more frenzied, they increase their speed and Robert is just about able to match it. In front of him, somewhere in the darkness, he hears a scream.

He rushes forward, holding the lamp over his head. Standing in an alcove, beating off the ever-increasing river of rats is Mordaunt, trying to hold his injured arm behind him and away from the rats.

When he becomes aware of Robert, with Christopher and Harry behind him, he screams out: '*Help me!*'

Robert approaches him with his blade extended.

'Why on earth should we?'

'*Please! I was lying when I said that I tortured your brother! He died like a true soldier!*' Mordaunt screams, pulling off a particularly large rat that has attached itself to the wound.

'You're a murderer, and a liar,' Robert says and brings the blade down on Mordaunt's other arm.

344

Mordaunt lets out a scream and tries to kick out at the rats, but it's a fruitless exercise. Finally, his survival instincts take over and he decides to try and outrun them. He turns to stumble his way further down the tunnel. As he moves away Robert lashes out with his sword towards his leg. The blade bites into the back of his upper thigh, cutting through the muscle and tendon. Again, he lashes out, opening another gash in the other leg. Mordaunt, now half-walking half-staggering stumbles forward deeper into the tunnel.

Robert follows close behind watching as more and more rats join in the hunt. Dark, furry bodies scamper up Mordaunt's legs and on up towards his face. Now he's covered in a swirling mass of rats shrieking with blood lust.

'*Please, have mercy, kill me!*' he screams out but his cries are cut off as the rats are now completely covering his head.

For what seems like an age Mordaunt stands upright completely covered in writhing, furry, bodies. Eventually he flops down onto his knees, then topples over onto his back, one arm extended into the air. Robert watches the feeding frenzy impassively until Mordaunt moves no more. He approaches what is left of his brother's killer and holds the lamp aloft. Mordaunt's face is almost completely eaten away, except for the mask which stares up at him. Behind him he hears the sharp intake of breath from his friends.

'*Rest in peace, Jonathan*,' he whispers.

'*Amen*,' say Harry and Christopher.

CHAPTER 36

Skagway, Alaska,
1897

They leave the town immediately, following the course of the Skagway River on into the hills, back the way they had come. Levon tries to explain to his father and apologises and pleads with him that he has learned his lesson. But his father just rides on, silent, staring ahead. Unlike the leisurely pace on the way down to the town he seems intent on getting home as soon as possible. It isn't until after dark that his father finally stops and they make camp beside one of the streams that bled into the river.

Levon unpacks their horses and makes a fire. He reheats the last of the rabbit stew they had brought with them and breaks off some stale bread, handing it to his father. But his father has already rolled out his blanket and lies down, his back to the fire.

The following day is worse and the two horses are reaching exhaustion and covered with a shiny sweat before his father finally stops. That night there is nothing to eat and Levon lies shivering under his blanket, more afraid of his father's silence than of his rage. Early the next morning they reach the small river where they branch off towards their cabin. They follow the trail until it peters out onto the plateau where their log cabin lies. In the distance he can see a plume of smoke rising from the chimney in the cabin.

His father reins in his horse and turns to face him.

'Get off your horse,' he says, his voice dull, his eyes staring somewhere over his son's head.

'But, Pa ....'

'I said get off your horse.'

Levon dismounts and stands, waiting, almost eager to get his punishment over with. His father gets off his own horse, opens his saddlebag and begins to rummage about inside. When he finds what he's looking for, the old family Bible, he turns. Levon begins to shake. The last time his father had taken out the Bible for punishment was when his mother, a Chilkoot squaw, had disrespected him in front of her brother. Her brother had been part of a hunting party that had paid them a visit. He still didn't fully understand why his father had gotten so mad. His mother's brother had four strapping sons and he joshed his sister about Levon being an only child. He guessed her mistake was to laugh along with the joke. But his father didn't. When her brother and his sons had ridden off, he had taken out his Bible and dragged her around to the back of their cabin. Levon had to bury his head under the blankets to drown out the screams of his mother.

Now his father stands in front of him, flicking slowly through the Bible. He comes to the passage he is looking for and begins to read out loudly, his voice cracking with rage:

> *'So the Lord God said to the serpent:*
> *Because you have done this,*
> *You are cursed more than all cattle,*
> *And more than every beast of the field;*
> *On your belly you shall go,*

And you shall eat dust
All the days of your life.'

When he finishes reading the passage, he places the Bible back into his saddlebag and turns to Levon.

'Get down into the dirt and squirm on your belly, boy.'

Shaking, Levon lowers himself onto his hands and knees, but it isn't fast enough. His father walks up behind him and he feels the full force of his foot into his lower back and it knocks him, face down, into the dirt. The ground, wet from the rain, smells of dread grass and earth. His father places his boot on the back of his head and kneads his face into the mud. When Levon feels his father's foot lifting from his head he begins to get up.

'Stay on your belly, boy. That's the only way you're goin' home. Crawling like a serpent.'

'But it's too far, Pa, I'll never do it!' Levon cries out. 'Have mercy!'

'*Then stay out here in the mud, where you belong!*' his father screams.

The afternoon has closed in and it is becoming bitterly cold. Levon knows that he won't survive a night outside on the plateau. If the cold didn't get him, the wolves would. He tries to picture the cabin: it's about two miles away. His mother would have a fire going and have some stew bubbling away. He starts to crawl. The thought of the warmth of the cabin and the food drives him on for the first few hundred yards, but even those thoughts are not enough. The effort of dragging and pushing himself forward on his stomach is too much and he feels his arms begin to weaken. When he stops his father kicks him in in the side.

'*Keep crawlin', boy!*' he shouts down at him.

Levon lifts his face and stares into his father's eyes. For a split second he recognises a flash of regret in them and this makes him hate him more. His father, he realises in that instant, is a coward and a weak

348

man. He had backed away from the men in Skagway and now he is taking his weakness out on him. He lowers his face again and this time he uses his legs to help him crawl forward. But more than his legs, he uses his hatred for his father. Grabbing handfuls of sodden grass and pushing backwards with his legs he finds it easier to make his way forward. After a few hours he realises that darkness is falling around them and his hands are bleeding. But he continues crawling. Only forty or fifty yards to go. He hears his father open the gate to the corral and lead the horses inside. Then he becomes aware of his father's legs in front of him.

'I guess you learned your lesson, boy,' his father says. 'Get up onto yer two legs before yer ma sees yeh.'

But Levon keeps crawling towards the cabin door.

'I said get up off the dirt,' his father repeats and this time he kicks him in the side.

But Levon becomes aware of a note of fear creeping into his voice and doesn't answer him. He ignores the kick to his side and keeps crawling towards the cabin door. Then he feels another kick, to his legs this time, less strong, and hears the cabin door open.

A wailing scream rings out in the darkness and then he becomes aware of his mother's legs standing in front of him and feels her arms under his arms, trying to raise him up off the ground. But his body is finally spent and he flops back down, unable even to raise himself. His mother runs back into the cabin and comes charging out again, running past him. He hears an angry shout from his father and then he hears his father's screams. Using his elbows, he pushes himself up onto his knees and turns.

In the weak light pouring out from the cabin he is just about able to make out the shapes of his mother and father to one side. They are a dark moving mass of limbs as his mother hits out repeatedly and his father struggles, trying to fend off his enraged wife. As he staggers backwards, Levon can make out the glint of a knife as it's plunged repeatedly into his body searching for that vital spot. As one they topple onto the ground, his mother on top. He can hear the sound of the knife as it strikes home again and again, but still his father struggles and almost manages to topple his wife off him.

Levon uses the last of his strength and throws himself towards the struggling pair. Grabbing hold of his father's bloodied arms, he forces them onto the ground. His mother places the knife just under his father's ribcage and pushes it upwards with all her strength, turning it at the same time. It makes a sucking sound, not unlike when Levon has to kill one of their winter pigs. As his mother forces it upwards again a gush of blood pours out of the wound. At last, his father's arms grow slack. His mother stands up, lets the bloody knife drop, steps away from his father's dead body and walks back towards the house, returning with a blanket. She places it around Levon's shoulders and raises him up from the ground.

EPILOGUE

Christopher, Robert and Harry sit in silence around the dining-room table. The mood in the mews at the back of Anna Macken's is sombre. It's early evening and the sound of a phonograph playing one of the popular street ballads drifts down from the main house. Nell sets cups and saucers down in front of the men and goes back into the kitchen, returning with a plate of sandwiches and a large teapot. The men watch as she pours out cups of tea but make no move to eat any of the sandwiches.

'Have you lost your appetites?' Nell tries to snap them out of their thoughts.

Christopher looks up at her and shakes his head.

'You should be happy to be alive,' she says impatiently.

'For how long?' Christopher says, and takes up his cup, holding it with both hands wrapped around it.

'What do mean? He's dead, isn't he?'

Christopher looks at the two men sitting across from him, but they avoid his gaze.

'Crotty gave me a gun with dummy ammunition. It was a trap.'

Harry Irvine rises up from his chair and begins to pace around the room. The others watch as he walks up towards the kitchen and back again, his eyes staring ahead. He stops in front of the table.

'I was thinking about that, Christopher. We don't know for certain who put him up to it or if he was working alone.'

'But Mordaunt said he was his new ally!'

'Mordaunt was a liar and a narcissist, with an urge for control and domination. He could have been lying.'

'So, what would *you* do?'

'I would get word to Crotty and apologise for losing his gun.'

'*Apologise?* It should be him apologising to me!' Christopher says, slamming down his cup.

'Listen to Harry, Christopher,' Nell pleads.

'And what are you going to do – take on the whole of the IRA?' Harry says. 'Because if you go after Crotty, that's what you'll be doing.'

'What about Collins? Could he have been involved? He said he had no qualms about using people. Look what he did to Nell.' Christopher points at his wife.

'*Did* to me! Grow up, Christopher, he did nothing to me!' says Nell. 'I did it with my eyes open.'

'But it's a betrayal.'

'Jonathan was betrayed, but he paid with his life,' Robert says. 'You were lucky. A United States senator said the first casualty in war is the truth. I believe him. Who knows any more who our real enemies are?'

Nell walks around the table and stands behind Christopher, putting her hand on his shoulder.

'I think it's for the best. For all of us.'

'Furthermore,' Harry says, 'you don't even have to mention anything about what occurred. You can say you went down into the tunnels and stumbled across the corpse. Somewhere, in the middle of your search, you lost Crotty's gun.'

'By myself?'

'It's the simplest way. If you say Robert went with you it would bring a complication into it. After all, even though Robert was Jonathan's brother, he is still British and ex-military.'

Christopher thinks through what Harry has suggested. The grandfather clock in the corner, donated by Anna, strikes six times. He looks over at Nell, imagining what would happen if he was not there to watch over his wife. He sighs.

'Very well. We'll do it your way, Harry.'

✳✳✳✳

Shanahan's pub is doing a brisk trade. Behind the bar Phil Shanahan, with a towel thrown over his shoulder, is talking to two customers, men, who are dressed in dark suits that have seen better days. A crowd of students sit in one corner, eking out their drinks.

Robert Byatt and Christopher enter the snug. As Christopher takes a seat, Robert goes up to the hatch and rings the bell. Shanahan turns, looks down and smiles. He walks down to the hatch and sticks his head through.

'What'll be, gentlemen?'

Robert claps his hands together and turns to Christopher:

'I think this calls for a celebration, what do you say?'

'It's been a good day for both of us, why not?'

Robert turns back to Phil.

'We would like a bottle of your best wine, Mr Shanahan. Champagne if you have it?'

Shanahan looks over at Christopher.

'I presume that you've good news.'

'Good and bad,' says Christopher. 'I finally caught up with him, but it was too late for me to kill the bastard. He was already dead.'

'Well, thank God for that!' Shanahan looks up towards the ceiling and blesses himself.

'But, there is another bit of bad news. I lost the Mauser that Crotty gave me. There'll be hell to pay when I tell him.'

Shanahan whistles under his breath.

'The Big Fella won't like losing a Mauser. They're hard to come by.'

'I can make up for it.'

'I dare say you can. Anyway, that's for another day. Now it's time for a celebration. I have some champagne left over from Anna's order. Things are slowing down for her now, what with the war on the streets getting hotter. And it'll be even slower when we get control of the country again.'

'Why's that?'

'I can't see pious De Valera putting up with the Monto. Its days are numbered. Between me and you, more's the pity.'

'Why would you say De Valera? He's in America. Isn't Collins in charge of the IRA?'

Shanahan shakes his head sadly. 'Christopher, you're going to have to learn some of the facts of life. Collins might be in charge, but it's Dev who gives him the money to pay the wages. And those who control the purse-strings wield the power.'

Shanahan's head withdraws through the hatch and they can hear him laughing at his own joke as he makes his way up the bar towards the storeroom. Christopher tries to imagine what life would be like in Dublin without the Monto. He used to believe it would be better, but now he's not so sure. Most great cities are a mixture of resentment and success, grievance and happiness. The rich live side by side with the poor and it's only in places like the Monto that they come together in pursuit of pleasure. In the brothels and bars, laneways and doorways, men seek consolation from the daily grind, leaving their own women behind to wait in sadness. What would happen if the Monto closed down?

A shot sounds from somewhere in the public bar. Instinctively he ducks his head. But when he hears the cheers from the people in the bar, he realises that it's only Phil Shanahan opening their bottle of champagne.

Ends

MURDER IN THE MONTO

TONY O'REILLY

I n the days following the 1916 Dublin Rising, Christopher Flinter, a young Dubliner, deserts from the British army and returns home from Flanders to avenge the death of his younger brother. Caught in the act of revenge, he is imprisoned in Dublin Castle. There he meets Major Jonathan Byatt, a British secret service agent who gives him two choices: be shot for desertion or work undercover for the British.

Christopher's mission is to infiltrate the Monto, the biggest red-light district in Europe, and locate an American agent. The agent, code-named Janus, has a darker side. He is also a depraved serial killer who roams the alleyways of the Monto, terrorising the prostitutes who ply their trade there.

Christopher then meets Nell, a spirited young woman who supports the rebels' cause, and their feelings for each other grow. He, with comrades fighting and dying in the trenches in Flanders, finds his loyalties divided.

Intent on honouring his promise to Byatt, he wanders blindly through the dark heart of the Monto, searching for clues, aware that he himself may be the next target of the faceless and brilliant assassin he seeks.

Praise for MURDER IN THE MONTO

'Tight of plot, sharp of dialogue, and gripping as a vice, O'Reilly's debut novel – based in part on his grandfather who signed up with the British army to escape slum life – is a cast-iron cracker.'
HOT PRESS

ISBN 978-178199-7093